I0608947

The Man With the Blue face

IN THE SAME SERIES

The Man With the Blue Face
and Other French Scientific Romances

translated, annotated and introduced by
Brian Stableford

A Black Coat Press Book

English adaptation and introduction Copyright © 2015 by Brian Stableford.
Cover illustration Copyright © 2015 Mandy.

Visit our website at www.blackcoatpress.com

ISBN 978-1-61227-386-0. First Printing. April 2015. Published by Black Coat Press, an imprint of Hollywood Comics.com, LLC, P.O. Box 17270, Encino, CA 91416. All rights reserved. Except for review purposes, no part of this book may be reproduced or transmitted in any form or by any means, electronic or mechanical, including photocopying, recording, or by any information storage and retrieval system, without permission in writing from the publisher. The stories and characters depicted in this novel are entirely fictional. Printed in the United States of America.

TABLE OF CONTENTS

Introduction

This is the ninth in a series of Black Coat Press anthologies of exemplary texts in the evolution of the French genre of *roman scientifique* [scientific fiction]. The stories it contains were first published between 1860 and 1928, although the item published in 1928—the title story—was written in 1907 and is placed at that point in the chronological sequence of the stories, with the title that it was originally intended to have rather than the one under which it eventually appeared.

Although the term *roman scientifique* already existed in 1860, it had previously been used as a pejorative term to dismiss scientific theories that the writer thought fanciful, but it acquired a new meaning during the following decade because of its application to the works of Jules Verne, which became the first archetypes of the newly-identified fictional genre. As with any such new definition, however, the term tacitly embraced various works produced before Verne's advent, which appeared to be responding to the same historical and cultural developments. Although Verne's first novel, *Cinq semaines en ballon* (1863; tr. as *Five Weeks in a Balloon*) set a new standard in terms of its treatment of the burgeoning science and technology of aerostatics, it was by no means the first works of fiction to employ a balloon as a narrative device; that had been a regular feature of French fiction ever since the Montgolfier Brothers' first epoch-making ascent manned in 1783, rapidly adopted as a useful feature of all kinds of stories featuring fantastic voyages, especially utopian romances.

The progress of aerostatics entered a new phase in the 1860s because of continued improvements in the design of balloons, their increasing use in atmospheric research, and considerable interest in their potential military uses, of which tentative experimentation had been made during the Crimean

War. All these factors had brought into sharp focus the key problem of making use of purposive use of balloons: the problem of their dirigibility. That became a key focus of research in the period, as various designers and inventors strove to find a means of steering balloons and liberating them from the tyrannical whims of the wind.

With the aid of hindsight, we now know how intractable that problem turned out to be, that no satisfactory solution would be produced before the end of the 19th century, and that by the time dirigible airships did become practical, they faced stern competition from fixed-winged aircraft, which soon swung decisively in favor of the latter. At the time, however, there seemed to be a realistic possibility that the problem might be solved at any moment, by some single ingenious innovation, which might open up a whole new world of opportunity in terms of the transportation of people and goods. We can now understand how wildly over-optimistic that hope was, because, even if the problem of dirigibility had been solved, any major revolution in transportation would have faced immense problems with the potential speed of aerostats and the amount of weight they could carry. While the whole issue consisted of castles in the air, however, the sky no longer seemed to the bold imagination to be closed to any kind of adventure, and the prevailing mood in France in 1860 readily permitted such cavalier literary endeavors as Alfred Assollant's novelette "Les Amours de Quaterquem," here translated as "The Amours of Quaterquem," which first appeared in book form as an adjunct to a novel in the volume *Brancas. Les Amours du Quaterquem* (1860).

Assollant's story is marginal even within the fledgling genre of *roman scientifique*, which is considerably broader in its inclusions than the subsequent genres indentified and developed in Britain and America under the rubrics of "scientific romance" and "scientifiction," the latter of which was swiftly renamed "science fiction." It was commonplace in Verne's work, and that of the great majority of the writers who followed in his wake, to fit the scientific innovations featured in their work into conventional narrative frameworks, often attributing them peripheral roles rather than placing them center-stage. Given that no writer could spell out how a method of steering balloons was actually going to work, there were good reasons for not making the invention itself the principal focal point of the story.

The revolution anticipated by Assollant's novelette is carefully left outside the range of the narrative, and it is envisaged in singular terms, but the Vernian era had not long got into swing when it was realized that the impending technological evolution would not be a matter of a single epoch-making discovery but of a whole host of new technological opportunities fostered by the domestication and diversification of the force of electricity. The character and exploits of Assollant's hero, Yves Quaterquem, was soon supplemented, and to a considerable degree replaced, by fictitious scientists cast in a very different mode, which stressed the eccentricities of scientific genius, and called into question the normality of their social and sexual relationships.

That developing notion of the distinctive personality of inventors, coupled with the potential that a multitude of new gadgets seemed to have for altering the texture of human communications, made the kind of love story featured in "Les Amours de Quaterquem" seem a trifle obsolete, and called forth such satirical examinations of the future of amour as Ernest d'Hervilly's "Josuah Electricmann," which first appeared in *Le Petit Parisien* in 1882 and was reprinted in his collection *Timbales d'histoires à la parisienne* in 1883. The story clearly reflects the French impression of the American inventor Thomas Edison, who was then approaching the height of his fame and success.

The first of the two short novels contained in the collection, Charles Guyon's *Voyage dans la planète Venus* (1888), here translated as "A Voyage to the Planet Venus," takes up the theme of rapidly-moving dirigible balloons, but uses it simply as a narrative device—and an extremely unconvincing one—for transporting its heroes to unexplored territory for the

9

purposes of adventure. Because of the rapid progress made in the previous century by geographers, the Earth had run out of such potential new worlds, save for the inconvenient polar regions, and Guyon followed the natural trend of shifting them to another planet within the solar system, imagined as an Earth-clone, with human inhabitants, although its megafauna is otherwise entirely "antediluvian." The book was marketed for younger readers, as many Vernian romances were, and the story has marked affinities with English "boys' books," not least in the complete absence from its pages of members of the female of the species.

Although the story is wildly implausible, in imagining that a balloon ascending rapidly from the Earth surface could travel all the way to Venus, the passengers in its unsealed nacelle merely falling into the state of suspended animation once beyond the atmosphere, it is not without a certain charm and interest as one of the most rapid developments of the ideas concerning life on Venus set out by Camille Flammarion in his popular illustrated guide to *Les Terres du ciel* (1884)—the influence of which is duly credited—and also in its contribution to the notion of using light signals for interplanetary communication, first popularized by Charles Cros in 1869. It is similarly naïve as a fantasy of prehistory, although its depiction of a pitched battle between a megatherium and a mastodon anticipated similar scenes in many later tales of marvelous survivals.

As an early "planetary romance," *Voyage dans la planète Venus* anticipates, albeit rather weakly, many of the tropes that were to become typical of that subgenre as it developed in British scientific romance as well as *roman scientifique,* and, in a later era, in American science fiction. Indeed, it shares so many motifs with earlier and later works that it deserves to be recognized as a significant illustration of the way in which the elaborate cocktail of ideas in question was indeed becoming generic, adding a further layer to relatively modest Vernian fantasies of terrestrial tourism and preparing the way for the more ambitious scope that British scientific romance adopted when it was copiously refueled by the imagination of H. G. Wells.

Bernard Lazare's "L'Offrande à la Déesse," here translated as "The Offering to the Goddess," which first appeared in *La Grande Revue* in 1889 and was reprinted in his collection *Le Miroir des Légendes* (1892) is an early contribution to the subgenre of prehistoric romances, which employs anthropological speculations to try to reconstruct something of the psychology and sociology of primitive human beings still on the threshold of consciousness.

Camille Debans' "Le Fou d'après-demain," here translated as "Tomorrow's Fool," first appeared in *La Science Illustrée* in 1899, the fifth contribution to that periodical's *roman scientifique* feuilleton slot by the author. It is set solidly in the tradition of speculative *contes philosophiques*, one of several that attempts to extend philosophical speculation to some kind of extreme, interrogating the ultimate purpose and possible boundaries of the scientific quest in a typically ironic manner.

The second short novel included herein has a curious history. It must have been written as a follow-up to the author's first speculative novel, *Le Docteur* Oméga (1906)[1] and was intended to be published as *L'Homme à la figure bleue*—for which reason it is here translated as "The Man with the Blue Face"—but did not actually get into print at the time, although Galopin appears to have deposited a sample of the text with the Bibliothèque Nationale, perhaps as a means of registering evidence of its existence for copyright purposes. He subsequently included that title in the lists of his works included in the prefatory material of his later books, and continued to do so even after it had actually been published, in 1928, as *Le Bacille*.

The latter edition contained a note explaining that the story was set in the past and that the monstrous crime it de-

---

[1] tr. as *Doctor Omega*, Black Coat Press, ISBN 978-1-0-9740711-1-4

scribes would no longer be practicable, thus suggesting the possibility that the reason why the novel was not published in 1907 was that the potential publisher feared that someone might actually attempt to carry out the act of terrorism featured in the story's climax. The non-appearance of the book might help to explain why Galopin's subsequent works—almost all aimed at younger readers rather than the adult audience of the present text—stuck much more closely in their speculative inventions to conventional Vernian devices.

The novel had lost some its shock value by 1928, and also some of its plausibility, because the science of bacteriology, especially in relation to pathology, had made considerable progress in the previous twenty years. Considered as an 1907 text, however, it is notable for its attempts to extrapolate a science then in its infancy, and also as an addition to the long tradition of stories attempting to focus on the unusual psychology of scientists. The book carried a dedication to the author's father, Augustin Galopin, "Professor of Physiology, pupil of Claude Bernard," which explained both its inspiration and its relative sophistication.

Like almost all stories in which scientists unleash disaster, it is routinely dismissed by historians and critics as a "mad scientist story," but it illustrates very clearly, albeit in rather garish fashion, that most stories of that kind are actually accounts of inordinately sane men who are driven to breaking point and beyond by the woeful incomprehension, willful stupidity, and coarse brutality of their "normal" neighbors. If they do eventually go mad, it is because their highly-refined minds fail to resist, in the end, the brutal insanity of the society that does not deserve them.

Gaston de Pawlowski's brief vignette "La faillite des sciences," here translated as "The Bankruptcy of Science," was first published in book form in the collection *Polochon, Paysages animés, Paysages chimériques* (1909) but was probably published some time before in *Comoedia*, the periodical that the author edited. It is, like "Josuah Electricmann," a somewhat sour reflection on the symbolic career of Thomas

Edison, which also has a certain affinity with the philosophical underpinnings of Camille Debans' story.

E. M. Laumann's "L'Alycon," here translated as "The *Alcyon*," was first published in the 15 juin 1923 issue of *Je Sais Tout* and was reprinted in issue 13 of *Le Visage Vert* (May 2003). It belongs to the same tradition of exotic adventure fiction as Charles Guyon's story, but illustrates the manner in which the stakes of exoticism were steadily raised by the pressure of "melodramatic inflation" as that subgenre evolved. The story has some affinities with the exotic sea stories produced by one of the leading writers of British scientific romance, William Hope Hodgson.

The translation of the Guyon novel was made from a copy of the book published by Lecène and Oudin, operating under the rubric of the Société Française d'Imprimerie et Librairie in 1888. The translation of the Camille Debans story was made from the undated Kindle edition of *Recueil de 7 nouvelles*, and the translation of *Le Bacille* was also made from the Kindle edition. The translation of the E. M. Laumann story was made from a copy of issue number 13 of *Le Visage Vert*. The translation of "La faillite des sciences" was made from the copy of *Polochon, Paysages animés, Paysages chimériques* reproduced on the International Archive Digital Library site at *archive.org*. The other three translations were made from the editions of the texts reproduced on the Bibliothèque Nationale's *gallica* website.

Brian Stableford

Alfred Assollant: *The Amours of Quaterquem*
(1860)

I

"Yes," said Quaterquem, "putting his pen down on the table, "the problem is resolved, and the balloon will fly like a swallow, replacing the diligence. I shall make millions...God, how expensive bread is!... duchesses will fall at my feet... that dirty Auvergnat ought to give me better-filtered water!... and the world is mine. What, then, am I going to do with it?"

At that moment the porter came in. "Monsieur," he said, "it's the fifteenth of April today."

"I don't mind that. Is it warm out?"

"Yes, Monsieur, warm enough. I've brought the monthly bill."

"Are the leaves beginning to grow?"

"Yes, Monsieur. The landlord..."

"And the birds are singing in the wood?"

"I presume so, Monsieur. I came up..."

"O potent Nature, always beautiful and always cheerful in her immortal youth."

"Monsieur, it's two hundred francs..."

"That you've brought me? Be welcome, my good man. And who is the generous person...?"

"Monsieur, it's the landlord..."

"Who has sent them to me? Oh, the worthy man!"

"No, Monsieur..."

"What? Your landlord isn't a worthy man?"

"I didn't say that."

"But you did say it."

"Monsieur, with all due respect, I didn't say it!"

"Am I a liar then?" said Quaterquem, leaping to his feet.

At that sight, the porter opened the door and recoiled on to the landing. "Monsieur," he said, "in the name of Heaven, don't get annoyed. I mean that my proprietor has not sent me to give you, but to ask you for, two hundred francs."

"Oof! And for what reason, pray? Is today his birthday?"

"No, Monsieur."

"Or that of his wife, who has a nose shaped like a small potato and as red as a cooked lobster?"

"No, Monsieur, it's..."

"Does he think I lend money at interest?"

"Monsieur owes him a month's rent."

"Already?"

"Yes, Monsieur. You arrived here on the fifteenth of January 1859; that was three months ago today."

"Three months! How time flies! *Life is a fragile vase/Easy to break, alas!* Life, my poor friend, is like a wall into which one hammers a few nails at intervals. Those nails are the happy days. From a distance, they seem innumerable; tear them out and there are not enough to fill the hand. Do you know who said that?"

"No, Monsieur."

"It was Bossuet. Have you read Bossuet?"

"No, Monsieur."

"Too bad. He was a great man, a true genius, an eagle of Meaux."

"Monsieur, I'm in a hurry. If you can just..."

"Pay you? If I can? Why, my poor friend, why didn't you say so sooner?"

Quaterquem took the key to his writing-desk from his pocket. As he put it into the lock he turned round. The porter was quivering with impatience.

"Are you sure that it's the fifteenth of April?" he asked.

"Look at the almanac, Monsieur."

"You know the proverb: *To lie like an almanac.* I mistrust almanacs."

"Here's this morning's paper."

"And you believe what a newspaper says?"

16

"Yes, Monsieur; I believe everything that is printed."

Well, my dear friend, I'll give you certain proof that the newspaper is lying. Sit down on that chair and lend me an attentive ear. My story won't take very long."

"Monsieur, the landlord is waiting for me."

"Go tell him to uncork a bottle of Sauterne. That will give him patience."

"Monsieur..."

"Oh, you're annoying me now. Are you going to listen to me, yes or no?"

"Monsieur, I want to be paid."

"Eh? I'm not deaf. Listen to me story first. It has more relevance to your request than you think. I was born on the banks of the Rance, which is the most beautiful river in Brittany, and, in consequence, the entire world. My father, who died last year, left me eight or ten hectares of land, which I sold for six thousand francs. I was expecting the money on the fourteenth of April. Now, it hasn't arrived. Therefore, we haven't yet reached the fifteenth. Thus, it's necessary to be patient, and to come back when the fifteenth arrives—which is to say, when I've received my six thousand francs. Do you understand?"

"Yes, Monsieur, and I'm going."

"Bonsoir, my friend."

"I'm going to see the landlord."

"Give him my compliments.

"Yes, Monsieur, and I'll tell him that you're refusing to pay your rent, and he'll have you thrown out."

"What?"

"Thrown out. Yes, Monsieur, out," said the porter, fleeing.

Quaterquem did not pursue him. He sat down in his armchair, his arms folded and his legs stretched out, and reflected profoundly.

"Decidedly," he said, "the condition of tenant is intolerable. I need to build a house. Bah! What's the point? When one can cleave through the air like a swallow, does one need a

17

cage like a canary? Can you imagine that notary, keeping my six thousand francs?"

Three raps on the door interrupted our friend's reflections.

"Come in!" he said.

Immediately, a man of mild and polite appearance presented himself.

"Monsieur," he said, refusing the chair that Quaterquem offered him, "is it to Monsieur Yves Quaterquem, professor of physics and chemistry, that I have the honor of speaking?"

"Yes, Monsieur, in person."

"I'm charmed to make your acquaintance, Monsieur. You are the man who has carried out savant research into the manner of directing aerostats?"

"Yes, Monsieur, and that research has just culminated, this very day, in a solution of the problem. Within an hour, I'll be certain of success. Is it to a colleague that I have the honor of speaking?"

"Not exactly, Monsieur, although I'm very interested in the sciences and hold scientists in particular honor. Your reputation, Monsieur, has reached me."

"Monsieur!"

"In the practice of my profession, I often have dealings with men of your genius—with inventors—and I dare say that they have never had anything but praise for me."

"I believe you, Monsieur. What is your profession, if you please?"

"I'm known by my exploits, Monsieur."

"You're an official?"

"Yes, Monsieur, a public official, or, if you like, a jurisconsultant responsible for citing notifying and signifying, at a just price, the ordinances of justice, judgments and warrants of the court and the civil tribunal."

"Ah! You're a bailiff, my dear Monsieur. I don't mind that. I've always liked bailiffs. Sit down, I beg you."

"Monsieur, I can't..."

At that point, the man took a legal document from his pocket, which was perfectly illegible.

"Believe," he said, "that I'm caring out a painful duty with regret. Monsieur Mardochée, my client, is claiming from you the sum of fifteen hundred and thirty-five francs forty-three centimes, comprising, in the principal, interest and expenses, the total amount of what is owed."

"Oh, yes, I remember. Six months ago, he sold my three or four scientific instruments. It came to seven hundred francs, if I'm not mistaken."

"Yes, Monsieur, and the expenses of recovering the aforesaid amount account for the rest. You've been condemned by default."

"And if I don't pay today, what will happen?"

"I regret to say it, Monsieur, but I shall be obliged to seize your furniture, your papers and your instruments."

"Seize? Who's talking about seizure?" cried someone in the corridor. "The furniture is mine, and guarantees the payment of the rent." At the same time, a large stout man came into the room.

"My word," said Quaterquem, sitting down in an armchair. "Let's see who'll prevail. We'll have something to laugh about. My dear proprietor, may I introduce my bailiff; my dear bailiff, may I introduce my landlord."

"Nobody plays games with me, Monsieur," said the landlord. "I want my money!"

"Of course!" said Quaterquem. "You never lose your taste for it. I ask Heaven for it every day, but I don't know how to obtain it. Would you believe that I was expecting six thousand francs yesterday, and that I haven't received a single guinea, piaster or copper coin?"

The bailiff had sat down, and was writing silently.

"What are you doing?" demanded the landlord.

"…*Having been and spoken to him in person*…," recited the bailiff. "As you can see, I'm drawing up a warrant of seizure."

"This furniture is mine!" cried the landlord.

"As soon as my client has been paid, yes, Monsieur."

The quarrel was about to become heated. Fortunately, the postman came up the stairs and appeared, holding a registered letter. Quaterquem broke the seal and took out six thousand-franc banknotes.

"Saved!" he said. "Dear postman, bearer of good news, take this five-franc piece, the last one in my purse, and drink to my health."

The postman saluted by putting his hand on his heart, and left.

"And you, generous friends, who have not abandoned me to misfortune, be blessed! Here's your money; give me the change. To the man who has lost everything, one last consolation remains, which is the afflicted visage of his creditor. His friends might forget him, his dog might search for another master, but his creditor, always faithful and devoted, will only quit him on the threshold of the cemetery."

When the landlord and Mardochée's ambassador had departed, Quaterquem became pensive.

"Well," he said, "I'm rich. Six thousand francs, minus the seventeen hundred and thirty-five francs forty-three centimes of which I've made a present to those worthy fellows, leaves me four thousand two hundred and sixty-for francs and fifty-seven centimes for tonight's dinner. It's a pretty penny, and my father's son is a powerful lord. How will I ever get to the end of such a sum?"

While speaking, he looked at the clock. "Well," he said, "it's three o'clock and I haven't had lunch. It's the effect of violent emotions. Let's go out. Strolling is the mother of ideas, and the Boulevard des Italiens is their father."

With that, he headed for the boulevard. He had no suspicion of the influence that stroll would have on his destiny.

II

Yves Quaterquem was one of the most civilized scientists ever to climb the stairs of the Institut. His father, an old

Breton mariner, who had earned a little money fishing for cod off the shores of Newfoundland, had had him educated with care, and young Quaterquem, who combined the firm determination of his race with a penetrating intelligence, became in a few years one of the most distinguished mechanicians in France. Always occupied in inventing new machines, however, and neglecting to care for his fortune, he lived with difficulty, with no money but almost devoid of debts, on the sixth floor of a house in the Rue Montmartre. He often dreamed of glory and of some discovery that would render his name immortal; such is the dream that nourishes unknown men of genius.

"God knows," Quaterquem said to himself one day, "everything that the human race owes to means of transport. Steam engines and railways are civilizing Europe and populating America. With balloons, who knows? Perhaps I'll put Oceania under the plow. Now, what do balloons lack? It's not the means of support and it's not the motor; it's the rudder. That's what it's necessary to search for. If I find it, compared with me, Christopher Columbus will only be a weekend sailor."

And he searched for two years.

On the fifteenth of April 1858, the day that this story commences, after a thousand experiments, the problem was resolved, and Quaterquem saw himself able to go around the world in twenty-four hours, spitting effortlessly on the highest peak in the Andes.

He was then twenty-six years old. That is an age for loving glory and enjoying it.

There are men of genius who strike the eye at first glance, who walk around Paris with the majesty of immortal gods. Our friend Quaterquem was not one of those. With his hands clasped behind his back and his hat tilted backwards, he walked slowly, full of admirable calm, without looking at anybody.

At the corner of the Rue Vivienne he made a reflection.

21

In truth, he thought, *I'm a terrible egotist. At three o'clock, I had a fortune. It's quarter past three, and already I'm forgetting my friends. Accursed money has extraordinary charms. What if I were to offer them a bowl of punch to redeem my sin? Why, there's the very bowl!*

He went into one of those brilliant bric-à-brac shops that one sees at the extremities of the civilized world, in which one encounters, pell-mell, suits of armor, helmets, sabers, daggers, épées, coffee-pots, Japanese vases and all the shiny gewgaws that are the specialty of Parisian industry.

"How much is that Sèvres vase?" he asked the merchant.

"Three thousand francs, Monsieur."

Quaterquem bit his lip.

"Monsieur," said the merchant, "just think that the vase is unique in Europe. As soon as it was made, the mold was broken. Look at the painting: it's a copy of Greuse's 'Young woman with a Broken Pitcher.' It's an admirable copy. It was made on the orders of the great Napoléon."

Quaterquem started laughing.

"Perhaps you doubt it?" said the merchant. "Are you in the trade?"

"No, I'm a geometer."

"Exactly, Monsieur. Napoléon made a present to if to Monsieur Monge, Comte de Péluze, who was a famous geometer and his great friend, as you know—and Monsieur de Péluze's heirs sold it to a Russian prince, from whom I obtained it."

"I believe you," said Quaterquem, "but three thousand francs is very expensive."

"Monsieur," said the merchant, "We have brand new Limoges porcelain much cheaper."

That was not what the buyer wanted. He made a tour of the shop, but only had eyes for the Sèvres vase. Finally, he paid for it, took it home, and wrote seventeen of his most intimate friends a circular letter which read:

My dear friend,

Archimedes only asked for a lever to raise up the universe. I've found something better; I can guide balloons as a coachman guides an omnibus. In a month I'm going to see Peking. Prepare your commissions for the leader of the Celestial Empire, brother of the moon and first cousin of the sun.

One joy never comes alone; money is flowing into my pockets, and I've just bought an old shaving-bowl of Napoléon's, born in Sèvres, in which we'll make punch. I'll expect you this evening at nine o'clock.

Entirely yours,

Yves Quaterquem

When the seventeen letters were written, he got up to look for a stick of sealing-wax. In that abrupt movement, he knocked over the Sèvres vase, which fell to the floor and shattered into numerous pieces.

Quaterquem remain motionless for some time. Surprise, despair and regret for the loss of the money and the broken masterpiece all overwhelmed him at the same time.

Finally, he made his decision, and sadly wrote a postscript at the bottom of all the letters:

P.S. Hell and damnation. I've just broken Napoléon's shaving-bowl. Don't disturb yourselves. The punch is postponed until better times. To the devil with the vase, the workman who made it, Napoléon who gave it to Monsieur Monge, Monge who gave it to his descendants, his descendants who sold it to the Russian prince, and the Russian prince who had the stupid idea of getting rid of it. Adieu. I'm going to the Opéra-Comique.

Then he sealed and posted is seventeen letters. At eight o'clock he went into the Opéra-Comique. As chance would have it, he could get only a seat in a box, and he sat down in the front row. That hazard was to determine the course of his life.

The box was empty, but a quarter of an hour later, an Englishman came in, flanked by two Englishwomen: one blonde and as ripe as an old apple wrinkled by the winter frost, the other not so blonde but as beautiful as a lily and as charming as a heroine out of Walter Scott. They were mother and daughter.

As for the Englishman, he was an Englishman. Everyone knows that energetic, gauche, intelligent, egotistical, formal and disagreeable race, which fills continental hotels for six months of the year. The Englishman of the box was one of its finest specimens.

Quaterquem, as polite as a Frenchman of the last century, stood up in order to surrender his seat to the young English-woman. The mother had already sat down, and our friend was compensated by a smile and a "Thank you" to which the purest British accent added new charms. The Englishman, as stiff as a pikestaff, sat down without deigning to look at the Breton, who scarcely cared about that, and leaned toward the young woman.

"My dear Alice," he said, in English, "Do you know that gentleman?"

"No," she said.

"No one has introduced you to him?"

"No one."

"If he hasn't been introduced, it's as if he doesn't exist; if he doesn't exist, why are you thanking him?"

Alice shrugged her shoulders. "If he doesn't exist," she said, "why are you talking about him? Let's suppose that I'm thanking the void, pure nothingness; would you be jealous of the void?"

"My dear Alice," said the Englishman, "you know very well that I'm not jealous..."

"Too bad."

"But..."

"Shut up. The overture's staring."

The overture of *Le Chalet* had indeed commenced.[2]

Quaterquem, who knew a little English and divined the rest, had not missed a word of that whispered conversation. He looked at Miss Alice and thought her as beautiful as the daylight. The music of *Le Chalet* lost something in consequence.

That's a pretty Englishwoman, he thought. *Is she the fiancée or the wife of that tall fellow, so red-haired and badly brought up?*

In the meantime, the beautiful Alice was listening very attentively to the opera. She wept for the fate of Austrian infantrymen when she learned from Max that "In the service of Austria/Soldiers don't get wealthier." She burst out laughing when she saw the drug take effect and pinched her nose as if with a wooden clothes-peg. In sum, she completely scandalized her mother and the Englishman with the russet sidewhiskers. During the entr'acte, the mother said: "What are you thinking, my dear Alice? You're laughing like a flighty little Frenchwoman. It's quite shocking."

"Shocking and inappropriate," added the Englishman.

"Sir," said Alice, with a sufficiently serious expression, "I'm well aware of your prudence, and I know that you wouldn't be out of place in the House of Commons. My father says so, and my father surely knows what he's talking about. But please don't waste that precious eloquence on a poor flighty girl. The English nation would lose too much by it, and I fear that I wouldn't gain enough. Let me laugh and sing at my ease, and least until I'm your wife. Later, we'll see."

"Alice!" said her mother, in a severe tone.

"Dear Mother," said the young woman, taking her hand, "Why is Mr. Harrison giving me lessons in propriety? Does he

---

[2] *Le Chalet*, a one-act comic opera with words by Eugène Scribe and music by Adolphe Adam, was regarded as one of the latter's finest works, had its première at the Opéra-Comique in September 1834, and became part of the theater's standard repertoire, reaching its thousandth performance in 1873.

think I'm unaware of the convention that it's utterly indecent to express any emotion whatsoever in one's words or gestures? That's all well and good in Oxford Street, but we're in Paris, not in London any longer; we're at a play, not in church. And I don't need sermons from Mr. Harrison."

This speech, which was not long, completed the conquest of Quaterquem. There are days when scientists fall in love, just like ignorant people. That day, it was our friend's turn. Until then, his heart had been empty, for science is a jealous mistress who does not leave room for other amours, and for two years, Quaterquem, fully occupied with his research on aerostats, had been living the life of an anchorite in the desert. In a matter of minutes, that long-extinct fire had been reignited, and was burning the heart of the poor mechanician.

What folly, he thought, *to fall in love with that young woman, already engaged to someone else! I'd consume myself in pursuit of that dream and put at risk a discovery that might perhaps change the face of the world!*

The reflection was as futile as it was sage. Carried away by his ardor, Quaterquem was no longer thinking about anything but getting closer to the young Englishwoman—but how could he overcome the barrier and violate all British conventions?

In the meantime, the entr'acte finished; already the auditorium was filling with spectators again. He made an effort of genius and found a question.

"Forgive me, Mademoiselle, but did you not pronounce the name Harrison?"

The young Englishwoman looked at him in astonishment. "Yes, Monsieur," she said.

The Englishman blushed to the ears, but Quaterquem had decided not to perceive that.

"Monsieur," he said, addressing him directly, "permit me to ask you whether you might be my cousin James Harrison, of Derbyshire?"

"I have no cousin in France, and I am not from Derbyshire but Lancashire," replied the Englishman, with a surly expression.

"Lancashire or Derbyshire. It's all the same. Anyway, I congratulate you, for the cousin of whom I speak is, it's said, a rather ill-mannered gentleman."

The young Englishwoman burst out laughing, and Mr. Harrison frowned.

Good! thought Quaterquem, *the ice is broken and the introduction accomplished.* "However, Monsieur," he went on, "the Harrison family with which I'm allied is a very good family, to whom any man of honor could be proud to belong. My aunt, Mrs. Margaret Harrison, was one of the most beautiful women in England. I've seen her portrait, painted by Lawrence; it's a veritable masterpiece. What astonishes me the most is the perfect resemblance to Miss Alice; one might think that she is her mother or sister."

All of that was rattled off in a single breath, with perfect simplicity. Miss Alice smiled graciously and was flattered by the compliment. Her mother listened to the Frenchman without saying a word or even twitching an eyelash; one might have thought her a statue of Prudery. Only Harrison, bristling like a bulldog, was stifling with anger at not being able to pick a quarrel with such a polite individual.

"Monsieur," said Alice, who took pleasure in poking fun at Harrison, "Are you English in origin?"

"Not entirely," Quaterquem replied. "my father was Low Breton and my mother Low Brette,[3] but in 1803 or thereabouts, one of my father's cousins, five times removed, married an Englishman named Harrison—hence our kinship with all the Harrisons in Lancashire. In Brittany, cousins of cousins are all one another's cousins."

"You've never met your cousin, Mr. James Harrison?" asked Miss Alice.

---

[3] A *brette* is a kind of rapier.

"No, but I'll go to see him as soon as my great enterprise is concluded."

"Excuse my curiosity, Monsieur," said Alice, "but what is the great enterprise that prevents you from visiting Mr. James?"

"Alice," said her mother, her gaze rigid. "Curiosity is impolite."

"Oh, Madame, it's not curiosity at all," Quaterquem hastened to reply. "In a month's time, the entire world will know about it. I intend to give France the empire of the world."

"Oh!" cried the old Englishwoman. "You'll leave a part of it for England, I hope?"

"Me!" replied Quaterquem, delighted with his success. "I won't leave her a single continent, a single island, or a single county."

"Monsieur," said Alice, laughing, "You've just made my mother indignant to the extent of speaking French, which she swore she would never do, out of patriotism."

Quaterquem apologized politely. The curtain went up, and *Le Domino noir* interrupted the conversation.[4]

It's all going well, our hero thought. *Alice is astonished, her mother indignant, Harrison is grinding his teeth and longing to bite.*

He waited confidently for the end of the first act, and appeared to be uniquely occupied by the play. He was not mistaken in his calculations. Scarcely had the curtain come down than the old Englishwoman turned to him and commenced the attack in these terms: "Have you ever heard of Lord Nelson, Monsieur?"

"It was my father who killed him."

"What! It was your father who killed that hero?"

---

[4] *Le Domino noir*, a three-act comic opera with music by Daniel Auber and a libretto by Eugène Scribe, was premièred at the Opéra-Comique in December 1837; like *Le Chalet*, it was added to the standard repertoire and eventually clocked up more than a thousand performances.

"In truth," said Quaterquem, "it wasn't his fault. Nelson shot at him, he shot at Nelson. My father was a brave matelot doing his duty aboard the *Redoubtable* at Trafalgar. When the *Victory*, with Nelson aboard, confronted the *Redoubtable*, my father, who was on the maintop, spotted the admiral, took aim at him and, as he was a good marksman, killed him with a rifle bullet."

The old Englishwoman uttered a sigh and covered her eyes with her handkerchief. Alice's eyes were shining with impatience: Clearly readable there was: *My dear Monsieur, you've just done something stupid.* Quaterquem saw that, and was disconcerted.

Fortunately, the young woman came to his aid. "Console yourself, Mother dear," she said. "We're all mortal, and if that invincible hero had escaped the French bullets, he would nevertheless not have lived forever. His death was well avenged."

"Alas, my dear Alice, you know as well as I do how much our family lost by that fatal death!"

"Forgive me," said Quaterquem, "if I have inadvertently reminded you of a dolorous memory."

"Monsieur," said Alice, "you cannot comprehend my mother's chagrin. It's a family secret."

My poor father, Quaterquem thought, *just had to fire his rifle at that English dog, only for that wretched rifle shot to cause me to fall out at the first utterance with an old madwoman!*

There was a silence that lasted several minutes. Quaterquem, very embarrassed, pretended to be looking at all the boxes through his opera-glasses.

Suddenly, the old lady resumed the conversation.

"Monsieur," she said, "You will grant me, I believe, that the fatherland of Nelson and Wellington will always be the foremost country in the world."

The Englishwoman's obstinacy made Quaterquem smile, and rendered him some hope.

"Be careful, Monsieur," said Alice, laughing. "My mother will extract your secret from you and make a present of it to

England. Be discreet, or you're doomed, and the empire of the world will pass to the children of Albion."

"Alice," said the mother "don't interrupt our discussion. Answer my question, Monsieur, if you please."

"Say nothing, Monsieur," said the young woman, laughing even more loudly, "if you don't want to see your secret published in the *Times* within forty-eight hours."

"I hope," said the old Englishwoman, "that it isn't an infernal machine to blow up London and our beloved queen?"

"No, Madame," Quaterquem replied, utterly reassured, "it's the simplest of inventions, which will make Paris the center of the world, and render all the arsenals of Portsmouth and all the fleets of Spithead redundant."

"I'm curious to see this marvelous secret," said the old Englishwoman.

"Nothing easier," replied Quaterquem. "I've invented the balloon-omnibus. Henceforth, people will travel from France to England by the road of the birds, where one does not encounter any mariners, soldiers of customs officers. I shall plant the tricolor flag on the dome of St. Paul's, and with that flag I shall bring justice, equality and fraternity, of which your compatriots only know the names, and borrow from you a few petty things that we no longer know. By means of those reciprocal loans, all people will be friends, and there will be no more heroes, who cost so dear and bring very little back."

"You know how to steer balloons?" said the young Englishwoman.

"I know."

"For a long time?"

"Since three o'clock this afternoon."

"You're doubtless going to make a great fortune?"

"I don't know," said Quaterquem. "I've never thought about it."

She looked at him with admiration. "In England," she said, "You'd become a lord and a millionaire."

"Frankly," said the Breton, "my invention is worth more than that."

"You want to be a Minister?"

"No."

"King or Emperor?"

"God preserve me from that! I believe that a little glory would suit me much better. We're vain, we Frenchmen, and we want, above all else, other people to admire us."

"I regret," Alice said, "that my father stayed at the hotel this evening."

Quaterquem did not have time to ask why. The second act of *Le Domino noir* was beginning.

During the following entr'acte, they chatted about all sorts of things, and Quaterquem was able to adapt his language to the opinions of the old Englishwoman. In a matter of minutes they became the best of friends. The Frenchman, still obliging and polite, was able to flatter her tastes and prejudices delicately. He deployed to the fullest extent the art, unknown outside France, of caressing the most resistant and obstinate mind, without baseness. He took no less trouble to seduce Harrison, who was looking into the auditorium without speaking, with his hands on his knees and his eyes staring, resolved not to respond to his advances.

The play concluded, however, without Quaterquem having found a means to see his inamorata again. The ladies got to their feet and left the box, accompanied by Harrison. He watched them climb into a cab, hoping at last to discover their address, but fortune, dogged in his pursuit, did not permit that. Harrison, who suspected his design, gave the address to the coachman in a low voice.

Meanwhile, the vehicle drew away, and Quaterquem was getting ready to follow it on foot, when cries of joy burst forth around him.

"There he is!" cried seventeen voices, at the same time.

The unfortunate found himself trapped by his seventeen friends, who surrounded him, retained him by force, and demanded an account of his conduct.

"Where's the punch, man devoid of faith, constancy and substance?" said the chorus.

"In Heaven's name, let me go!" cried Quaterquem. "I'm in a hurry."

"Where's Napoléon's shaving-bowl?"

"Let me go!"

"Where's the balloon-omnibus?"

"Let me go!"

During this argument, Alice's carriage had disappeared round the corner of the boulevard.

"Oh well," said Quartequem, despairingly. "Come with me, if you must. Let's drown my misfortunes and my amour in waves of punch."

Everyone followed him to the nearest café. They were already turning off the gas-lamps, and the weary waiters were getting ready to go home. He ordered the punch, took the ladle in his hand, and, in the midst of general attention, he made the following speech: "Workers and gentlemen of my good city of Paris, you see in me the happiest of men and the least fortunate..."

"Bravo! Very good!" said the chorus of friends.

"My happiness is unlimited, like the Ocean, and my misfortune is endless, like eternity..."

"You've already said that!" cried the chorus.

"Well, I'm repeating it—don't interrupt me or I won't say anything. I'm in love with the most beautiful of women..."

"Listen! Listen!" cried the chorus.

"She's blonde, with emerald eyes, coral lips, and teeth as white as the fine pearls fished from the isles of Bahrain..."

"Well then, marry her!" said the chorus.

"She doesn't know that I love her..."

"Tell her."

"I can't talk to her..."

"Write."

"I don't know where she lives..."

"Search for her."

"I don't know her name..."

"Are you mad?" said the chorus. "You're telling us fairy stories, and the punch is going cold."

Quaterquem poured the punch, sighing. "Alas, he said, "I'll never see her again. She'll go back to London..."

At those words, the chorus, whose members had already raised their glasses to their lips, put them back on the table. "She's an Englishwoman!" they exclaimed, with one voice.

"I admit it..."

"Poor fellow," said the chorus.

"She's in Paris," said Quaterquem.

"How do you know?"

"She was at the Opéra-Comique this evening, and but for you, I'd have followed her. But for you, barbarians, I'd know where she lives and her name. You held me back..."

"Well," said the chorus, "we'll repair our fault. Let's drink up, and disperse to search for the address. How will we recognize your beloved?"

"By her unrivaled beauty..."

"That description is a trifle vague. Is she alone?"

"She's lending her arm to her mother, and a bulldog with red hair named Hercules Harrison, who is her future husband.…"

"Very good" cried the chorus. "Three snarls for Hercules and three cheers for Quaterquem!"

III

Miss Alice was the only daughter of Mr. Cornelius Hornsby, a principal associate of Hornsby, Harrison & Co, whose painted fabrics cover the steps of Germany and the United States. Hercules Harrison, Alice's future husband, was the son of his associate, and the two businessmen, in order not to separate their interests, had arranged the marriage long ago.

That arrangement displeased Miss Hornsby immensely. Poor Hercules, although he was neither ugly, nor malevolent, nor devoid of intelligence, was no romantic hero. He was a fine, stiff, proud, taciturn, almost brutal gentleman of a type of which England manufacturers hundreds of thousands a year, for whom the principal object of life is to make money, and, once having gained a great deal of it, to make even more. Solidly built, a distinguished boxer, as perpendicular in his morality as in his physique, he was one of those who please the majority of young women. Such as he was, for want of anything better, Alice had not refused to marry him, and contented herself with delaying the marriage under various pretexts. She was waiting for that imaginary and perfect lover, the accomplished gentleman with the Byronic gaze of whom every young woman has a right to dream, and of whom she does, indeed, dream in the depths of her heart.

That day, when she returned from the Opéra-Comique, she was humming the famous "Rule Britannia!" As, among all her perfections, she sang rather badly, she was rarely heard to do it, and that sudden desire to sing astonished Mrs. Hornsby.

"You're very cheerful this evening," she said to her daughter. "Why is that?"

"I was thinking about the presumption of that Frenchman," Alice said, "who wants to take the empire of the world away from England with his balloons. And how you reminded him, to confound him, about Nelson and Wellington! I was laughing at his aerostats."

It is true that Alice was thinking about Quaterquem, but she disguised the truth slightly in saying that she was making fun of him. The whole truth is never good to tell, and the real truth is that she was very preoccupied. Quaterquem, with his smiling face, his good humor, his affability and casual ease, was as dissimilar as possible from the grim Hercules, and the latter gained nothing by the comparison. Furthermore, she had seen Hercules every day for fifteen years, and such a long familiarity is not conducive to the birth of amorous feelings.

Mrs. Hornsby took Quaterquem's side. "You're wrong to laugh," she said to her daughter. "Perhaps he's a man of genius, even though he wasn't born in England."

"Oh, Mother, what are you saying? A man of genius who doesn't wear gloves, knots his cravat like a piece of rope and leaves his waistcoat half-unbuttoned?"

"You must have looked at him very attentively, Alice," said Hercules, with his customary gaucherie.

She bit her lip. "What do you mean by that, Harrison?" she demanded, sharply. "Have I said anything improper? Are you looking for a pretext for another sermon?"

Profoundly wounded, Harrison remained silent, and all three of them soon got down outside the Hôtel Meurice.

Cornelius Hornsby was waiting for them. He was a tall, stout gentleman whose imposing gait announced to all the passers-by that he was worth several millions. Apart from himself and his money he did not love anything in the world as much as his daughter, and after his daughter, what he liked more than everything else was his museum—for he had a museum.

In England, that is the sign by which one recognizes a true gentleman and a true millionaire. To the swords of one's ancestors—if one has ancestors—one adds stuffed Nile crocodiles, blackened old canvases by Italian painters, old Etruscan pottery, old sculpted dressers, old enamels, old stained-glass windows, missals, and all the pious bric-à-brac that twenty-five or thirty extinct peoples have left in the ruins of Babylon, Nineveh, Athens and Rome.

Cornelius Hornsby had come to France to augment his collection and show off his daughter. That very day, the desire to buy an old Persian inscription engraved on a fragment of wall from the great temple of Persepolis had prevented him from personally escorting his wife and Alice to the theater. Unfortunately, a more fortunate art-lover had obtained the inscription and was about to bury it in his own museum—with the result that Cornelius Hornsby was the unhappiest manufacturer of painted fabrics in the whole of Europe that evening.

He was pacing gravely back and forth under the arcades of the Rue de Rivoli when he saw Mrs. Hornby get down from the cab with his daughter and the downcast Harrison.

"You're back very late," he said.

His daughter's only response was to throw her arms around his neck.

"Dear Father," she said, "I hope you bought your inscription, and that it's even more cuneiform than all those in Korsabad. I can read in your eyes that Colonel Rawlinson will die of jealousy. Thank you, Hercules, and good night."

Sadly, Harrison shook the hand that she held out to him, and went away, despairing of ever understanding his fiancée's caprices.

As soon as he had gone, Mrs. Hornsby said: "You treated him very badly this evening."

"In revenge," said Alive. "He annoyed me enormously; we're quits."

"Alice!" said Mr. Hornsby.

"My God, Father dear, don't be so severe, and don't frown like that. I'm not the mistress of my impressions. He annoyed me. He's a very honest man, a very good citizen, and a very rich man, who will be even richer in future; I'll grant you all of that. Grant me that he's annoying. As soon as he opens his mouth he says something stupid, and on rainy days, the sound of his voice alone gets on my nerves."

"Do you want to marry him, yes or no?" demanded Cornelius Hornby.

"Certainly I want to, since it's inevitable, but don't rush me. Who knows whether, by dint of time and patience, I might succeed in liking Hercules? It's necessary not to swear to anything. The Great Turk might convert to Christianity and become Pope. I might also fall in love with someone else."

"Do you think so?" said her father. "Do you want me to break my word to my associate, so that, for the first time in his life, Cornelius Hornsby of Hornsby, Harrison & Co., fails to honor his signature?"

"Oh, my dear Father, Hercules is an honest man and would release you from your promise."

"Let's not think about that," said the old gentleman. "Take your time, if you wish, and make up your mind. It's time that Harrison went back to England; our business is suffering from his absence."

"Well then, let him go, and we'll stay in France. I like Paris; I've lost the habit of yawning here, and you're entirely rejuvenated by the air of the boulevards. I like the Parisians too; one doesn't see those long puritanical faces here that abound in the streets of London."

"Alice," said Mr. Hornsby, "You're becoming spoiled on the continent; you're taking on the language and the manners of this flighty nation. Look at the casual manner in which you made the acquaintance this evening with the young man who was in the same box as us at the play."

"Was it necessary to take his seat and not thank him, then?" said Alice. "You thought him very amiable and very polite yourself, Mother."

"Who is the young man of whom you speak?" asked Mr. Hornsby.

"He's a physicist who's found a means of steering aerostats," said the young woman, "and who wants to give the empire of the world to the French people. Can you imagine such madness? Mother put him in his place."

"He's a fantasist," said the father.

"The worst of it," added Madame Hornsby, "is that his father, who was present at the battle of Trafalgar, is the very matelot who killed Nelson with a rifle shot."

"And he dared to boast about that?"

"He had no idea of the extent to which that death was fatal to our family."

"Damn it!" said Cornelius. "He hasn't asked me for my daughter in marriage, but I'd have taken pleasure in refusing it. The son of Nelson's murderer!"

"And what if I loved him?" Alice said.

"If you loved him? How can one love the son of..."

"But in the end, what if I did?"

"Get away—it's absurd! You don't love him."

"No, but what if I did?"

"Well, you'd remember that you're my daughter, and you'd marry Harrison."

Alice fell into a profound meditation.

"It's time to go to bed," said the mother, and Cornelius retired to a nearby room.

As soon as she was in bed, Alice, wide awake, dreamed about Quaterquem.

IV

Quaterquem's seventeen friends spent the next day searching for the young Englishwoman's abode. That evening, at eight o'clock, they met up at the physicist's apartment, and said: "Her name is Alice Hornsby."

"Alice, oh, what a sweet name!" Quaterquem exclaimed.

"Her father is the noble Cornelius, who gives the world, in change for a great deal of money, several million meters of cotton cloth, in order to obey the catechism, accomplishing one of the seven labors of penitence by 'Clothing those who are naked.'"

"Good for Cornelius."

"Her mother is the worthy Kate, and her future, Sieur Hercules, is a worthy man, very stubborn, very much in love and a crack shot with a pistol."

"I shoot quite well myself," said Quaterquem. "The advantages are even."

"The entire family is leaving tomorrow."

"O Heavens!" said Quaterquem, going pale.

"They're going to Tours, a city of great renown."

"That's good. I'll go too. What are they going to do in Tours?"

"Old Cornelius, who's an antiquarian, is going to search the battlefield where Charles Martel fought the Saracens.[5] A

---

[5] At the Battle of Tours in 732 A.D., which earned the Frankish leader Charles his nickname (the Hammer), the Saracen leader Abdul Rahman al Ghafiqi (shortened to Abderam in some contemporary Frankish accounts) was killed, but the exact location of the battle and thus the location of any relics thereof remains unknown. Subsequent historians decided that

practical joker in London showed him Abderam's helmet; he wants to find his burial place."

"Who told you that?"

"The chambermaid, who spends all day long listening at doors."

"Wretch! You seduced her!"

"Oh, not much," said the chorus. "I scarcely kissed her."

"One more thing. Where is the beautiful Alice staying?"

"At the Hôtel Meurice."

"Thank you, my friends, bless you!" exclaimed Quaterquem, "and come embrace me. I'll bring you back a ham. My heart will never forget..."

He was interrupted by a single voice: "And wine?"

"Bacchus and Ceres will not be forgotten. To table! I drink to my imminent marriage to Alice."

Early the next morning, Quaterquem, clad in traveling costume, was strolling in the Rue de Rivoli. The chorus of seventeen friends was following him at a distance. One of them, detached as a scout, brought the next that the Englishman was climbing into a cab and was about to leave.

"The moment has come," said Quaterquem, "to render yourselves immortal forever by your devotion to friendship. Make sure that Harrison doesn't leave."

"Don't worry," said the chorus. "Leave Hercules to us."

They arrived at the railway station. Quaterquem, having come without luggage in order to be more agile, hastened to sit down in the waiting room. Behind him, but without seeing him, Mr., Mrs. and Miss Hornsby advanced. Hercules, laden down with heavy luggage, remained in the rear.

Suddenly, the bell sounded the last call. Anxiously, Hercules, increased his pace in order to get to the waiting room.

---

the battle was the crucial turning point of the Islamic invasion of Europe, which saved Christendom from annihilation and paved the way for the eventual expulsion of the Moors from what is now the south of France and from Spain.

Unfortunately, he bumped into a young man. He tried to continue his route.

"Pay attention, Monsieur if you please."

Hercules continued on his way without responding, but the passer-by with whom he had collided made a detour and planted himself in front of the waiting room door. "In France" he added, "when one has done something stupid, one apologizes."

The Englishman blushed, and tried to move his adversary aside with his hand, but a neighbor of the other intercepted his arm. In a trice, a group had formed around him.

"What's this?" said the chorus.

"It's an Englishman who's trying to pick a quarrel with me," replied Hercules' adversary, "who bumped into me and doesn't want to apologize."

"Let him apologize," said a voice.

"No, let him fight," said another.

Harrison clenched his fist furiously. "Messieurs," he said, "I'm not trying to pick a quarrel with anyone. Leave me alone. The bell is ringing and the train is going to leave without me."

But he could not get out of the circle in which he was confined. In his fury, he seized his adversary by the collar as if to strangle him; the latter freed himself, and a punch in the chest made him let go.

"Good! The Englishman's boxing now," said one of the audience.

"No, he's kicking," said another.

"Someone ought to fetch a policeman," said a third.

As he was speaking, one of the modest and useful functionaries in question appeared, and demanded explanations. The Englishman opened his mouth, but seventeen voices rose up at the same time to drown his out. That racket lasted for several minutes, and the policeman had great difficulty trying to understand what it was all about. As soon as he had understood, he laid his hand upon poor Harrison, who was struggling like a demon.

"You can explain it to the Commissaire," he said.

The chorus of friends laughed, and sang: *Never in France/Shall the English reign.*"

At the police station, the explanation was neither long nor stormy. The Englishman's principal adversary had disappeared. All the others declared that they had not seen or heard anything, and poor Hercules was released—but the train had gone and the perfidious Quaterquem was weaving his web tranquilly.

V

The physicist saw Cornelius Hornsby come into the waiting room with his wife and daughter, and resisted the violent desire that he had to greet Alice—prudence prevailed. He turned to the wall and read the railway timetable with avid interest. Meanwhile, he watched the young Englishwoman from the corner of his eye, and had the pleasure of seeing that he was being examined intently.

As soon as the double doors of the waiting room were opened, Cornelius advanced toward an empty carriage, and immediately installed himself comfortably in a corner. Facing him was his wife, and beside him, his daughter. A fourth seat remained empty, reserved for Hercules.

Quaterquem stuck his head into the carriage in an insouciant fashion.

"Get in quickly, Monsieur," said a guard, giving him push. "The train is about to leave."

"The seat is reserved for a friend!" exclaimed Cornelius Hornsby.

"Your friend can go into another carriage," said the railway employee, who thought that the Englishman was employing a ruse to keep a seat for his overcoat. "And you, Monsieur, hurry up,"

Quaterquem hastened to enter, and the employee closed the door.

"Excuse me if I'm causing you any difficulty," our friend said, graciously, taking Hercules' seat. "All the other carriages are full. The railway administration is unpardonably negligent."

Cornelius Hornsby muttered a few words, which Quaterquem pretended to take for polite assent. In the meantime, Mrs. Hornsby looked at him attentively and Alice, her eyes lowered, concentrated on reading a book that was open on her lap.

Suddenly, our friend appeared to recognize them. "By what fortunate coincidence do I find you here, Madame?" he said to Mrs. Hornsby. "I didn't expect the pleasure of seeing you again so soon."

At these words, Alice raised her eyes and smiled. Quaterquem saw that he had been divined, and that his boldness did not displease her. He took that as a good augury.

"We're going to Tours and Poitiers to look for the burial-place of Abderam," said Kate Hornsby, who, having no great credit in the company, was not reluctant to amuse herself at the expense of her lord and master Cornelius.

The Breton noticed that nuance, but did not want to equip one of the spouses with arms against the other. That was too dangerous a game.

"Archeology," he said, in a serious tone, "is an admirable science, and I regret to say that it owes great progress to the genius of your nation."

Cornelius' frown vanished.

Good, I have him, Quaterquem thought. Enthusiastically, he continued: "To whom do we owe the statues of Rome, the bas-reliefs of the Parthenon of Athens, and all the debris of the most beautiful monuments of antiquity? To whom, if not to English hands, filled with English money and directed by English genius?"

The most gracious of smiles strayed over Cornelius' lips. "Well, Monsieur," he said, interrupting Quaterquem. "That glory is disputed. I know a Norman who boasts of having taken molds of all the inscriptions of Korsabad, and there are thirty thousand of them, Monsieur, thirty thousand—which is to say, enough to cover the British Museum from top to toe. You can't believe how far the presumption of those people extends."

"Have you visited Nineveh?" asked Quaterquem. "It's said that Monsieur Place, the French consul, has left nothing for his successors to do there?"[6]

"Nothing to do!" said Cornelius, indignantly. "Monsieur, everything is to be done. Yes, I've seen Nineveh, its palaces and its temples, the debris of whose brickwork covers three or four square leagues of terrain. I have done better, Monsieur: I have seen Ecbatana, the city of the famous Dejokh, the city with seven walls, behind which the king's palace was found."

"Ecbatana!" said Quaterquem, struck with admiration. "Is it possible?"[7]

"Everything is possible for an Englishman," said Corrnelius, swelling up with pride. In 1857, I was at Khiva and I dined with the khan of the Tartars, with Prince Barovsky, the governor of Archangel. Suddenly, I perceived among the slaves who were serving us a big fellow with a tanned face that I thought I recognized. I made him a sign to approach and I said to him: 'Bourdaké Pharana'—which is to

---

[6] In 1855 Victor Place took over the excavations begun by Paul-Émile Botta, the French Consul in Mosul, who believed (wrongly, as it turned out) that he had discovered the location of the ancient city of Nineveh. Most of the artifacts that Place tried to send back to Paris were lost when the boats carrying them were sunk in the Tigris.

[7] No, it isn't possible. Ecbatana, a city in the Persian Empire, is nowadays believed to have been on the site of the modern town of Tell Hagmtana, but that site was not excavated until 1913 and the attribution remains controversial. Herodotus attributed to founding of the legendary city to "Deioces," referred to in cuneiform inscriptions as Daiukku, which Hornsby renders as Dejokh. The story that Hornsby tells is pure fantasy.

say: 'Are you not a former English servant?' He replied: 'Krack'—which is to say: 'I'm a Frank.' As you can imagine, we were speaking pure Turcoman. 'Burnes perodhé barnaiâ,' he continued, which is to say: 'I served with Colonel Burnes, who as massacred in this dog of a country by the Tartar in whose home you're dining today, and I'm the slave of that ferocious scoundrel.' It's necessary to tell you that Turcoman is he most energetic and concise language in the world."

"I can see that," Quaterquem replied. "Continue the story, I beg you; I'm curious to hear the rest."

"The confidence of that poor devil—for he had spoken to me in a whisper, cut off my appetite. I replaced a piece of roasted horse on my plate—that was the best part of the feast—and started thinking about ways to set him free.

"Just then, the khan, who was facing me, noticed that I was no longer eating. Now, among those worthy people, it's an unpardonable insult to let the master of the house drink and get drunk alone. 'You're not drinking,' he said. 'Don't you like mares' milk?' I defended myself forcefully, and drank four or five bull's-horns to the health of the khan and the sultanas. After dinner, the khan, already considerably softened up by the mares' milk and the brandy that Barovsky had brought as a present, set my protégé at liberty, and I left immediately, in order not to give him time to repent of his generosity."

"What was the slave's name?" Quaterquem asked.

"Mahmoud. He was a lascar, born of an Indian woman and an Englishman. Under the leadership of Burnes he had visited all of central Asia, the Khorazan, the Mazanderan and the shores of the Caspian Sea. He took me to see Ecbatana. I alone, I Europe, Monsieur, have seen the ruins of that superb city, by comparison with which even London is nothing but a vast anthill. I recovered the preliminary title of the codex of the famous king Djemshid, that abridgement of all wisdom."

"And you haven't published anything?"

"What's the point? Would I have spent two hundred thousand francs, risked my life, crossed seas, traversed the highest mountains in the world, wandered in the Gobi desert and the vast solitudes of ancient Arya; would I have braved the sands of Tartary, thirst, hunger, fatigue and the burning sun to give millions of idlers the pleasure of becoming as knowledgeable by paying three francs to read my book? No, no. If they want to know Ecbatana, let them go there, let them expend their money and their health; then they'll receive the price of their fatigues."

"By God!" said Quaterquem. "I admire you."

"You're very kind. I don't care about being admired, but simply act on my whim, and my whim is to discover the monuments of ancient history. The late Napoléon called us shopkeepers; for me, that is a glorious title. I want to prove that with my money I can have everything, even a taste for the arts, if it pleases me. The shopkeeper is a king in his shop, and receives every day the homage of artists and writers of books. He stirs the gold in his drawers, and everyone bows down to that noise. If he wanted to, he would be a god..."

The conversation continued for some time in that tone. Quaterquem took great care not to contradict Cornelius even feebly, in order to give him the pleasure of talking victoriously. He had the pleasure of seeing that the beautiful Alice understood the tactic and was grateful to him for it. The worthy Kate, bored by Ecbatana and a overly detailed discussion of the various genres of antique pitchers, had drifted off into the sleep of the just.

In the meantime, they arrived at Étampes, and the train stopped for a few minutes. The young Englishwoman wanted to get out of the carriage and stretch her legs. Cornelius and his wife remained seated, and Quaterquem went with Alice. His heart was beating violently. It was the decisive moment.

"Miss Hornsby," he said.

"You know my name?" she exclaimed, astonished.

"Oh, I know a great many things. I know that you're engaged to be married to Mr. Hercules Harrison, the gentleman with the red side-whiskers who gave you his arm the day before yesterday. It's about him that I want to talk to you."

"Has something happened to him?"

"Oh, nothing much. He missed the train, but you'll see him again tomorrow. He picked a quarrel with seventeen of my best friends, and he was taken to the police station."

"With seventeen of your best friends?"

"The bell is about to ring," said Quaterquem, "And I don't have time to explain that mystery. Only know that it was on my instructions that he was retained in Paris."

"But Monsieur, what is this folly? What do you have against Hercules?"

"He loves you."

The young Englishwoman blushed, lowered her veil over her face, and climbed back into the carriage without saying a word.

Quaterquem followed her, slightly anxious about the success of his audacity. Without being entirely inexperienced in amour, he was certainly no Don Juan, and he was already too much in love not to be fearful, Fortunately, the first glance that he cast at his traveling companion made him see that she was not harboring any resentment for such a bold and abrupt declaration.

"Have you seen Hercules on the train?" Cornelius asked his daughter.

"No, Father." She blushed and looked at Quaterquem.

Good, he thought. *She's not in love with Sieur Hercules. All's well; I've gained half my suit.*

Meanwhile, old Hornsby, charmed to find such an obliging listener, had formed the project—rare and extraordinary for an Englishman—of making a more ample acquaintance with Quaterquem, and he came straight to the point.

"Monsieur," he said, "I can see by your speech that you're a distinguished archeologist; have you traveled in the Orient?"

"No," said the Breton, "but I've traveled from Saint-Malo to Paris and from Paris to Saint-Malo. That's sufficient for my happiness."

"You must at least by a member of the Institut, or one of its correspondents?"

"I'm not even the doorman," said Quaterquem. "I'm a pure X, and I have a thousand francs in my pocket, which is the bulk of my wealth."

While speaking, he examined the physiognomy of the young Englishwoman, in order to see whether that news might lower him in her estimation, but Alice, although astonished by such an unexpected confidence, did not appear overly moved by it. Mr. Hornsby was less satisfied, and his faced clearly showed that he had imagined that he was speaking to a more respectable—which is to say, richer—gentleman. Alice divined by Quaterquem's proud gaze that he was scornful of Cornelius, and she hastened to intervene.

"Monsieur," she said, "what is an X, please?"

"Open your pocket dictionary," said Cornelius.

Quaterquem smiled. "Miss Hornsby," he said, "won't find that information in her book. One doesn't find in dictionaries that for which one needs to consult them. An X, Mademoiselle, is an annoying man, like all the useful men who do all the difficult work of creation. A geometer is an X, a physicist is an X, a chemist is an X, a naturalist and an algebraist are Xs. It's an X who invented steamships, another who invented railways; it was a third X who invented printing. Everywhere that something great and useful is done, you'll find an X. Hiram, the famous architect who built the temple of Solomon, was an X, like Albertus Magnus, who found the secret of transmuting a ray of sunlight sealed in a tomb into gold.

"Did you live for a long time in Saint-Malo?" asked Miss Hornsby.

"Until the age of fifteen, and I've been in Paris for ten years. The name of Quaterquem is well-known in Saint-Malo.

"Quaterquem!" exclaimed Cornelius, astonished. "What a singular name!"

"It is one of the most noble in France," the Breton replied, "although my father, who did not know how to read, was a matelot all his life. Our nobility dates back to King Saint Louis. During the Egyptian crusade, my ancestor, who was a brave Breton peasant, killed thirty or forty Saracens in a single battle. Four times the mamelukes riddled him with saber thrusts and trampled him under the feet of their horses; four times he got up again and laid about him more even murderously, before the eyes of the marveling King. Saint Louis, who was as knowledgeable as a clerk, turned to his chaplain and said to him in good Latin: 'Iste Quaterquem vidimus occisum fortior renascitur.'[8] The chaplain repeated the king's words, and the entire army called my grandfather Quaterquem. The king made him a Baron and made him a present of a beautiful Barony, which melted away more than a century ago into the hands of usurers. Since that time my grandfather and my father fished for cod in Newfoundland, which was not lowering themselves, and spent their lives at sea—and I, in order not to be unworthy of them, have sought the means of navigating in the air."

"What!" exclaimed Mr. Hornsby. "It's you about whom my daughter talked to me all day yesterday?"

"Oh, very little, Father," said Alice, blushing.

Quaterquem was the happiest of men. She had talked about him all day; therefore she had been thinking about him; therefore she loved him, or would love him one day; therefore...

His presumptuous imagination did not stop in that series of therefores.

"Yes," he said. "I've found the means of steering balloons."

"A reliable means?"

"Perfectly reliable. I carried out the experiment the day before yesterday."

"Monsieur," said the Englishman, "if your secret is proven, if it's infallible, I'll give you a million for it."

"In order to exploit it?"

---

[8] It is a matter of opinion as to whether the Latin is good or not, but the king is asking the identity of the man who was seen to fall down four times and be reborn again. "Quaterquem" runs together *quater* [four] and *quem* [whom].

"Yes, and to put my name on it. I don't want it to be said that such a discovery was made by anyone but an Englishman."

Quaterquem started laughing. "A billion wouldn't buy the secret," he replied. "In ten years the human race will do the work of twenty centuries. England, all of whose strength is in her ships, her iron mines and her coal mines, will no longer be anything but a little corner of the habitable world. Her ports will be deserted, her shipyards deserted, her factories deserted. The crows will be croaking in the House of Lords, and magpies chattering in the House of Commons."

Miss Hornsby's expression stopped him in time. He realized that he had gone astray. Cornelius was unworthy of his audacity, but he wanted to confound him and he continued the conversation. Quaterquem was able to regain his good graces and talked about archeology as much as the Englishman desired.

Meanwhile, they were approaching Orléans. Kate opened her eyes and her mouth.

"At which hotel are we staying?" she asked.

Mr. Hornsby opened his Bradshaw. "The Hôtel du Loiret," he said. "That's the one preferred by His Grace he Duke of Bedford, and Hercules knows that we'll be staying there."

"My God!" said Quaterquem. "That's a fortunate coincidence. I plan to stop over in Orléans myself. If you wish I can show you the antiquities of the surrounding area."

"I'd be delighted," replied Cornelius, who held the Breton in high esteem now that he knew that he was the possessor of such a precious secret.

Miss Hornsby did not say a word, but Quaterquem could see that he was making progress in the young Englishwoman's heart. The worthy Kate, as mute as a fish, was only occupied with the hope of a good dinner.

That hope was not deceived, and two bottles of excellent wine completed Mr. Hornsby's joy.

"My word," he said, putting his elbows on the table, "you're a good companion, my dear Monsieur Quaterquem, and I'm delighted to have met you. Without your being aware of it, I had an extreme antipathy toward you, and I'm very glad to find that I was mistaken."

"Really—you hated me?" said Quaterquem. "For what reason, if you please?"

"Because, if it weren't for your father, I'd be in the House of Lords."

"What? In what country did you meet him, if you please?"

"I've never even seen a picture of him, but listen to my story. In 1806, my father, Lucius Hornsby, was the intimate friend and right arm of Nelson. He commanded under him one of the vessels of the squadron, and had Nelson's promise that he would be made a vice-admiral at the next vacancy. Unfortunately, your father killed Nelson and took away the promotion promised to Lucius. The Lords of the Admiralty retired him instead of giving him command of a squadron. My father, furious, married in Northumberland, and never wanted to hear any more talk of the peerage, and I, who ought to have been a lord and Secretary of State, am only five or six times a millionaire."

"It's true," said Quaterquem, "that that's a deplorable fate, and you have every reason to curse destiny; for myself, I shan't try to justify my father. It's inexcusable to have killed Nelson and hindered the advancement of Lucius Hornsby. Reflect, however, that we are all mortal, and that Nelson, if he had escaped my father, would doubtless have perished by someone else's hand."

"I know that," said Mr. Hornsby, "and that's what makes me indignant against your nation. So I've sworn that my daughter, come what may, shall never marry a Frenchman."

"That's very sagely thought," said Quaterquem, "and I approve, especially if you have a good English son-in-law already prepared."

"I have my friend Hercules, who would be the pearl of sons-in-law if he didn't yawn so much when I talk about archeology."

"Do you mean Mr. Harrison?"

"Yes—do you know him?"

"I think so. Isn't he the tall red-haired young man who was struggling with all his might in the vestibule when the train left? Between the two of us, and saving the honor that he has of being Miss Hornsby's fiancé, I believe that he'd had too much to drink."

"Too much to drink! That's impossible, Monsieur. Hercules only drinks port. You're surely mistaken."

"Let's admit, if you wish, that he only drinks port. There are, to be sure, very dangerous ports. I saw him picking a quarrel with fifteen or twenty people who were trying in vain to calm him down."

"In fact," said Cornelius, "his absence is very singular; he must have had some kind of accident. In any case, I'm not worried. He'll soon catch up with us."

"What are we going to do in the meantime?" Alice asked.

"What if we were to begin a game of whist?" said the placid Kate.

Quaterquem shivered. Among numerous good qualities, the poor fellow had the terrible fault of being unable to tolerate tedium. Now, whist, as everyone knows, is the finest incarnation of tedium. I shall say no more for fear of annoying several of my friends who have not been able to steer clear of it, but I deem every whist-player to be faint of heart and a ferocious egotist.

Fortunately, Cornelius Hornsby, as frightened as his new friend by the thought of whist, hastened to pick up his hat. "The weather's fine," he said. "Let's go and explore the surrounding area. Will you come with us, Monsieur?"

Quaterquem did not need the offer to be repeated, and offered his arm to the beautiful Alice.

They took the road to Olivet. Scarcely had they reached the Pont d'Orléans when a bellboy from the hotel ran after Mr. Hornsby and handed him a telegraphic dispatch. The English man broke the seal and read:

Paris, 27 April 1859, 11 a.m.
My dear Mr. Hornsby, a stupid quarrel I have just had with a stranger, which caused me to remain under arrest for an hour, made me miss the train. I am free now and am going to sue the policeman for illegal arrest. I'll teach these Frenchmen that they can't lay hands on an English citizen with impunity. My regards to you and my dear Alice.
                                            Hercules Harrison
P.S. The lawsuit obliges me to remain in Paris until tomorrow.

Quaterquem had a great deal of difficulty not bursting in- to laughter on seeing the fortunate effect of his intrigue. As for Miss Hornsby, she frankly made fun of her fiancé.

"Hercules," she said, "is scarcely in a hurry to rejoin us."

"He's right, my dear," replied Mr. Hornsby. "It's neces- sary that such an offence against the liberty of an English citi- zen doesn't go unpunished."

The incident was not without consequence. The Breton, delighted with his good luck, and seeing that he had time to spare, resolved to get straight to work. He increased his pace and, leaving Mr. Hornsby and Kate some distance away, was finally able to speak freely to his inamorata.

"Are all English lovers made on that model?" he said, laughing.

"Very nearly," Alice replied. "The gentlemen have such perfect mastery of their passions that one never sees them quit a business meeting for a lovers' rendezvous. Harrison won't think of anything today but his revenge on the policeman who felt his collar. He's drag him through every court in France until he's had him condemned to prison and a fine."

"Poor policeman!" said Quaterquem. "He's put his hand on a real porcupine. Fortunately, he has nothing to fear from that pursuit, and Mr. Harrison will have to pay all the costs."

"But what about you, Monsieur, who boasted to me of having played that trick on my future husband? What would you say if I repeated that confidence to my father and mother?"

Quaterquem could see, by Miss Hornsby's tone and merriment, that she was not sorry about his audacity, and he replied cheerfully: "I confess, Mademoiselle, that my crime is unforgivable, but I hope that you will show me mercy in view of the intention."

"And what is that fine intention?" she said, in a tone that as half light and half serious.

"I neither dare to speak nor to remain silent. I fear that my frankness might displease you."

No matter how much effort he made to remain calm, his heart was beating so violently that she perceived it sensed the sweet amorous emotion communicate itself to her.

She tried to maintain her bantering tone, however. "Speak, Monsieur; am I so fearsome?"

"A thousand times more than you think."

"You're making me die of impatience and curiosity. Whatever it is, Monsieur, speak; I pardon you in advance."

"Well then, Miss Hornsby, permit me one question?"

"Interrogate me if you wish, but I don't promise to answer you."

"Have you read any novels?"

"Oh, very few—two or three thousand at the most."

"That's not very many."

"Isn't it, Monsieur? Alas, life is so short!"

"Do you believe that a sincere and passionate man can fall in love suddenly, in a single minute, as a result of an encounter at a ball or the Opéra?"

"I don't know, Monsieur. My cousin Charlotte eloped five years ago with a lieutenant in the hussars with whom she had waltzed twice the previous evening."

"And did their love endure?"

"Certainly. In France, do people sometimes weary of loving?"

"I'm not saying that. One can, therefore, fall in love at first sight and for life—that you admit."

"What do you want me to say, Monsieur? I don't know. I have no experience in such matters."

"Well, Madame, let's suppose that someone fell in love with you in that fashion, and that the man in question was ready to give his life for you. Let's suppose that he has never loved anyone but you, and, in spite of all the obstacles that ought to discourage him, he dared to tell you. What would you reply?"

"Monsieur," said Alice, "I don't like to examine pure hypotheses."

"But in the end, if all that were true—if the life, the future and perhaps the glory of that man depended on you alone?"

"You're forgetting Mr. Harrison."

"I'm not forgetting him. He's the one who's forgetting you, for a ridiculous lawsuit."

"It's true that he'd have done better to follow us; but you, Monsieur, unless you have as much passion for archeology and rusty old daggers as my father, what are you doing here?"

"You haven't guessed?"

"No, I swear."

"Well, you see, I'm examining hypotheses with you."

"And you're speaking ill of my poor Hercules. What has he done to you?"

"Look, Mademoiselle," said Quaterquem, "let's talk seriously. I love you and I sense that I will love you all my life..."

"You're very prompt, and you ought to have consulted me before committing that folly. Seriously, my dear Monsieur"—while speaking she leaned gently on Quaterquem's arm—"you can't love me. Setting myself aside, what would my father think and do, who has given his word to Harrison, and who has an invincible antipathy for you and your nation?"

"Bah! The pleasure of talking archeology will outweigh the despair of giving his daughter to Nelson's murderer."

"But Monsieur, in order for him to give me to you, it would be necessary for me to give myself, and I'm still far from that."

"You don't love Harrison."

"How do you know? He's an excellent man who does everything I wish and who loves me madly."

"The fine merit of loving you and obeying you! The sun, the moon and the stars would do as much, if you deigned to command them."

"I don't doubt it, but who will convey my orders to them? In the meantime, is it not very comfortable to have in hand a good husband, ready-made, accustomed to all my caprices, who knows my faults as I know his, and who will love me tranquilly and eternally?"

"Very tranquilly, in fact!"

"My God, it's not ideal, I know, and Lord Byron's heroes have an altogether different style, but that honest Englishman, devoid of passions, weaknesses and vices..."

"And virtues..."

"Let us add, if you wish, devoid of virtues…will fill his role of husband very well in London."

"Yes, he'll have money, credit, importance, perhaps reputation. A thousand others are worth no more than he is—but he'll bore you to death. To him, you'll be like a beautiful item of furniture; you'll preside over the parties he gives, if he gives any; you'll be envied for your beauty, your irresistible grace, your charming intelligence—but you'll dry up inside with ennui and distaste, and you'll curse a thousand times over the day when you accepted an English husband from your father's hand."

"Perhaps; but who will guarantee that you will love me more, and that this declaration, so gallant and so unexpected, is not the effect of a ray of fresh spring sunlight, or the singing of the nightingales in the woods, and that your love won't be as brief and fugitive as the great reawakening of nature that is exciting it today?"

"Alice," said Quaterquem, taking her hand, emotionally, "I swear to love you eternally. From the first day that I saw you, my soul has been yours entirely; I no longer have any thought that is not of you. You shall be my life, or I shall die."

"You're forgetting Mr. Harrison and my father."

"Harrison! I'll kill him. Your father I'll convert, and if necessary, I'll surrender my secret and my glory to him."

"Your glory! If you do that, I shall know that you love me, and that day..."

"Finish! That day?"

"Well, I'll permit you to hope."

Overwhelmed by joy, Quaterquem kissed her hand passionately.

"Be careful," she said, swiftly withdrawing her hand. "My father is looking this way and might see us."

If anyone thinks that Miss Hornsby is a trifle prompt in disposing of her heart and her hand; that it would be more appropriate to wait for the consent of her father and mother; and that such precipitation does no great honor to the perfect education that the worthy Kate had given her, I would respond to that impertinent critic that Miss Hornsby is English—which is to say, very free in her actions—that she is in love with Quaterquem (which is, after all, neither improper nor unprecedented in the annals of nations), that she is not in love with Harrison, and that she has for that poor man the perfectly natural distaste that a rich, intelligent, pretty and willful young woman cannot fail to have for a savant automaton like the brave Hercules; I would add that a husband presented by a father does not have nearly the same savor and the same attraction as a husband who presents himself of his own accord and whom it is necessary to let in through the hidden door; and finally, I will agree, if you wish, that my heroine is not perfect and would do much better to read the Bible or listen to the pious sermons of the Reverend Spurgeon than to welcome so favorably the speeches of a very sincere, very amorous, very honest, and, at the same time, very dazed young man such as our friend Quaterquem. At any rate, whatever judgment one might make, the fact is certain, historic and authentic. It is therefore not me who will reproach the somewhat flighty conduct of the amiable Miss Hornsby, only daughter of the learned Cornelius.

VI

No incident marked the end of the stroll. Cornelius Hornsby and the placid Kate drew closer, and the conversation became general. Quaterquem, drunk with joy, replied at hazard to all questions. They went up the Loiret as far as the source; he took the oars and guided the boat with such skill that the Englishman complimented him.

"It was my first métier," he replied, simply. "When I was very young I went fishing with my father and I maneuvered the boat while he attended to the nets."

In the evening, the four travelers dined at the same table, and Quaterquem had the joy, as he withdrew, of pressing the divine fingers of the beautiful Alice. Love, in its commencements, is timid and content with very little. However, our friend was well aware that that exceedingly happy life could not last much longer, and that Harrison was going to come back and reclaim his property. He quivered with anger at the thought that another man lived in an almost intimate familiarity with the woman he loved more than life, and as he was not a man to deliberate for long, he resolved to ask Mr. Hornsby for his daughter's hand the following morning.

Unfortunately, the first person he saw was the jealous Hercules, who went past him without greeting him.

There's an encounter that doesn't augur anything good, the Breton thought.

A few moment later, the beautiful Alice appeared, who extended her hand to the two rivals and smiled very graciously at Quaterquem.

"Back already!" she said to Hercules. "You didn't initiate a lawsuit against the policeman, then? You allowed him to insult the name of England with impunity?"

"There was nothing to be done. Even the advocates said that I would lose my case."

"All the same, it would have been a fine gesture to try. We amused ourselves greatly yesterday, and we took a charming excursion with Monsieur Quaterquem. Monsieur Quaterquem, Mr. Harrison; Hercules, Monsieur Quaterquem."

They both bowed to one another with a cold politeness. The situation became embarrassing, and Miss Hornsby no longer knew what to say, when old Cornelius came into the lounge, very happy to have touched the forty or fifty patellas and tibias of monks that fill the crypts of the Église Saint-Aignan, the sight of which delights all Englishmen.

"Monsieur," said Quaterquem to the old Englishman, "I've discovered, on the other side of the Loire, three leagues from here, an old château that is a marvel. Would you like to come to see it with me?"

"I'm ready. Are you coming, Hercules?"

"No, I'm tired," he replied. "I'll stay with the ladies."

Cornelius and Quaterquem climbed into the carriage alone, and took the road to Sologne."

"Well," said Cornelius, "What is this fine château? What date? In what style—Byzantine or Gothic?"

Quaterquem was so emotional that he was unable to reply.

This, he thought, *is the master of my destiny. By what arguments can I convince him, or even reach him?*

"Monsieur," he said, "I don't want to hide the truth from you any longer. This journey is a ruse that I invented in order to be able to speak to you freely. The château does not exist."

"Really?" said Cornelius, who thought he was dealing with a madman. "And for what reason?"

"Monsieur, I'm passionately on love with your daughter, and I'm asking you for her hand in marriage."

The Englishman burst out laughing. "That's why you're dragging me away into the wilds of Sologne? My dear sir, you could have saved yourself the trouble. Firstly, my daughter isn't available for marriage; secondly, however much I think of your rare talents, and whatever esteem and sympathy I have for your character, I've sworn only to marry my daughter to an Englishman, and I shall keep my word."

"But..."

"Come on, Monsieur, let's reason a little, if you wish. You say that you love my daughter; in conscience, do you think you're the only one? And that it's necessary that I give her to just anyone, on the pretext that he loves her? Are you English, first of all?"

"No."

"Are you at least rich?"

"I have a thousand francs in my wallet and an invention that can make the fortune of a people."

"Yes, but which hasn't made yours. Are you noble?"

"I've told you that my nobility dates back to Saint Louis' crusade."

"Very good, but your father was a sailor and your grandfather too?"

"They were very honest men," Quaterquem replied, proudly, "who served their fatherland courageously."

"I don't blame you," the Englishman said, "for being proud of their name, but in all justice, do you think that my daughter and I are charmed by it? Is it something to say in a drawing room in Paris or in London: *My father-in-law was a matelot…*?"

"Oh, Parisians don't care very much about that."

"Perhaps not, especially if you're rich, but in London? That's not all. You're asking for my daughter's hand. By what entitlement? Your father killed Nelson, and, by the same stroke, stole the peerage to which I might legitimately have aspired if Lucius Hornsby had become an admiral. That's something I'll never forgive, and no Englishman will ever forgive you. Believe me, my dear sir, let's remain good friends; forget this bizarre idea that you've got into your head—I don't know why—and let's go to lunch. It's a little chill, and the air of the banks of the Loire has given me an appetite."

"That's all you have to say, Monsieur?"

"That's all. What more do you want? You're not a child to whom one offers a sweet to help him swallow a bitter potion. You're a man of intelligence and heart, and you know how to reconcile yourself to inevitable disappointments."

"Monsieur," said Quaterquem, "I shall love Miss Hornsby until death, and I swear to you that she shall have no other husband than me."

"My dear sir, you're mad. My daughter will marry Harrison."

"She will not!"

"She will! And for greater assurance, I shall send her back to England tomorrow."

"Send her wherever you like. I'll follow her, and provoke Harrison."

"What madness! If you kill Hercules, I'll be even more certain to refuse you Alice's hand."

"I'll elope with her. You won't want to condemn her, and you'll consent to the marriage."

"I won't consent to anything. I've promised my daughter to Harrison, and he shall have her."

"Harrison is an idiot, who would bore your daughter, and already bores her."

"How do you know?"

"She told me so."

"That's impossible! Alice knows that she is to marry him, and she loves him."

"She doesn't love him."

"She loves him!"

"She doesn't, I tell you."

"Well, love isn't necessary in a marriage. Alice is a virtuous girl, and well brought up, who will obey me willingly."

"She's virtuous and well brought-up, but she won't obey!"

Gradually, Cornelius was getting heated, and the discussion was about to degenerate into a quarrel when Quaterquem, who realized that, turned the carriage around and took the road back to Orléans.

That's enough for once, he thought. *It's necessary not to make the old man dig his heels in.*

Deep down, he was not too discouraged. He had expected and prepared in advance for the Englishman's reply, so he was no longer searching for anything but a way to get around the difficulty. When he arrived at the hotel he went to find Hercules.

The worthy gentleman, clad in a Scottish jacket and a cap without a peak, had the grace, casual manner, ease and nobility of an English palfrey. As soon as he perceived Quaterquem, he raised his eyes to the ceiling and appeared to be contemplating the moldings very attentively.

"Monsieur," said Quaterquem, "Will you, pray, walk with me for a quarter of an hour? I have a very important matter to discuss with you."

"I do not have any matter to discuss with you," said the Englishman.

"That's possible," said Quaterquem, "but I have one to discuss with you. Come on."

Hercules followed him, not without reluctance, and the two walked along the bank of the Loire.

"Do you love Miss Hornsby very much?" asked Quaterquem.

The Englishman stared at him without answering.

"I can see that my question astonishes you slightly," Quaterquem continued. "It's necessary for you to know that I'm passionately in love with Miss Hornsby, and that I too want to marry her. Now, Mr. Hornsby has got it into his head to give you preference, and that bizarre idea is so profoundly screwed into his skull that I'll never be able to unscrew it without your help. Come on, speak sincerely: do you love Miss Hornsby?"

"What business is that of yours?"

"So, you persist in wanting to marry her?"

"Of course! And I think you're very bold, sir, to talk to me in that tone."

"As to that," said Quaterquem, "one speaks as one can; the essential thing is to explain oneself. In plain terms, you bore Miss Hornsby."

"Did she ask you to tell me that?"

"Not exactly; but I've divined it, and I thought I ought to let you know."

"Are you trying to pick a fight, sir?" asked Harrison.

"Not at all. I've recognized by certain signs that you bore Miss Hornsby; furthermore, I love her, and I please her..."

"You please her!"

"I please her. She hasn't said so yet, but it's evident. Well, I'm informing you charitably, in your own interest, to make an honorable retreat. Is that a bad thing to do, I ask you?"

"Sir," said the Englishman, "do you know that you're beginning to warm my ears?"

"I didn't know," replied Quaterquem, "but I believe you. One last time, will you renounce marrying Miss Hornsby?"

The Englishman shrugged his shoulder, making no reply.

"Do you know," said Quaterquem, "that someone made a fool of you in Paris?"

Hercules reddened with anger. "Who is the insolent fellow who dared?" he cried.

"The insolent fellow," said the Breton, "is me." And he explained the trick of which Hercules had been the victim.

"Sir," said the Englishman, "You will give me satisfaction."

"Get away!" exclaimed Quaterquem. "That wasn't so hard. When shall we meet?"

"Tomorrow."

"What time?"

"Six o'clock in the morning."

"Where?"

"Here. Mr. Hornsby will be my witness."

The two friends separated. Quaterquem, having returned to the hotel, wrote to his seventeen friends.

Orléans, 18 April 1859.

Dear Seventeen,

Tomorrow, at six o'clock in the morning, I have to send the noble, sage and amiable Harrison to a better world, or go to take my own place there. Would you believe that the ill-bred Saxon has the bad taste to dispute the heart and hand of the most beautiful of the daughters of Albion with me? In truth, it's incredible!

You can imagine that I'm too wise to let myself be killed like a hare in a furrow, but it's necessary to be prepared for any eventuality. I'm sending you in this enclosure all the figures, plans and explanations necessary for the construction of my aerostat-omnibus. It's necessary that the human race doesn't suffer from my folly. I don't have the right, in dying, to take my glory and my secret with me.

Adieu, my dear and beloved Seventeen, my only loves after the divine Alice. Admire the way in which everything in this world is connected. If I hadn't received money on the fifteenth of April, I wouldn't have bought the great Napoléon's shaving bowl; if I hadn't had the bowl I wouldn't have broken it and I wouldn't have gone to the Opéra-Comique; if I hadn't gone to the Opéra-Comique, I wouldn't have seen Miss Alice Hornsby, the daughter of the learned Cornelius; if I hadn't seen her, I wouldn't be in love; if I weren't in love, I would have let the surly Harrison of Hornsby, Harrison & Co. alone, and finally, I wouldn't be in danger of being imminently placed in the Panthéon—for I fully expect, my dear and faithful Seventeen, that you will make sure of my glory, if I have to cross the Styx.

You are all in my heart. Yours,

Yves Quaterquem

Our friend spent the rest of the day very sadly. Alice did not appear at dinner, and stayed in her room with the placid Kate. Cornelius tried to talk about archeology, but Quaterquem was not listening, and yawned pitilessly in the face of Hornsby, Harrison & Co. As for Harrison, he did not pronounce a syllable.

That evening, while the Breton was searching everywhere for a witness for his duel, he went into a café where the French army was playing billiards, drinking absinthe and discussing the merits of young Jenny, who was not the same one as "Jenny the seamstress/Her heart content, content with little..."

Jenny was an amiable Solognote who was the delight of the officers, sergeants and enlisted men of the seventh-fifth line regiment, and thus enjoyed a great popularity in that noble regiment.

Of all the officers who were in the café, only one was not taking any part in the conversation. He was a young man with a blond moustache and a melancholy face, who was sitting with his feet on the table, level with his chin. He was smoking peacefully, with his eyes upraised to the heavens—which is to say, the blackened ceiling above his head.

Good, thought Quaterquem. *That's my man.*

And he went straight toward him.

"Monsieur," he said, bowing politely, "would you permit me to ask you for a small favor?"

The young officer put his feet down, gazed pensively for a few seconds and, doubtless content with Quaterquem's physiognomy, replied with the same politeness: "Sit down, Monsieur, I beg you, and tell me what you need."

"Monsieur," said the Breton. "Would you be kind enough to be my witness? I'm fighting a duel tomorrow morning with an Englishman."

"Gladly, Monsieur. Can the affair perhaps be settled?"

"In no way."

"Even better. Without being too curious, might I ask...?"

"Why I want to kill the Englishman? Listen, pray, and judge between us."

"Waiter!" shouted the officer. "Two glasses of absinthe and cigars. I'm all yours, Monsieur."

"The Englishman and I love the same woman. Now, the aforesaid Englishman was the earlier on the scene, and is absolutely determined to marry her. I've asked him politely to leave. He's holding firm and won't let go. What would you do in my place?"

"Precisely what you're doing. I'd ask him to line up and fight it out."

"Well, Monsieur, that's the whole question. Do you need any further enlightenment?"

"What's the point?"

"I can count on you for tomorrow morning?"

"It's agreed."

The next day, the two combatants and the two witnesses appeared on the battlefield. Mr. Hornsby wanted to reconcile the two adversaries and approach Quaterquem. To the first overtures of peace the Breton was content to respond: "That depends on you. Give me Miss Alice in marriage, and I'll answer for everything. Fundamentally, I don't hate Harrison. Let him renounce your daughter and go away, and I'll guarantee that we'll be the best of friends."

"I don't want to pay the expenses of the war," said Cornelius.

"As you please."

"I've sworn that I'll never give my daughter to a Frenchman."

"And I've sworn to marry her."

"But Monsieur, after all, a charcoal-burner is master in his own home. Harrison pleases me."

"Well then, let's not talk about it anymore."

"He's my best friend."

"So much the better. Let's load the pistols."

"This marriage has been decided for two years."

"Load the pistols!"

"And to make me break my word, it would be necessary for Harrison to have committed the most horrible treason."

"Load he pistols!"

"In any case, Monsieur, whatever happens, I shall never see you again."

"In the name of Heaven, load the pistols!"

This time it was necessary to yield; and the two adversaries took their positions facing one another at a distance of twenty paces. Harrison, favored by the draw, fired first.

The pellet, poorly fitted in the breech, did not fire.

"Goddam!" cried Harrison, furiously, and threw his pistol on the ground in despair.

Unfortunately, the first impact had moved the pellet into position; the second caused it to fire. The shot departed, so awkwardly that it struck the foot of Cornelius Hornsby, who was calmly watching the combat.

Cornelius uttered a cry of rage.

"Animal! Clumsy oaf! Churl! Imbecile! Murderer! Imbecile! Utter ass!" he cried, for a start.

Harrison ran toward him to catch him in his arms, but the old gentleman, agonized by his wound, shoved him away violently and say down on the grass, moaning.

"Oh, the triple idiot who fires at me instead of at his adversary! Ow! Ow! Has such a blockhead ever been seen!"

"But my dear friend...," said the desolate Harrison.

"You, my friend? Double traitor!"

"Please, my dear father-in-law..."

"Father-in-law, me! Oh, you can look for a wife elsewhere, I'll guarantee that. Father-in-law! You were counting on my inheritance I'll wager, and were in a hurry to murder me. Father-in-law! You need a father-in-law for target shooting! And I was about to give my daughter to my murderer! Great God, I thank you for having spared me that remorse!"

During this speech, Quaterquem and his witness, who had great difficulty in preventing themselves from laughing, gave first aid to the wounded man. Harrison was motionless, as if stunned by his disgrace. He turned the fatal pistol over and over in his hands, and completely forgot about the duel that had brought him to the terrain. Unfortunately, the old Englishman perceived that.

"Well," he said to Quaterquem. "What are you waiting for to get on with the affair? It's your turn to fire; deliver justice for me to this miserable wretch who tried to murder me."

Harrison recovered his composure, and positioned himself in front of the Breton again, ready to stand up stoically to his shot—but Quaterquem unloaded his pistol and offered him his hand.

"My dear Monsieur," he said, "you can go."

"I don't want mercy," said the Englishman.

"No, no mercy for that murderer!" cried Cornelius, taking off his boot. "Blow his brains out, as he deserves."

"Go to the devil, you old fool!" cried the exasperated Harrison. "For a bullet that misfired and might perhaps have tickled your foot, you're making an infernal racket."

"Monsieur," said Quaterquem to Hercules, "go away. You can make your peace another time. He isn't in any state to listen to you."

"I won't go," the stubborn Hercules replied, "until you've fired at me."

"Are you mocking society, and do you think I'm thirsty for our blood? Your engagement is broken and won't be renewed. That's all I needed. Adieu, my dear Monsieur; if you see Queen Victoria, please give her my regards."

The Englishman went away, without any reply.

"My God, but that poor boy is badly brought-up!" said Quaterquem to his witness. "Now it's a matter of transporting Mr. Hornsby to the hospital."

They each took one arm, and took him, limping, to his room. Having arrived there, the officer saluted, exchanged a handshake with the Breton, and left.

Alice and Mrs. Hornsby had great difficulty comprehending what had happened and, in accordance with custom, shed abundant tears, which greatly consoled the unhappy Cornelius. After the initial examination, the surgeon reassured the ladies, and promised to have the wounded man back on his feet within a month.

Harrison, who was hiding in the antechamber timidly awaiting the surgeon's response, opened the door cautiously, and, thinking the moment favorable, said with his habitual gaucherie: "It's nothing. You were more frightened than hurt."

At these words, the wounded man leapt out of bed so abruptly that the unfortunate Harrison recoiled.

"More frightened than hurt!" he cried. "Do you want to finish me off, torturer? Get out, scoundrel! Get out! Get out!"

Alice signaled to him to leave the room, and followed him. "Tell me, if you please, my dear Harrison," she said, "why you picked a fight with Monsieur Quaterquem?"

"I didn't go looking for the fight," Harrison said. "I submitted to it." And he repeated the conversation that he and his adversary had had.

"You're two rare idiots," she said, laughing. "I forgive you because no blood was shed, but never let me see you again."

"Alice, you'll help me appease your father?"

"It's impossible; he's too irritated with you."

"Or you're too prejudiced in favor of that Frenchman."

"Me?" she said blushing. "Where did you get that idea?"

"He told me."

"A fine authority! Monsieur Quaterquem is conceited, and you're impertinent to claim to divine whom I love or hate."

"Alice, I love you so much and I'm unhappy! In the name of Heaven, get your father to forgive me!"

She remained silent. Hercules was condemned. He sensed it, and without insisting any further, he left for Calcutta that same morning.

The next day, Quaterquem received the following letter from his friends:

Man of genius!

Leave the English and their daughters and take the train. Don't stop to cut the surly Harrison into little pieces. It's a waste of time and you owe it to the human race. Your invention is a stroke of genius, which all the men in the business think sublime. In less than a month your aerostat-omnibus will be carrying the glory of your fatherland, and your own, to every corner of the globe.

Don't say that you lack money. A hundred thousand francs will suffice for your first aerial omnibus and we already have six hundred thousand to offer you. The sum is ready and deposited with the notary.

This evening, immense genius to whom Christopher Columbus will be unable to hold a candle, we'll be waiting for you at the Gare d'Orléans.

Yours truly,

The Seventeen

Immediately, he went to old Hornsby's room. His daughter received him on her own.

"Alice," he said, "I have to leave at noon, and might never see you again. Do you love me?"

"Yes. And you?" she replied

"Until death."

"Well then, trust me, and come back. Whatever happens, I'll have no other husband but you. But why do you have to go?"

Quaterquem showed her the letter from his friends. She read it and said: "You're right; you have to go. Trust me to take care of softening up my father."

She held out her hand.

Quaterquem left full of love and hope, and several days went by without Miss Hornsby hearing any mention of him. In the meantime, the old Englishman was visibly getting better, and was astonished by the beautiful Alice's melancholy silence.

"Are you missing Harrison?" he said, one day.

"Not in the least, my dear Father," she replied.

"Are you tired of France?"

"Even less."

"Do you want to go to Naples and see Vesuvius?"

"No."

"Do you want to go back to London?"

"No, Father, London bores me."

"Ah!" He fell silent, divining his daughter's thought.

Does she really love that Frenchman? he thought. *To marry the son of Nelson's murderer would be a sacrilege! Oh, how unfortunate fathers are!*

In that extremity, he resolved to return to London, and to leave for Paris that same evening.

When he arrived, he found the following article in an evening newspaper:

Everyone is talking about the immense discovery that is due to the genius of one of our most distinguished professors, Monsieur Yves Quaterquem. It is a balloon-omnibus that can be directed at will, and which can cover immense distances in a matter of moments. The first trial carried out yesterday before a committee of the Académie des Sciences was a total success. Never has human genius made a discovery more useful and more beautiful. Adieu diligences and railways! People will be able to go around the world in a matter of hours.

The newspaper fell from his hands, and was picked up by Alice.

"Well," she said, "am I wrong to love him?"

"You do love him, then?"

Her only response as to throw her arms around his neck and lavish the most tender caresses upon him. He allowed her to do it because, after all, old Hornsby of Hornsby, Harrison & Co. was not a malevolent man, nor a barbaric father, nor a maladroit calculator, and he knew full well that the inventor of the balloon-omnibus would not remain poor or obscure for long. What do all fathers want? To enrich themselves and to

70

seek out for their daughters even richer husbands; that is the Gospel of all families.

That is why, having weighed and calculated the pros and cons, he wrote the following note to our friend Quaterquem on the sixth of May:

Mr. Hornsby of Hornsby, Harrison & Co. has the honor of requesting Monsieur Yves Quaterquem to favor him with a visit tomorrow morning at eleven a.m.

His very devoted

Cornelius Hornsby.

Quaterquem took care not to be late. You can guess the rest.

They will be married on the twenty-fifth of May at the Mairie of the 2nd arrondissement, at eight o'clock in the evening. Their happiness is cloudless. In a year, Quaterquem will be the most illustrious man in the two hemispheres. His balloon is admirable and functions marvelously.

On the twenty-sixth of May, immediately after the nuptial ceremony, our friend will set forth with his wife for China, where he will arrive that same evening, in order to spend the honeymoon in a house in the country, rented in advance.

Ernest d'Hervilly: *Josuah Electricmann*
(1882)

Everyone knows that Josuah Electricmann, the prodigious American scientist, has just announced that he is on the point of inventing a machine destined to take the place of the father of a family in society, and which he has already named the Household Galvanomaster.

One of my friends, who lives in New York, has been asked by me to visit the astonishing inventor of the photoplumographer.

This is the portraitgram that our distant friend has sent us:

Thirty-seven years old. A heart much further to the right than Molière thinks. A black beard. Excellent eyes. They were once poor, but he has improved them by replacing them after their ablation under ether—an operation that is a veritably pleasure party—with a double hooked prunelloglass, his first invention: an instrument that permits one to be, at will, myopic for micrographic studies, or presbyopic for the manipulation of colored disks on railway lines.

I found that unparalleled man sitting in the middle of his vast study on a seat (patented in Paris, London, Philadelphia and Vienna) that can, according to need, be transformed into a parrot's perch or a bottle-rack, and which can also serve as a sled in snowy weather or a linen-press on washing day. It is extremely comfortable.

The walls of the tireless inventor's study are dotted with innumerable constellations of ivory buttons, the departure-points of an immense network of conductive wires connected to all the telegraphic stations in the world. Its only ornament, in the middle of a panel replete with electric switches, is a vast golden border framing a polished mirror on which, thanks to the next-to-last inventions of the celebrated electrician, the colorofix and the vultugraph, one is able, whenever one has the desire, to have the most marvelous picture in the world painted instantaneously: living and animate pictures of the most incontestable naturalism.

Thanks to that magical combination of the two items of apparatus, which are reminiscent at first sight of two obscure irrigators, Josuah Electricmann enjoys an unrivaled collection of splendid panoramas and delightful urban scenes.

It is also a painted newspaper of the greatest interest. The news appears there in the flesh and bone. The most secret vitriolizations are revealed there in all their horror.

A simple flick of the thumb on button number 4334, for instance, and the vultugraph of Borneo, abruptly allied with the same station's colorofix, instantly reproduces in Electricmann's study what is happening in an absolutely virgin or recently married forest, where a monkey spree is being troubled by the protests of a tiger disturbed in its siesta.

By pressing button no. 22, however—two little ducks, as Bingo callers say—Josuah Electricmann can follow the monkey blow-out with one of Parisian students during "Happy Hour."

Electricmann invents while eating lunch, or eats lunch while inventing. Nothing is easier. At meal-times, he places a tube in his esophagus, without leaving his desk, and through the orifice of the tube he threads a chaplet of pearls of all kinds of extracts: beef grog, concentrated beefsteak, vegetable essences, cheese pills, wine capsules, solidified coffee aroma, etc., etc.—all products patented in Paris, London, Philadelphia and Vienna.

While he ingurgitates and swallows, he dictates inventions to his scribograph, a mechanical secretary, never ill and always smiling.

The scribograph, one of the discoveries that does the greatest honor to Josuah, is a fortunate graft of the stylocurse and the phonograph. The scribograph, the cradle and point of departure of the galvanomaster, writes, draws, paints, sculpts, counts shirts, arranges books on bookshelves, reupholsters old umbrellas—in short, night and day, it plays the role of the henceforth-redundant individual who, in rich families, was primarily occupied in paying court to the demoiselle of the house.

It is a veritable treasure! Two hundred francs with nickel springs, a hundred and fifty in copper.

Having eaten well, like Jacquot, the honorable Josuah Electricmann consults, by applying it to his pulse, his medicofere, an electric physician with a mobile dial, and if the pointer indicates seventy-five degrees—which is to say, a perfect equilibrium of the faculties—the great scientist gives thanks to God with the aid of a very curious theotelegram, which permits one to pray even while exercising on a trapeze. It renders great service to Protestant acrobats throughout the territory of the United States.

Thanks having been given, he gives a flick of the thumb to button no. 1027, which brings forth a reading by the poetogene, combined with the vaporistroph, of one of the most remarkable passages by one of our best authors.

A month ago, as he was activating the chemification of his lunch with a strong dose of Vichy pastilles, manufactured in Chicago by the threadworms of which one no longer hears talk in Europe—another coup mounted by the cod merchants who want to annihilate the consumption of ham!—while Monsieur Electricmann's digestive apparatus was performing its function, the proprietor of that apparatus felt a very particular kind of void, or vacancy, in the region of the heart.

That vacancy, or void, was produced by the banal effect on the reverdisant nature of the luminary, so old-fashioned nowadays, and which few people any longer venerate, known by the name of the Sun.

In a word, Spring was renascent (old style).

Incited by that circumstance, Monsieur Electricmann, addressing his scribograph, exclaimed:

"The damnation of Cromwell be upon me and on you, but it's true—I've completely forgotten to think about perpetuating my race. I need to get married while inventing. What shall I do? Reply."

The scribograph replied, with its bizarre voice, in which the acerbic grating of goose-quills and iron and the obscure hoarseness of an indisposed ventriloquist are mingled:

"Press buttons 4 and 8; switch off current; return to button 4; press pedal 3603; adapt radiometer; press 6, 29, 33. Ring no. 39; switch off current. Fix 1-6034-24-110. The way is open."

Such is the formula, it appears, to obtain, with the apparatus of the prodigious Josuah, a marriage uniting all conveniences.

For ten minutes, there was an infernal manipulation. Nothing was heard but resonating buzzers and alarm bells ringing madly.

It was a matter of combining, by connecting them up to one another, the vultugraph, the phonograph, the telephone, the colorofix, the poetogene, the scribograph, the medicofere, the auriculophile and an infinity of the marvelous Electricmann's other inventions.

During the operation, while still inventing, he savored the odor of a delicious Havana, which one of his machines, the autocigarofume, paraded under his nose. At the same time, a capillophobe, a barber powered by pulverized chloroform vapor, shaved the American man of genius dexterously.

A quarter of an hour later, without having left his study, Electricmann knew the hair-color, surname and forenames, the sound of the voice, the weight, the number of pulsations, the tastes, the state of hygiene, the talents, the age, the strength, the tendencies, the moral resistance, the aspirations, the shoe-size, the waist-measurement, the knowledge and the odor of every unmarried woman in the five continents of the world who was already dreaming of a union with a man as practical as him.

He had even telegrammed the moon and the stars, those pale candles.

The moon opened her eyes.

She opened them with even greater astonishment when, for three nights running, she perceived gigantic advertisements in the sky, visible everywhere in the universe: advertisements projected by means of brushes of intense galvanic colored light invented by Electricmann.

Those advertisements requested a wife for the famous inventor of the United States, and concluded uniformly with the specification: "No round shoulders!"

The required woman was found and married the day before yesterday. In three hours, the affair was done and dusted.

They were married, of course, by telegraph; the spouse lives in Greenland.

The witnesses, old and dear friends of the groom, one of whom lives in Australia, another in Romainville, the third in Tehran and the last in the Transvaal among the Boers, were alerted by telegram, and while a pastor duly alerted by the same agent, without ceasing to work in his garden, confided the words necessary in such circumstances to the telephone, the fortunate husband laid down the foundations of his future and world-changing latest invention, the household galvanomaster, while pronouncing the sacramental "I do."

And in the evening...

That was the snag.

Eletricmann did not have the time to go and see his wife in Greenland, and it was not for a semester that her parents thought that they would be able to send her to him, even by employing the most rapid means of high-speed land and sea travel.

Oh, if only the Aeroveloce—which is to say, Josuah's express balloon—had been finished, everything would go smoothly; but alas, the aeroveloce was not yet finished.

So, keenly annoyed by the forced delay to which his marriage plan has been subjected, the celebrated Electricmann is seeking, at the present moment, while continuing work on his household galvanometer, a means of collecting the Greenlandian orange-blossom without disturbing himself.

It is whispered in the United States that Josuah Electricmann would regard himself as dishonored, and would commit suicide by volatilization, if he does not succeed in inventing an apparatus indispensable to men of science, which has already been baptized, in his mind, with the name of the amouradistanceophone.

Charles Guyon: *Voyage to the Planet Venus*
(1888)

I. The Marvelous Ascension

On the twentieth of June 1885, an extraordinary animation reigned in Chicago, the queen of the Great Lake Michigan.

All the hotels and restaurants had been obliged to turn people away. The rooms, the lounges and the dining rooms were all full of luggage. Blankets had been laid on the floor to serve as beds. People were placed wherever possible; comfort was not an issue.

In all the private houses the owners had taken advantage of the opportunity to rent out rooms and make serious profits. The smallest rooms, from the ground floor to the seventh, had not been disdained, and some porters were cited who had rented their lodges for between twenty and twenty-five dollars a day.

It had been necessary to bring food in from all the neighboring towns, and a veritable city of stalls, where nourishment of every sort and all the beverages in the world were being sold, had sprung up along the streets. The Chinese were displaying dog flesh, shark fins and swallows' nests; the English were offering plum puddings and rump steaks; the Italians macaroni and Modena zampetti; the Spanish Valencia oranges, toasted garbanzos and sugared wines; the Brazilians were presenting perfumed maté to the pedestrians, which they drank with bombillas as they walked. In sum, one found specimens of every cuisine in the world. But French cuisine was admired most of all, and our culinary art could be judged there in all its forms, for Parisians, Flemings and Marseillais had established restaurants that were always full of eager crowds, and from beef *à la mode* to bouillabaisse, no national dish was missing from the menu.

People were also camped in all the public places, in the streets and the squares, and the immense docks, whose magnificent houses alongside the blue waters of the lake resembled a vast bazaar, where the most bizarre individuals were rubbing shoulders in an inexpressible tumult.

There, one could encounter amiable and elegant Canadians; rude inhabitants of the western plains, trappers armed to the teeth; grave Anabaptists from Pennsylvania; and Texas planters in Mexican attire of the most brilliant colors. Englishmen, Frenchmen, South Americans, negroes from Haiti, Spaniards from Cuba, proud and grim Malays and wily Chinese had come, attracted by the same curiosity. One even encountered Redskins, majestically draped in their multicolored garments.

What motive, then, had brought that exceedingly various crowd from all the corners of America?

It was the fact that the ascension of the *Franklin*, the most powerful aerostat that had ever been seen in the States of the Union, was due to take place that day. No one knew the aeronaut's name, but he was assumed to be skillful and audacious, for he had promised not to bring his balloon down until he had traveled the 1,200 kilometers that separated Chicago from New York, in a straight line, and then the Atlantic Ocean itself, in order to go all the way to Paris.

The Yankees, gathered in noisy groups around tables, with glasses full of whisky in front of them, affirmed that the bold voyager must be American, and they drank enthusiastically to the success of an enterprise that was sure to be an aerostatic triumph for the United States.

The Canadians and the English shrugged their shoulders, convinced that only an Englishman could attempt such a voyage. The French said that it was doubtless a Gascon. At any rate, everyone wanted to be a compatriot of the valiant aeronaut of the *Franklin*.

Enormous bets were laid on the probably nationality of the aeronaut. Homeric duels took place. One newspaper, the Chicago *New Scientific Herald*, having called the unknown hero a charlatan in a leading article, and the ascension a ridiculous farce, saw its headquarters attacked by an exasperated crowd. The doors and windows were broken, the presses were smashed, and the reporters owed their life to a flight as rapid as it was prudent. The editor had to appear before the crowd and apologize humbly in order to be authorized to return to the city.

Among the strangers attracted to Chicago by curiosity was a Frenchman named Henri Landal. He was a Parisian in every sense of the word; elegant and distinguished, he combined an agreeable face with an amiable and cheerful character, a solid education and an ardent and adventurous spirit. At the age of thirty, he found himself in possession of an immense fortune, which he employed in traveling, as much for the profit of science as for his own pleasure.

He had arrived the previous day by the midday train coming from Niagara Falls, where he had spent a few days admiring the famous falls at his leisure. There he had made friends with a young American named Charles Madison, who had rapidly acquired his sympathy because of his frankness, his piquant and original intelligence, and the varied knowledge he possessed.

Madison was, in fact, a veritable scholar, but he also possessed a brave and generous heart. One day, while walking near the falls with Landal, he had dived into the water in the midst of the rocks in order to save a young Canadian woman who was being dragged away by the current.

Madison was tall but well-built, with broad and solid shoulders and arms capable of felling a bull, and yet his features were fine and delicate, redolent of a great energy combined with benevolence. Cool and calm in appearance, he was quickly moved to enthusiasm by a new idea or an extraordinary enterprise; nothing frightened him. In sum, his was an elite nature, which inspired sympathy from the start.

Madison had been in Chicago for several days—on important business, he had told his friend Landal, whom he had arranged to meet on the twentieth of June at the Great Lake House Hotel.

That day, early in the morning, the Parisian, leaning on the balcony of the hotel, was admiring the marvelous lake, covered by numerous boats. On the horizon, a warm, bright sun had just emerged from the gilded waves, announcing a delightful day. Charmed by the spectacle, Landal, only expecting his friend later in the day, decided to go out to take an excursion in a boat on Lake Michigan.

Imagine his surprise when a domestic introduced Madison. The latter, after a cordial handshake, without giving Landal time to ask him any questions, said to him: "Today, at four o'clock in the afternoon, the most superb balloon in the United States is being launched. Would you like to take part in the ascension?"

At first, Landal was amazed by that unexpected question, and a few seconds passed without any response, while he was uncertain whether Madison might be joking. Finally, having recovered from the astonishment caused by such an abrupt introduction of the subject, he replied: "I've always wanted to go up in a balloon, and I wouldn't be sorry to satisfy my desire one day, but I'm absolutely unknown here, and I heard it said yesterday that only the aeronauts will be allowed to take their places in the nacelle for the voyage, which promises to be extraordinary.

"I'm the sole owner of the *Franklin*," Madison replied.

"What! You're...!"

"Yes, my dear friend," said Madison, laughing. "I'm the famous aeronaut, whom you perhaps consider audacious and reckless, and about whom there's so much talk in America today. I'm going to set off, first of all, with one of my oldest friends, Samuel Dixton, Professor of Natural History at the University of Boston, who guided my youth and to whom I've always conserved the most profound gratitude. He is, in truth, a great eccentric, but he's a very knowledgeable man. He has a keen desire to carry out experiments in the atmosphere, and I couldn't possible refuse him a place in my balloon. Secondly, I'm taking my faithful servant Tom, who has already accompanied me on numerous ascensions and can be considered a very skillful aeronaut. He's more of a friend to me than a servant, and he's demonstrated an inalterable devotion on more than one occasion. We'll be three, unless you're disposed to come with us. I've sworn to cross the Atlantic in the *Franklin*, and I shall keep my promise. I'd like to take you back to Paris, my dear Landal.

That promise seemed to be made with so much confidence, and Madison spoke in such a natural and resolute tone, that Landal did not think any objection was possible.

"I'll go with you," he replied.

Madison shook his hand cordially. "I was sure," he said, "that a Parisian wouldn't refuse such a beautiful opportunity to return to his country gloriously, and that you would prove your friendship by accepting my offer."

Madison certainly inspired the greatest confidence; his courage and coolness were known throughout America. He had already accomplished more than one extraordinary expedition. He had been the first to cross the Gulf of Mexico between New Orleans and Cuba. Everyone knew his fine book on aerial voyages, which had caused a veritable revolution in aerostatic science.

His audacity, always fortunate, had, however, attracted the hatred of a few American scholars jealous of his successes, and, in keeping his name secret from everyone until the last moment, he had wanted to avoid the violent attacks of a few newspapers directed by his enemies.

"Let them argue when I've gone," Madison said. "I'll reduce them to silence with a telegram sent from Paris."

That afternoon, Madison introduced his two companions to Henri Landal.

Professor Samuel Dixton was a veritable type specimen of the scientist who neglects absolutely everything mundane in order to live in the world of science. Tall, thin and formal, he was clad in a long frock-coat whose form had been forgotten by fashion a long time ago. His narrow trousers would have needed gaiter-straps to reach his boots; a top hat whose silk had disappeared since time immemorial seemed to be riveted to his head. His long, thin nose supported a pair of blue-tinted spectacles at its extremity, over which he often peered with a searching gaze. He was, in sum, a worthy man who had but one passion: incessantly to be learning something new.

Tom was, by contrast, a stout and hearty fellow with a round, pink and cheerful face. He felt happy to be alive, and if he had ever heard of Epicurus, he would certainly have declared himself to be his disciple. But that love of wellbeing did not inspire any egotism in him, and he had proved on more than one occasion that no sacrifice was too much for him when it was a matter of his master or his friends. He was a Pennsylvanian, and as such, he had a depth of common sense and natural intelligence that rendered him precious to the aeronaut, to whom he was capable when necessary of lending his assistance in an ascension. Madison considered him a friend, but Tom did not abuse that condescension.

Such were the two new companions that Madison introduced to Landal a few hours before the ascension; the acquaintance was rapidly made.

At four o'clock, all four of them were on the quay to preside over the inflation of the balloon.

Barrels filed with zinc granules, water and sulfuric acid were placed next to one another. They communicated via pipes with a larger barrel whose bottom, which was open, was plunged into a vat full of water. The hydrogen gas produced by the reaction of the water and the sulfuric acid on the zinc passed through that vat in order to purify it of the sulfuric acid, and then went to pass through the orifice of the aerostat through a long canvas tube.

The balloon was suspended from several masts by means of ropes and pulleys, in order to permit the gas to enter more easily. Its immense envelope, at first piteously limp, was soon dilated by the gas; it was then possible to take account of its enormous dimensions. It was thirty meters high and twenty-two meters in diameter.

An innumerable, agitated crowd covered the quays. The windows, balconies and roofs were full of men and women, waving their hats and handkerchiefs frantically to salute the valiant aeronauts. Even the lake was covered with boats that were creaking under the weight of spectators.

Several people came to beg Madison to admit them to the nacelle that was about to be raised into the atmosphere. A rich Mexican immediately offered him a thousand dollars to have the right to accompany him in his extraordinary voyage, but Madison did not want to grant any favor. The Mexican retired, proffering terrible threats.

"That's the third or fourth time that man has sought me out," said the young aeronaut. "No matter how often I reject him he won't let my balloon alone; he seems as interested in the inflation as if the aerostat belonged to him."

While the final preparations were being made, Tom stocked the nacelle with everything that might render the voyage as pleasant as possible. He also added all the objects necessary for a long and distant expedition. He took the greatest care in placing baskets full of provisions of every sort in the bottom, including liters of water, wine and liqueurs. He hung up the compasses, barometers and astronomical instruments, and did not forget the box that contained a complete pharmacy.

Finally, the balloon was ready. It was swaying, gracefully retained by the ropes attached to its equatorial circle and the sacks of ballast suspended from the nacelle. The voyagers took their places in the aerostat to the acclamations of the crowd, which was cheering frantically. The nacelle was a small square room, softly quilted and surrounded by a balustrade about a meter high.

The solemn: "Cast off!" rings out, and the balloon rises with vertiginous rapidity into the upper layers of the atmosphere.

What a splendid panorama unfurls before the voyagers' eyes! There is Lake Michigan with the thousand vessels furrowing its waters, the city of Chicago with its long boulevards as straight as a ruler, and in the distance, the immense plains irrigated by the Mississippi; in sum, a spectacle that the brush of the most skillful artist could not have painted.

Soon, however, everything disappears into the void. A thick, moist cloud envelops the balloon; it seems to be stationary, but pieces of cigarette paper thrown out of the nacelle indicate that the aerostat is traveling eastwards, and the barometer proved that it is still rising rapidly.

"Six thousand meters!" Madison exclaims.

The blood is buzzing in his ears; he seems dazed. Tom, standing in front of him, has eyes open immeasurably wide, is moving his jaw up and down in a mechanical fashion, with an astonishing noise; one might think it were that of a crocodile breathing out of water. Samuel Dixton seems to be lunged in a profound stupor. Only Henri Landal still conserves his presence of mind; he is admiring the magnificent landscape displayed beneath the balloon.

"Seven thousand meters," says Madison, again.

He tries to pull the cord to open the valve and stop the ascension, but he trips and falls to the bottom of the nacelle. Tom seems helpless; the Professor is still motionless.

Landal hurries to Madison to lift him up; in passing he glances at the barometer, and reads *nine thousand meters*.

And he falls, inanimate, beside his companions.

How long did the voyagers remain plunged in that faint, similar to death, in which air was no longer necessary to them, since they were no longer breathing, and in which everything, including cold and hunger, was insensible to them?

No one could say...

Henri Landal was the first to return to life. He was extremely weak. At first he was scarcely able to open his eyes and move his head. Marvelously, however, he was breathing easily enough, and felt a devouring hunger tugging at his stomach. Soon, by supporting himself on the ropes, he was able to raise himself half-upright and look around.

Madison was still lying motionless in the bottom of the nacelle. Samuel Dixton appeared to be profoundly asleep. Tom, sitting beside him, was beginning to stir and to rub his eyes, as if emerging from a long slumber.

"Come on, courage!" Landal said to him. "Get up! You need to help me to save your master, who isn't showing any sign of life."

"Brute that I am!" exclaimed the worthy fellow, opening his eyes. "I'm snoring like a bison while my master is ill!"

He tried to stand up, but could only get to his knees.

"Pass me the pharmacy, which is beside you," said Landal.

Tom immediately handed the box to the Frenchman. The latter took out a small bottle containing a cordial, and slid a few drops into Madison's mouth. The aeronaut seemed to re-animate slightly; a little color returned to his pale and hollow cheeks.

Finally, he opened his eyes. Samuel Dixton, to whom Tom fed the same cordial, did not take long to come round, and seemed amazed to find himself lying in the nacelle. He started wiping his spectacles furiously—a serious operation, which always announced that the professor had to study a phenomenon or to elucidate an embarrassing question.

"Where are we?" Madison asked, raising his head.

At that moment, Landal, who looked over the balustrade of the nacelle, perceived distinctly beneath the balloon the snowy summits of an immense mountain range, toward which the aerostat seemed to be descending with great rapidity.

"We're going down," he said. "I can see the ground."

"We must be a long way from our point of departure," said Madison. "It seems to me that I've been asleep for a long time. I really don't know what happened at our departure. It's the first time that anything like that has happened to me. Until now, I've always been able to moderate the velocity of my balloon, and it's never gone up with such vertiginous rapidity. It's an accident, and it's certainly due to some extraordinary reason."

Suddenly, Samuel Dixton, who, having cleaned his spectacles thoroughly, had made a violent effort to look over the edge, uttered an exclamation.

"That's too much!" he said, immediately. "All the ballast sacks have gone, and the cords are still attached to the balloon. They must all have escaped at the same time, at the moment of our departure. That must have been arranged in advance. The sacks can only have been attached in appearance, with slip-knots. At the last moment their weight detached them, without a shock, and we set off like a flash of lightning, without having time to see anything."

Madison leaned over to take account of the extraordinary fact. He recognized the exactitude of the information given by the professor.

"It's an infamous treason," he said. "It's a vengeance on the part of that Mexican whose offers I rejected. I remember the threats he made. He was capable of corrupting the men responsible for maintaining the balloon and attaching the sacks."

"We'll be able to find him one day," said Tom, "and then he'll feel the strength of my fist."

"Those are the Allegheny Mountains," said Madison, studying the landscape displayed beneath the balloon. He pointed at the peaks. "We've deviated toward the south, my friends," he added. "We're flying toward Charleston, or at least toward Baltimore…hurrah! That's my homeland; we'll get a good reception there."

"I'd be glad to satisfy my stomach," said Tom, patting his epigastrum. "It's as hollow as a dry gourd."

"We'll rest here for a few hours, my dear Tom, and you'll have time to get your strength back before we cross the Ocean."

When the voyagers had recovered slightly from the shock they had experienced, Madison wanted to put the instruments in order; they had been deranged during the terrible lethargy.

"What!" he suddenly exclaimed. "The chronometer has stopped, and marks today as the thirtieth of June, which is already ten days of travel, not counting the time that might have elapsed since it stopped. That's a good joke on the balloon's part, which has doubtless made a few jumps while we were drowsy. Besides which, everything here is in disorder."

"I'll soon put it all back in order," said Tom, "but first, I'll ask for permission to prepare lunch. I'm as hungry as a man who hasn't eaten for a year."

As he pronounced those words, Tom—who, being a true American, always had a formidable appetite—opened the box of provisions in order to take out what he had placed inside it before the departure.

But the voyagers were utterly amazed!

Everything had dried out. The ham was reduced to leather; the bread seemed as hard as stone; the cold veal and conserved meat had been reduced to crumbs.

Only the bottles of Burgundy and Bordeaux wine had remained intact. The aeronauts rank a few glasses delightedly, and felt their strength returning.

"Long live Bacchus!" exclaimed the joyful Madison, swallowing a few large gulps. "He alone remains victorious in the midst of our catastrophe."

"Yes," said Tom, enthusiastically. "Without Bacchus, we'd be sticking out our tongues like the hanged men of Green Park."

Everyone however, was keenly intrigued by the state of dilapidation in which the crate of provisions had been found.

"What does all this signify?" Landal asked. "Why are your food supplies so dried out? Do such things sometimes happen during aerial voyages?"

"I don't believe," Madison replied, "that any similar phenomenon has been produced in previous ascensions, and I think it's enough to confuse the mind of more than one academician."

"It's a phenomenon of which I'll make a note," said Samuel Dixton gravely. "I'll make a report to the Scientific Society of Boston."

"Could someone have played a trick on us on our departure?" Landal asked. "Might someone have replaced our food supplies with this ham and this bread, which are at least a year old?"

"Perhaps it's another vengeance of that accursed Mexican, who nearly caused us to rise all the way to the stars. It doesn't seem very probable to me, though, for Tom and I put the food in the box at the moment of departure. It's marvelous!"

"Fortunately," said Tom, who was nursing hopes of consoling his forced fast, "we'll find a good table when we come down to earth."

"Yes—and we're nearly there. I can already make out the trees on the mountain-sides. First of all, let's try to land in an inhabited area. I don't want to have to walk a long way to find a hotel or a good inn. I'd have preferred to come down in Baltimore, but I don't know where we are. I don't recognize this region."

While he was speaking, Madison was following the course of the balloon attentively. Suddenly, he uttered a cry of surprise.

"I don't know whether I'm dreaming," he said, "but surely I can see another balloon out there, which is advancing toward us, and it certainly must be a giant among aerostats, because it's enormous…look, gentlemen."

They all directed their gazes toward the indicated point.

A monstrous balloon was, indeed, coming toward them, descending in a gracious curve to catch up with the *Franklin*.

It seemed to be steering very easily. One might have thought that they were looking at a terrible monster threatening he audacious individuals who had dared to enter its domain.

"Sunk, my poor *Franklin*!" exclaimed Madison, with chagrin. "There's a balloon ten times as big as you, which is maneuvering like a New York ferry-boat. I'm curious to meet the mysterious rival who has just cut the grass from under my feet."

That metaphor, so out of place in an aerial situation, was scarcely concluded when the strange balloon, gliding through the air with ease, came to place itself alongside the American balloon and let a light bridge fall upon its nacelle, with a grapnel that brought the aerostat forcibly to a halt.

Beneath the balloon was a veritable cabin, in graciously sculpted wood, ornamented with balconies and windows. An elevated door gave access to the bridge that ended at the *Franklin*. Several people came through that door, with very dark complexions, clad in white tunics, their heads covered with a kind of Roman helmet made of an almost-transparent fabric.

One of them advanced toward the American balloon, in front of Madison—who, stupefied by the marvelous adventure, had already climbed on to the bridge, holding on to the rigging of the nacelle.

The unknown individual was a young man with a very pleasant and very expressive face. He extended his hand to Madison, and pronounced a few words in an unknown language, as soft as they were harmonious—but neither the young American nor his companions could understand them.

Having recovered from his surprise, without advancing his hand, Madison exclaimed: "You're terrible audacious, sir, to put a grappling-iron on my property like that! I ought, for the honor of the American flag, to punch you, but I forgive you, for two reasons: firstly your ignorance of our customs, since I can see that you come from a long way away; and secondly, and more importantly, because I'd like to know your system of steering aerostats."

After this little speech, inspired by national pride, which was greeted with numerous bows on the part of the young stranger, Madison extended his hand to the latter and advanced toward the giant balloon.

His companions were preparing, for their part, to climb on to the bridge, when the *Franklin*, suddenly relieved of Madison's weight, tore itself free from the claws that were holding it, and departed through the clouds at a terrific velocity, carrying the frightened Landal, Tom and Samuel Dixton with it.

At first, the shock caused them to fall into the bottom of the nacelle, and for a few minutes they stayed there, unmoving, almost choking.

Gradually, the ascent relented; it was possible for them to breathe more easily, and they were able to stand up, to take stock of the situation and see whether they could still perceive the foreign balloon.

Nothing!

All around them, solitude, silence and empty air!

It seemed to them that the incident had merely been a dream, a hallucination caused by the state of weakness into which their initial overly rapid ascent had plunged them. It was soon necessary to yield to the evidence, however; the unfortunate Madison was no longer with them.

In vain, Samuel Dixton wiped his spectacles in order to examine the surroundings more clearly; in vain, poor Tom climbed the rigging in order to be able to see further; nothing appeared.

All three of them looked at one another, full of anguish, not daring to express the anxieties that were agitating their minds.

Finally, the professor was the first to break the painful silence.

"There's no point," he said, "in allowing ourselves to be depressed by futile chagrin. It's better to make a decision. Either our friend has been the victim of a treason, and has been abducted by enemies jealous of his glory, or that sudden, unexpected departure was a simple accident. In either case, there's only one thing for us to do: we must set out without delay to search for Madison. If it was an accident, we'll find him again in Chicago or Baltimore; if not, we're in the presence of an infamous trap, and it's necessary that all the United States are warned—that they know that in free America, it's no longer possible to travel in safety even in the air. It's necessary that the authorities are mobilized everywhere, and that the abductors of our glorious friend are tracked like wild beasts! So, it's important to go down right away."

Landal and Tom gave their assent to those wise and generous words.

Meanwhile, a very pronounced movement of descent made itself felt, as they were able to take account by the agitation of the silk streamers attached to the nacelle. At the same time, however, the wind was rapidly pushing their aerostat in a direction they could not determine because the compass was turning crazily in all directions and no longer providing any information.

They had resolved to land in spite of everything, wherever hazard took them. Tom tugged violently on the cord connected to the valve situated at the summit of the balloon, and it did not take long to begin descending in a more tangible manner. They soon perceived beneath the nacelle all the details of a picturesque landscape. The mountains were still visible in the distance as a blue line.

"If those mountains are really the Alleghenies, as Madison thought, or the Blue Mountains," Samuel Dixton said, "we must be above the rich plains of Virginia or Carolina."

"That's a region I know very well," Tom replied. "We've made more than one ascension there, Mr. Madison and I. My worthy master has many friends there, and if that's where we are, we can easily find him."

"We'll find him," said Dixton, "And we won't separate until we've brought him back aboard this balloon, which he created for the glory of the United States."

"I was about to make the same proposal," said Landal.

"Me too," added Tom. Mr. Madison will find his balloon intact and his friends ready to continue the voyage that he'd sworn to make. This will only be an episode in our ascension, a delay of a few days."

While the voyagers were chatting among themselves, the balloon drew nearer to the ground. They could make out the green color of forests very clearly, and an expanse of water whose limits were lost beyond the horizon.

"The sea!" Landal exclaimed. "The Atlantic Ocean!"

Madison's estimations were justified, then; the balloon had not strayed very far from its route during the aeronauts' lethargy. They were about to land in a civilized country, where they would be able to calm the hunger that as beginning to weaken them, and find the companion from whom they had been separated by such an extraordinary adventure.

The air was warm, in spite of the altitude they were at. The light that illuminated the vast scene displayed to their gaze was dazzling, but without fatiguing the eyes.

They admired the high peaks of the mountains situated to the north-west.

"I'd never imagined," said Samuel Dixton, "that the United States had chains as high and as rugged. Those are covered in snow, even though it's June. They must be prodigiously high—which is astonishing, for the Alleghenies don't exceed two thousand meters, and their snow disappears with the winter. Another phenomenon to note; our voyage will decidedly by very fruitful for science. Oh, my colleagues in Boston, how astonished you'll be when I return!"

As he spoke, the professor took out his notebook and began to take notes.

The three voyagers were plunged into admiration in the presence of the magnificent spectacle that developed before them, when a violent shock brought them back to reality.

"Land!" cried Tom. "Help me, sirs—we've touched down; we have to disembark."

To seize the anchor and throw it to the ground was the work of a moment, and after a few seconds, during which the balloon was dragged along, it suddenly came down to earth. The anchor had caught in a tree.

The voyagers immediately leapt out of the nacelle, which they filled with large stones they picked up in the surrounding area. In any case, the *Franklin*, reached by the tree-branches, had been ripped in several places, and the gas was escaping with a shrill whistle. It did not take long to deflate and settle on the ground.

"Poor balloon," said Tom. "It's very sick. It'll take days before it's ready to be inflated again. It needs repairs."

"We'll take advantage of the forced rest to search for Madison," Landal replied. "In any case, we can't think of setting off again without him."

"Before anything else, let's look for people to help us fold up the *Franklin* and transport it to a safe place."

II. It's Venus!

When Madison and his companions had emerged from the faint into which the *Franklin*'s rapid ascent had plunged them, they had found that all their watches has stopped. It was, therefore, impossible for them to know that time it was, and they were unable to calculate it even approximately.

They had left Chicago at about five o'clock in the afternoon. Assuming that they had been plunged in their lethargic slumber for at least an hour, and adding the time that had probably passed since their awakening, it ought now to be about seven o'clock in the evening.

Marvelously, however, the sun had scarcely risen a few degrees over the horizon, and, given the season, it ought to be about nine or ten o'clock in the morning.

In that case, their slumber must have lasted seventeen or eighteen hours. If that was the case, what distance ought the balloon to have traveled? In what region had they come down?

That was the question they asked themselves as they examined the place to which hazard had brought them. They found themselves on the edge of the sea, on a shore bordered by magnificent forests. It seemed to them that they were in a tropical region, where the plants all had enormous proportions.

Arborescent ferns could be seen everywhere, as tall as poplars, and Lepidodendrons[9] like coral reefs, together with Sigillarias with cylindrical stems, as straight as immense candles, redoubtable cacti with bizarre forms, gigantic horsetails whose sporangia resembled massive clubs, and multicolored geraniums the size of oak-trees.

In some places the trees, rising up to a prodigious height, formed a consistent vault; the superb trunks that supported it described splendid porticoes, displaying their branches majestically. The branches were themselves charged at their tips with a host of parasitic plants, which mingled their flowers agreeably with the foliage of the trees. Lianas of an incredible extent snaked from tree to tree, covering the branches with flowery garlands. Elsewhere, climbing and winding around the trunks and blooming, they saw granadillas, dracontiums, begonias and lichens of colossal dimensions. The mosses, which humbly presented their verdant carpets in other places, formed mysterious thickets here, in which the three friends could hear a host of invisible animals agitating.

What a fête for a naturalist!

Samuel Dixton, in consequence, was flabbergasted by the unexpected spectacle. He knew the flora of the United

---

[9] "Scale trees" of the genus *Lepidodendron* thrived during the Carboniferous Era and were long extinct by the modern period, so it is perhaps odd that their presence does not attract more astonishment and comment from Dixton than the mere suspicion that they might be in the tropics. The same is true of *Sigillaria*.

States, and even the whole of America, well enough to take full account of the strangeness of such a spectacle.

"Where are we, then?" he said, as he examined the forest. "Could we have been transported to Mexico, or Brazil? Are we in Hindustan or some forest in Java? Whatever country we're in, there are certainly plants here that are not recorded in modern botany. The *Franklin* must have carried us into an absolutely unknown region...but in that case, how long...?"

At the same time, the worthy professor raised his eyes to look at the sun and take account of the hour.

His companions saw him stop suddenly; he seemed to have plunged into a profound stupefaction. He polished his spectacles, adjusted them on his nose, and then took them off again to rub them again. Undoubtedly, however, they did not render him the service he required, for he put his hands over his eyes to form a kind of visor, and then rounded them out in the form of a pair of binoculars.

Finally, unable to solve the problem he was posing, he ran toward Landal and Tom, who were watching him, very intrigued.

"Have you noticed the sun?" he asked them

"We haven't thought of studying it."

"Well then, look, my friends. Look at a further phenomenon: the sun is a quarter of the way through its course, and it's enormous, similar to its appearance when it's near the horizon. It's the first time I've seen that marvelous fact, and I've never seen it reported in any scientific work. Today, the sun is twice its normal size!"

Landal and Tom could not suppress an exclamation of surprise on confirming that verity.

"Perhaps the magnification is due to a particular condition of the atmosphere," said Landal.

"The atmosphere is perfectly clear at present, my friend," the professor replied. "I've studied the question from every point of view just now, and I can't find a good solution. It only remains for me to observe the fact and inform the knowledgeable Robin Jeffrey, the professor of astronomy, our illustrious president, who'll be glad to have such an extraordinary event to explain."

"If this goes on, your notebook won't be sufficient," said Tom, laughing. "You'll need volumes to record so many mysteries..."

"Yes, Tom, that's true...mysteries, unfathomable mysteries. I'm confounded by them! And this marvelous forest..."

He was interrupted by an exclamation from Tom. The Pennsylvanian took Samuel Dixton by the arm and pointed into the sky.

"Look," he said. "That gigantic bird, which seems to be heading toward us! It's still a long way off, but it's already possible to see that it's colossal. If I had a rifle, what a fine shot I'd have—and what a fine morsel we'd have to roast on a spit!"

"And where would we find the spit, my dear Tom?"

"We'd do what the Redskins do that I've often seen near the Missouri. We'd make one out of tree-branches."

"Yes, but the main thing is to have the bird, and that one doesn't seem to me to be of a size to let itself be captured easily."

Indeed, the closer the bird came, the more monstrous it seemed.

The professor was contemplating it with evident signs of satisfaction, no missing a single one of its movements.

"It's doubtless a condor," he said, "and a condor of rare size, even so; it's at least as big as an ostrich."

"A fine subject of study or a professor of natural history," added Landal. "There, at least, Monsieur Dixton, you'll be on your own turf, and will find the key to the mystery."

"Hmm! Who can tell? I've seen things so prodigious in the last few hours that my science has run out of resources. If that's a condor, it's come from a long way off, because I don't know of any in our country. But is it a condor? I'm beginning to doubt that it's even a bird..."

The flying monster was almost directly above the three voyagers, but at an immense height, and although they could see its long wings and enormous body, they could not make out any details.

Suddenly, the bird stopped, and they saw it descend toward them, describing graceful curves.

The professor had no thought of any danger; he was studying the animal, and repeating, in a low voice: "It's prodigious! It's prodigious!" Then, suddenly, he cried: "But it's a man! It's a flying man!"

"Better and better," said Tom. "Perhaps he's bringing us news of Mr. Madison."

In the meantime, the strange being that the three friends had initially taken for a bird came to settle gently on the ground a few paces away from them. They were the able to examine him easily.

He was, indeed, a perfectly constituted human, with a venerable face, a burnished complexion, a long white robe and a light helmet, reminiscent of those worn by the mysterious aeronauts who had taken Madison away.

He was simply equipped with a very ingenious aerial apparatus. It consisted of two wings about three meters long, made like those of birds with large plumes sewn together with fine thread. The wings, which seemed very light, were surrounded by a ring of shiny metal. They were attached to the shoulders by two steel belts; one circled the breast, passing under the arms, and the other was fixed around the waist. To the left and the right, handles were visible that caused four or five small cog-wheels to rotate, and set the wings in motion as rapidly as desired, without any difficulty. They deployed or folded up along the body like a vast mantle. Finally, the belt was also attached to a large tail, woven like the wings, which a small lever moved to the right or the left like a tiller. To either side of the body one could also see two iron stirrups suspended; they were used to maintain the feet in rear, for the mysterious individual flew almost horizontally.

The three voyages were able to consider this strange and admirable apparatus rapidly. The wonderstruck Dixton approached the stranger, who was similarly considering the aeronauts curiously. The flying man also came forward to meet the professor, and offered him his hand, while speaking to him in an unknown language.

"I don't have the honor of understanding you," Dixton said. "Let's speak English, if you please."

The stranger did not appear to grasp the meaning of those words.

"Perhaps Monsieur can speak French?" said Landal, in that language, drawing closer.

There was the same ignorance on the part of the flying man, who still replied in his own mysterious language.

Dixton, who could speak several of the world's most widespread languages, thought he ought to try them all.

"*Hablemos español?*" he tried first.

The same silence on the stranger's part.

"*Parliamo italiano?*"

No response.

"*Sprechen wir deutsch?*"

Nothing,

"Damn!" said the knowledgeable professor, scratching his nose. "It's enough to make one lose one's head. What country is this person from, then? Oh! I forgot the language I should perhaps have started with, which every educated man ought to know. *Latine loquamur, domine?*"

Still nothing. Greek met with a similar fate.

"All my science is decidedly going to waste," said the exasperated professor.

Tom, seeing these fruitless efforts, stepped in. "I'll speak to him in a universal tongue, Dr. Dixton, that he'll understand right away."

"You, Tom? Perhaps you mean Volapük, which, unfortunately, I don't know?"

"I don't have the honor of knowing that idiom, but you can judge my knowledge."

Approaching the stranger, the Pennsylvanian pointed to the balloon and the sky, and, by means of the most expressive mime, explained to him that he and his companions had arrived in the nacelle. Then, passing on to a pantomime familiar to all peoples, he testified by means of eloquent gestures that he was hungry and thirsty. He brought his hand rapidly to his mouth, imitating a person eating, and then simulated a thirsty drinker.

Those gestures were very easy to understand, for the old man grasped their meaning immediately; taking Tom by the arm, he gestured to him and his companions to follow him.

After having passed through a dense thicket, the voyagers arrived at a broad elevated roadway. It was paved with square blocks of wood framed in fine cement.

"More and more astonishing," said Landal to Samuel Dixton.

"And I thought the United States was the most advanced nation in the world! Here we are, thoroughly humiliated!"

The stranger stopped, and produced a long, shrill note by means of a small whistle suspended around his neck.

A few moments later they saw a vehicle coming toward them along the road at great speed, containing several young people. One of them, placed in front, was directing its course by means of an ivory lever that he turned to the right or the left, in accordance with the direction in which he wanted to steer the vehicle. The carriage was as elegant as it was light; it was made of a shiny metal that appeared to the voyagers to be silver.

The marvelous vehicle was powered by electricity, as the professor—who thought he was dreaming—was able to assure himself. Underneath, at the rear. there was a small box housing the electricity generator, which communicated with two electromagnetic coils. Alternately magnetized and demagnetized, they attracted two iron pistons, which, placed at opposite ends of a seesaw, imprinted it with a regular up-and-down movement. A crank shaft attached to the seesaw turned the wheels. The latter spun with great facility, they could attain excessive speeds, and stop almost instantaneously.

The young people manning the vehicle greeted the three friends politely, and got down from their seats without delay. The old man, followed by Landal and his companions, led them to the *Franklin*, and gave them an instruction to fold up the balloon and carry it to the vehicle, along with the nacelle and the instruments.

That rather awkward operation was accomplished with admirable skill and great rapidity; one might have thought that the men were skilled aeronauts, and Tom, who was ready to give them advice, had to be content to watch and admire them.

When everything was ready, the flying man invited the three friends to climb aboard with the young men, and while the vehicle departed at frightening sped, the old man, deploying his wings, launched himself like a bird in the same direction.

Al these details had greatly surprised the voyagers of the *Franklin*. They remained mute, observing everything they saw and wondering whether they might be the victims of an extraordinary dream.

"Marvelous, prodigious, miraculous!" murmured Samuel Dixton. "When was the means found to drive vehicles by means of electricity? Are we a thousand years behind the times in the United States? What about the academicians? Have they no idea what's happening outside their meeting-halls? John Rigthon, who claims to be the foremost physicist in the world, has never mentioned this discovery to us in his reports?"

The worthy professor was not unaware that numerous attempts had been made for several years to employ the motive force of electricity—which is to say, to make electrical engines as one makes steam engines. People had succeeded in theory, being able to imagined ingenious mechanisms put in motion by an electric motor, but without any serious result for industry, and without it being possible to employ them on a large scale, at least for an extended period of time. Page,

Bourbouze and Froment had invented remarkable apparatus that might serve in time as models for electrical machinery, when generators more powerful than those currently in use had been developed—which is to say, less expensive piles with superior power.[10]

One of the most curious attempts had been made by the Russian physicist Jacobi in 1838, who had been able to go up the river Neva in a boat carrying a dozen people.[11] For several hours the small vessel had vanquished the wind and the current, moved by an electrical machine that turned the paddle-wheels, but the trial had not been repeated because of the enormous expense involved.

Samuel Dixton was up to date with those matters—that was why his amazement was so complete in the presence of a discovery that no one had yet made in the United States.

Tom and Landal shared his bewilderment.

"So much for the Jockey Club," said Tom. "Its fastest racehorses are miserable nags by comparison with this carriage. These are practical people! Here, at least, one doesn't need straw, and grooms don't have horses to look after. It's an economical and agreeable system, which I'll recommend to Mr. Madison!"

"Poor Madison! How surprised he'd be if he were here!"

"Let's hope we'll soon have news of him," Dixton put in, "for we're doubtless going to arrive in an inhabited place and we'll find someone who speaks English."

"Or French, my dear professor."

"We haven't crossed the Ocean yet."

---

[10] Charles Grafton Page (1812-1868), Jean-Gustave Bourbouze (1825-1889) and Paul-Gustav Froment (1815-1865) all constructed early electric motors between 1840 and 1860.

[11] Moritz von Jacobi (1801-1874) was born in Germany, but spent most of his career working for the Russian Academy of Sciences in St. Petersburg. The electric motor boat he demonstrated carried 14 passengers up the Neva in 1839 at 3 m.p.h.

"That isn't necessary. The French language is known throughout America."

"Not here, at any rate," said Dixton, a trifle piqued.

"I could say the same about English," Landal replied, taking pleasure in teasing the naturalist.

"That's what we'll soon see," said the latter, not wanting to yield any of his American pretentions. "It seems to me that we're reaching our destination."

In fact, the vehicle had just arrived in front of a strangely-formed edifice, the aspect of which was as imposing as it was picturesque. The flying man arrived at the same time. In a matter of seconds he had take off his wings and handed the apparatus to one of the young men. Taking Samuel Dixton by the arm, he indicated by signs that he and his companions should go into the building.

The edifice was calculated to cause further astonishment. Imagine a tower about fifty meters high, oblong in form, formed entirely of shiny metal. Gold, silver, iron and other metals were perceptible, variously employed in accordance with the necessities of construction or the needs of decoration. At a height of about fifteen meters there was a first gallery, magnificent sculpted and ornamented, which circled around the monument, and on to which splendid apartments opened. Ten meters higher up there was another similar gallery, but with different sculptures, connecting other apartments. Finally, higher still, there was a further galley, whose luxury ceded nothing to the other two. The tower terminated in a broad and specious terrace surrounded by a beautiful colonnade. From there, numerous iron wires extended through the air in all directions, doubtless to connect it to other monuments.

The entrance to the edifice was an immense door in the form of an arch, which led into a broad and well-lit vestibule. There, several richly decorated elevators, forming veritable rooms, led rapidly to the various floors. A single person, even a child, could direct them at will and without the slightest effort; it sufficed to press a button to activate an electric motor that caused the apparatus to go up or down without any danger to anyone.

On the various floors, numerous and comfortable apartments communicated with the galleries, from which the view extended into the distance, toward the mountains on one side and the sea on the other. All around the edifice, gigantic trees of an unusual species deployed their bizarre foliage. An ordinary New York house would have seemed tiny, like a child's plaything, in the midst of that majestic nature, but the grandiose monument that the foreigners had just entered seemed perfectly proportionate to the surrounding trees.

An apartment was graciously put at the disposal of the three friends, and they were immediately served with a table loaded with very agreeable foodstuffs, but which bore no resemblance to ordinary nourishment. There was the meat of unknown animals, sauces seasoned with deliciously perfumed spices, and roasted birds that ornithology had not yet classified.

At each course, the professor incessantly made exclamations of surprise. He forgot to eat; he would have liked to dissect and study the specimens of natural history that were set before him—but Landal, and Tom most of all, who were dying of hunger, did not listen to his scientific explanations. As the proverb says, a hungry stomach has no ears; that was certainly the case for Samuel Dixton's companions.

They therefore did full honor to the feast supplied by their unknown host; they ate several succulent fruits that they had never encountered before on any table, even in the most renowned restaurants in the world, and they drank white and red wines whose fumes made them merry.

After that meal, as fantastic as everything else that they had seen since their ascension, they went to take the air on a gallery on the same level as the dining room, which overlooked from a great height an immense bay over which the first shadows of dusk were beginning to spread. They remained plunged in a profound contemplation for some time.

"Tom," said the professor, suddenly, "be so kind as to bite my thumb."

Tom started laughing, looking at Samuel Dixton.

"I'm being serious," said the naturalist. "I want to assure myself that I'm not dreaming."

"In that case, it'll be necessary for us all to bite one another's thumbs," the worthy fellow replied, "for all three of us are having the same dream."

"Perhaps we've ceased dreaming since this morning," said Landal, offering his companions cigars that he had just found in a portfolio. "It's possible that until now our lives have just been a dream, and that we've only just woken up. You remember, my dear professor, the ancient philosopher who claimed that life is just a dream, and that one day, one wakes up in another world."

"I prefer to think that I'm on Earth," replied Samuel Dixton, "and I'd be in despair at no longer being in the company of ordinary living beings—or dreamers, as your philosopher says. I hope that we'll soon find ourselves back, you in Paris and me in Boston, where we'll have many things to tell our friends..."

"Who'll say to you: a fine liar, who's come so far."

"They can say what they want; we'll be able to prove the truth to them, because we won't forget the way to this marvelous country. We'll be its Christopher Columbus, and nothing will prevent the incredulous from coming here to verify our discoveries."

"We'll make it an American colony," said Tom.

"Why not French?" said Landal.

"I think, my friends, that there's no point in starting an argument on that subject, for a country as civilized as this one must be, according to what we've seen, has no need to be colonized. We'll simply have opened a new State to American and European commerce. But what is this country? It can only be located in one of the parts of the world still unknown, in one of the regions that voyagers haven't yet penetrated."

"Perhaps we're at the North Pole," said Tom.

"It's possible, my friend," Landal replied, "since certain geographers claim that there's a sea free of ice at the pole and a habitable region where the climate must be mild."

"However," added Samuel Dixton, "I think it more probable that we're near the equator, in the torrid zone. The exuberant vegetation, the tropical heat and the dazzling light, seem to confirm my opinion. In that case, the balloon must have carried us a long way while we were unconscious, and if it weren't for that immense sea, I'd believe that we're in central Asia in Tibet or in one of the little known regions in the middle of the Himalayan mountains."

"Yes, but in that region there's no sea or lake that can compare to that expanse of water," Landal replied, pointing at the bay. "I rather think we're in the heart of Africa; there are immense countries there into which Europeans have never penetrated, and there might be a vast inland sea there, in the opinion of some geographers."

"Wherever it is," said Tom, licking his lips, "it's a magnificent place; the inhabitants are hospitable and the cuisine doesn't lose anything by comparison with the best hotels in New York. It's unfortunate that we can't converse with these worthy people, because I'd like to know the menu of our marvelous diner."

"What's that by comparison with the other marvels we've seen?" retorted the professor.

"Tomorrow, my friends," said Landal, "we might perhaps be enlightened regarding the mystery that surrounds us. Perhaps, too, the day will bring us news of our dear Madison, who can't be far away from this region, since the people in the balloon that carried him away were exactly similar to those who are giving us hospitality."

It was in vain that Samuel Dixton had hoped to find someone able to speak the English language, Neither English, nor French, nor any other European language seemed to be known in the country.

The three voyagers of the *Franklin* had been obliged to remain in Sarimak—that was, as they soon learned, the name of the splendid dwelling in which they had been received. As they could not communicate with the inhabitants or ask for any information regarding Madison, they had decided to learn the language of their hosts. That was the sole means of getting out of difficulty.

Landal and Samuel Dixton had a very considerable aptitude for the study of languages. Tom had a little more difficulty, but in sum, it was not great, for the language of the Kirimonians—that was the name of the people occupying the unknown region—was as clear as it was simple. In any case, the benevolent old man who had offered such generous hospitality to Landal and his friends, whose name was Fertinist, put himself at the service of his guests in the most obliging fashion.

Thanks to his collaboration, Samuel Dixton was able to compose in a matter of days a comparative dictionary of the English and Kirimonian languages, which he entitled: *A New Pocket Dictionary of English and Kirimonian, by S. Dixton.* He asked Fertinist to name each object that was presented to him, and immediately inscribed it in his book. Every day, the three friends learned a great many words in that fashion, and at the end of a month they spoke Kirimonian sufficiently well to be able to maintain an everyday conversation and circulate in the locality.

That facile progress is not astonishing, when one knows that the language has no grammar, which would render it very dear to our schoolboys. Landal often said that it must be the language of the first humans. This is an extract from a little note that the professor put at the beginning of his dictionary:

All substantives, except for proper nouns, end in A, all verbs in O, and they only have the infinitive mode and the participle.

The adjectives and participles are always invariable and terminate in I; finally, the adverbs, prepositions conjunctions and other words, without exception, end in U.

There are no different genders; everything is masculine. There is no article.

Only nouns and pronouns have a plural, which is made by adding the letter K.

There are only three pronouns: as (me); al (you) and at (oneself, it, or him). Add K and you have us, the plural you and them.

That is all the grammar; one can see that even volapük is a very complex language compared with such a primitive idiom. The writing is a kind of elementary stenography. The alphabet only has 19 characters, for the letters G, H. J, Q, Y and W do not exist, the Q and the hard C being replaced by K and the soft C by S.

In sum, the Kirimonians speak like certain negroes who want to explain themselves in French. They say:

Me greet you.

We have much hunger.

They must leave tomorrow.

What news today?

You want eat?

Are you ill?

Him has lost him purse.

Me want be you friend.

By means of these examples one can see how easy it as for Samuel Dixton and his companions to speak in a very short time a language whose words were easily recognizable by the final letter, never vary and have no syntax. In spite of that, however, the language is soft, harmonious, clear and poetic. One can hardly believe what a host of ideas and knowledge it can express; when a Kirimonian sings a ballad, one thinks one can hear the charming murmur of bees when they are playing in a garden around the flowers on a mild summer morning.

As soon as the three friends felt capable of expressing themselves with assurance, they resolved to quit Sarimak and set out in search of Madison. It was then that they learned that they were, as we have said, in the land of the Kirimonians, thus named for its capital, the illustrious city of Kirimon, as it was called by Fertinist, who often spoke about it to his guests.

When Samuel Dixton heard that name, he exclaimed: "Kirimon! Without flattering myself, I can say that I know my geography, but I've seen the name Kirimon in any atlas, nor read it in any book."[12]

"Perhaps that name," Landal replied, "proper to the inhabitants, is translated among us into another term. It's a habit that the majority of geographers have to transform the names of the countries hey describe. Would some voyager, transported by a balloon to the Far East, recognize in the kingdom of Chung-Kuo the great empire that our maps call China? In any case, how much even the name of China varies, I accordance with the provinces in which it is found! The archipelago that we call Japan bears the name of Dai-Nippon among the indigenes. I could cite many other peoples who would scarcely recognize their nation if they heard it named by Europeans. However, what makes me believe that we're in a region still unexplored, among a civilized people who have thus far kept themselves apart from the entire world, is our ignorance of the marvelous inventions that have astonished us since we have been here."

"The more I think about it," the professor said, "the more convinced I am that the *Franklin* has transported us either to the center of Africa, to the shores of an inland sea, or to one of the islands of Malaysia, to one of the unknown coasts of Borneo, or perhaps New Guinea or Australia.

"Madison must undoubtedly be in the same region and, unless he has been able to get back to America, we may hope to encounter him in one of the cities of the Kirimonian State—large and populous cities, according to Fertinist. There, we can at least seek information as to whether a stranger has appeared in the land.

---

[12] Which is perhaps odd, given that it is the name of the Government Seal of Japan, as reported in Sir Richard Alcock's account of his three years in that country, published in 1863.

The three friends thought about making their preparations for the journey. It was a matter, first of all, of obtaining garments in the Kirimonian style, in order to travel more freely. That was what delayed the departure by several days.

In the meantime, they improved their knowledge of the language. Every evening, they liked to walk with Fertinist in the vast and beautiful gardens of Sarimak, illuminated by electric light.

For some time, in each of these strolls, Samuel Dixton had seemed preoccupied; he seemed always to be expecting something. He looked at all the parts of the sky and spent entire hours examining the stars and making numerous calculations.

One evening, he said to Fertinist: "When will the moon appear? It seems to me, according to my calculations, that we ought already to be seeing its first quarter, assuming that we arrived at the new moon; that part of its phase must have gone by."

The worthy Kirimonian looked at him in surprise; he did not seem to understand.

The professor assumed that the word he had used was insufficiently clear, and he explained, as best he could, that he was talking about our globe's satellite."

"I've never seen such a planet in the sky," Fertinist replied.

Imagine Samuel Dixton's surprise. It was considerable, for he took off his spectacles several times, wiped them for a long time, then replaced them on his nose and peered t his interlocutor intently, as if the other were making fun of him.

"What?" he said, finally. "You've never seen the moon?"

"I don't know what heavenly body you're referring to."

"Stranger and stranger," said Landal, who had just drawn closer with Tom. "An enormous sun, no moon! It's the world turned upside down!"

"It is, indeed, turning me upside down," replied Samuel Dixton.

"Poor Musset," said the Parisian. "His ballad to the moon would be out of place here."[13]

"At least we're sure of not encountering lunatics hereabouts," added Tom, laughing.

"No moon? Is that possible?" repeated Samuel Dixton, scrutinizing the sky, as if he were unable to admit such a phenomenon. "Where are we, my friends? Where are we?"

Seeing the worthy professor's anxiety, Fertinist said to him: "I've invited a few scientists from Vornam, the nearest city to Sarimak, to dinner tomorrow. Among them, I have a friend who is the most knowledgeable astronomer at the Observatory. He will be able to talk to you about the star that you mentioned to me and explain the reasons why it cannot be seen from this region."

The next day, in fact, there was a numerous gathering in Sarimak. The three friends were able to sit down at table with the most illustrious scholars of the neighboring city.

After the meal, they went for a walk in the gardens. Fertinist introduced the professor to Molvistik, the astronomer from the Observatory of Vornam.

They quickly struck up an acquaintance.

Samuel Dixton recounted his marvelous voyage to the scientist, who reflected for a long time before replying to him.

"All that you have just old me," he said, eventually, "is most extraordinary. You come, you say, from a land where the nights are illuminated by a star whose phases are regular. It is the first time I have heard mention of a satellite attached to the course of our planet, and if I did not know that everything is to be expected in this world, I would think that you were laughing at my simple science. However, you seem to me to be speaking seriously and in good faith. I shall therefore submit your appreciation to the scientists of our Observatory."

---

[13] "Ballade à la lune" (1840) by Alfred de Musset, nowadays best known by virtue of a song adapted from a few of its numerous stanzas.

"It's possible," said Samuel Dixton, "that the moon does not appear above the horizon of the land of Kirimon, and is thus unknown to its inhabitants."

"That cannot be the reason, for we know all the inhabited lands of Miriom—that is the name we give to this globe—and our navigators have often traveled around it. They have never heard mention of any satellite of our sphere."

The professor from Boston thought that the astronomer from Vornam was not as learned as he wanted to appear, and that what he called a voyage around the world was simply a tour of the land of Kirimon, which American maps did not even identify. However, as a well brought up individual, he kept his observations to himself.

"Come to Vornam tomorrow," the old astronomer added, "with your companions and Fertinist. You can attend a meeting at the Observatory. You will hear interesting communications from our scientists, and you can explain to them what you have told me about the satellite that illuminates your homeland."

The next day, all four of them made arrangements to leave for Vornam. The city was situated twenty leagues from Sarimak. That distance was traveled in less than two hours by means of the electric vehicle.

Fertinist took his guests directly to the Observatory, where the meeting was about to begin. The meeting hall was situated on the fourth floor of a tower even higher and larger than that of Sarimak. They reached it in a matter of seconds by means of one of the numerous elevators that were going up incessantly, filled with people going to attend the meeting.

When the voyagers arrived, the galleries were full of spectators, and near the armchairs were some fifty astronomers, who were holding grave discussions around Molvistik. They were talking about the moon, for when Fertinist and his companions came in, everyone turned to look at them curiously, and Molvistik came to welcome them in order to introduce them to his colleagues.

All of them, after having greeted the foreigners, went to their seats at a signal from the President, and the session was opened.

"Sirs," said the President, "before hearing Molvistik's report on a new planet, of which the estimable strangers who are in our audience today have spoken, I must make you aware of a few communications. I have received from Kirimon a letter from our esteemed correspondent Sormil, who has confirmed by new and very precise calculations the distance between our planet and the sun. The minimum distance is exactly 26,575,800 leagues, and the maximum distance 26,925,000 leagues."

At these words, Samuel Dixton could not help rising to his feet, and, as Fertinist had informed him that all observations were welcome, even on the part of foreigners, he asked for permission to say a few words.

Permission was granted with the most gracious immediacy.

"Pardon me, sirs," he said, "if the figures that I've just heard cause me a great surprise. In my country, the United States, where we have several renowned observatories and astronomers have obtained a well-merited glory by means of their discoveries and their science, I have always heard it said and have read in all the books that the mean distance of the Earth from the sun is 37,000,000 leagues. Our figures do not match, and I am surprised by such a great difference in a matter that is so easy to elucidate."

"Our honorable contradictor," replied the President, "doubtless by virtue of distraction, is attributing to our world the distance that exists between the sun and Karim, the third planet of the solar system. The mean distance of Karim, our neighbor, from the sun is, indeed, 37,000,000 leagues, and the mean distance of Miriom, our planet, the second in the solar system, is, according to the calculations that have just been determined, 26,750,400 leagues."

"Pardon me, Mr. President," said the professor, "but there's some confusion between us. You give our planet the second rank in the solar system, but all astronomers know that before us there is Mercury, situated at a mean distance from the sun of 14,400,00 leagues, and then Venus, placed in the second rank, at a mean distance of 26,750,400 leagues; then comes the Earth. You name the planet we inhabit Miriom, and you say that it is in the second rank; you are in complete opposition to our European astronomers...what am I saying?...with the astronomers of all epochs and all nations."

"The slightest knowledge of the heavens shows you that we are the second planet!" exclaimed the President, in a tone marked with some impatience, "and you, sir, have been talking for a quarter of an hour as if you were from the third planet, Karim—the Earth, as you call it."

"But of course I'm from the Earth," repeated Samuel Dixton, laughing. "How do you think that I could be elsewhere?"

He had scarcely pronounced those words than one of the members of the Observatory, who, like his colleagues, had been listening attentively to the conversation, rose to his feet and asked to speak.

Permission was granted; he took a manuscript from his pocket and said: "Everything about the words of the scholar that we have just heard seems prodigious. I don't know what idea had got into my head, but however bizarre it appears, I'll express it. Everything seems to support the belief that this stranger and his companions come from Karim, the third planet in our solar system: the balloon that brought them, so different from ours; their extraordinary costume; their pale skin, which does not exist among us; their unknown language, whereas the Kirimonian language is spoken all over our globe; the satellite of which they speak to us, which does indeed orbit the third planet; the distance so exactly given, which really is that of the world that the strangers call the Earth; and finally, the profound conviction that they have of not being on the second planet of the solar system, all confirm my opinion. Besides which, I have just received a letter from my friend and correspondent Kisbol, who announced to me the discovery of proof that the planet Karim possesses an atmosphere like ours—from which we can conclude that it is inhabited."

"How can Karim—which is to say, your Earth—be inhabited?" cried Molvistik, impetuously. "Can organized beings like us lives on a world on which the temperature must be glacial? Would they not perish immediately at such a great distance from the sun? Could humans live on a globe where the light must be only half as intense as it is on ours?"

"Our dear colleague's arguments," replied the first speaker, "are not sufficient to prove that Karim and other worlds are uninhabited. The planets have not been created simply to rotate around the sun. Everything in the universe is useful, and I maintain my opinion, which is that as the third planet has an atmosphere, it can and ought to be inhabited."

At that moment a young man came in, who handed a packet to the President. The latter opened it, read a few manuscripts, and his face suddenly lit up.

"My dear colleagues," he exclaimed, "great news has just reached me! Our celebrated astronomer Bustrinop, of Kirimon, thanks to a new telescope brought into use the day before yesterday, has discovered seas and continents on Karim. He and all his colleagues have recognized the form of lands. He has even sent me an admirable photograph of the hemisphere that he has been able to observe. Judge for yourselves."

At the same time, the President sent round a map of fairly large dimensions, which Fertinist almost immediately placed before the eyes of the three voyagers of the Franklin.

"But that's the Earth!" exclaimed Landal, excitedly. "That's the exact design of Europe, north Africa and a part of Asia! I recognize the form of France, my homeland! Is it possible? Is this not, Messieurs, a photograph of one of our European maps?"

"Europe, Africa, Asia, France...we don't know those names at all, sir," said the President. That photograph was taken from the height of the Observatory or Kirimon, with the improved instruments with which we have recently been provided."

"In that case, the balloon must have transported us to Venus, eleven million leagues from our own world!"

"Ah! I understand now," said Samuel Dixton in his turn, "why our food supplies dried out, why our watches were no longer working and why the chronometer marked the thirtieth of June. It had stopped after ten days, during our lethargic unconsciousness, and our balloon, transported through the ether, has run aground on Venus! It's amazing, incredible! I'm not sorry, though, for I'm proud that an American, a professor of the University of Boston, has been the first to set foot on this new world, and I'm going to...."

"You're forgetting, my dear friend, that there's a Frenchman here," replied Landal.

"That's true! I forgot. How I regret not having noticed which of us jumped out of the *Franklin* first."

"That's just like an American!" said Landal, laughing. "We have a lot better things to do than argue about a platonic priority."

"You're right, sir," replied Samuel Dixton, recalled to reality. "First, let's think about finding our dear Madison, and then we'll try to find a means of getting back to Earth."

The astronomers listened to the strangers in astonishment, and the President took notes in order to submit the case to the Observatory of Kirimon.

Finally, Fertinist and his guests took their leave of the scientists, and set out back to Sarimak.

During the journey, Tom remained mute; he seemed to be reflecting profoundly.

"So," he suddenly said, "We're no longer on Earth?"

"Alas, no," replied Landal.

"Then it's as if we were dead?"

"Not absolutely, since we're quite well and we're in a land which, in sum, has nothing lugubrious about it."

"Lugubrious or not," replied the worthy Pennsylvanian, "for my part, I confess that I regret the United States keenly, and I don't know what I'll be able to do on this new world. Long live the Earth!"

"We'll get back there, my dear Tom, we'll get back," said Samuel Dixton, "and we'll return in triumph. What a glory it will be for us to return to Chicago, having come back from the planet Venus! What an upheaval in science! What a revolution in astronomy! What amazement among the members of the University of Boston! The descent from a star— that's never been seen before! We'll be able to bring back rare and curious objects, perhaps even a specimen of Venusian humankind!"

"So we're on the beautiful star we call the Shepherd's Star," said Tom. "Truly, Mr. Dixton, I can't get used to that idea, and I'd rather believe that these so-called scientists know absolutely nothing."

"Astronomy," said the professor, gravely, "cannot be mistaken. Its calculations are immutable, and that photograph we saw leaves no doubt. Venus greatly resembles the Earth, but there are differences that are easy to observe. First of all, it's a little smaller; its diameter is about 3,000 leagues, and it's only 9,500 leagues around. The sun seems twice as large to the inhabitants of Venus as to those of Earth. That's what explains the phenomenon that surprised us so much when we arrived. This planet has no satellite, and we searched for the moon in vain. Thus, everything is clarified now. And those prodigious mountains can't astonish us any longer, when we know that there are some on Venus that attain heights of forty kilometers.

"The day is only 23 hours, 24 minutes and 22 seconds— which is to say, 34 minutes less than the day on Earth. The seasons are only 566 days long; the year only has 231 instead of 365, as on Earth—it only lasts seven and a half months. You can see that it's much shorter than ours, so the inhabitants of Venus live to be much older than those of Earth."

"Ah! That, at least, is a consolation for us," said Tom.

"Yes, but they arrive at old age more rapidly."

"Damn!"

"So, when an Earthly human reaches the age of twenty, a Venusian human born at the same time reaches thirty-two, Thirty years on Earth corresponds to forty-eight on Venus, thirty-five to fifty-six and fifty to eighty. A person aged sixty on our world has reached ninety-six on this one, and an old person on Venus who has lived a hundred and fourteen years would only be seventy on Earth."

"So," said Tom, pulling a face, "I, who am only twenty-five, am already forty in this country?"

"Exactly, my friend."

"That's not very reassuring, and doesn't please me."

"But you also have the chance to live to be a hundred and thirty or a hundred and forty."

"I like our earthly system better; one stays young for longer."

"If, as I hope, we can return to Earth," said Landal, "you'll have the advantage of having lived until forty and re-verting to the age of twenty-five!"

"Let's try to get back as soon as possible!"

"There'll be time to think about that when we've found Madison."

"As to that, yes. I'd rather stay here all my life than leave without my master."

During this conversation, they arrived at Sarimak. The preparations for departure were resumed immediately, for Samuel Dixton and his companions were determined to set out in search of Madison the following morning.

III. A Little Astronomy

We have seen that the knowledgeable professor of the University of Boston has said a few interesting things to his friends about the planet Venus, to which, perhaps for the first time since the commencement of the universe, a balloon had just transported inhabitants of the Earth. We believe that we ought to complete the information given by Samuel Dixton with a few further details.

Venus is the magnificent star, the most beautiful in our sky, that one often sees shining in the evening in the west and in the morning in the east. It is very popular, and the crowd, which in general does not know the names of stars and can scarcely recognize them, is never mistaken on the subject of that one.

It has long been given the name of the Shepherd's Star; that is its most familiar name. Hardly anyone but authors, especially ancient poets, make mention of "Venus." It is often cited under the name of Vesper, and the shepherds of Italy regards its appearance as the signal for the return of the flocks: *Vesper ubi e pastu vitulos ad tecta reducit,*[14] says Virgil, who loved to recall that beautiful star frequently.

Venus is the second planet in our solar system. Its mean distance from the sun is about twenty-six million leagues, while that of the Earth is thirty-seven million. Our globe is thus at a mean distance of eleven million leagues from the shepherd's star.

The brilliant star rotates around the sun in 224 days 16 hours 49 minutes and 8 seconds; that is, therefore, the duration of its year. It is 231 days counting in accordance with the length of the Venusian day. Its orbit covers a total of 168 million leagues. While orbiting the sun Venus travels about 750,000 leagues a day, which is 34,600 meters per second. It has phases similar to those of the moon. Sometimes, like our satellite, it presents its entire disk, resplendent with the light of the sun, sometimes it disappears like the new moon, and sometimes it appears as a crescent, but these various phases are rarely visible to the naked eye because the planet is too far away.

The sun and the moon are not the only stars that can produce shadows. Venus is bright enough to project a person's

---

[14] The quotation is from the *Georgics*; the line actually refers to oxen, but the following one adds in lambs.

shadow on a white wall. Monsieur Flammarion proves that very well. "The light of Venus," he says, "is so strong that it sometimes casts a shadow. One evening, I observed that fact without expecting it and without having any thought of it. Returning from a journey to Italy in the spring of 1873, I stopped at Ventimiglia, which the train from Italy passed through at about nine o'clock in the evening. It was the twenty-third of March. Conducted through the dark city by a guide, I perceived at one moment three shadows following us along a garden wall alongside which we were walking.

"Very surprised by that shadow, produced without any moonlight or street-light, I pointed it out to my two companions, who also recognized the fact. It was quite clearly and distinctly marked out. The sky was populated with bright stars, but there was only Venus to our right as a star of the first magnitude, and shining moreover with such a glare that its light seemed brighter than that of all the others stars in the firmament combined. The wall was a dirty white, almost gray; if it had been white, our shadows would have been even more distinct.

"During the following weeks, in Nice, I renewed the experiment on paper; the shadow of fingers, or a pencil, or any other object, was outlined there with the greatest clarity."[15]

The dimensions of Venus are similar to those of the Earth; its diameter is about 3,000 leagues and its circumfer-

---

[15] Author's reference: "Camille Flammarion, *Les Terres du ciel*, p. 242." The handsomely-illustrated book in question, published by Marpon et Flammarion in 1884, and subtitled "*voyage astronomique sur les autres mondes et description des conditions actuelles de la vie sur les diverses planètes du système solaire*" [An Astronomical Voyage to other worlds and a description of the present conditions of life on the various planets of the solar system], was enormously popular, and became the primary reference text of several notable French interplanetary romances written in the late 1880s and 1890s.

ence 9,500 leagues. Its volume and surface area are slightly less than those of our globe.

Our neighbor rotates on its axis in 23 hours 21 minutes and 22 seconds, which means that the duration of the day and night are almost the same as on Earth; the difference is only 34 minutes.

The seasons, shorter than ours, since they only last 56 days each, are much more varied than on our terrestrial world, by virtue of the inclination of the axis, which is about fifty-five degrees, whereas the Earth's is only inclined by twenty-three degrees.

Astronomers have recognized that Venus is covered with mountains much higher than ours; some of its gigantic chains include peaks that reach heights between thirty and forty kilometers. One can see that the Himalayan mountains, the highest on Earth, are mere pygmies by comparison with the mountains of Venus.

The sun, seen from that planet, appears twice as large as when seen from the terrestrial globe. The light and heat there are superior to those of our world. However, the geographical researches that have been carried out in its regard are sufficiently in accord to inform us that its seas extend principally along the equator and that they are more akin to the Mediterranean than to vast Oceans. The extremes of heat and cold are tempered by those waters, and we can presume that the most favored regions are the coasts of those interior seas. One can admit without temerity that there are civilized peoples there, and that it is in those nations that the most flourishing nations of the planet are located. Those seas have tides much feebler than ours, caused by the sole attraction of the sun, and their waves are agitated like ours by the breeze.

The effects of light and shadow that are admired there, the coloration of the clouds at sunset, the undulating evening breezes, the plaints of the wind in the woods, the murmurs of streams—in sum, the thousand noise of life—must develop panoramas, situations and scenes there offering infinite harmonies with the terrestrial and maritime vistas of our planet.

"The atmosphere and water exist there as here. In accordance with what we have seen previously regarding the planet's rapid and violent seasons, we can presume that the agitations of wind, rain and storms must surpass those that we see and feel here, and that its atmosphere and its seas must be subject to continuous evaporation and the continual precipitation of torrential rains: hypotheses confirmed by its light, doubtless due to the reflection of its superior clouds and by the multiplicity of those same clouds.

"To judge by our own impressions we would find those lands much less pleasant than ours, and it is even quite probable that our physical organization, very elastic and complaisant as it might be, would not be able to acclimatize to such variations in temperature. But it is not necessary to conclude in consequence that the world is uninhabitable and uninhabited. One can even suppose, without exaggeration, that it natural tenants, organized to live in their environment, find themselves at ease there, like fish in water, and judge that our Earth is too monotonous and too cold to serve as an abode for active and intelligent beings."[16]

Bernardin de Saint-Pierre, in his *Harmonies de la Nature*, depicts Venus in a very different aspect from Monsieur Flammarion.

"Venus," he writes, "must be dotted with islands that each bear peaks five or six times more elevated than that of Tenerife. The brilliant waterfalls that flow there irrigate their flanks coved in verdure and refresh them. Its seas must offer both the most magnificent and the most delightful of spectacles. Imagine the glaciers of Switzerland, with their torrents, their lakes, their meadows and their conifers, in the bosom of the Southern Seas; add to their flanks the hills on the banks of the Loire, crowned with vines and all kinds of fruit trees; add to their bases the shores of Molucca planted with groves from which bananas, nutmegs and cloves are suspended, whose

---

[16] Author's reference: "Flammarion, *Les Terres du ciel*, p. 311-312."

sweet perfumes are transported by the wind; hummingbirds, the beautiful birds of Java, the turtle-doves that build their nests there, and whose sings and gentle murmurs are repeated by the echoes.

"Imagine their shores shaded by coconut palms, strewn with pearl-oysters and ambergris; the madrepores of the Indian Ocean, the corals of the Mediterranean, growing in a perpetual summer to the height of the tallest trees, in the bosom of seas that bathe them, marrying their scarlet and purple colors with the green of palm trees, and finally, the currents of transparent water that reflect those mountains, those forests, those birds, coming and going from island to island—and you will only have a feeble idea of the landscapes of Venus!

"The poles must enjoy a temperature much more agreeable that that of our mildest spring. Although the nights of the planet are not illuminated by moons, Mercury, by virtue of its glare and its proximity, and the Earth, by virtue of its size, take the place of two moons there. Its inhabitants, similar in statue to us, since they inhabit a planet of similar diameter, but in a more fortunate celestial zone, must devote all their time to amours. Some, tending flocks on the slopes of mountains, lead the lives of shepherds; others, on the shores of their fecund islands, devote themselves to dancing, feasting, delighting one another with songs and competing for prizes in swimming, like the happy islanders of Tahiti."[17]

---

[17] Henri Bernardin de Saint-Pierre's posthumously-published *Harmonies de la nature* (1818; tr. as Harmonies of Nature) is a massive study of natural history, which concludes with an account of the solar system, offering naïve accounts based on astronomical observations and the then-common assumption, based on a principle of divine economy, that all the other plants must be inhabited by beings made in God's image, offering suggestions as to how that life might be adapted to variant physical conditions. Flammarion's accounts in *La Pluralité des mondes habités* (1868) and *Les Terres de ciel* are obvious attempts to update Bernardin's account with the aid of

Let us hope that the extraordinary voyage of the aeronauts of the *Franklin* will bring us new information on the subject of Venus.

IV. In Search of Madison

The next day, early in the morning, the three friends were in their apartment, waiting to be informed that everything was ready for their departure. Fertinist had promised to accompany them at least as far as Kirimon, to which he was summoned by important affairs.

Suddenly, they saw him running toward them urgently. He seemed very joyful, and was carrying a little metal box in his hand.

"My friends," he said—that was the name he had been pleased for some time to give to his guests, who also had the greatest affection for him—"I've just received a phonogram..."

"A phonogram!" interrupted Samuel Dixton.

"Yes—let me tell you the news, first, and then I'll give you all the explanations you desire."

"Speak. My dear Fertinist."

"I've received a phonogram from one of my friends in Rimink, who tells me that a white man, a foreigner, has been seen in that city, where he stayed for a few hours with people who came in a balloon. He is tall, slim, blond and had a full beard. His clothes are similar to yours."

"That description fits Madison very well," said Landal. "It can't be anyone but him."

"Hurrah!" cried Tom, transported by joy. "We're going to see my dear master again. Long live Mr. Fertinist!" And the worthy Pennsylvanian threw his arms around the old man, surprised by that abrupt accolade.

---

more recent data obtained from better telescopes, albeit by observers still prejudiced and deluded by similar assumptions.

Samuel Dixton also manifested his joy, but he was profoundly absorbed by the sight of the little instrument that the Kirimonian was holding.

"It's by means of that box that you learned the news that is giving us so much pleasure?" he asked.

"Yes, my dear professor," Fertinist replied. "It's a phonograph, which received the information I've just communicated to you by means of one of my most powerful telephones. I could simply have made you aware of the telephonic news that reached me, but I preferred to record my friend's own words, and for that I only had to place the telephone over the mouth of this little portable phonograph."

"But that's marvelous!" exclaimed Samuel Dixton. "How far is it from Sarimak to Rimink, from which the phonogram reached you, I believe you said?"

"Only four hundred leagues."

"Damn! Only, you say! We're a long way in America from being able to transmit words and sounds over such a distance, let alone of being able to record telephonic news on a phonograph. The Earth is decidedly behind Venus!"

"Are the words easy to understand?" asked Landal.

"Listen, sirs."

The old man put the phonograph down on a small table and turned a little handle. Words immediately became audible, quite distinctly.

"Amicable greetings to my dear Fertinist. In response to your questions, I can tell you that a white man, tall, slim and blond with a long beard, wearing tight black clothing, with a long black tube on his head, has been seen in Rimnik. He arrived with several foreigners from the land of Nirmul in a balloon. After a few hours, he disappeared. The foreigners who accompanied him searched for him in the city for a day, in vain, and were obliged to leave without him. I have learned that the white man was seen again yesterday in the area. That's all I know. Adieu!"

Those words, come from four hundred leagues away, contained in such a small instrument, were perfectly understandable; one might have thought that a man was talking to his listeners.

Samuel Dixton and his companions marveled.

"A little more," exclaimed Tom, "and we'd have been able to hear Mr. Madison's own voice!"

"Perhaps that will happen sooner than you think," said Fertinist. "Courage, my friends! Everything is ready for the journey. We'll soon find your compatriot, but it's necessary to change our itinerary. Before receiving that news I thought it would be preferable to go directly to Kirimon, where I hoped that we might perhaps find Mr. Madison. Then I summoned one of my ships, which would have transported us to the capital of the Kirimonian States, about four hundred leagues from Sarimak—but it's necessary to abandon that plan. The city of Rimnik, where your friend has been seen, is also four hundred leagues from here, to the south of Kirimon, on the beautiful River Kerib, beyond the Sorem Mountains—which is to say, in the direction of the land of Nirmul, which is independent of ours but not much different.

"Until the other side of the mountains we shall have to traverse an almost uninhabited, wild region covered with forests, where communications only take place by means of balloons, wings or, where there are roads, by means of electric carriages. I don't have a balloon here; it's a means of large-scale transport one used for regular voyages. A carriage can only go as far as the foothills of the mountains, and it would be necessary to abandon it. I therefore propose that you make use of wings, like me, which are easily to manipulate and provide comfortable travel. It's a rapid means of locomotion, agreeable and very advantageous in a country like the one we have to traverse. Beyond the Sorem Mountains, on the Kerib, fifty leagues from here, we'll find the city of Kimislam, where we'll find any means of transport we desire—balloons, boats, mechanical vehicles, and many others that would take too long to list. If my proposal is agreeable to you, I am at your disposal; we have only to depart."

Samuel Dixton and his friends thanked the worthy Kirimonian and told him that they would yield entirely to his experience, accepting him from that moment on as the leader of the expedition that they were about to undertake.

After a light meal they all went down to the beach, where four servants were waiting for them with the apparatus and items necessary for the journey.

It was not without difficulty that Samuel Dixton and his friends were able to equip themselves with the gigantic wings, to which they were not accustomed. They were astonished, however, by the facility with which they were able to rise up; scarcely had they turned the handle and set their apparatus in motion than they launched forth into the air like birds, and felt an incredible lightness.

Tom was full of enthusiasm. "This," he said, "is a real means of travel. This way, there'll be no more need of railways or ships; one can go long distances without undoing the purse strings, and without fear of derailment or shipwreck."

In the meantime, Fertinist gave his companions some advice.

"Keep careful track of your direction," he said. "Nothing is easier than to start your wings moving, rising up into the air and flying to the right or the left, as you wish, thanks to that tail, which serves as a rudder and which you direct by means of the lever set in your belt—but be careful. It requires considerable skill to land where you want; one often comes down more rapidly than one desires, and falls to the ground. It's also necessary to avoid trees and bushes. Extend your wings fully and let yourself descend gently, like the birds that soar above the plain. At some distance from the ground, a little flick of the tail will take you to the place that seems suitable."

He combined the lesson with examples, and rose up to a great height in a matter of seconds; then, spiraling around Sarimak, he alighted on the top of the tower, before descending on an immense conifer and coming back from there to rejoin his friends.

"For the moment," he said, "we have only to fly in a straight line. I'll go on ahead, and my servants, who will carry my luggage, will follow close behind us.

Indeed, the four servants were carrying sacks attached to their back; they were carrying food, spare wings and wooden lances armed with steel tips. A lance of the same kind was given to each of the voyagers.

"Why the weapons?" asked Samuel Dixton, the most peaceful man in the world.

"To defend ourselves in case of attack."

"Are we going to travel through enemy territory?"

No, but the forests and the mountains harbor a few dangerous animals, and we might encounter one. These weapons can also procure game, if he needed arises."

"What a pity we don't have a rifle or a revolver," said Landal. "What marvelous hunting we could do in the air." He asked Fertinist whether he had any firearms.

The Kirimonian replied that those weapons were unknown in the region, and that people only used, in general, bows, spears, hatchets and swords.

"Large-scale hunts," he added, are mostly undertaken with electrical machinery. That's how we kill the enormous animals that populate our forests. You haven't yet had the opportunity to encounter them, since they avoid inhabited regions, but you'll certainly see some. Many, in any case, have been reduced to a domestic state, and serve for public works and transporting heavy materials."

During this conversation, all the preparations had been concluded, and in response to a signal given by Fertinist, they rose into the air. The old man took the lead, and made them rise, initially, to an altitude of about fifty meters. Then he headed toward the mountain chain while blue line marked the distant horizon.

Nothing was more picturesque than the group of eight individuals gliding through the air with excessive speed, deploying their immense wings beneath the blue sky, like wild ducks traversing the plains of Champagne. One might have thought, seeing them at a distance, that they were gigantic migratory birds heading for distant regions.

Fertinist, a few meters ahead of the others, was directing the column; then came Landal, alongside Samuel Dixton, and a little further way Tom, preceding the servants.

They soon lost sight of Sarimak and its verdant bay; the sea disappeared from the horizon, and nothing remained beneath their feet but a somber carpet of forests, which extended as far as the eye could see. Sometimes the tall trees almost reached their height and it was necessary to raise a few meters to avoid their pointed summits.

They flew like that for several hours. Fertinist apparently experienced no fatigue; he was accustomed to that exercise— but Samuel Dixton was beginning to find it less easy to maneuver his wings. His limbs were exhausted, and he felt himself sinking slowly downwards. His younger companions were maintaining themselves more vigorously.

Fertinist noticed the old professor's deceleration and drew closer to him.

"We're going to descend to the ground for a little while, Mr. Dixton," he said. "You need to rest. We've already covered a long distance, and we need to renew our strength before sitting off again."

He let himself down gently into a sort of clearing in the middle of the forest. His companions imitated him, and they had soon touched down on the ground without the slightest shock.

They place where they had landed was admirably beautiful. Nature deployed all the riches of a flora unknown to our terrestrial globe, which recalled the descriptions naturalists furnish of the primitive world. Plants of all epochs seemed to have been preserved there and brought together. Lepidodendrons five meters in circumference, of an immense height, with bark ornamented by regular diamond shaped decorations, like scales similar to those of pine cones. Gigantic mushrooms looked like huge umbrellas deploying their caps over our heads; Sigillaria—colossal ferns—graciously formed a thick vault with their foliage; there were admirable cycads, taller than our palm trees, elegant araucarias of the conifer family, palms, bamboo, eucalyptus, magnolia, sequoias, pines and plane trees.

The voyagers sat down on the edge of a stream, in order to preserve themselves, do far as was possible, from the heat. The sunlight was, in fact, overwhelming, and the freshness of the water murmuring softly beneath the trees, invited repose.

The professor set down his wings; he could not sit still; that nature was too tempting for a lover of natural history. He went from one flower to another, and from tree to tree, studying all the marvels of the unknown land, and thus drew some way away from his companions without perceiving it.

Suddenly, a frightful roar resounded a few paces away. He heard branches creaking, as if under a terrible pressure; and ground resonated dully.

Samuel Dixton stopped, and threw himself behind a cycad, gazing fearfully in the direction of the redoubtable racket.

He saw a gigantic animal appear between the Sigillaria, which it were bending and breaking.

Monstrum horrendum, ingens![18]

One might have thought that it was an enormous rock, a gray mass nearly ten meters high and longer still, moving slowly thought the vegetation. Compared with that monster, an elephant would have seemed no bigger than a dog. Its legs and body were coved with long hairs armed with pointed tips, more than a meter long. Its black head was hairless, and its nose was elongated into a short, stout trunk like that of a tapir. Its tread was heavy and awkward. It tore up entire trees in order to eat their foliage, as elephants do with tender reeds.

The professor, trembling behind his frail shelter, scarcely dared breathe. He gazed curiously at that specimen vanished

---

[18] Virgil's *Aeneid*, IV, 181, with reference to two Giants, thus indicated as "monstrous, horrible and vast." A similar reference to the Cyclops Polyphemus, which adds *informe* [hideous] is more frequently quoted.

from our fauna. He recognized the primitive animal known naturalists as a Megatherium.

He knew that pachyderms are herbivorous and not very agile, but were they any less savage and ferocious for that? That was what the worthy American did not know.

The monster was little more than twenty paces away, and was heading straight toward Samuel Dixton. The latter could see only one resource: attempting to flee. That was what he was about to do when a cry even more formidable than that of the Megatherium rang out behind him. Chilled by fear, the poor professor turned round and saw another animal a few paces away, more terrifying than the first. It was much taller, although less bulky. It resembled an elephant, but it possessed four tusks, two exceedingly long upper ones above the mouth and two smaller ones beneath it. Its trunk was tearing branches from trees, and its immense ears were threshing the air.

The professor had recognized a Mastodon, the precursor of the elephant, one of the most terrible pachyderms of the primitive world.

He thought that he was doomed, for every escape route seemed to be closed, and he was between the two monsters, but the mastodon paid no attention to the paltry human being hidden in the undergrowth. He had seen his enemy the megatherium. The latter, for its part, had just perceived the mastodon.

They headed toward one another, giving voice to the most frightful roars. The mastodon raised its redoubtable trunk to the height of the summits of trees. It scored the grounds with its tusks. The megatherium, by contrast, remained where it was, raising it elongated muzzle in a threatening manner. It scratched the ground with its terrible claws.

Samuel Dixton understood that a terrible, exotic duel was about to take place. Curiosity might perhaps have caused him to stay where he was if he had not been afraid that he would fall victim to an error on the part of one or other combatant before the end of the fight; instead, he took advantage of the moment when the monsters were commencing the attach to plunge into the forest and try to rejoin his companions. But which way should he go? How could he find the clearing again? Everywhere, the trees and plants formed a dense thicket, into which the sunlight could hardly penetrate.

He arrived at a stream, however, which must, he thought, be the same as the one to the banks of which Fertinist had brought his companions.

Were his friends upstream or downstream? Should he follow the current or go the other way?

He did not know, for in his eagerness to look at the plants, he had not paid attention to the slope of the stream.

At hazard, he followed the course of the water.

He walked in that direction for some time, troubled in his flight by the ferocious cries with which the two animals were filling the forest. He still feared that he might encounter another monster, and stopped at the slightest sound.

Suddenly, several detonations reminiscent of rifle-shots rang out some distance away.

Samuel Dixton stopped, utterly surprised. He remembered that Fertinist has told him that firearms were unknown in the hand of Kirimon. What, then, did those gunshots signify, which continued to resound nearby like a veritable fusillade? At the same time he heard shouts, and thought he recognized Tom's voice. In fact, the later son appeared to the professor's eyes. He was covered in yellow dust; his face and hands were dotted with red, round bumps like those caused by a hail of small stones. He seemed utterly bewildered and frightened.

"Finally!" he exclaimed, on seeing the professor. "Here you are, Mr. Dixton—we've been looking for you everywhere, and I was afraid I might find you dead in the midst of all this racket, this frightful machine-gun fire."

"Are we in the middle of a battle, then?" asked the professor, anxiously.

"I don't know what it is," poor Tom replied, "but look at my wounds; I've been peppered by bullet, and I don't know how I'm still alive. There must be invisible enemies behind every bush."

As he spoke, Tom held out his arm and touched a bush in front of him. Immediately, new detonations were heard, and a hail of pellets launched in all directions struck Samuel Dixton and the Pennsylvanian.

"Ow! Ow!" cried Tom. "It's starting again."

He threw himself down on the ground to escape the projectiles. The professor, hit in the face himself, recoiled in fear. At first he thought, like his companion, that enemies hidden in the wood had just fired bullets aft them, but he soon pulled himself together and looked around.

He saw that he unexpected bombardment was coming from a tree situated in front of him, from which seeds the size of a hazelnut were escaping, Launched with great force, with a detonation like a rifle shot, they were flying in all direction, piercing the nearby foliage. The knowledgeable naturalist immediately took account of the phenomenon, recognizing in the redoubtable tree a euphorbia of colossal dimensions, whose species, much diminished, bears in America the name *Hura crepitans*, or the sandbox tree. The tree is known in the present-day flora; it still makes an explosion like a gunshot heard, and launches its seeds more than fifty meters, but in the primitive nature of Venus it had retained its colossal size, and its enormous fruits, projected long distances, were capable of causing veritable wounds.

Dixton immediately understood the cause of the marvelous fusillade, and reassured poor Tom, by giving him a brief explanation of the phenomenon that had just occurred.

They were then rejoined, almost immediately, by Fertinist, Landal and the servants, who had come from some distance away and did not seem at all frightened by the extraordinary din. Landal had understood what enemy they were dealing with right away, and the Venusians, habituated to their forests, were long familiar with threes whose properties had frightened the Pennsylvanian so much.

When they got back to the bank of the stream where the wings and luggage were, Samuel Dixton told his companions about the terrible spectacle that he had witnessed; he described the horrible monsters he had encountered.

"Our forests," said Fertinist, "contain a large number of those animals, and some even more terrible, but they're not as redoubtable as you think, because they rarely emerge from their lairs, and unless they're attacked they pay very little attention to any humans they might encounter."

"Redoubtable or not," the professor replied, "those monsters surpass anything that can be seen on our world; I've never encountered any more frightening; our lions and tigers are charming creatures by comparison with your pachyderms."

"As for me," said Tom, "I don't understand forests where one can't take a step without being bombarded. Not only is one risking running into ferocious animals, but even the trees shoot bullets at you, like the cannons at Charleston. I don't know how I got away from that machine-gun fire. I'm aching all over!"

During that conversation the voyagers had picked up their wings and the servants had taken charge of the luggage. Fertinist gave the signal to depart, and the band flew away lightly, like grouse surprised by a hunter.

After a few hours they arrived in the foothills of the mountains that had been looming on the horizon since they had left Sarimak. It was a chain of prodigious height; a few snowy summits disappeared entirely into the clouds. In general, pointed peaks appeared, with the most bizarre and rugged forms. The mountains were reminiscent of the Pyrenees, but on a much larger scale. There were the same profound gorges, in which foaming trickles flowed, the same sheer rock-faces carved into the mountains, like the blackened ruins of collapsed castles.

"On the other side of the mountains," said Fertinist, "is the city of Kimislam, near the sources of the River Kerib. There we can change our system of locomotion and proceed much more rapidly—but we need to be prudent in crossing this gigantic boundary; we'll be forced to go up to a very high altitude, and the tempests hereabouts break out frequently and unexpectedly.

Everything went well for the first hour. The voyagers were able to pass over the summit of the chain, and perceived a splendid valley in front of them irrigated by a river of imposing width, on the banks of which extended, as far as the eye could see, a series of towns and villages with scintillating houses. They all seemed to be made of metal, like Sarimak. Numerous boats were cutting through the water in both directions, and enormous balloons were circulating in the air.

The entire landscape appeared in a vaporous distance, like all those perceived from the tops of high mountains. It was a grandiose spectacle, whose beauties struck Dixton and his friends with admiration. Even so, they were preparing to fly toward the plain when Fertinist, who was still leading the way, shouted: "Look out! Get your weapons ready! Here comes a band of Kermis!"

"What are they?" asked Dixton.

"Big birds, quite frequent in these parts, and I'm only astonished to see so many of them together. They sometimes attack flying travelers. It's best to be on one's guard.

Everyone held his lance tightly, ready to defend himself in case of an attack.

"This," said Landal, "is a kind of combat unknown on Earth.

"I don't think it'll ever catch on," said Tom. "The cowshed floor, as our soldiers say, is more reliable!"

The birds were approaching rapidly. There were only five, but their gigantic size authorized the presumption of redoubtable strength. Their red and brown wings had a span of more than ten meters; a black and white hooked beak terminated each ruddy head; their powerful feet were covered in scales, as were the claws armed with talons. They seemed to be eagles, vultures and condors all rolled into one.

"Those," said the professor, "are probably what our scientists called *Dinornis*.[19] They're monstrous birds of the primitive world, which disappeared from the Earth a long time ago. I'd be glad to have a specimen to offer to the Museum of Boston."

"Here's the opportunity, my dear Dixton," said Landal, laughing. "They're coming to offer themselves."

"Let's get as close to the ground as possible!" shouted Fertinist.

He and his companions allowed themselves to descend rapidly, their motionless wings extended. But the dinornis plummeted after them impetuously, and it was necessary for them to maintain themselves in the air with the left hand alone, while defending themselves with the right.

Fertinist and his servants, full of self-confidence, doubtless used to aggressions of this sort, had soon wounded three of the animals. Tom and Landal defended themselves bravely, while Dixton struggled in isolation against a terrible adversary that launched itself at him furiously. The bird was able to seize the lance and break it in two; the brave professor was about to be torn apart by the dinornis' claws, when Landal came to his rescue. He plunged his lance into the bird's belly; but in his haste, he was hurled into the monster, which inflicted a deep wound in his arm with a thrust of its break.

Three birds had been killed; the other two, wounded grievously, fled with mighty wing-beats, while he voyagers gathered around Landal. Weakened, he could no longer steer his winged mechanism. Fertinist and his servants supported the Frenchman under the arms while descending gently to the ground, where they arrived without any accident in a few seconds.

The professor then took the brave Frenchman's hand and squeezed it emotionally. "You saved my life," he said. "I'll never forget it! You must be in great pain..."

---

[19] This is unlikely; the *Dinornis*, or giant Moa, was flightless.

"It's hardly worth mentioning," Landal replied. "A mere scratch. I'm lucky to have got out of it so lightly!"

Samuel Dixton, who was a skillful physician, bathed the wound with water from a nearby spring, and bandaged it carefully. It was not dangerous, but Landal would not be able to maneuver his wings for several days. It was therefore necessary to change the mode of locomotion they had been using since the morning.

They were on an elevated plateau, half way down the Sorem Mountains.

"We're going to try to reach the city of Kimislam in the valley," said Fertinist. "From there it will be easy for us to continue our route rapidly. Unfortunately, I don't know the paths of these mountains, which I've always overflown. It will be necessary for us to move somewhat at hazard through the rocks and cacti. Let's get going, then, sirs, for darkness might catch us before we reach the plain.

All the wings were folded up and given to the two servants, who, laden with part of the luggage, went on ahead and flew rapidly toward Kimislam. The other two, who stayed with the little group, were only carrying a few food supplies that would be useful if they had to spend the night on the mountain.

The difficulties proved to be greater than the voyagers had anticipated. On all sides there were rocks, slippery or sharp, standing sheerly over profound precipices. The ground was littered with sturdy euphorbia and cacti with dangerous spikes. It was also necessary to proceed prudently, to avoid injuries or falls into the fissures.

Night began falling; the red sun as already descending beyond the horizon, but Fertinist and his companions had not yet reached the foot of the mountain. It was necessary to think about finding shelter for the night. The voyagers stopped on a small platform only a few meters square, situated at the base of perpendicular rocks. The black entrance to a grotto, about three feet high and as many wide, opened there. It was like the arched doorway of a Gothic cathedral, whose immense columns were formed by lepidodendrons.

The voyagers only penetrated a few meters inside; it was simply a matter of being sheltered from the humidity of the night and surviving the rather sharp cold that succeeded the heat of the afternoon every evening.

They sat down, therefore, on tufts of grass next to a stream that flowed from the depths of the grotto, and started eating the food that had been brought by the servants with a hearty appetite.

The crimson light of the dusk gradually disappeared; the voyagers were no longer able to make out one another's silhouettes. A good fire was lighted with branches and dry grass, and everyone, fatigued by a day of travel and varied emotions, got ready to go to sleep.

Only Samuel Dixton remained awake.

By the vacillating light of the flames, he had immediately noticed brilliant gleams of all colors in the walls and ceiling of the cave. They were like the scintillation and sparkling of precious stones. The blue, green, red and yellow colors formed admirable rainbows.

The professor was too curious to remain insensible to that spectacle and could not sleep until he had taken account of the phenomenon.

It must be rock crystal, he thought, *or perhaps something better. Let's see!*

He made a torch out of an enormous conifer branch and got up quietly in order to examine the cave. The vault was still as high and the walls as brilliant. He moved closer and found that the gleam was produced by veritable diamonds. He picked up several of the precious stones, which he studied attentively. They were diamonds of the greatest beauty and of a size hitherto unknown.

"What a fortune!" he said aloud. "What a revolution this would bring about in American jewelry! I must take a few of these magnificent stones for the collections of our museums."

"Are you quite sure they're diamonds?" asked Landal, suddenly, who, seeing what the professor was doing had come to join him, with Tom. They were each furnished with several torches.

"Oh, you're spying on me!" replied Samuel Dixton. "You're afraid that I'm enriching myself without you. Have no fear, there's enough for everyone. They're true, authentic, magnificent diamonds!"

"Then we have a veritable fortune before us!" exclaimed Tim, wonderstruck.

"Millions, my brave Tom—billions."

"I'm going to fill my pockets."

"That's easy," said Laval. "But how are we going to get them back to Earth."

"That's the question," replied Dixton.

"At any rate, I'm still going to lay in a provision," said Tom, who was picking up as many stones as he could. "One never knows what might happen."

The three friends moved further into the grotto in this fashion. It became narrower, and he vault became lower, full of admirable stalactites that formed bizarre shapes or imitated Gothic sculptures.

Soon, one might have thought that they were looking at cathedrals with pointed, delicately sculptured steeples. In some place, magnificent draperies hung down, the long pleats of which fell gracefully to the ground. Elsewhere, organs with regular pipes seemed to have been assembled for giants to play in a marvelous chapel, or stalagmites ornamented by the finest sculptors formed colossal colonnades.

Samuel Dixton went from room to room, unable to weary of admiring those marvels, and forgetting that they were drawing further away from the place where Fertinist was.

Suddenly, Landal, who was marching slightly in the lead, signaled to his companions to stop. He was at the entrance of a chamber vaster than the others. The vault was so high as to be out of sight; the stalactites were magnificent.

"Look!" said Landal, pointing at the middle of the chamber.

An unexpected spectacle struck their eyes. There, placed in various positions, was a series of immense skeletons. Some were lying on the ground, others, back against the wall, seemed to be seated; yet others were standing upright, attached he stalactites. A few measured more than fifteen meters in height. Various bones lay scattered on the floor all around; the carcasses, from which the heads had been removed, indicated animals of a prodigious size.

Fearful at first, the three friends remained nailed to the spot for a while. Soon, however, the professor of natural history, seeing in the extraordinary collection a mine of great richness for his favorite science, drew his companions into the center of the chamber.

"Admirable!" he exclaimed. "Sublime! Oh, my sympathetic listeners in Boston, why aren't you here? I could introduce to you in the natural state what I have so often depicted for you in theory. You could see the finest specimens of the fauna of the primitive world!" He draw Landal and Tom toward him. "Yes, my dear companions," he added, you have before your eyes specimens of animals that we call antediluvian."

He pointed at a skeleton standing upright against and enormous column. "Here," he said, "is the ichthyosaur;[20] its length surpassed twelve meters; it resembled an immense lizard equipped with fins instead of feet; it was covered with a

---

[20] But the description is surely more akin to the one that inevitably follows, of a plesiosaur. A similar mistake was made by S. Henry Berthoud in "Le Château de Heidenloch" (1865; tr. as "Heidenloch Castle" in *Martyrs of Science*, Black Coat Press, ISBN 978-1-61227-229-0) and both authors appear to have been drawing on the description drawn up by Georges Cuvier, whose interpretation of the early skeletal discoveries made by Mary Anning was based on mistaken assumptions, although they were out of date by 1865, let alone 1888.

thick carapace, like the saurians of the Nile; its enormous jaws, armed with sharp teeth, recall those of a crocodile, and its round eyes were larger than a human head. In sum, it represents the dragons depicted to us in fable, minus the wings.

"Do you see these gigantic bones? They're those of a plesiosaur. Imagine a duck of prodigious size, a monster larger than our elephants, with a very long neck terminated by a relatively small head—and yet armed with redoubtable teeth a foot long. Its large fins permit it to move rapidly through water, which is its ordinary habitat.

"This immense carcass is that of an atlantosaurus, the largest animal of ancient times; it is a veritable lizard, whose stature was no less than thirty meters

"The skeleton that you see standing near that stalactite is that of an iguanodon. It was a horrible monster about ten meters long; it walked like a man, standing upright on its enormous hind feet and its tail. Its forelegs are very short and resemble arms. They are terminated by veritable hands, armed with enormous spurs.

"In the middle of these animal remains, which are only fund in our homeland in the most ancient rocks, I'm surprised to discover a paleotherium, from a more recent epoch. That pachyderm resembled a tapir, but it was much larger.

"I can also see a dinotherium, a colossal elephant with two curved tusks, the megatherium and the mastodon, which I saw fighting a horrible duel a few hours ago, and many other monsters that science has been able to reconstitute with great difficulty on our globe, and might still be alive on Venus."

The savant professor thought he was in his amphitheater in Boston; he was speaking with enthusiasm, and his companions were listening attentively, momentarily transported back into the midst of primitive life, when a violent shock suddenly recalled them to reality.

Frightened, they would have liked to get out of the chamber to return to the cave entrance, but a second shock even more violent than the first stopped them.

"Damn!" cried Tom. "One dances the polka whether one likes it or not in this place!"

Indeed, the voyagers were shifted from right to left, backwards and forwards; then they rose up, and subsided again. Around them, stalactites cracked; several were detached from the ceiling, noisily; the very walls of the cave seemed agitated, by an oscillatory movement that was not at all reassuring.

"It's an earthquake," said Samuel Dixton.

He had scarcely pronounced those words than there was another shock, more terrible than the others, which threw him to the ground, along with his companions. The torches went out in the midst of a frightful din caused by the falls of stalactites, the collapse of rocks and a subterranean rumbling, like thunder.

The voyagers remained stunned for three or four minutes. Landal, who was the first to recover his senses, got to his feet and groped around. He had not sustained any further injury, but as the obscurity was complete he could not tell what had happened to his companions.

"Samuel? Tom?" he said, in a firm voice.

"Present," Tom replied.

"I can't be far away from you," replied Dixton.

"That's good, my friends; we're still safe and sound in the middle of the cataclysm. Now it's a matter of getting out of the cave."

"Let's try first to link hands," said Dixton. "It's necessary, as much as possible, not to become separated."

It was not difficult for the three friends to come together, for they had fallen almost on top of one another. To guide themselves through the darkness was, however, another matter. For a start, which way should they go? In which direction was the exit?

It was impossible to know.

"Let's follow the wall in one direction," said Landal. "I remember that about a hundred meters from here, in a rather narrow chamber, we encountered a row of stalagmites stuck to the side-wall of the cave, forming kind of double colonnade to either side, about a man's height. We need to go that way. There was an abundant stream flowing there, which you doubtless noticed too."

"Yes," said Tom and Samuel Dixton.

"Well, if, by following the wall, we arrive at that stream and those columns, we'll be on the right track, and we'll only have to keep going. If, on the contrary, after a hundred or a hundred and fifty paces, we haven't found anything, we'll retrace our steps and march in the opposite direction."

"That's perfectly reasoned," the professor replied. "Let's go."

They walked slowly, holding one another by the left hand, while Landal, in the lead, steered along the wall with his right hand.

"Damn!" said the Parisian, after thirty paces or so. The route's closed by a wall. We've gone the wrong way"

"We've arrived at the back of the cave, then," said Samuel Dixton.

"Probably," replied Landal.

"It only remains for us to retrace our steps."

"That's what I'll do, following this wall to reach the one parallel to the one we've worked our way along. It's necessary to make sure that the barrier has no issue."

He turned along the wall that had stopped them and followed it, guiding his friends. After a few steps, they found the main wall of the cave. The obstacle they had encountered sealed the tunnel completely in that direction.

The three voyagers retraced their steps, groping their way, the other two following Landal. It was difficult to move forward, because the way was continually hampered by fragments of stalactites, stone blocks and landslides.

After having taken two hundred paces, Landal stopped. "Nothing," he said. "No colonnade, no stream."

"And yet it's our only route," Tom replied.

"Yes, our only route."

"Perhaps the earthquake has dislocated the stalagmites and dried up the stream," said the professor. "That often happens during earth tremors."

"In any case, let's keep going forward," said Landal. "It's our only resource. We'll soon arrive at some issue."

The three friends continued walking in darkness, in the midst of numerous obstacles that roe up continually to oblige them to make detours.

Suddenly, Landal stopped.

"Well," said Samuel Dixton. "Aren't we going on?"

"Impossible, my friend. "This route is closed too, either by a collapse or a wall of rock."

"So?"

"So, we're prisoners."

Imagine the situation of the poor voyagers: they were imprisoned at great depth in dark and narrow corridor, without any hope of getting out.

What had become of Fertinist and his servants? Might they not have perished in the earthquake, crushed beneath the rocks that must have fallen from the top of the mountain. Ordinarily, earthquakes are more terrible on the surface than they are in caverns or mines, where they are sometimes scarcely detectable.

If the worthy Kirimonian had not perished, he would make every effort to find his friends. He would go to seek reinforcements in the nearby city in order to penetrate into the grotto and try to pierce the rockfalls. Could they reach the voyagers in time? Could the latter stay alive long enough for them to complete what might be a difficult task? On the other hand, if Ferminist and his companions had perished, there was no more hope. Samuel Dixton and his friends would soon succumb to a horrible death; they would die prey to the cruel torments of hunger, or die of asphyxia when the air contained in the subterranean chamber became deficient.

Thus, in either alternative, the situation was terrible.

The three voyagers were sitting down, sad and silent, on fragments of stalactites. The most somber reflections were agitating their minds, but they dared not communicate them to one another. None of them had the courage to entertain his companions with a hope that they no longer had.

The sat there without speaking for a long time. Finally, Tom, who could not resign himself to losing hope entirely, broke the painful silence.

"Are we going to let ourselves die," he asked, "without making one last effort? Perhaps we haven't explored every point of the cave. The stalactites and the rocks getting in our way sometimes drew us away from the wall. We might have gone past an exit without noticing it. Before despairing, let's carry out another inspection."

"You're right, my dear Tom," Landal replied. "We won't stop until we've explored everywhere, or fatigue obliges us to rest. Forward, my friends!"

All three resumed their difficult march through the debris in order to traverse the width of the cave and reach the parallel wall, which they had decided to follow first.

They had only taken a few paces when Landal suddenly slipped downwards, letting go of Samuel Dixton's hand and sliding into a deep hole.

He was drawn down a rather steep and very damp slope, over which cold water was flowing abundantly, and only reached flatter ground at a considerable depth. He was able to hang on there by holding on to projections in the rock.

That fall, or slide, had not caused him any damage because of the inconsistency of the terrain, but it had been so rapid that he had not had time to utter a cry.

Samuel Dixton and Tom had remained motionless in the cave, unable to take account of what had happened, and waiting for Landal to speak to them. No longer hearing and sound, however, Dixton called out to his friend: "Landal!"

After a few seconds, he heard the Parisian's voice. "Don't worry, my friends; I'm not hurt."

The voice seemed to be coming from a long way away, but all the words were easily understandable.

"Where are you?"

"I slid down a narrow tunnel, whose slope, until I reached the place where I am, which is quite steep, but formed of soft earth. There's a stream flowing abundantly here."

"Can you climb up again?"

"Let me study the situation. Don't move until I tell you to. I can sense cool air—a sort of ventilation coming from below. Perhaps there's an exit in that direction. I want to make sure."

"Be careful."

"Have no fear, my friends."

The brave Frenchman started walking, slowly and carefully following the wall of the tunnel. The slope became steep again, and in order not to slide, Landal had to hang on to stalactites or stone outcrops. He made a rather long descent in that fashion, with his feet almost always in the stream.

His friends had called to him several times, but their voices could no longer reach him.

Suddenly, he perceived a small bright dot in the distance. It was daylight!

What a joy that was for the poor Parisian! How glad he would be to tell his friends that they were saved, that they would be able to quit the prison that had almost become their tomb! He did not want to go back, however, until he had made sure of the possibility of getting out of the tunnel through the hole that he could see,

He had to continue his descent for a long time. Gradually, the bright dot grew; the sun's rays gilded the walls of the tunnel, and it became possible to walk with more security. Soon, Landal fund himself close to the issue, which was almost the size of a man. He was content to recognize that it was possible to get out that way, and, eager to make his friends party to the discovery, he returned into the darkness in order to go back to the cave.

It seemed to him that the return journey was less difficult; he was climbing through the winding tunnel when he suddenly heard footsteps. He stopped in surprise at first, but soon realized who it was. It was Samuel Dixton and Tom, who, impatient to know what had become of their companion and not receiving ay response to their repeated calls, had let themselves slide down the slope. After numerous bruising collisions, they had been able to penetrate the tunnel.

They soon met up.

"We're saved, my friends!" Landal exclaimed.

"Finally! We've found you!" said Samuel Dixton. "What anxiety you caused us!"

"I wanted to explore the tunnel," Landal replied. "And I was right, because I've found a way out. In a few minutes, you'll see the sunlight."

Having rejoined the Parisian, the professor and Tom embraced him effusively, thanking him for his devotion. Then, guided by him, they descended toward the exit. After half an hour of walking, they arrived in daylight, and were able to get out of the black fissure without difficulty. It opened almost at the foot of the mountain.

The sun was already high above the horizon, and its warm light inundated nature. The contrast between its resplendent rays and the darkness scarcely permitted the voyagers to see the landscape surrounding them.

"We've spent an entire night in anguish," said Samuel Dixton. "It's a night that it will be difficult to forget."

"I want to forget it, since we're back in the sunlight," replied the ever-optimistic Tom. "It seems to me that after escaping such a danger, we have nothing to fear from the future."

"May that hope be realized!" said Landal.

While taking, they had become accustomed to the bright daylight and were beginning to take stock of the place where they had arrived.

The tunnel had brought them to the base of the mountain. The stream that had hollowed out the subterranean conduit traversed a small cactus wood and went to flow into a larger, seething watercourse that flowed down from the nearby heights.

First they followed the stream to the bank of the river, which ran alongside a broad road paved with long pieces of wood, like the one at Sarimak. They thought that it must be the Kerib, which they had perceived from high on the mountain, the course of which ought to lead to Kimislam, a city that could not be far away, as it was close to the bottom of the chain.

They set forth, therefore, along the picturesque path, which formed gracious curves as it descended, bordered on one side by the foaming water, and on the other by a dense wood of euphorbia, eucalyptus and cycads.

After walking for an hour, they suddenly found themselves confronted by the city of Kimislam.

It was less a city than an aggregation of towers similar to Sarimak. They were separated from one another by magnificent gardens, the varied trees of which formed splendid arbors. The road divided into numerous forks, which passed under vaults of verdure to connect the habitations to one another marvelously. The river, wider and deeper, separated the city into two parts. They could not see any bridge, but thousands of bats of all sizes were incessantly going from one bank to another or following the stream.

When the voyagers arrived at the first houses they saw a numerous crowd gathered in a verdant park close to the main road. As soon as they were seen, a venerable old man, dressed like Fertinist in a long white robe, with a felt hat on his head advanced to meet them. After greeting them, he asked the whether they were Fertinist of Sarimak's companions.

Samuel Dixton replied affirmatively, and questioned him as to the fate of the worthy Kirimonian and his servants.

"Fertinist escaped the earthquake," the old man said. "Frightened by your disappearance, he came with his servants at daybreak to ask for help. A troop of young people equipped with the necessary apparatus left immediately to fly up the mountain in order to search for you. You haven't encountered anyone, then?"

Samuel Dixton recounted what had happened, and how they had been able to escape from the horrible danger that had threatened them.

The old man and all the other listeners congratulated the voyagers of the fortunate outcome of their adventure, while messengers rose into the air in order to go find Fertinist and inform him of the arrival of his friends. The old man, whose name was Koreb, and who was related to Fertinist, took Dixton and his companions to his house, where they enjoyed the most generous hospitality.

In the evening, Fertinist and his little troop returned. The joy with which he greeted his friends, and the emotion with which he heard the story of the terrible adventure they had had during the night, are easily imaginable.

The next morning, the voyagers were fully rested, and even Landal, in spite of the pain of his wound, whose healing had not been favored by the previous night's events, wanted nothing but to continue the journey. They were impatient to reach Rimnik, where they hoped to find news of Madison, and perhaps to see him again.

"We have several means of locomotion available," said Fertinist. "Wings, public electric carriages, isolated or formed into long convoys, ships, similarly moved by electric force, or even balloons. You'll find better in Rimink; we're still in a remote region here."

"Damn!" said Samuel Dixton. "What more do you want? I believe that's already quite complete."

"Which is the most rapid mode of travel, and the most comfortable?" Landal asked.

"That's certainly the balloon."

"Well then, let's go for the balloon," said the three friends. "When can we leave?"

"Whenever you please. Balloons come and go continually."

"In that case, we're ready."

The voyagers took their leave of their host, old Koreb, and headed for the departure-point of the balloons, situated in the city center on the river bank. There was a huge, busy crowd there. Ships with several decks could be seen, like floating hotels, stationed along quays where passengers were waiting. There were elegant and light carriages, convoys consisting of long tall wagons, and colossal balloons of various models attached to long platforms reached by means of magnificent stairways.

Nothing was more picturesque that that square, shaded by leafy trees and surrounded by houses more than fifty meters high, shining with the rarest metals. What struck Samuel Dixton and his companions most were animals of prodigious size in the midst of the crowd. Nothing of what they encountered there was reminiscent of the Earth; only the humans were the same as on our globe. Horses of colossal size, monstrous elephants with long hair armed with curved tusks and other unknown animals were circulating, laden with goods or passengers.

"Look!" said Samuel Dixton. "A Mammoth! And that's a Hipparion, the antediluvian horse! In front of us that immense llama with soft eyes and a slow gait, carrying women and children, is a *Palaeotherium magnum*.[21] And there are others even more extraordinary!"

"These animals," said Fertinist, "are primarily used to transport local families or goods brought to market."

What astonished Samuel Dixton and his companions most of all was not seeing any animal similar to those of Earth.

---

[21] Georges Cuvier originally identified *Palaeotherium* as a kind of tapir, but when more skulls had turned up speculative paleontologists began to reconstruct them as more akin to horses, although the long neck suggested to others that the species was related to modern-day llamas. *P. magnum*, the largest species, was about the size of a horse.

"Venus," said the professor, "is still in the state that the Earth was in before the deluge, but humans, warmed by an ardent sun, have made immense progress, and are a thousand years ahead of us. We can therefore see here, simultaneously, the ancient Earth and the society of the future. Oh, my friends, what things we'll be able to relate if we're fortunate enough to return to our own world!"

The worthy scientist would have continued his explanations if he had not been interrupted by Fertinist, who invited the voyagers to climb up to one of the platforms, above which a gigantic aerostat was suspended. It was already filled with people and was about to leave.

Fertinist and his companions took their places without delay on the lower deck, and the machine rose into the air with extreme rapidity.

The aerostat taking them to Rimnik was formed of ten balloons placed one beside the other, each having the form of a long fat cigar. They were linked together by an enormous network of ropes. They were steered by means of powerful helical propellers and rudders, which caused the electrically-powered mechanism to turn. Ten meters beneath each balloon, an elegant gallery of light wood was suspended, where everything necessary to the wellbeing of the passengers was found. That was where the passengers usually remained, either seated or walking along the galleries. The balloon could carry a hundred people at a time.

The professor and his companions never wearied of admiring the magnificent aerostat, which a few man maneuvered with the greatest facility. Dixton especially never ceased manifesting his astonishment.

"I wonder," he said, "how Europe and the States of the Union, where people consider themselves so advanced in the arts and industry, have not yet discovered this beautiful invention, and I'm ashamed to see that a people whose existence the inhabitants of Earth deny has arrived well before us at the perfection of the aerostatic art, and all these other inventions. I know that among us, devoted men are making every effort in the cause of scientific progress; some of them even sacrifice their fortune, their health and their life to the dissemination of an invention due to their genius, but how are they recompensed? Ordinarily, blind, incredulous people attached to ancient errors mock the new discovery; people ridicule or insult the inventor, and he, discouraged and rejected, often dies in poverty and abandonment. His idea remains static for a long time, and then gradually begins to catch on, and finally, a luckier man cause it to blossom; the great and sublime invention overcomes the incredulous mockers, and people erect a statue, albeit too late, to the memory of the poor martyr who was the first to find what later became the joy and glory of the human race."

"Among the Kirimonians," said Fertinist, who had listened to the professor attentively, "it is not the same. There is a permanent jury, maintained at the expense of the State, made up of honest and experienced men, who study all the inventions submitted to them at length and seriously. Before rendering a definitive judgment on a new discovery, it is tried out, and its advantages and defects weighed up; if the invention seems to be useful to society, the State pays all the expenses to ensure its success; if, without being useful, it proves the talent of the inventor he is encouraged to continue his research by a recompense."

"Yours is a land of sages," replied Samuel Dixton, "and I promise to sing the praises of the Kirimonians to the Boston academy."

"And if you persuade them to grant a prize," said Landal, laughing, "who will take responsibility for bringing it here?"

"The planets will arrive in conjunction eventually," the professor replied, "and perhaps we'll be able to take advantage of this voyage to establish a means of communication with the Earth. Has electricity said its final word?"

During this conversation the balloon has made rapid progress. Kimislam had disappeared over the horizon some time ago, and nature deployed her most splendid spectacles beneath the balloon. A powerful favorable wind was driving the voyagers in the right direction.

The weather suddenly became cloudy, however; the sun as veiled by black clouds and the wind began to blow through the rigging of the balloons violently.

"We're going to have a storm," said Fertinist.

"That's not reassuring, when one's in a balloon a thousand meters from the ground," said Landal. "Are we going to continue our route in this bad weather? I can see house down below where it would be easy to stop."

"We'll only go down if the tempest is too strong and becomes dangerous," said Fertinist. "Thus far, we have nothing to fear."

In spite of that assurance from Fertinist, however, the travelers were manifesting considerable anxiety. The clouds were becoming progressively thicker; the sun's rays could no longer penetrate them; a dense shadow spread around the aerostat, and the plain was no longer perceptible. The wind was sighing in a lamentable fashion in the rigging and the balustrades of the gallery; the balloons, shaken by a terrible force, seemed to want to tear free of the bonds retaining them; they bumped against one another violently, threatening to burst.

The pilot gave the order to go down, but a gust more powerful than the rest carried one of the rudders away, and the balloon started to rotate on its axis in a frightening manner. It was making fearful bounds; sometimes its flight carried it away into the thick darkness of the clouds, sometimes it plunged downwards as if it wanted to crash into the ground. It was impossible to steer it; the wind alone was the master. The gallery was swaying like the deck of a ship on a stormy sea; the terrified passengers were hanging on to the rigging, and having great difficulty maintaining themselves in place. The obscurity was so intense that they could only see by means of the lightning flashes that furrowed the clouds with their sinister glare from time to time.

However, the aerostat suddenly began to descend in a visible fashion; two balloons had burst and the weight of the passengers was too great for those that remained intact.

"Look out!" said Fertinist to his companions. "We're about to touch down! Let's hold on tight and not get separated."

At the same moment, the aerostat plunged violently into water.

"Into the water! Into the water!" cried the passengers, diving into the river together.

Fertinist and his companions were quick to follow that advice, and threw themselves into the Kerib. It was, in fact, that river's waters into which the aerostat had just plunged. The waves, driven by the tempest, were rising up furiously in foaming mountains. It was impossible to see the banks of the river, and the travelers, having returned to the surface, did not know which way to go.

Tom, who was a very strong swimmer, cleaved through the waves energetically, easily maintaining himself on the surface of the water. He darted a rapid glace around to see where his friends were. He perceived a boat some distance away, which was approaching rapidly.

"This way!" he shouted using a few of the Kirimonian words he knew. "Help!"

The boat stopped almost immediately. "A boat, my friends!" shouted the Pennsylvanian. "A boat close by!"

Landal and Fertinist had heard him; they headed rapidly toward the vessel, which picked them up. Tom perceived Samuel Dixton in the distance, who was not making any progress and could hardly maintain himself on the surface; he swam toward the professor and supported him with his left arm while propelling himself with the right. So much effort had fatigued the brave fellow, however, and he felt his limbs growing weak. Samuel Dixton was not making any movement; he had fallen unconscious.

They were still some distance from the boat, which could not hold its position because of the enormous waves, and Tom could already feel his strength running out.

Poor Tom! He was thus about to perish, a victim of his devotion, and with him the old scientist for whom he had risked his life in vain.

Those bitter thoughts ran through his mind, and he was imagining himself falling to the bottom when two solid arms gripped his shoulders, while two others lifted up Samuel Dixton.

It was Landal and Fertinist, who, perceiving the danger that their friends were in, had jumped back into the river and come to their aid. That unexpected help changed the situation, and a few minutes later, Tom and Samuel Dixton were hoisted on to the vessel.

The professor was soon returned to life by diligent care; as for Tom, he was on his feet as soon as he touched the deck.

There is no need to describe here the warm thanks that Samuel Dixton addressed to the courageous Pennsylvanian and his friends when they told him what had happened.

"My dear Tom!" he exclaimed. "The University of Boston will be informed of your noble devotion with regard to one of its members. I want your name to be inscribed in its golden book."

The worthy fellow replied that the best recompense was to have saved the life of his master's old friend.

"His friend and yours, my dear Tom!" the professor added, swiftly.

Meanwhile, the boat continued its progress through the agitated waters of the river. The tempest had eased somewhat, and the sun's rays penetrated the cloud from time to time. The majority of the balloon's passengers had been able to take refuge on the vessel, which was going to Rimnik. It was a magnificent ship, with four decks, surrounded by open galleries, permitting the passengers to enjoy, in calmer weather, the marvelous spectacle provided by the two river banks.

The travelers were able to pass from one deck to another by means of broad staircases, and went to place themselves on the platform of the vessel, from which the view extended a long way. Varied flowers were disposed there tastefully, forming a kind of hanging garden where a delightful freshness was to be found. The long-distance passengers had private cabins at their disposal aboard the ship, as well as lounges, dining rooms and libraries. In the lowest section were the electric piles that powered the vessel.

After a few hours of navigation, night fell—a calm and black night, which had succeeded the day's storms. Having recovered from their emotion, the voyagers stayed on deck, savoring the charms of a pleasant evening.

Suddenly, at a bend in the river, a beam of light of extraordinary brilliance appeared in the distance; it was like a marvelous star whose light traced a long broad furrow through the darkness.

"What is that light?" Samuel Dixton asked Fertinist.

"It's the electric lighthouse in Rimink," the Kirimonian replied.

In fact, the city was soon announced by the watchman, and half an hour later, the boat stopped at one of the city's quays.

The light was almost as bright as broad daylight; towers of an immense height, equipped with electrical apparatus, dominated the whole city and illuminated its every detail.

"That's what Paris needs," said Landal. "With those magic suns, the police would no longer have to pursue malefactors."

"It will come," said Samuel Dixton. "Several cities in America already have electric lighting."

"Yes, but what a difference!"

As the voyagers descended on to the quay, a balloon rose up laden with passengers. It was passing over Fertinist and his companions at a low altitude when Tom grabbed Samuel Dixton by the arm and said to him, excitedly: "Look at that passenger in the balloon! It looks like Mr. Madison!"

Astonished, the professor looked.

It was, indeed the aeronaut. He was standing on the gallery, looking down at the city; his black clothing and top hat distinguished him from all the other passengers. His arms folded and his expression pensive, he seemed absorbed by the view of the grandiose spectacle.

"It's him! It's him!" said the professor, immediately. "It's our friend!" At the top of his voice he shouted: "Madison! Madison!"

Landal and Tom added their appeals to his.

It was a waste of effort. The balloon drew away rapidly, and no one replied.

The voices had been lost in the din of the waters, the movement of the boats and the thousand voices of the agitated crowd. It must be noted, too, that Samuel Dixton and his friends were dressed in Kirimonian costume, and that Madison would have had great difficulty recognizing them in the midst of the other travelers, especially at a distance.

"We have no luck," said the professor, chagrined. "A few minutes sooner and we'd have arrived before our friend's departure."

"We need to find out where that balloon is going and try to catch up with it," said Landal.

They went to a platform where another balloon was suspended, ready to depart. There, they learned that the balloon that had just risen into the air was bound for Kirimon, where it was due to arrive that evening. Another departure was scheduled to take place in a few hours' time.

"That will be too late!" said Tom, who was desolate. "We'll lose track of Mr. Madison. I'm sure that, impatient as he is, he won't stay in the same place for ten minutes."

"There's one means," said Fertinist.

"What's that?" the three friends asked, simultaneously.

"Taking the tube-express."

"The tube-express?"

"Yes—we'd be in Kirimon in a quarter of an hour; we'd have crossed the two hundred leagues separating us from the city and we could wait for Mr. Madison's balloon to arrive this evening."

"A quarter of an hour! Two hundred leagues!" stammered the professor. "My dear Fertinist, I'm too sad to listen to jokes."

"It's not a joke. We'll go to the departure station, but since we'll have plenty of time to arrive in Kirimon, permit me to take you before then to the house of my friend Sirinom. It was him who sent me the phonogram about your compatriot that I showed you. He's a wealthy businessman, with a noble and generous heart. He lives nearby, on the quay. I wouldn't be surprised if, desirous of pleasing me, he's taken other steps to find Mr. Madison, and can give us fuller information."

So they went to see the rich Sirinom, whose splendid dwelling was not far away. He welcomed the voyagers with great cordiality.

Fertinist asked him immediately whether he had learned anything new about Madison.

"Not knowing about your departure from Sarimak," Sirinom replied, "I sent you another phonogram there, in which I informed you that the foreigner you call Madison had just returned to Rimnik. I sent some of my servants to look for him; they told me that he was at the Karima. I was about to go in person to ask him to accept the hospitality of my house, where he could have waited for our arrival, when I was told just now that he had left on the Kirimon balloon. I was able to find out that he had left a letter at the Karima written in an unknown language, with strange characters."

"A letter from Madison!" exclaimed Dixton. "Let's go find it, quickly! What is this Karima?"

"The State hotel, where travelers receive national hospitality."

"Be kind enough to take us there," Landal said, on his friends' behalf.

"No need, sirs. I was able to procure the letter by saying that I knew where to find the foreigner's friends an promising to ensure that it would reach them. You can see that nothing has escaped me, and I haven't been wasting my time. Here is the letter."

So saying, Sirinom took a piece of paper from an elegant writing-desk, which he presented to Samuel Dixton. The latter, tremulous, unable to hide his emotion, wiped his spectacles, adjusted them carefully on his nose, and read in a loud voice:

"I'm writing this letter at hazard, my dear friends, in order that if the *Franklin* brings you to this city, you'll know what has become of me and what I intend to do. Carried away, as you know, by the giant balloon that accosted ours, I was the object of the most amiable attentions on the part of the people among whom I found myself. We sought in vain to find you again, traveling through the air in all directions; a contrary current had doubtless borne you away. After a long search, the young man in charge of the balloon gave the order to resume its route.

"In a matter of days we visited marvelous lands, traversing broad rivers furrowed by boats, and encountered aerostats even more monstrous than ours, al laden with passengers. In sum, I went from one surprise to another.

"I would dearly have liked to get to know the marvelous lands over which we were traveling, but the aeronauts refused to go down. In spite of their enthusiastic cares, they had the intention of keeping me prisoner—me, a citizen of free America! That thought irritated me, and I would have protested frequently against the restriction put on my liberty if I had known the language of those strangers.

"One day, for the first time since our separation, the balloon came close to the ground; the aeronauts were doubtless obliged to descend. It was in this city that the balloon came down. I accompanied the strangers, who did not leave me, but it was easy for me to escape.

"Since that time, I have received the most generous hospitality in this land. I have been living in the State house, where travelers of every nationality are welcomed. I learned enough of the language to get me out of difficulty.

"What country am I in? I don't know. In any case, this nation is certainly the most civilized on Earth, and I'm in haste to get back to the United States in order to prepare an expedition to come and study the marvelous inventions that I encounter at every step. The discovery of this region, hitherto unknown to our geographers, will cause a veritable revolution in the scientific world.

"I'm leaving tomorrow morning in order to look for a means of returning to the United States. I'm going to try to reach the borders of a great State they call the land of Nirmul, to which, it appears, my aeronauts belonged. Perhaps I'll find a better known region there; perhaps I'll encounter Americans or Europeans, and will be able to find out to what part of the world I've been transported.

"Will this letter stay here, lost, forever? Will hazard ever bring you to Rimnik? Perhaps the *Franklin* has already carried you back to our dear homeland? In any case, I'm leaving this document. It will always be a proof that it was an American who first set foot in this new world."

The reading of that letter caused Samuel Dixton and his friends the keenest emotion. The professor immediately translated it for Fertinist and Sirinom.

"Poor friend!" he said. "He still believes that he's on Earth, and he hopes to be able to return easily to the United States! We need to catch up with him without delay; he needs to know where we are, so that we can combine our efforts in searching for a means of returning to our own world."

"My master has enough genius for that," said Tom, proudly. "He's capable of anything."

Sirinom tried in vain to retain his guests; they were determined to depart immediately, and, having bid the rich merchant farewell, they headed for the tube-express station.

Imagine a vast hall, in which a numerous crowd is gathered, and where everything that comfort and wellbeing require can be found. A kind of tunnel opened there, absolutely circular, like the opening of an immense pipe; it was the opening of the tube-express. There was a vehicle at the entrance, long and rounded in form, constructed in such a way that it could easily penetrate into the tube, to which it was adapted exactly, and in which it slid like a piston in its cylinder. But what a cylinder! It was six meters in diameter and two hundred leagues long! It crossed rivers on solid bridges, mountains in profound tunnels and valleys on grandiose viaducts, always horizontal and always as straight as a ray of sunlight.

Samuel Dixton had Fertinist explain the invention to him, and his admiration rose to the highest degree.

"This," he said, "surpasses everything else we've seen. It's the most beautiful and the most marvelous of inventions."

As the departure time was approaching, they went into the vehicle. It was vast, comfortable and very elegant; banquettes were placed all around it. An electric lamp lit the cabin as brightly as daylight—a necessary arrangement, because, once the apparatus was in motion, the vehicle was hermetically sealed. Between the horizontal floor of the lounge and the circular envelope of the vehicle were the receptacles containing the air necessary to the passengers during the short time that the journey lasted.

When all the passengers had boarded, the doors at the rear of the vehicle were solidly closed. Then a powerful mechanism caused an enormous breech, like that of a cannon, to slide to the opening of the tube. The breech adapted perfectly to the end of the cylinder, closing it completely. When everything was ready, an electrical signal was transmitted to Kirimon, announcing that nothing any longer retained the vehicle. In that city, a gigantic vacuum pump immediately removed the air from the tube, and with a frightful rapidity, the projectile—if it can be described thus—sliding along the barrel, was launched toward the capital of the Kirimonian States. The travelers did not perceive the progress of their vehicle at all, and yet it crossed the eight hundred kilometers in less than sixteen minutes—which is to say, at fifty kilometers a minute.

Tom was surprised not to see the vehicle set off.

"Aren't we going to leave then?" he asked.

"We've arrived," Fertinist replied.

Indeed, the electric light had just gone out, and rays of sunlight were penetrating into the vehicle. The doors opened immediately.

The travelers had therefore arrived without any shock. How had that happened?

A few seconds earlier, air had been allowed to penetrated the tube gradually. The vehicle, encountering that elastic resistance, had slowed down, and, still drawn by the slowly-diminishing acquired speed, it had arrived at its goal gently. The travelers had not been able to perceive the speed with which it had been drawn along because, being completely sealed in, they had not had any reference point, and the vehicle, attracted by an immense, regular and uniform force, sliding like a bullet through the barrel of a rifle, had not experienced any oscillation that might indicate that it was in motion.

That was why Samuel Dixton and his friends were so astonished when they were told to disembark.

"But that's impossible!" exclaimed the professor. "We haven't left Rimnik!"

"You're traveled two hundred leagues," Fertinist replied, laughing.

"That's railways sunk!" said Tom, enthusiastically. "That's the ultimate in speed. To cover two hundred leagues in a few minutes, without even noticing it!"

"Railways," said Dixton, "are a long way from attaining such speeds. An express train covers about seventeen meters in a second—which is to say, a kilometer a minute—while we've just been traveling at fifty kilometers a minute, a little more than 833 meters a second. We'd have been able to cover 750 leagues in an hour. We were, therefore, going fifty times faster than an express train."

"Flying like a cannonball," said Tom.

"Even more rapidly, my friend! A 24 centimeter cannon-ball is only traveling at four hundred meters per second when it emerged from the cannon—which is to say, twenty-four kilometers a minute, only half the velocity of the tube-express. It's almost the same for the Earth, which, in its rotational

162

movement, is traveling at 464 meters per second at the equator. Thus, we've surpassed all those speeds, although they're extraordinary. The most curious thing is that, if the distance permitted it, we could hear from here the explosion of a cannon that we'd fired ourselves on departure from Rimnik, and we'd be able to be killed by the cannonball that we'd personally loaded into that cannon!"

"That's something that has never been seen on Earth," said Tom. "A man killed two hundred leagues away by a cannon he's fired himself! That's an original means of committing suicide!"

"It's comprehensible, since sound only travels at 331 meters a second. Only light leaves us far behind, because it travels at 300,000 kilometers a second."

"Boom!" said Tom. "We'd soon be back in the United States at that rate."

"In half a minute, very nearly."

"If only I could sit astride a ray of sunlight!" replied the brave fellow.

During that conversation, Fertinist and his friends had arrived on the quays opposite the magnificent bay along which the capital extends.

They marveled at the admirable spectacle that was offered to their eyes. They quays extended as far as the eye could see, covered in splendid houses, all constructed in the same manner as those of Sarimak, but they different from one another in the richness of their metals and the splendor of their ornamentation. Gold, silver, steel and precious stones appeared everywhere, and the sunlight made all those marvels resplendent with dazzling gleams. The animation on the quays was immense; vehicles of all kinds and convoys laden with passengers were circulating incessantly in every direction, alongside the houses, while the river was furrowed by magnificent vessels and the air was filled with numerous balloons and bands of flying humans.

After pausing momentarily to admire the sublime panorama unfurled before them, the voyagers resumed walking.

"Where are we going first?" Samuel Dixton asked Fertinist.

"To the Karima," the old man replied.

"It's the same here as in Rimink, then?"

"Yes, my friend, you'll find everything at the Karima. Every city and every village possesses something similar, in which everyone can find all possible comfort in exchange for a small retribution. Once, individuals kept hotels in which travelers found lodging and nourishment at exorbitant prices. Their owners rapidly made fortunes, at the expense of strangers who had abundant grounds for complaint. Poor people could no longer find shelter, the prices were so high, even in modest houses. Then the government founded these public hotels, which immediately rendered everyone great service and ruined the private hotels completely.

"People must be poorly lodged and fed in those establishments," said Dixton, who, as an American, was a partisan to the utmost degree of private enterprise in all matters.

"You'll be able to judge for yourself," Fertinist replied.

While chatting they had arrived at the Karima. There was nothing cleaner, more elegant and more agreeable.

Imagine an immense garden, filled with trees and the most varied plants, with shady pathways and occasional ponds. In the middle stood a tower of great height, in which there were private apartments, lounges and libraries, which were reached without difficulty by means of elevators. The ground floor was occupied by the kitchens and the dining rooms. The majority of the travelers, however, preferred to eat in the gardens, where cool arbors furnished a delightful shade. Only foreigners were admitted to the Karima, but they could invite their friends in during their stay.

As soon as they were inside, Fertinist and his friends sat down at a table placed in the shade of the trees and a waiter brought them a menu from which they could choose the dishes most agreeable to them.

The old Kirimonian read the menu to his companions and, after a few detailed explanations he gave them regarding the animals and plants of which the dishes were composed, Samuel Dixton was able to translate it into English:[22]

Cutlets of Palaeotherium parvum.
Jugged dichobune.
Spit-roasted Adapis ribs.
Chaeropotamus head.
Haunch of Xiphodon.
Leg of Sivatherium.
Puréed cycad flour.
Equisetacea Sporangia in sauce.

And many other dishes with strange and fantastic names.

"What is all that?" Landal interjected. "There isn't a single name there reminiscent of the dishes usual in our homeland."

"It is, in fact," the professor replied, "a meal such as our ancestors might have made, a hundred thousand years ago!"

"They must be tough!" said Tom, pulling a face.

"Those kinds of meat are excellent," Fertinist replied, "and you won't find cooks anywhere else as skilful as those in Kirimon."

"In any case," Samuel Dixton added, "although the names seem bizarre, the animals that bear them are less different than you might think from those that serve four our nourishment. So, for instance..."

"Suppose we eat first," said Landal, who had a keen appetite and, fearing a long digression, thought he ought to interrupt his friend. "We'll have more pleasure in listening to you, my dear professor, as soon as we're less hungry. An empty stomach has no ears. Since you're so well-informed about the local nourishment, choose what seems to you to be the best."

---

[22] It is not obvious how Dixton is able to translate the names without reference to the actual animals and plants.

"A few slices of Xiphodon," said Samuel Dixton, "will, I think, give you great pleasure. I know you like game, and I'm very fond of it myself."

"So you know that this meat is a kind of game?" asked Tom, displaying a slice from a gigantic leg that a waiter had just brought.

"Yes my friend, the Xiphodon is a colossal gazelle, which stands nearly as tall as our elephants."

"Damn!"

"It's the ancestor of the present-day roe deer and fallow deer of our forests; it's a light, svelte and very graceful animal."[23]

"Its descendants haven't degenerated much," said Landal.

"Like almost all other animals," replied Samuel Dixton, serving each of his friends a slice of the leg. "Thus I see, among the names cited on the menu, the Lophiodon, which is an enormous tapir, whose flesh must be as good as that of its American relatives, highly valued by Indians. The Sivatherium is a deer of monstrous size; the Dichobune is the predecessor of our hares; the Adapis of our rabbits, and, the Chaeropotamus ought to be reminiscent of the pork prepared with so much skill in Chicago."

"And in Paris," said Landal.

"The Chaeropotamus," Dixton continued, is the antediluvian pig; the Palaeotherium parvum is a little llama the size of a sheep, whose flesh ought to be very tender. You see, my friends, that we discover on this menu many of our ordinary kinds of meat. As for the plants I see cited here, they still exist on our world, but they're only paltry herbs today."

During these explanations, which the worthy professor made without missing a thrust of his teeth, they had eaten the thigh of the Xiphodon with pleasure, and found it delicious.

---

[23] It is now thought that *Xiphodon*'s nearest living relatives are probably camels, although the animal in question was much more slimly built.

Several other dishes that Fertinist and his friends requested obtained the same success. They were washed down with a generous wine, which, ripened in the rays of a marvelous sun, surpassed the best vintages of our world.

Tom declared that Kirimonian cuisine was not inferior to that of America.

"At any rate, I prefer it to that of China," said Landal. "Although it's composed of antediluvian animals, it seems to me to be very appetizing."

"The nourishment of the Chinese ought not to differ much from ours," said Tom, "since their animals and their products are almost the same as in our homeland."

"Well," said Landal, "in spite of the resemblance of the climate, nothing differs more from our nourishment than that of the inhabitants of the Celestial Empire. They eat everything that we reject; and here, by way of comparison with what we've just been served, is the menu of a meal that I was served in the home of a Cantonese mandarin. I'll proceed in order of the service: sugared cakes; fried locusts; fruits and jam..."

"What! They begin with dessert in that country!" exclaimed Tom, laughing.

"I'll continue," said Landal. "Poached pheasant's eggs; bird's nest soup; stewed sturgeon gills; sugared whale sinews; freshwater tadpoles; sparrows' gizzards; sheep's eyes spiced with garlic..."

"I wouldn't like that much," murmured the Pennsylvanian.

"Bamboo-shoot salad," Landal continued, "chopped shark-fins; roasted dog's ears; apricot kernels; toads' legs stew..."

"Pooh!" said Tom, disgustedly.

"Salted almonds," Landal continued, without pausing, "fricasseed rats' tongues; melon pips; millet seeds; ginseng jam and unsugared tea. That, Messieurs, was the menu; you can see how varied it is."

"Well, Mr. Landal," said Tom, "I share your opinion. I'd rather eat palaeotherium, as Mr. Dixton calls it, old though it is, than rats' tongues and toads' legs."

Evening had arrived. Fertinist and his friends had spent the day visiting the city, the center of Kirimonian civilization. After admiring the marvels of the extraordinary capital, they had returned to the quays, near the stage where the balloon from Rimnik on which Madison was traveling, was about to arrive.

They waited with feverish impatience. It was, in fact, a solemn moment. They were about to see their friend again, their dear Madison, from whom they had been separated for such a long time. They were about to meet up with the man of genius who might be able to take them back to Earth, and return them to their homeland. It seemed to them that without Madison, nothing was possible.

Darkness had begun to fall; the electric lamps lit up all over the city, and their white light had succeeded the sunlight when the Rimnik balloon was announced by the watchmen.

It descended gracefully toward the ground and stopped above the platform on which Fertinist and his companions were standing. They ran toward the balloon, and searched the crowd that was descending on to the platform, but they did not see Madison.

They looked everywhere, and scrutinized all the groups.

No one!

Fertinist questioned the arriving passengers, asking them whether they had seen the mysterious foreigner; he gave them a description of the American aeronaut, whose costume could not have gone unnoticed.

"The foreigner you're talking about didn't come all the way to Kirimon," one of the passengers replied. "He disembarked at Kobil, a village situated near the frontier of Nirmul. As he manifested the intention of visiting that nation, we urged him not to go there without passing through Kirimon, where he would have been able to make contact with

Nirmulians and go among those suspicious people with less danger, but the stranger persisted in his plan."

After giving them this information, the traveler went on his way, leaving Fertinist and his companions very disappointed by that new mishap.

"It's a fatality that's pursuing us," said Samuel Dixton. "At the moment when we think we're reaching the goal, Madison escapes us, like the beloved individuals we see in dreams, who flee before us incessantly."

"Is there danger, then, in traveling to the land of the Nirmulians?" Landal asked Fertinist.

"That people is as civilized as ours," the old man replied, "but it has a suspicious and mistrusting government. In general, the Nirmulians are untrustworthy, cunning and vindictive. On occasion, they are generous in their hospitality—but it's necessary, in order to be welcomed by them, to have an authorization to travel in their country, or to be accompanied by an important individual. Any stranger that crosses the border without having taken precautions risks not coming out again; he'll be treated with care, but he'd be a prisoner."

"That's what happened on the balloon that took Mr. Madison away," said Tom.

"Exactly. The Nirmulians acted on a small scale on their balloon as they're accustomed to do on a large scale in their country."

"Mr. Madison was able to give them the slip," said Tom. "He'll be able to find a way of getting out of the country."

"In any case, we'll go to fetch him ourselves," said Landal, "and we'll see whether the Nirmulians can stop us, as free individuals!"

"Bravo!" said Samuel Dixton. "Spoken like a good Frenchman!"

"And a good American," added Tom.

"My friends," said Fertinist, who was looking at things with a calmer eye, "the best means of succeeding is to address ourselves to the Nirmulian representative to the Kirimonian government. He lives in this city. I can, if you wish, obtain an introduction for you from some powerful friends I have in Kirimon. With his authorization, you'll be able to go to Nirmul and travel without any danger."

"We'll accept your offer with pleasure, my dear Fertinist," replied Samuel Dixton. "You've always been our Providence, in the midst of our difficulties."

The following day, the worthy Kirimonian did not lose any time in putting his friends in contact with the representative of the Nirmulian nation. He visited people who might be able to help in the matter, and was able to maneuver so successfully that events took on a more favorable turn.

In the meantime, Samuel Dixton and his companions, obliged to stay in Kirimon, toured the city exhaustively, and took advantage of their leisure to study the mores of the Kirimonians.

To explain in detail the differences that exist between the habits of those people and those of the inhabitants of Earth would take too long, but it will be useful to say a few words about the subject.

The Kirimonians are administered by a Council composed of ten members, who divide up the various branches of administration and are appointed by a general vote of the population for a period of ten years. If a member of the Council is found guilty of some criminal action he can be deposed by his colleagues, with the assent of at least eight of them. The people elect a new minister immediately. The Council is both the executive and the legislative power. The ten ministers, however, elect a President for ten years, who is always a man esteemed for his wisdom and experience. He convenes the Council, presides over it, represents the country with regard to foreign powers and marches at the head in all the ceremonies in which the Council must participate.

The army is not established on the same basis as those of the majority of terrestrial nations. Every Kirimonian is a soldier from the age of eighteen onwards, and has to do an hour of military exercises every day in his city or village, under the orders of a chief chosen from among the oldest, bravest and most knowledgeable soldiers in the locality. When that hour is over, the citizen returns to his work, which is thus uninterrupted. One is a soldier until the age of forty, but officers can serve until fifty if they so wish.

In case of war—which has not happened for more than a century among that peaceful people—the troops gather initially in their locality, and then go to the cities, and from there to the capital, directed by their respective chiefs, who appoint a commander-in-chief by common accord. Young men between eighteen and twenty-five, married men and soldiers aged between thirty and forty guard the regions where they live. Only men aged between twenty-five and thirty go one campaign, but the others are called up in case of dire necessity. It is evident that with that system the army is not permanent, and not a burden on the State, even though everyone is a soldier and trained in the use of weapons. Every month, the soldiers undertake a march of several leagues with a heavy burden, in order to accustom themselves to fatigue, in case of war.

Meanwhile, an army of ten thousand volunteers remains in a permanent state in order to form a police force and maintain order. It is disseminated in equal portions in all the cities and towns. It replaces our police and gendarmerie. Like everyone else, those soldiers wear a white robe and a felt cap, but are distinguished by a red belt, which also serves to lift up the robe in order that they can walk more easily. Their arms consist of a short sword, a lance and a hatchet. Gunpowder is unknown, which caused Tom to say: "These people are clever, but they haven't invented gunpowder!"

As has been said, no war has broken out for more than a hundred years; that is because differences between nations are, for the moment, settled by a General Council formed by delegates from several nations, who meet in a city designated for that purpose. There, the arguments, complaints and grievances of the counties at odds are weighed, and an impartial judgment rendered, which is almost always respect and carried out with exactitude. That avoids many wars and calamities.

"Ah!" exclaimed Samuel Dixton, on hearing that information. "If only we had the same wisdom on Earth, too often devastated by atrocious and unjust wars. And to think that, back there, we believe that we're arrived at the peak of civilization! To think that we regard our globe as an abode of wisdom and reason!" He shook his spectacles and added: "Come to Kirimon, O poor inhabitants of Earth! Come to Venus!"

In spite of the great simplicity that reign in matters of costume, however—a costume that is similar for all citizens—certain official ceremonies exist in which those wise men forget their natural modesty. In that case, what characterizes rank is a wig, which seems grotesque to foreign eyes. The inferior functionaries only have an ordinary peruke, but it grows and gets higher by degrees with rank in order to distinguish the importance of an individual. People say: "He wears a one-foot wig," or "a two foot wig" or "a three foot wig!"

What astonished Samuel Dixton and his friends was seeing how seriously and with what pride those functionaries advanced, maintaining their fantastic perukes vertical.

It is also necessary to cite another habit rather bizarre in a knowledgeable people. To testify great respect for someone, one lifts one's right leg up for a few seconds. That custom seemed so droll to Dixton and his companions that they could not help laughing to begin with on seeing the most earnest individuals lift their leg in the course of the most serious conversations. Fertinist, who excelled in that fashion of standing on one leg, was wounded by that inappropriate laughter, and asked Samuel Dixton what people did on Earth to salute people they met to whom they wanted to testify respect.

"We politely take off our hats," the professor replied, "and hold it in our hand. One also makes a gracious salute by lowering one's head and bending one's back."

"Do you think," Fertinist said, "that your customs are less ridiculous than ours? Do you think they seem any wiser in the eyes of strangers? What does your hat have to do with questions of politeness? Are these profound curves that you make with your back any more natural than the movements of our legs? Believe me, every people has its mores and only prejudice can make us believe that ours are better than those of others."

Samuel Dixton and his friends admitted that Fertinist was right, and did not laugh again on seeing the Kirimonians stand on one leg to salute one another.

V. Further Adventures

For several days, Samuel Dixton and his friends remained in Kirimon. Thanks to Fertinist, they had been received by the representative of Nirmul, and the latter had seemed entirely disposed to assist with their journey to his country.

One morning, that important individual, whose name was Konian, summoned the strangers.

"I have just received orders to return to Nirmul, the capital of my country," he said, "situated four hundred leagues from Kirimon. Make your preparations; I shall be setting out tomorrow at daybreak."

Samuel Dixton and his companions took advantage of the few hours that remained to them to render a final visit to the numerous friends they had already made in Kirimon. All of them expressed fears with regard to their journey, and reinforced the information that Fertinist had given them regarding the character of the Nirmulians."

"Decidedly," said Landal, "the Nirmulians are the Chinese of Venus!"

The next day, Fertinist went with them to the representative's residence. After having embraced the poor old fellow—who was weeping copiously—several times, the voyagers climbed aboard Konian's private balloon, and an in a matter of seconds, Kirimon disappeared from view.

They were to travel in that fashion to the frontier of the land of Nirmul, where another mode of transport had to be employed.

The representative was very amiable in their regard, and questioned them about the impressions they had retained of Kirimon and its people. Samuel Dixton told him frankly how wise and good he had found the Kirimonians to be. Konian approved that opinion, and made several observations that proved the fineness of his judgment. He took a particular pleasure in questioning the voyagers about Earth, and the government, mores and civilization of their nations. Landal sang the praises of France in terms as eloquent as possible, and Samuel Dixton neglected nothing in trying to prove to the Nirmulian that the United States was the foremost nation in the world.

"That's prodigious!" the representative exclaimed, incessantly. "I would never have thought that other worlds were inhabited. I thought that our globe was the only one that could harbor living beings. At least, I thought we were the only beings organized as we are, and that our arts and our knowledge could not exist elsewhere. Yes, it's prodigious!"

The voyagers conversed in that manner while traveling through the air, while simultaneously admiring the splendid landscapes that unrolled beneath their feet. Cities succeeded one another; rivers, lakes and hills passed by rapidly, as in a brilliant panorama.

At times, balloons passed nearly, and the passengers waved to one another eagerly.

"What a pleasant people the Kirimonians are!" said Samuel Dixton. "They're the French of Venus."

"They're also the Americans, in their knowledge and practical mentality," replied Landal, bowing.

After several hours of rapid and pleasant travel, the representative showed the voyagers a long chain of high mountains in the distance. "There is the frontier of the land of Nirmul. "At the foot of those mountains we'll be obliged to leave our balloon in order to continue our journey on Kiraback."

"What is that animal?" asked Samuel Dixton.

Konian gave a description of it.

"That's the mammoth!" cried the professor. "It's the ancestor of the elephants."

"Then we're going to be traveling like Hindu princes," said Tom.

"Yes, my dear Tom, but our elephants will be more than six meters tall, and their tusks will be no less than four meters long."

"Is that your usual method of travel?" Landal asked the representative.

"Here," replied Konian, "only the sovereign and his family have the right to wear the white robe and make use of balloons to travel. Ordinary individuals have the kira, carriages, boats and all the other means of transportation, according to their wealth. Thus, men of low extraction, clad in red robes, can only go on foot. Soldiers, merchants and any citizen who is not a simple artisan or mendicant, wear a blue robe and have a right to the service of electric vehicles. People of noble families, functionaries and officers, recognizable by their yellow robe, can make use of boats and carriages. Ministers and representatives of the nation wear a white robe, like the court, while exercising their functions, and have the right to use any means of transport except balloons."

"Those distinctions of caste and obligations must hinder social progress," said Landal.

Konan laughed. "One can see," he replied, "that you've just been visiting an absolutely free nation. Mores change with peoples, and we're so accustomed to our way of life that we don't experience any inconvenience from the servitude in which we're plunged."

They had arrived. The balloon settled gently on the ground and deposited the travelers near an isolated house set in the middle of a little wood agreeable in its coolness.

"That's the last of the Kirimonian Karimas," said Konian. "I'll leave my balloon there with the operators, and we'll find kiras a league from here, at the first Nirmulian post. I expect to come back before long and recover my balloon, in order to return to Kirimon. The prince has summoned me to

Nirmul, without my knowing the reason that necessitates the journey, but I hope that I won't be kept away from my post for long. I'll tell you frankly, because you're foreigners, that I'd rather be in Kirimon than Nirmul."

When Konian had made his arrangements, they all set out on foot to go to the Nirmulian frontier at the town of Kirmust, where there was a military post. The country gradually changed its aspect; instead of verdant plains dotted with an infinite number of houses, there was nothing to be seen but somber and menacing rocks; the route was difficult and badly traced. That first sight gave a very poor impression of the land of Nirmul.

After walking for an hour, the voyagers arrived at the walls of the town, where they were stopped by soldiers. Scarcely had Konian given his name than they threw themselves upon him and bound his hands.

He looked at his companions and sighed.

"I should have expected this," he said. "Courtiers envious of my position have calumniated me to the prince. I'm doubtless accused of some crime. As they feared to give me any suspicion and see me stay in Kirimon, they've made me come back under the pretext of political business."

Samuel Dixton and his companions responded by commiserating with the poor representative.

"That's a beginning that's scarcely reassuring for us," said the professor.

An officer interrupted him by seizing him by the arm and speaking to him in Nirmulian.

"I don't understand your language," Dixton replied, in Kirimonian.

The officer immediately questioned the voyagers in that language. He asked them where they came from, and how they came to be with the Nirmulian representative. The worthy professor answered as clearly as possible, but his responses must not have seemed very conclusive to the officer, who said to him: "I'll keep you and your companions prisoner. You'll be taken to Nirmul to explain yourselves to the police there."

They were placed on the backs of several mammoths, which were already standing by and equipped with all that was necessary for the journey. The enormous pachyderms with the huge curved tusks seemed very docile, and allowed themselves to be led meekly by their mahouts. A kind of tent was set on their backs formed by four poles attached to a sturdy saddle, supporting a large white cloth. One climbed on to the animals by means of rope ladders that remained suspended at their sides.

In sum, that mode of locomotion was not unpleasant, and, in spite of the natural ponderousness of pachyderms, their tread was very rapid. Samuel Dixton, his friends, Konian and the officer traveled together on one of the mammoths; the soldiers followed behind on two others.

The first days of the journey passed without incident. They traversed a mountainous region along broad, well-maintained roads, but which often had steep slopes and frightful bends. It was necessary to cross narrow ridges above unfathomable precipices that bordered the road to either side.

Konian soon recovered his cheerful insouciance; he was no longer thinking about the high position that he had lost, and did not worry about the future that was in store for him. He abandoned himself to the course of events with an indifference that astonished his companions.

"Everything in life is fated," he said. "I could lament or resist, but it wouldn't change the march of things. What will be, will be, and often turns out to be better than we expect. I've always been in the habit of letting events flow and adapting myself to them."

Samuel Dixton tried in vain to show him how unreasonable that theory was and how sad its consequences might be, but Konian laughed and replied: "Why be anxious in advance? So long as I have an hour before me, I don't think about what might happen thereafter."

"An odd fellow," said Landal. "He talks like a veritable Turk. I'm sure that if he saw his house on fire, he'd fold his arms and watch it, saying: 'It's either written that it will burn entirely or that it will be conserved; if it is to burn, there's no point in trying to put the fire out; if it is to be preserved, the fire will go out of its own accord. Conclusion: I shall calmly let events take their course.'"

"That's a fashion of reasoning that could go a long way!" said Tom, laughing.

"Not too far, my friend, for it easily leads men to death. When one is ill, one can say: 'It's written that I shall die, or that I shall not, If I'm to die...'"

"There's no point in taking care of myself...," Tom put in.

"Exactly. If I'm not to die..."

"There's still no point in taking care of myself," Tom added, again. "That's a reasoning that's very favorable, to physicians."

"And to those who adopt it," Landal replied, "for it scarcely facilitates a cure."

If Konian had been less fatalistic, he could have escaped easily on several occasions and returned to Kirimon, but he did not take advantage of them.

On the third day of the journey the little troop emerged from the Vorim Mountains.

"I understand," said Samuel Dixton, "what a separation that barrier must contrive between two peoples, and why their mores, their languages and ideas can be so different."

No one will be surprised by the savant professor's astonishment when they know that some of those mountains are no less than eleven leagues high. Their summits, covered in snow, are lost in the midst of the clouds; Konian told them that several years often passed without them being perceptible.

The voyagers had reached a beautiful plain in which there were numerous villages on the banks of a broad and profound watercourse named the Sirile, as they learned from the Nirmulian officer. The river flowed into the Southern Sea two hundred leagues away, after irrigating the city of Nirmul.

"We'll take the public boat," said the officer, "and we'll be in Nirmul tomorrow morning."

Those words caused Samuel Dixton and his friends considerable emotion.

"Tomorrow," said Tom, "perhaps we'll see my excellent master. A presentiment tells me that we'll soon be reunited."

They forgot that they were prisoners, thinking that they might be able to embrace a friend, a brother and a compatriot the next day.

"Madison's American, and I'm French," said Landal, "but here, so far from our homelands, our two nations are adjacent, and only form a single fatherland."

"Those words are very true," the professor replied. "How surprised those who are so proud of vast empires on Earth would be if they could see, as we can, the brilliant star that is known here as Karim, and which is our Earth. Thus, in that little dot circling in the sky, confounded with all the other stars, are so many immense lands, so many rich and populous cities! In that little dot, millions of people are agitating, filed with pride and passion, each of whom thinks himself the king of creation and dares to discuss the laws of the universe and casually solve the most unfathomable problems! In that little corner, how many vices and lies there are, how much ambition and vanity, malevolence, ignorance, prejudice and baseness! And how little virtue!

"In that little corner, an almost invisible atom of the universe, there are men still foolish enough to attach importance to petty everyday intrigues. There, people are loving and hating, and people are isolating themselves within their personalities, which are so tiny by comparison with the globe, which is itself nothing compared with the universe! There, scientists, poets and artists are ambitious for a glory that they think immense and immortal, but which doesn't surpass that little yellow star, where it only lasts for a few moments, very brief if one compares them to the immobile eternity. To understand the negligibility of human being, it's only necessary to see the Earth thus!"

"And yet," Landal added, laughing at that philosophical tirade, "we desire nothing more than to return that little globe,

179

vicious and miserable as it is! And you, my dear professor, will be the first to be proud of the glory that your extraordinary voyage will be worth to you."

"I admit it," replied Samuel Dixton. "I'm no better than other humans." One cannot imagine the incredulous amazement of Konian and the officer when Tom, pointing out a magnificent star in the sky, similar to Venus as seen from Earth as the evening star, told them: "That's our world. That's where we were born."

The two Nirmulians could not admit that the foreigners had come from another planet. They believed that they had come from a nation situated on Venus, but very far away from the land of Nirmul. They said that the stars could not be inhabited, that men could not fall through space, and could not live so far from the sun.

"How do you expect us to believe," they said, "that there can be water, seas and houses on Earth? Is all that possible? We're too polite to make fun of you; you come from far away, you've had misfortunes and you have a right to our pity, but we beg you not to say such things to the other inhabitants of Nirmul—they'll take you for madmen."

The voyagers made no reply, for they knew that nothing is more difficult than uprooting prejudices, and that one often risks one's life in trying to combat them. Do not even the wisest inhabitants of the Earth have a host of prejudices? Do we not see some who believe in ghosts, who are afraid of traveling on Fridays, who fear the number 13 or put their fortune in a piece of rope by which someone has been hanged? Have we not seen the most eminent men die victims of the ignorance of their compatriots? Do we have any need to cite Gutenberg, Christopher Columbus, Galileo, Denis Papin, Jacquard, and many others?

Such were the reflections that Samuel Dixton and his friends often made in listening to the arguments of the two Nirmulians.

The rest of the journey was completed rapidly. The boat was full of people going to Nirmul. The professor and his companions were astonished to see the variegated costumes that signified the different classes of society. All the passengers looked at the three strangers with a curiosity that was often bold and disagreeable. It was far from the amiable and affectionate politeness of the Kirimonians, who had only glanced at Samuel Dixton and his companions in passing, without affectation, in order not to cause them any embarrassment. The Nirmulians, by contrast, often pointed fingers at them, formed a circle around them in order to look at them more closely, and would even have gone as far as maltreating them if the officer had not often responded by pushing them away brutally.

Eventually, they arrived in Nirmul.

The first impression that the city gave our voyagers was far less agreeable than the one made by Kirimon. The houses were all very low, built in wood and placed without order or alignment.

"We're going directly to the prince's palace," the officer said to the voyagers. "I'll put the representative in the hands of the police. If the compatriot that you've mentioned to me is in Nirmul, he can only be in the palace.

Dixton and his companions followed an immense, narrow and tortuous street. The numerous and noisy population rendered movement difficult, but they were not disturbed. Children, however, and even a few men and women, followed them curiously, at a distance.

"This reminds me of certain small towns in Europe," said Landal. "Any rogue being taken to a police station draws the entire population in his wake, all the way to the cells."

What annoyed them most, however, were the enormous dogs that followed them in numerous packs, barking relentlessly in spite of the blows with which the soldiers administered to them.

"Those dogs are aggravating," said Tom. "If I get one by the ears, it'll spend a bad quarter of an hour!"

"They could easily devour us," said Landal. "They're real monsters."

"Those animals," replied the professor, are the species that natural history calls Amphicyonids: antediluvian dogs, of which those of our era are only diminutives."

"If ours no longer resemble their ancestors in stature, they haven't lost their mores and habits," said Tom, looking down at his legs.

After a good hour's march, they arrived outside a kind of citadel with exceedingly high walls. A somber arch, guarded by soldiers, served as an entrance. At a word from the officer, the little troop was allowed to go through the door that led to an initial courtyard surrounded by walls. Beyond that was a further vault through which it was necessary to pass. Then they arrived at a tower surrounded by leafy trees, constructed in the Kirimonian fashion.

"This is the prince's palace," Konian told the voyagers. At the same time, he saluted them with his hand, and added: "Goodbye. I would have liked to be of some use to you, as I had hoped, but I can no longer serve you now. Be prudent, and always on your guard."

"If the Nirmulians aren't worth much, that one, at least, is an exception," said the Pennsylvanian.

"Exactly—the exception confirms the rule," said Landal.

The officer had gone into the palace. He soon emerged again with several individuals in yellow robes and one in a white robe, who must have been a minister. The poor representative was seized and taken away to a remote part of the citadel.

As for Samuel Dixton, he was taken with his friends into an immense hall, bare and somber. There were two solemn individuals there. One, dressed in a yellow robe, was sitting in front of a round machine fitted with a large handle, on which his hand was placed. Several silver funnels attached to the top of the machine were curved in the direction of the voyagers, seemingly placed there to absorb all their words.

The other Nirmulian, whose white robe identified him as someone highly placed in the Court, was sitting on an elevated seat behind the fantastic apparatus, which attracted the professor's keen curiosity. He made a sign bidding the stranger to approach, and proceeded with a kind of interrogation, addressed to Samuel Dixon—probably because he was the oldest.

"Who are you?" he asked, in the Nirmulian language.

The professor replied in Kirimonian that he did not understand, and that if the other cared to speak in Kirimonian, he would be able to reply.

While Samuel Dixton spoke, the man in the yellow robe turned the handle, to the great amazement of Tom, who could scarcely hold back a burst of laughter.

The functionary in the white robe then addressed the professor in Kirimonian, and asked him numerous questions about himself and his companions, their homeland, their voyage and their intentions.

Samuel Dixton gave a complete account of their adventures, and told him that he would be glad to find Madison, their traveling companion; that that was the only motive that had brought them to Nirmul, under the safe conduct of the country's representative.

The man in the yellow robe never ceased turning the handle, and Tom held his stomach in order not to laugh.

"What's that one doing turning his barrel-organ?" he whispered to Landal. "He seems to be going to a great deal of trouble to make very little noise."

Landal smiled but did not reply, being occupied in following the interrogation.

"I am the chief of police," said the man in the white robe. "Prince Movori, our master, having learned of your arrival in Nirmul, instructed me to interrogate you. The prince met your compatriot Madison several months ago, in a balloon of an extraordinary form. The prince, who has a veritable passion for aerostats, desired to investigate the one you were manning, which seemed different from ours. Your companion was welcomed generously into the prince's balloon. It was at that moment that, by means of a ruse unworthy of a virtuous man, you detached your balloon from Prince Movori's and fled through the air, doubtless to avoid making known to him the inadmissible aim of your voyage."

At those words Samuel Dixton protested sharply against the accusation leveled at himself and his companions. He replied that none of them had any evil intention to hide and that if they had had anything for which to reproach themselves they would not have come to the land of Nirmul to surrender themselves to Prince Movori. He explained to the chief of police how the aerostat had been torn away from the grapnel because of the abrupt removal of Madison's weight.

In the meantime, the chief of police repeated incessantly to the man in the yellow robe: "Turn the handle, Disko, turn the handle."

The professor added: "We would have come to the prince as eagerly as our companion if the balloon had not been suddenly wrenched away."

"In spite of that insolent flight," replied the chief of police, "Prince Movori showed the greatest generosity with regard to your companion. He would even have forgiven him, if Madison had not toyed with his confidence by telling him similar fables to those you have just recounted. Knowing perfectly well that the star Karim, which you call Earth, cannot be inhabited..."

"How do you know?" the professor interrupted. "How dare you contradict us with so much assurance?"

"Turn the handle, Disko, turn the handle," said the chief of police. And he continued, calmly: "Knowing perfectly well that it cannot be inhabited, for reasons that there is no need to explain here, we have every reason to believe that Madison wanted to conceal by his lies the true objective that brought you to this region. The Prince, always full of indulgence, did not, however, want to maltreat that insolent man, and contented himself with keeping him prisoner on his balloon. One day, he took advantage of a forced landing in a Kirimonian town to escape, without testifying any gratitude to our master."

"He should doubtless have thanked him for having held an American prisoner!" murmured Tom, in English. "Rogue if you weren't on a star, you'd find out what Union bullets are worth!"

"A short time after that flight," continued the Nirmulian, who had not understood what Tom had said, "your compatriot came imprudently to surrender himself by penetrating into the land of Nirmul. He was rapidly arrested and brought here. He has been treated in the most courteous fashion and only retained in an isolated building in the midst of the vast gardens that the citadel surrounds. You will join him..."

"That's the best thing he's said so far," said Tom, in a low voice.

"And when you have admitted frankly what country you come from and what is the objective that brought you to Nirmul, you will be set free. Be glad that you are being hidden from the irritated crowd, for you would be torn apart by the people if you were allowed to go out."

"Charming, the people of Nirmul!" murmured Tom.

The professor replied to the chief of police: "We cannot give any other reasons than those that I have already explained, and which Madison has explained himself."

Disko had not ceased turning the handle.

"Reflect on what you ought to do," replied the magistrate, "for the prince's patience will run out, and you might soon be punished by delivering you to the fury of the people."

Samuel Dixton made no reply, and turned to his companions.

"You have nothing to add?" asked the chief of police.

"Nothing."

"Disko," said the magistrate to the man in the yellow robe, "allow the strangers to hear their deposition, in order that they can make their observations, if they have any."

Disko immediately pulled a small lever, brought the funnels of the machine closer together, and slowly turned the handle. The phonograph—for that is what it was, combined with a microphone—immediately made the questions asked by the chief of police and the professor's answers head with the greatest exactitude.

When everything had been reproduced, the machine stopped.

"Do you recognize the accuracy of that reproduction?" asked the chief of police.

"Perfectly," said Samuel Dixton.

"That's sufficient."

The handle had turned again, and registered the professor's approval. It was like a signature attached to a legal document.

"That's an admirable invention," said the professor, forgetting his situation in the presence of the scientific marvel he had just heard. "I'd like to make it known to all the courts in the United States."

He did not have time to look at it more closely because, at a sign from the magistrate, the soldiers took him out of the room with his companions. They went along several long corridors, across courtyards planted with trees and surrounded by high walls, and, after passing through one final vault, found themselves in an immense garden, where the soldiers abandoned them, closing the entrance to the tunnel firmly behind them.

Samuel Dixton and his companions were at the end of a splendid pathway, at the far end of which, seemingly a long way away, was a detached building, too far away for them to make out the details. To either side were bushy hedges, interrupted by narrow canals, above which the trees formed shady vaults. Further away, paths plunged into the bushes in all directions.

The voyager's first impulse was to head straight for the building, where, in accordance with what the Chief of Police had said, they hoped to find Madison. They therefore went along the path that ought to have taken them there. After a hundred paces or so, however, they were stopped by a broad stream without a bridge, which obliged them to take a path to the right, which led into the wood. They thought that they could still reach their goal, but new obstacles stopped them incessantly, which seemed to have been calculated to mislead unfortunate prisoners trapped in the labyrinth.

They walked for more than an hour; they had crossed over several bridges and traversed several clearings, but had not reached the building. Wearied by the long course, they sat down under a tree whose foliage provided a beneficent shade.

"The Cretan labyrinth," said Samuel Dixton, "could not have been more ingenious than this one, and we could certainly do with Ariadne's thread to get us out of difficulty!"

"What must Mr. Madison think about being in the middle of this garden?" asked Tom. "He only likes straight lines."

"Do you really think that he's here?" said Landal. "Haven't we been deceived by the Chief of Police, who seemed to me to be as rascally as he is pig-headed?"

"I'm beginning to fear so," said Samuel Dixton. "Our worthy Fertinist was right to tell us to mistrust these wicked people."

They had been chatting in that manner for a few minutes, while admiring the marvelous prison they had been given, when they heard someone nearby whistling an English tune that Madison often repeated.

Tom sprang to his feet. "It's him!" he said. "It's my master!"

They immediately caused the garden to resound with their appeals.

After a few minutes, Madison, who had been surprised to recognize his friends' voices, joined them, and embraced them with the greatest effusion.

Tom shed tears of joy.

"What! You, here?" the aeronaut said to them, when the initial emotion had calmed down.

"Yes, my dear friend," replied Samuel Dixton, on behalf of his companions. "We learned that you were in the land of Nirmul, and we came to find you."

"But I'm a prisoner here!"

"We know that, and so are we, since an hour ago."

"What! You're prisoners? Why?"

"Why are you, my dear Madison?"

"I confess that I have absolutely no idea, and I swear that as soon as we're free, I'm going to make vigorous complaints to the government in Philadelphia. These savages will see what it costs to infringe the liberty of a citizen of the United States! Do you at least know what accursed country we're in? How did you get here? Was it in the *Franklin*?"

The voyagers could not help smiling at their friend's threats. Landal rapidly recounted the adventures that had happened to them.

Imagine the stupefaction of the aeronaut when it was demonstrated to him that he was on the planet Venus!

"I understand now," he exclaimed, "why these stupid people accused me of lying when I told them that I was a citizen of the United States—from Baltimore, if you please! They replied that there was no such place in the world. You can understand how flattered I was! In any case, I'm content now. I'm proud of having been the first, along with you, to plant the flag of the Union on another planet! Three cheers! We'll give a famous report to the Chicago Observatory!"

They could not help bursting into laughter on hearing the joyful American's jokes.

"Before thinking about that," said Samuel Dixton, "it's necessary to think about freeing ourselves. If we can get back to Kirimon, the friends we have there will help us to build an aerostat that might be able to transport us back to Earth."

"Recovering our liberty might be more difficult," Madison replied. "We'll do it, though—I promise you that. How? That's the question. I've already been all over this immense garden. It's surrounded by high walls whose exceedingly long circuit prevents us from seeing anything. Once over the wall, we'd still be surrounded by palaces and citadels full of soldiers. Let's study the terrain again, though. Inhabitants of the Earth certainly can't remain slaves of these evil Nirmulians!"

"Bravo!" said Tom. "That's well said!"

"We're doubtless being watched?" asked Landal.

"Thus far, Madison replied, "I haven't perceived the surveillance of my jailers. Every day, servants bring my food to a building not far from here, to which I'm taking you. I've been able to make friends with Koro, the young man who is primarily responsible for me. He tells me, as much as I can understand it, what's happening in the palace. Perhaps he'll be able to give us some useful information one day."

While talking, they arrived at the building, to which they had been quite close, without being aware of it. In order to reach it, however, it had been necessary to make a few detours that would doubtless have deceived Madison's friends had they been alone.

The building was very pretty. It only had a ground floor, formed by several rooms, the furniture of which consisted entirely of carpets and cushions.

"Here, gentlemen, it's necessary to sit, eat and sleep like Turks," said Madison, laughing. "No tables, no chairs, no beds. In the end, one can get used to anything."

"Let's hope that we won't have time to get used to it," said Tom.

"I assure you that I'll do my best to ensure that you won't be obliged to get a taste for this life," Madison replied.

"In that case, I'm certain that we won't wear out these carpets," said Tom.

However, the aeronaut's friends, fatigued by their long journey, lay down on the cushions and slept until the evening.

When they woke up, Madison was chatting to a young man whose yellow robe made him recognizable as a palace officer,

"May I introduce my page, Koro," said Madison, still disposed to humor. "He's a little better than his fellows, and doesn't have any entirely stony heart. It's a pity that I can't communicate with him more fluently."

The young Nirmulian greeted the prisoners. Samuel Dixton said a few words to him in Kirimonian; Koro spoke that language very well, and as Madison already knew a little Nirmulian, they were all able to engage in a fairly coherent conversation.

Koro told them that the lords of the palace were exciting the Prince against them and urging him to deliver them to the people, who were demanding the "white spies," as they called them. The Prince, wiser and more humane than his subjects, wanted to be informed in a certain manner as to the nationality of the prisoners and the objective of their voyage. Prince Movori would come in person to visit the newcomers the following day, to see whether his questions could obtain more success from them than they had from Madison.

What explained the conduct of the Prince and the Normulian people was that a few months earlier, ships sent to the north-west had been brutally seized by a people of those regions known as the Karaki. A few sailors, who had been able to escape and return to Nirmul, frightfully mutilated, had given a description of the clothing, appearance and features of that barbaric people, which fit Madison and his companions perfectly. It was therefore believed that they were emissaries of that people, and that they had come to keep watch on the departure of further ships and balloons.

This information shed new light on the prisoners' situation, and they were able to hope that some circumstance might prove that they were not from the Karakian nation.

The next day, as Madison and his friends were chatting on the grass in front of the house, a balloon similar to the one they had encountered aboard the *Franklin* appeared overhead, seemingly descending slowly in their direction.

"That's what we need to free ourselves," said Madison, with a sigh.

"The same thought occurred to me," relied Landal.

At the same time, the aerostat touched down, and the young man they had perceived on the first day of their awakening on the *Franklin* jumped to the ground and advanced toward them. It was Prince Movori.

A single aeronaut was manning the balloon, which remained stationary, as if fixed to the ground.

The Prince greeted the prisoners graciously, swinging his right leg like a Kirimonian.

"It's you," he enquired, "who were in the balloon with Madison when the encounter occurred?"

"In person," replied Samuel Dixton, on behalf of his companions.

"I didn't have time to see you."

"It was the same for us."

"It's your fault. I've read the report of the chief of police and the explanation you gave of our precipitate departure. It hardly seems credible."

"We can't give any other, for we've told the simple truth."

"Always the same response! You interest me, however, and if you had told me frankly that you were envoys from the Karaki people, I would have forgiven you, as enemies serving their fatherland who had the misfortune to be captured. But this absurd story you've old about the star Karim irritates me and excites my suspicion. You can't think that we're stupid enough to admit such fables without complaint? What has become of your balloon? I would have liked to study the details of its conformation..."

Samuel Dixton replied that it had remained in the land of the Kirimonians, at Sarimak, near the city of Vornam.

"That's more than eight hundred leagues from here," said the Prince. "I know that place."

Then he asked them curiously how their balloon was composed, how they steered it and what instruments they used. He embarked on a long interrogation on that subject, which proved the great interest he had in aerostatic science.

Madison, so expert in such matters, gradually drew nearer to the balloon as he explained to the prince the differences that existed between terrestrial aerostats and those of the Nirmulians. Prince Movori was so attentive that he went into the nacelle, followed by Madison and his companions, in order to be able to follow the aeronaut's explanations more closely.

Madison understood the mechanism of Nirmulian balloons perfectly, having examined it attentively during his first excursion with the Prince.

Suddenly, the friends saw him push a lever abruptly, and the balloon rose up into the air with frightening rapidity.

The two Nirmulians attempted to shove Madison aside and stop the aerostat's ascent, but the American gave the lever one last thrust, imposing a circular movement on it. The balloon rose up with new force, and moved horizontally. At the same time, he maintained the stupefied Prince at a distance with his strong arm, while Landal and Tom grabbed the other Nirmulian.

At first they followed a crazy, dizzying course at a great height. The features of the ground fled beneath them like clouds driven by a storm wind: towns, rivers and mountains al vanished successively, and the balloon continued to move with the same rapidity.

Finally, Madison said to the Prince: "You see, Sire, that we're the stronger. You've held us prisoner unjustly; we're reclaiming our liberty. We have no intention of abusing the advantages that fortune has put in our hands, nor of taking you too far from your country. I render homage to the courtesy with which you, very particularly, have always treated me. We're therefore going to set you and your companion down— but I warn you that if either of you makes any attempt to re-take the balloon, I'll take you to the Earth of whose inhabitants you deny the existence."

That slightly risky threat struck the two Nirmulians sharply, who wanted nothing better than to be deposited on the ground.

The balloon, skillfully guided by Madison, descended to within a hundred meters of the lain. He examined the terrain attentively; it was necessary not to land in an inhabited region, exposed to the danger of an attack. The aerostat was traveling over a vast sandy plain. A few habitations were visible in the distance, but the area where the voyagers were at present was deserted. The place seemed propitious to the aeronaut, and, turning the lever, he took the aerostat down to within a meter of the ground. He refused to go any closer, but the two Nirmulians did not have to be begged to jump and run away, while Madison cried, as he took the balloon up again:

"Hurrah! Hurrah! Hurrah!"

They were free again, in an immense space, with a balloon much easier to direct than the *Franklin*. Once their initial joy had calmed down, however, they were not without anxiety, thinking that they had no food supplies. They resolved to continue their progress until the sun reached its zenith. They calculated that, at their present speed, they would cross the Nirmulian frontier in a matter of hours.

"What country will we reach?" asked Samuel Dixton, always anxious about the future. "Will we find a hospitable people? Will it be possible to procure the necessities of life?"

Those fears were agitating the worthy professor, but they did not seem to affect Madison, who, leaning his elbows on the well-cushioned rim of the nacelle, was admiring the landscape unfurling beneath his feet.

In the meantime, the weather had deteriorated. A brisk wind was pushing the balloon with greater velocity, and thick clouds were forming around them. Sometimes they disappeared, lost in a thick fog that hardly permitted them to see out of the nacelle.

Madison accelerated the progress of the balloon in order to flee from the storm, but the wind pursued the voyagers, and lightning was already furrowing the clouds around the aerostat.

"We have to go up," said Madison. "It's the only way of escaping the storm."

He pulled the lever vigorously, and he balloon was launched upwards through the dark clouds. At first, the aeronauts were enveloped by complete darkness. Their clothes were soaked, as if they had been plunged into water.

Finally, the aerostat went through one last layer of vapor, and the sky appeared, limpid and resplendent with ardent sunlight. Beneath the balloon the clouds were agitating, like the furious waves of an angry sea; lightning races long zigzags through that turbulent ocean, and the dull rumble of thunder rose up to the voyagers.

Several hours went by, during which the storm continued to growl as terribly as before.

Finally, the black clouds disappeared in the distance; the sky beneath he voyagers clears, and although a thick veil still separated them from the ground and prevented them from making out the terrain, they thought about going down.

Hunger was beginning to make itself felt.

We must be far away from the land of Nirmul," said Madison, "and I don't think we have anything more to fear from our enemies."

"I wouldn't be sorry to encounter another Fertinist disposed to give us hospitality," said Tom. "My stomach—and yours too, I'm sure—would be very glad at present to find a table laden with antediluvian dishes, as Mr. Dixton calls them."

"A leg of palaeotherium no longer frightens you, then, my friend?" queried the professor, laughing.

"Not even a leg of mastodon," replied the worthy fellow, whose appetite was formidable.

"Let's hope that your wishes will be granted," said Madison. "We'll soon be able to see in what sort of region we've arrived."

In fact, the balloon emerged from the clouds, descending rapidly.

A terrible noise suddenly reached the aeronauts' ears.

Fear gripped them as they saw beneath them the rolling waves of the sea. They looked in all directions, but in vain; no land appeared on the horizon. They were in mid-ocean, and did not know which way to steer in order to reach land. And their stomachs were complaining of famine!

"Which we shall we go?" the professor asked Madison.

"Straight ahead," the American replied. "It's better to continue on our course than waste time tacking in all directions. This ocean can't be infinite."

They held their course, therefore, maintaining an altitude of about a hundred meters above the water. The professor was at the front of the nacelle, searching for land, as Christopher Columbus had once anxiously awaited the appearance of the New World.

But nothing appeared.

Long hours went by like that, and the sea continued to growl beneath the balloon—always the sea!

The sun descended toward the horizon; its light, which had always seemed so brilliant and pure since the voyagers had been on the planet Venus, seemed to become pale and dull for the first time. The temperature diminished gradually; gusts of cold wind struck the aeronauts' faces from time to time.

Finally, night fell. Madison and his companions were exhausted by fatigue and hunger. They had crossed five hundred leagues since the morning.

"Who sleeps dines!" exclaims Landal. "Let's lie down in the bottom of the nacelle and forget our appetite. It's said that fortune arrives while one sleeps, and perhaps, by taking a long nap, we'll each a continent where we'll find something to satisfy our hunger."

"Sleep, rest yourselves, my friends," Madison replied. "As for me, I'll stay awake; the duty of an aeronaut is always to keep his eyes open. It only requires a malfunction of the aerostat's mechanism to plunge us into the sea. I'm accustomed to such fatigue, and I still feel sufficiently solid to pass the night without weakening."

Those words reanimated the brave American's friends. They shook Madison's hands emotionally, and felt the drowsiness that was making their eyelids heavy dissipate.

"We'll stay awake with you," they said. "We'll feel less fatigue and tedium if there are several of us."

How long did that terrible night last? No one could say. The hours succeeded one another; the time went by with desperate sluggishness; it seemed to Madison and is friends that daybreak ought to have appeared several times over, and yet the sun still remained hidden beneath the horizon. The poor voyagers remained lying in the bottom of the nacelle, plunged into a semi-sleep. They were no longer talking, and were scarcely able to think. Madison, the strongest of them, was still monitoring the progress of the balloon, but in a mechanical fashion.

Samuel Dixton, his eyes dilated, had noticed a glimmer in the distance that seemed to presage the sunrise, but the star so ardently desired remained below the horizon.

The night still went on, so somber and black that the voyagers had difficulty seeing one another in the nacelle. The cold had become very intense, and a heavy numbness invaded the aeronauts' limbs.

Suddenly, a terrible shock stopped the balloon. The aeronauts were hurled out of the nacelle, which hit the ground a little further on, along with the wreckage of the balloon.

Curiously enough, Madison and his friends did not come to any harm. They had fallen on to a soft carpet, into which they had sunk profoundly, feeling a cold humidity.

That freshness reanimated them. Madison was the first to try to take stock of the situation.

"Where are we, my friends?" he exclaimed. "For myself, I'm up to my neck in snow."

"I'm in a veritable well," said Landal, "And I don't know how to get out."

Tom announced that he could eat snow at will.

Only the professor did not make himself heard.

"Samuel?" Madison shouted. "Where are you?"

All they heard was a dull groan.

Frightened, Madison made great efforts to extract himself from the hole in which he was buried, and, extending his arms to the left and the right in the dark, he felt feet agitating desperately above the snow.

They were poor Samuel Dixton's feet; he had fallen head first into the snow, and was trying vainly to right himself. The more he moved, the deeper he sank.

Madison employed all his strength to pull him out of that unfortunate position, and finally succeeded in getting him back on his feet.

At the same moment, the sky lit up with a magnificent glow; it was an aurora borealis of incomparable beauty. Rockets sprang from the horizon in all directions, like those of a firework display; then curtains of fire seemed to be deployed in the sky, forming gracious undulations. Soon, luminous sprays, broad, diffuse and irregular, rose slowly toward the zenith; fiery streaks of various colors sparkled vividly, forming a gigantic rainbow that rose majestically toward the upper regions of the celestial vault.

That aurora borealis had dissipated the shadows of the night, illuminating it with a pale gleam.

Wonderstruck by that grandiose spectacle, Madison and the professor had forgotten their sad situation. They were surprised, however, when they lowered their eyes to the ground, to see an immense, limitless plain extending before them, covered in snow. Not a single object interrupted the monotony of that polar landscape: not a tree, not a house, not even an undulation of the snow disturbed the regularity of that white expanse. Behind them rose high rocks covered with ice, against which the balloon had crashed, and broken. They were sheer, absolutely insurmountable, and it had required a deep layer of snow for the voyagers not to be crushed by their fall.

Landal and Tom, having succeeded in freeing themselves from their envelopes of snow, were able to join their companions, and they gazed dazedly at the vast winter shroud that had suddenly succeeded the luxuriant verdure and humid warmth of a tropical summer.

"That's a singular transformation," said Tom. "It's like in the theater—burning sun one minute, now snow as far as the eye can see."

"I believe that the balloon has transported us to the pole," said Madison.

"I remember having read," the professor said, "that in the polar regions of Venus the most intense cold succeeds tropical heat, and that the nights there last several months."

"Then we're in a fix!" said Landal.

"Not very solidly," said Madison, laughing. "It's difficult to stand in this snow."

In fact, a terrible squall had just succeeded the calm of a few minutes before. The snow, whipped up by the wind, was flying around in fine clouds, and a sharp chill was beginning to grip the voyagers.

"The situation seems serious to me," said Samuel Dixton. "What are we to do, my friends? To travel over this snow seems hardly possible to me, and in any case, I can see no sign of any habitation. On the other hand, the cold won't take long to stiffen our limbs if we don't keep moving. Finally, our stomachs can scarcely support a longer fast."

"We have to walk," said Madison. "For the moment, that's the sole means of not perishing. Come on, my friends—an effort. Perhaps, by going forward, we'll discover some habitation that distance prevents us from perceiving at present."

The debris of the nacelle was lying a few paces away. Madison and his companions picked up pieces of wood that might serve them as staffs and help them maintain themselves on the snow, and they immediately started walking.

The tempest increased. The wind stirred up great masses of fine and icy powder, which filled the air and hid the glam of the aurora borealis. The voyagers sank into the snow at every step, and it often required a common effort to bring one of them who had fallen to his feet again. They marched silently, in single file, Madison in the lead, sounding he snow with a long staff and only advancing slowly.

After a few hours, Samuel Dixton stopped, exhausted. He could no longer put one foot in front of the other; a gradual numbness had invaded his limbs, and an invincible need for sleep gripped him in spite of his determination.

"Keep walking, my friends," he said. "For myself, I'm exhausted by fatigue; I can't go on. I'll never leave this spot. March, march! Any delay might be fatal for you."

"We won't abandon you, my dear professor," Madison said. "Are you capable of a supreme effort?"

"No," replied Samuel Dixton, who was losing consciousness.

"It's impossible for the moment to continue our route," said Landal. "We're heading for certain death."

"If we remain still, we'll perish anyway," said Madison.

"We still have one resource," said Landal. "To dig down into the snow. Let's try to reach the ground; we might find a few lichens that will give us a little nourishment, and we can establish a shelter against the intense cold that's killing us."

It was the only thing to do in the midst of that glacial desert.

So they started digging into the snow, courageously. Thanks to the staffs they were carrying, aided by their hands and feet, they first formed a mound several feet high, which presented a gentle slope to the direction of the wind, and had a vertical face on the other side about four or five feet deep. There they established a kind of doorway and a corridor, which descended deeply into the snow. That labor, for which they employed al the strength remaining to them, warmed them up and reanimated them. Even Samuel Dixton, sheltered from the gusts of cold wind, felt himself revive, and helped his companions roll enormous balls of snow extracted from the interior to the entrance.

Suddenly, Tom and Landal, who were in the forefront, disappeared into a hole that had suddenly opened beneath their feet. They fell several meters on to more solid ground covered with fine moss.

Madison and the professor, who were close behind them, slid in their turn into the same hole, and all four of them soon fund themselves in a tunnel similar to those of the salt-mine of

Wieliczska. Large columns of ice supported the vaults, and a pale light illuminated them, making the crystals of the magical palace scintillate.

A sound of voices reached the voyagers, and seemed to announce that human beings inhabited that mysterious abode. Madison and his friends headed toward the place from which the extraordinary sound seemed to be coming, and after a rather long walk they found themselves on the edge of a square, around which the facades of magnificent wooden houses could be seen, ornamented with plaques of various precious metals. Metal pillars supported an immense roof of wood, which also rested on the roofs of the houses. On all sides, streets covered in the same fashion extended into the darkness of the subterranean world. Electric lights placed at equal distances furnished a sparkling light, replacing the absent rays of the sun. The temperature was cold, but quite tolerable.

An animated crowd filled the square and the streets; electric carriages were circulating in all directions; one might have thought it a large American city at nightfall. The inhabitants did not have the same appearance as those that Madison and is companions had so far encountered in the planet Venus. They had pale complexions, blond hair and blue eyes; their thick, warm garments resembled those of the inhabitants of North America.

The voyagers had stopped at the entrance to the square, admiring the beautiful monuments that surrounded it, not knowing which way to go.

A young man was just passing nearby. Samuel Dixton approached him politely and asked him, in Kirimonian, whether the city possessed a Karima for foreigners.

"Those establishments are unnecessary here," the young man replied, in the same language. "Our houses are open to all foreigners who come here, especially to Kirimonians, whose friends we are. I can see that you are not of the Karakian nation. Follow me; you'll find everything that you might need."

"You mentioned the Karakian nation," said Madison. "Are we in a town belonging to that people?"

"You're in Monoka, an important city of the Karaki States."

"I'm glad of it," said Madison, following the young man.

The latter led the strangers to a house situated in the middle of a broad and well-lit street. There they received hospitality that reminded them of the benevolent Kirimonians.

After a sleep necessitated by their fatigue and weakness, they were able to study the country to which hazard had transported them. They leaned that the Karaki lived in a large region situated to the north of the Nirmulian lands, along the Occidental Sea. The Karaki capital was in the south, on the shore of the sea, about five hundred leagues from Nirmul. The Karaki, placed in the glacial zone, were exposed twice a year to a rigorous winter succeeded by two scorching summers, but the industry of the inhabitants had succeeded in vanquishing that veritable nature. It was a fertile land in spite of the cold, irrigated by great rivers that carried the waters produced by the rapid melting of the snows to the sea. The Nirmulians, a mercantile and seafaring people, had tried several times to found a number of colonies there, but their malevolence and avidity had always led to them being expelled from the coast by the Karaki.

Their cities were immense glasshouses; in summer they received a refreshing cooling from the watercourses that irrigated them and the trees under which the houses were constructed; in winter the snows, which rose up everywhere to a prodigious depth, could cover them entirely without stifling them, thanks to roofs formed of solid wood and crystal, which protected entire towns and were supported by thousand of metallic columns of grandiose effect. The air was incessantly renewed by means of corridors that communicated with the exterior via immense chimneys.

Those marvelous cities were linked together by broad, high tunnels illuminated by electric lights; they were subterranean roads whose center was Karaki. Electric vehicles, mammoths, hipparions and other means of locomotion transported travelers rapidly from one place to another.

Such was the information that Madison and his companions received from their host, whose name was Nostir.

They were astonished to find so mild and polite a people that the Nirmulians had depicted to them as barbaric and bloodthirsty. The understood that the inhabitants of Nirmul, by accusing that peaceful nation of having murdered its sailors and pillages Nirmulian ships, were seeking a motive to attack the Karaki and steal the wealth that they had accumulated during a long period of peace. That often happens on Earth, where many good and peaceful peoples have been destroyed without any motive by avid and ferocious conquerors who do not hesitate to charge the weak people they are attacking with imaginary crimes.

Madison and his friends spent several weeks resting in Monoka, studying the language of the mores of the country, and waiting before going to Karaki until the thaw that was about to commence was entirely concluded. The passage from winter to the ardent hat of summer was so abrupt that the snows melted in a matter of days; then all circulation was suspended; the profoundly hollowed-out river beds were filled to the brim, and the waters hastened noisily toward the sea. Soon, the sun's rays dried out the ground; nature decorated it in a matter of days with her most beautiful ornaments and life resumed everywhere with a new activity.

It was at that moment that the voyagers resolved to set out. Besides which, strange rumors were circulating in the city; there was talk of war, and it was said that the Nirmulians were heading toward Karaki, intent on invading the country.

Madison, who had retained a considerable hatred for his oppressors, was dreaming of nothing but battles and combat; it was important to go to Karaki and find out what was happening.

The stranger consequently took their leave of Nostir, who had recommended them by telephone to several friends in the capital. They departed by electric vehicle and rapidly covered the distance separating them from Karaki.

As they approached that city, they were surprised by the extraordinary movement that reigned everywhere; the entire population was afoot; on all the roads immense convoys could be see arriving laden with armed men.

Madison questioned one of those warriors, who was proudly sporting a double-headed ax in his belt and carrying a long Kirimonian lance.

"You haven't heard the news?" he replied. "In spite of the Council's conclusions, a Nirmulian fleet has just disembarked warriors on our coast. That people has commenced a war without any preliminary declaration, and is threatening to march on Karaki. The order to gather all men capable of bearing arms has been given in all districts, and the army is to concentrate as soon as possible around the capital."

That news, confirmed in such a precise manner, caused the voyagers some anxiety, except for Madison, who seemed filled with enthusiasm. When they entered Karaki they had a god deal of trouble fraying a passage through the crowd cluttering the streets. They went to the home of an important individual in the city named Kiomo, a particular friend of Nostir. Warned by the latter, Kiomo had been expecting the foreigners for several days, and hastened to put his dwelling at their disposal. It was situated on the shore of the Occidental Sea, whose foaming waves broke at the foot of the house.

From there, Madison and his friends could see in the distance the Nirmulian fleet, anchored some way off shore, and also the enemy army that had been landed , which had set up camp while awaiting reinforcements in order to attack the city. The Karakian ships were in harbor, preparing for combat.

Two days after their arrival, early in the morning, they observed a great stir in the Nirmulian army. The Karaki were massed at the entrance to the city, and the two fleets were slowly drawing closer to one another.

The battle was imminent.

Suddenly, Madison who had almost always been out-doors, in conference with Karakian officers, since their arrival, came to find his companions.

"My dear friends," he said. "I have a grudge against those malevolent Nirmulians, and I have a strong desire to help the Karaki expel them from their country. Would you like to go with the army?"

"What!" exclaimed Samuel Dixton. "You're going to take part in the war?"

"Oh, yes! Wouldn't you be glad to lend your collaboration to these good people, against a nation that is attacking it so unjustly?"

"Meager collaboration!" said the professor, the most peaceful of men, who was trembling most of all because Madison might be risking his life.

"I know, my friend, that you once fought bravely for the United States in the War of Secession."

"Yes, once. I was young then."

"Well, you're still sturdy."

"Hmm!"

"For my part," Landal said to the aeronaut, "if I can be useful, I'm ready to go with you."

"Bravo, my dear Landal; a Frenchman could not speak otherwise."

"And me," said Tom. "Do you think I could stay here watching you from a distance?"

"If everyone wants to fight, then," said Samuel Dixton, "I must do the same."

"I knew, my brave professor, that you wouldn't take long to make up your mind."

"All right, all right…but try not to risk your life recklessly."

"Ah! I'd guessed it—that's why you wanted to dissuade us from combat," said Madison, laughing. "It's not for yourself that you're afraid, but for me."

"It's because I know you…"

"I'll be careful, my dear Samuel," said Madison, embracing the worthy professor, who could scarcely hold back his tears. Let's go, my friends; I've asked the Karaki commander to accompany the army and fight with it; he'll give us every latitude for that. The moment has come—who loves me, follow me."

All four joined the Karakian army, whose battalions were beginning to move off. They were given axes and lances, and they followed the combatants.

After a rapid march, they recognized the varicolored robes of the Nirmulians. That sight reanimated Madison's anger.

"There," he said, "are the inhospitable people who treated us unworthily and held us prisoner. They're going to receive the correction they deserve."

The Nirmulians advanced in good order, and the battle was soon engaged with great fury. The four friends kept as close together as possible, but, surrounded by numerous Nirmulians, they were soon separated and obliged to defend themselves energetically.

Suddenly, Tom and Landal, who were at odds with several enemies, heard Madison's voice.

"Help us, my friends!" he cried. "Help us!"

They disengaged, with difficulty, from the Nirmulians that surrounded them, and tried to find the place from which the aeronaut's appeal had come. Fraying a path with blows of their axes, they reached Madison's side. He was on his knees, covered in blood, fighting desperately against three Nirmulians, who had knocked him down. Next to him, Samuel Dixton was lying motionless.

Tom and Landal felt armed with an invincible strength, and hurled themselves upon the enemies, felling the first and wounding the second; the third ran away.

"Thanks!" said Madison. "See to our friend." And he fell unconscious.

Several Karaki helped Tom and Landal to carry the two wounded men away from the battlefield, into a nearby house, where hasty cares brought them round.

Samuel Dixton only had a bad cut on his head; he was not in any danger. Madison, however, who had devoted himself to saving his friend, had been struck by several spear-thrusts, one of which had punctured his lungs.

"My dear friends," he said, in a feeble voice, "I'm mortally wounded. I only have a few minutes to live. If you return to Earth one day, go to embrace my aged father in Baltimore, and tell him how I died. I would have been glad to go back with you and tell my compatriots..."

The wounded man was unable to continue. A mortal pallor covered his face. He shook his companions' hands in one final effort, while they all burst no sobs.

Madison was dead.

At that moment, the Karakian army gave voice to cries of joy. It was victorious. The enemy fleet was fleeing in shame. But the poor voyagers remained beside the body of their dear companion, utterly drained. They wept bitterly for the friend who had died so tragically on a strange planet, far from his homeland and his family. They wept for that frank and honest heart, that bold and generous nature, the brother to whom they had linked themselves in a constant and devoted amity forever.

The Karakians surrounded Madison's cadaver, and seemed deeply afflicted by the death of the hero who had sacrificed himself for their cause. The commander of the army expressed his condolences in noble and touching terms, and promised the aeronaut's friends to honor their brave companion with a funeral worthy of his courage.

The following day, in fact, the entire army, emotional and silent, attended Madison's funeral. He was not burned, as was customary in the country; the friends wanted him to be buried, as he would have been in America. With common accord, the soldiers brought stones collected from the plain and formed a high pyramid. Samuel Dixton placed an inscription on top of it, which read:

Here lies Charles Madison, citizen of the United States of America, who traveled by balloon from Earth to Venus and died bravely in combat, for the independence of the Karaki people.

Trees were planted to form a little grove around the poor tomb and thus isolate it in a shelter full of shade and silence.

Oh, what a void Madison's companions felt around them when they returned to the city with the victorious army. Sad and discouraged, they had incessantly before their eyes the image of their poor compatriot, who lay alone in is abandoned tomb. They reproached themselves for not having dissuaded him energetically from taking part in that deadly war, and almost criticized themselves for not having died with him.

In spite of their extreme sadness, however, it was necessary to occupy themselves with finding a means to leave the lands of the Karakians and return to Kirimon, where they wanted to go back to Sarimak, to the home of the kindly Fertinist. They considered it a duty to repair the *Franklin*, as Madison would have wished, and attempt another ascension; they wanted to return to Earth, if they could, with their friend's balloon.

They were obliged to wait for a few more weeks, in order to take advantage of an opportunity that would facilitate their voyage to Kirimon extraordinarily. A gigantic project as just being completed in Karaki, in fact, to install an absolutely new means of locomotion, even more marvelous than the ones that had been employed thus far. It was a matter of establishing direct communication between Karaki and the city of Kirimon, passing over a part of the land of Nirmul and the Occidental Sea.

That invention, by two Karaki engineers, consisted of a mortar a hundred meters long, which, by means of a newly-discovered explosive of prodigious force, was to launch a projectile weighing 15,000 pounds, which could accommodate ten people.

That mortar would, according to a perfectly established calculation, launch the shell two hundred leagues, as far as Kerbil, a city on the Kirimonian frontier, which the tube-express put in direct communication with Kirimon. Thus the capitals of the two States, united by a close amity, would be able to communicate with one another henceforth without traversing Nirmulian territory, which had previously been obligatory. It is true that they could also reach Kirimon by ship via the Northern Ocean, but the voyage was very long and almost impossible in winter.

On the seventh of December 188*, the knowledgeable astronomer Robin Jeffrey was on the terrace of the Boston Observatory. He was examining the stars with great attention, devoting himself in particular to studying the course of Venus, which was then showing its full brilliance. His immense telescope was directed toward the bright planet, whose phases he was tracking with great care.

Suddenly, he seemed to be struck by a profound astonishment, and began staring at the Shepherd's Star with a very particular interest.

After having observed it for some time, he pressed a number of the buttons close at hand that caused electric bells to ring, and soon saw several people arriving with serious a magisterial expressions, who gathered around the director, awaiting his explanations with all due deference.

"My friends," Robin Jeffrey said to them, "I've just perceived an astonishing, marvelous phenomenon, in the reality of which I can't yet believe—so I'm appealing to your experience." He addressed himself to the oldest member of the group, and added: "Please look into the telescope, Sir John Krigthon."

John Krigthon applied his eye to the instrument with the most serious attention. After a few seconds, a vivid surprise was painted on his placid face.

"What have you seen?" asked the director.

"I don't know whether I ought to say it," the professor replied, "but it seems to me that I perceived, at a point on the planet Venus, the American colors perfectly designed."

By turns, the other astronomers came to place themselves at the telescope.

"There's no doubt about it," they aid. "There's an immense American flag there, reflected with a prodigious glare."

"Is it a phenomenon due to light?" said Robin Jeffrey. "Is it a combination of colors? Is it an illusion? We can't say—but our eyes are not mistaken. Our flag is admirably displayed at a point on the planet."

The news of that prodigy soon spread throughout the United States; thousand of curiosity-seekers flocked to Boston in order to admire the American flag planted on the most beautiful planet in the solar system. Eccentric projects were soon in formation.

"It's necessary," said the astronomers, "to establish a powerful electric source, illuminating a colossal flag that can be perceived on Venus. If it really is the American flag we can see, direct communication can be established between the inhabitants of the planet and Boston Observatory."

No extraordinary enterprise can stop the Yankees, so all the engineers in the country were invited to submit plans for an electric lighting apparatus of marvelous power. Harry Jenson's plan was adopted, and immediately put into execution.

It consisted of establishing a vast mirror composed of an infinite quantity of little mirrors combined in the form of a funnel; a hundred magneto-electric machines of the greatest force, using the system of the Alliance Company,[24] were placed in front of the mirrors, and immediately produced a

---

[24] The Alliance Company was an Anglo-French enterprise set up to exploit an electrical machine designed in the early 1850s by the Belgian physicist Floris Nollet to decompose water into hydrogen and oxygen. F. H. Holmes and Michael Faraday adapted the device to produce light and installed it in two English lighthouses in the late 1850s.

light equal to 30,000,000 candelas. Mobile mirrors of various colors designed the American flag.

A few days sufficed to establish the colossal machine.

As soon as the planet Venus appeared on the horizon, the powerful beam of electric light was launched in its direction, forming an immense cone in the dark sky.

From the height of the Boston Observatory, the astronomers, with the aid of one of the most powerful telescopes of our era, carefully observed what was happening on the planet.

An enormous crowd, which had come from all parts of America, surrounded the Observatory buildings, impatiently awaiting the information that the savant Robin Jeffrey was to give them.

A few hours passed without any result. The resplendent star conserved its ordinary appearance; no particular light was any longer to be observed there, and the American colors that were believed to have been seen previously had disappeared.

The astronomers were already embarrassed by the disappointment. The crowd became agitated, giving evidence of considerable discontent; mocking remarks and gibes rose up to the terrace of the Observatory. The misadventure might have cost the director and his colleagues dear.

Suddenly, however, the feverishly nervous Robin Jeffrey, who had not quit the telescope, uttered a cry of joy. The sparkling radiance previously seen on Venus had just reappeared; the American flag was once again visible on the Earth's sister planet!

The news was immediately announced to the crowd.

Thousands of hurrahs rose into the sky.

By means of a clever mechanism, the mirrors making up the American flag were set in motion and simulated the flag salute.

A few minutes later, the flag on Venus saluted in the same fashion.

When the director made this new fact known, the enthusiasm reached its peak; there was a sort of delirium. The Observatory was invaded, and for several hours, it was necessary to let the entire crowd file past the telescope and allow every member to see the planetary phenomenon.

Only daylight put an end to the interminable procession

The news of the discovery made by the astronomers of Boston spread throughout the world. Naturally there were numerous arguments. In general, people were incredulous, and, in spite of the testimony of numerous eye-witnesses, the scientists of all countries claimed that the astronomers and residents of Boston had been the victims of an epidemic hallucination or a simple trick of the light.

In the meantime, what was happening on Venus?

Samuel Dixton and his friends, obliged to wait for the monstrous mortar that would link Karaki and Kirimon to be completed, had spent their time studying the arts of the nation and visiting the capital's most remarkable establishments.

One of the most interesting experiments attracted them to the Observatory situated some distance from Karaki. It was a matter of launching toward Karim, the third planet of the solar system—the Earth, in other words—an extremely intense electric beam, and to try to attract the attention of the inhabitants of the plant, who ought to be able to see it by means of newly-constructed optical instruments.

The haste with which the voyagers went to the Observatory is understandable; they received the most gracious welcome there.

The electric apparatus had been installed on a vast platform; it consisted of a colossal machine of incalculable power; it produced a luminous beam which, projected by an immense metallic mirror, equaled the brightness of the sun.

That light was directed at the Earth.

Samuel Dixton, with his eye to the telescope, examined the terrestrial globe attentively; the form of the continents appeared in a very clear fashion, but neither he nor his companions could see anything that indicated the slightest movement on the planet. Everyone meanwhile, was waiting anxiously.

"I'm certain," said the professor, "that such a radiance might be noticed by our astronomers, but it's necessary for one of them to be observing Venus particularly for his attention to be drawn to the electric beam, which can't fail to strike the gaze of an experienced astronomer."

He urged the Karakian astronomers to be patient, and the experiments were continued for several days. The savant naturalist then had the idea of launching colored rays by means of various metals, which, perfectly combined, imitated the national colors of the United States.

It was at that moment that the electric light on Venus was perceived by the director of the Boston Observatory, and a response as made to the signals of the Karakian astronomers. The joy of Samuel Dixton and his friends is easily imaginable. They could, in consequence, correspond with the inhabitants of Earth, and soon they hoped, by means of a colossal alphabet, to converse with them and make their presence on the planet Venus known.

The professor and his companions could not remain for long at the Karaki Observatory. The work undertaken for the new communication link with Kirimon was reaching its conclusion.

"We'll find an observatory in Kirimon," said Samuel Dixton, "where it will be easy for us to repeat the experiment that has just been carried out here. I hope that we'll soon be able to engage in conversation with our friends in America."

"If we could only go to shake their hands as well!" said Tom, with a sigh.

"Perhaps that will soon be possible, with the curious system of locomotion invented by the Karakians."

Samuel Dixton was curious to try that new method of travel. After having seen so many marvels on Venus, he did not doubt the success of the Karaki invention. He was surprised, most of all, that they had been able to discover an explosive substance powerful enough to launch such an enormous projectile over such a great distance.

When the voyagers were informed that the cannon was complete, they went to visit it. It was a magnificent machine, cast in gilded bronze; it was located in one of the major squares of the city, and reposed on an immense terrace that served as its gun-carriage. It was placed obliquely, and the shell was alongside it, ready to be lifted up and slid into the enormous mouth by means of powerful cranes. It was a colossal cylinder, surmounted by a conical cap. One might have thought that it was one of those little towers of the Middle Ages, placed alongside a feudal castle. One penetrated into the interior by means of a small door that could be hermetically sealed. It was to be illuminated by electricity, and a sufficient provision of air had been made in the inferior section.

All measures had been taken to prevent the slightest accident and to avoid the effects of shock. According to the calculations of the engineers, the shell ought to slow down gradually in its course and fall softly near Kerbil, in the middle of a vast esplanade prepared for that purpose and covered to a depth of twenty meters with a soft and elastic substance. The passengers ought, therefore, to arrive without danger.

Our voyagers, especially Samuel Dixton, marveled at the audacity and the genius of the Karaki engineers.

"The inhabitants of Earth," said the professor, have found gunpowder, guncotton, nitroglycerine, dynamite, panclastite, forcite, roburite, picrate, melinite..."[25]

"All those names make us jump!" Tom put in.[26]

---

[25] All these explosives were real; roburite was invented by the German chemist Carl Roth in 1886, the same year that Jules Verne published *Robur-le-Conquérant* (tr. as *The Clipper of the Clouds*). The coincidence probably results from the fact that *robur*, the Latin for oak, is used figuratively to mean "strength."

[26] Tom is making a pun that is by no means unconnected with the purpose of the device, the French *sauter* meaning both "jump" and "blow up." Although it seems a trifle surprising from a modern viewpoint, travel by cannon-fire was a com-

"I'd be proud," the professor continued, "to make known to the Boston Academy an explosive agent far superior to those we know..."

"And what would you call it?" asked Landal

"Venusite—in memory of this marvelous world! What I'd like most of all to make known is the application of the agent as a motive force in place of steam."

"Your discovery wouldn't be absolutely new on Earth," said Landal. "Someone has already thought of making a boat move by means of an explosive mixture. One of my compatriots, Monsieur Just Buisson, is the inventor of that apparatus, which is put in motion by a force of recoil furnished by a series of successive explosions. His machine functioned perfectly at first, and when he perished as a victim of his invention, it was by virtue of a simple imprudence."[27]

"I know about those attempts," said Samuel Dixton. "I also know that the United States is not lagging behind in that regard. An American engineer, Mr. Berdan, has invented a

---

mon motif in French scientific romance, pioneered in a satirical fashion by Charles Nodier and Émile Souvestre before being applied in earnest by Jules Verne, and frequently copied thereafter. The plausibility of the notion was doubtless fostered (misleadingly) by the advent of "human cannonballs" in circus acts, first deployed in 1877.

[27] The device in question, demonstrated in 1886, is nowadays usually credited to Buisson's collaborator, the Rumanian inventor Alexandru Ciurcu (1854-1922), who had the good fortune not to be aboard the rocket-powered boat in question when it blew up in Paris in December of that year. Their ultimate aim was to employ the device for air travel, so their citation in a story about space travel is by no means inapt. Who knows what they might have achieved had Buisson's death not brought their experiments to a halt?

torpedo whose propeller is powered by explosive gas, and the same gas is used to launch the torpedo."[28]

"Weapon and locomotive at the same time!" exclaimed Tom. "That's magnificent!"

"But what are all these little-known trials," said the professor, "compared with the grandiose result obtained by the Karakians? We're going to see more than all of that today—we're going to see the carriage-shell."

"As in Jules Verne," said Landal, laughing.

"Absolutely."

"I've always thought that was a dream, impossible to realize," said Tom.

"Dreams are realized every day, my friend."

When all the arrangements for the departure of the carriage-shell had been made, a large number of people asked to take part in the journey. Samuel Dixton and his companions were the first to present themselves, but all the requests were flatly refused. The engineers and the inventor of the new means of locomotion wanted to make the first journey alone.

The cannon was therefore loaded in the regulation manner, and before a large crowd gathered for the occasion, the shell, in which ten people had taken their places, rose into the air in the midst of a mighty explosion.

An hour later, the telephone announced that the travelers had crossed the two hundred leagues and had arrived safe and sound at Kerbil. People would be able to go even faster by increasing the quantity of the explosive substance—that was the opinion of the engineers—but the result was already mar-

---

[28] The inventor and sharpshooter Hiram Berdan (1824-1893) was one of those American inventors who liked to publicize his inventions before they had actually been tested, so it is unclear whether his rocket torpedo, advertised in the pages of the *Scientific American* in 1885, ever really existed. Many designs for hypothetical torpedoes were published in that decade, including others powered by rockets, but very few got off the drawing board.

velous, since the projectile had traveled two hundred leagues in less than forty minutes.

That brilliant success filled everyone with enthusiasm. From that moment on, everyone wanted to make the journey by carriage-shell.

They prepared a second projectile for launch, and, by a courtesy worthy of that intelligent people, Samuel Dixton and his friends were, as gusts of the Karakian nation, admitted to the party making the second journey, which was to take place the following morning.

"What a rapid transit we're going to make!" said the professor. "Less than forty minutes after our departure, we'll be in Kerbil. A quarter of an hour later, the tube-express will have transported us to Kirimon, and from there, in a matter of hours, by electric balloon, we'll rejoin our friend Fertinist in Sarimak."

"And what distance will we have traveled?" asked Tom.

"More than eight hundred leagues, if we can believe the information that has been given to us."

"Almost the distance from San Francisco to Omaha City?"

"Yes, my friend. The distance that our best railways take five days to travel."

"What a connection we'll be able to establish between France and America when we get back to Earth!" said Landal.

"It's necessary to hope that we will get back there," the professor replied.

Samuel Dixton and his companions took advantage of the few hours that remained to them to make one final visit to Madison's tomb and say a final farewell to that beloved friend, whose loss left them inconsolable.

The next day they went into the carriage-shell with seven high-ranking Karaki who were going to Kirimon.

The small door was firmly shut and the projectile, lifted by an enormous crane, slowly descended into the mortar. They had been careful, following the advice of the engineers, to increase the quantity of the explosive substance in order to give the shell a greater velocity. The carriage was richly carpeted inside, and a circular banquette permitted the travelers to sit down during the few minutes that the journey lasted.

Samuel Dixton and his friends were chatting as they admired that comfortable installation when a frightful din interrupted their conversation. The travelers felt themselves lifted into space with a frightful velocity.

The professor had calculated that the shell would arrive in Kerbil in less than forty minutes, but several hours passed and the projectile was still in motion.

What had happened, then? Had a mistake been made in the calculations? Had the quantity of explosive substance been augmented excessively? Was the second carriage-shell not equilibrated like the first? An error in a single figure in such delicate combinations might lead to a horrible catastrophe.

Such were the reflections that Samuel Dixton communicated to his friends.

"This means of travel is good," said Tom, "but it lacks variety."

"It is, indeed," said Landal "not ideal for geographical societies. What fine views must be escaping our admiration!"

The provision of air made for a short interval of time was beginning to run out. The travelers could scarcely breathe.

"Open the door!" said the professor to his friends.

Landal leapt to the door and opened it wide, but it was in vain; no respirable gas came in. On the contrary, the little air remaining in the room escaped.

"One…might…think," said Samuel Dixton, as he suffocated, "that…we…were…outside…the…atmosphere."

Already, however, no one could hear him. The travelers, lying to his right and his left, were no longer conscious of their situation.

Life abandoned them…

Epilogue

On 3 December 188*, it was reported in Budweiss in Bohemia:

Yesterday morning, miners going to work found the bloody cadavers of ten men near the town. Metallic debris was scattered nearby reminiscent of the shards of an immense shell. Three of the people, dressed in long linen robes, had European features; the others had brown skin like Hindus.[29] A manuscript written in the English language, which concluded with the words: I'm choking...I'm choking...lack of air prevents me from continuing... *was found near the bodies. This marvelous document has been translated by Herr Kammer, a professor at the University of Prague; it has caused great excitement, by making known to the population the strange catastrophe that led to the fall and the death of those unfortunates.*

That news, spread by all the newspapers, was soon known in America, where it made a deep impression. The entire United States, and in particular the University of Boston, went into mourning in honor of the valiant aeronauts.

Thus was explained to the world the marvelous appearance of the American flag on the planet Venus. The astronomers of Boston Observatory, in spite of their grief, achieved a double triumph, firstly because they had been the first to discover the phenomenon that appeared on the planet, and secondly because one of the principal heroes of the extraordinary voyage was one of their colleagues.

They propose, in any case, to renew the experiments with electric light imminently, and to seek to enter into communication with the inhabitants of Venus.

The remains of the unfortunate voyagers, as well as those of those of the inhabitants of the planet who perished with

---

[29] The author seems to have forgotten that the Karaki have pale skins.

them, were transported to Philadelphia, where a magnificent mausoleum was built for them, on which Madison's name was inscribed alongside those of his three friends.

The incomplete manuscript written from day to day by Samuel Dixton was placed in the national archives. It is from that manuscript that we have extracted the details of the marvelous voyage that you have just read.

Bernard Lazare: *The Offering to the Goddess*
(1889)

> *Echo of great primitive evenings.*
> Jules Laforgue.

Twice already, covered by its thick shroud of ice, the young globe had gone to sleep; twice it had wandered through space, cold and wan. One day, centuries ago, it had shaken its white cope, and now, crowned with forest tresses, the earth smiled again in the dawns, and quivered mysteriously in the dusks. But beneath the woods of beeches and oaks, the grave tread of the mammoth with the silky fleece was no longer heard; the ancient colossi were all dead; dead the heavy mastodons and the gigantic rhinoceros; dead the enormous tigers and the prodigious bears. Slowly, the wapiti and the reindeer retreated toward the poles; the lions and the leopards went in search of warmer climes. Only the aurochs with thick horns remained in these valleys, with the elk and the red deer.

Humans from the East had subjugated the old races. Tall blond people with long heads, broad foreheads and bright eyes ruled Europe. They lived in profound caves and sometimes built towns on the waters of blue lakes.

It was evening.

The sun was descending toward the horizon, brushing the skies with its bloody flowers, and its declining rays deposited sparkling bands of gold, rutilant with cinnabar, on the hills; in the east, white clouds spread out their carpet; here and there, light snowflakes floated as if in a lake. The blue of the firmament, ardent near the luminous nucleus, passed from deep lapis lazuli to pale sapphire and extinct gray, dotted with red and yellow clouds, sometimes giving birth to monstrous islands the color of bright rust, which darkened, elongated and changed shape, reminiscent of long serpents covered in brown scales.

Meanwhile, the star sank on to a bed of violet mist, and in the distance, the darkness was already displaying its black veil. Tenuous vapors, which sublimated as they reached the heights, rose from the meadows. Beneath the foliage of obscure forests, vague noises shivered; first there was birdsong, timid notes, sketched trills, frail piping and interrupted clucking; then stags belled, and the lowing of oxen and the whinnying of horses was heard, and above those voices resounded the laughter of hyenas and the yapping of jackals.

The people of the tribe had quit their rocky shelters; they were squatting on the ground and, with their elbows on their knees, supporting their heads in their hands, their eyes fixes and haggard, they watched the dazzling orb disappear. As if devoured by an invisible monster, the disk was rapidly eaten away; then it threw off brilliant rockets, agonizing in an ocean of blood.

The terrified women cried out, extending their arms toward the flamboyant cavalier, to appeal to him and hold him back—but the king was vanquished; one last time he launched a sigh of flame, and then he disappeared, which the pink gleams flcw into the empyrean. The old men uttered a plaintive groan, and the entire horde, prostrate, wept for the dead sun for a long time.

Now night enveloped the forests; its black waves had submerged the floating clarities, and even the luminous down gilding the mountain peaks had vanished; no spark palpitated over the somber verdure of the pines scaling the slopes. The birdsong had ceased, the horses and the familiar oxen had lain down in the grass, and the stags were no longer belling in the clearings; only the plaints of the hyenas burst forth, and suddenly the dogs, guardians of the herds, began to howl.

Arranged in a circle, spines arched, legs agitated by tremors, necks extended, mouths drooling, they ululated lugubriously, their sobs casting gloom over the heights and the plains, the meadows and the woods. Like an agonized appeal, the lamentable cries sounded, spreading terror; and yet, the pale and trembling beings cowering on the ground stood up with a clamor of joy.

On the horizon, the moon had just appeared, opening her red eye. Clarity was reborn.

Then, two young men having given the signal by crashing round stones together, the tribe marched away. First came the chiefs, clad in fabrics made from linen bark; they had staffs of reindeer horn pieced with holes, the insignia of their dignity; on their heads glittered nets covered with nacreous shells; their breasts were ornamented with ivory plaques, and over their bellies hung symbolic triangles made of red porphyry or green jade.

Next came the warriors, covered by the skins of wild beasts. They were armed with javelins tipped with sharpened flint, daggers with flat and diamond-shaped hilts, and arrows whose polished stone heads were encased in deer-antlers. A few were brandishing smooth barbed lances; others preferred serpentine, jasper or simple quartz axes; a few could even be seen who carried clubs in the form of cockleshells, carved in white granite speckled with black mica. All of them were protected by precious amulets; there were pierced teeth, crescents raising their obsidian horns, bizarrely engraved strips of schist, and most of all, roundels cut out of human skulls.

In the rearguard, the women had been placed. They were clad in short garments of linen, with fringes, and adorned with numerous items of jewelry. The majority wore ornaments composed of gray and light brown shells, two pairs falling in the middle of the forehead, two surrounding each arm, four circling the knees and two displayed on the feet. The richest wore rings, pendant and bracelets for which alabaster, callais and yellow amber had been worked, necklaces in jet or violet fluorine, the pearls of which were round or cylindrical, elongated like spindles or sculpted into double cones.

The old men and children remained under the guard of the most valiant men.

They went northwards. Rapidly, they traversed the meadows bathed with the bleached light of the moon, and, when they had been marching for an hour, they stopped in a circular valley surrounded by bald hills. In the middle of the circle was the entrance to a cave; to the right and left of the opening, two menhirs raised up their rigid masses, meaning the heavens. Already-numerous groups were squatting around it.

Gradually, the valley filled up. Confused rumors rose up from the crowd; all eyes turned toward the stone colossi. Suddenly, a muffled noise resounded in the grotto; a mysterious terror passed over the valley; heads bowed; the crypt was illuminated; an old man appeared on the threshold. He made a sign, and, slowly and silently, the people went in.

They went through a vestibule devoid of ornaments and entered a vast chamber. The walls, carefully polished, were decorated with designs: bizarrely tangled arabesques, parallel lines and others that were divergent met one another and intersected one another, and the symbolic triangle appeared everywhere. Lamps hung from the vault, made of earthenware and cups rounded like eggs or skulls; in the middle, a schist crescent was suspended.

At the back of the lair stood the goddess. She was sculpted in a block of white granite; her eyes were made with two black pearls; she had a bird's beak and pointed breasts. Her bosom was ornamented with a large necklace carved in the block, with an encased amber cylinder at its center.

To the right and left of the divinity were two enormous axes; above, in the rock, in elevated relief, an ill-formed statue of a woman was visible, her legs immodestly open; below, a long stone lay, narrow and rectangular, pitted with cupules representing vaginas, connected by a furrow.

Further down, a porphyry table had been set.

One by one, in order of preeminence, the men sat down on the ground: the chiefs in the first row, then the warriors; the women were crowded under the portico. The old man who had led them stood in front of them; he took hold of a vase; he

223

drank slowly, and the myrtle wine was passed around. Then the first, the ancestor, turned to the sacred bird and uttered a bizarre clamor.

Strange moans emerged from the crowd; in a mysterious language, every one chanted hymns, measuring the word rhythmically, unfurling litanies. Gradually, they became agitated, their cries became shriller, more violent; convulsions shook their limbs; their faces were disfigured by ecstatic grimaces; and abruptly, a young man launched himself forward. He lay face down before the goddess, remained immobile momentarily, then got up and went to lie on the porphyry table.

The old man approached him; with his right hand he took a long flint knife, with his left he seized the hair of the voluntary victim; the weapon glinted, the man stood up, circled by a bloody tonsure, and the sacrificer brandished the red roundel. The howls of the faithful redoubled; a warrior presented himself. Already, when younger, he had offered himself, and the yawning gap in his skull attested his faith; he prostrated himself at the feet of the idol, surrendered himself to the old man and got up again crowned with a red diadem, while the crowd cheered.

Then there was madness. They precipitated themselves forward in dense columns, and the first alone adored the image, the others being in haste to have the rutilant blade plunge into their brains.

The strong brutally made room for themselves; the weak could not reach the altar and lamented plaintively or rolled on the ground, foaming at the mouth and writhing; some even smashed their skulls against the walls.

The ancestor's arm fell and rose, stained red; an insipidly acrid odor filled the chamber; fuming blood spread out in a black sheet over the ground; the devotees with soiled hair bent lower down.

And that lasted for a long time; for hours the holocausts presented themselves freely; the immolator felt weary.

But the lamps sputtered, a pale ray of light slid into the cavern, the initial sound burst forth again; the sacrifice ceased, the vociferations of the women announced the renascent star, and they all went out to greet the day. They extended their arms toward the east.

In a prodigious enthusiasm they danced, glad to see the god they had thought dead alive again. Their clamors of joy resounded in the valley. They forgot the bleak moon and the evil divinity, avid for palpitating flesh; even those whose wounds were dolorous were trembling, singing with ardor, and no longer felt their wounds, for the new light had abolished their suffering.

In the same order in which they had come, they left the valley. Shivering with an immense delight, they went through the meadows embalmed with balsamic effluvia, though the forests where awakening creatures were murmuring, and, without dread, marched beneath the rising sun.

Camille Debans: *Tomorrow's Fool*

(1899)

There cannot be anything more extraordinary than the life of Doctor Hombre.

First of all, he was born a phenomenon. To be sure, one has to be wary of legends when it is a matter of such an abnormal individual, but it cannot be denied, apparently, that he was able to smile from his earliest days, and was possessed of an embryonic knowledge within a matter of months.

Two hundred days after his birth, he began to talk. At a year and half, it was perceived that he was able to read. At four he was able to give a concert, at six he was drawing from nature. His assiduity, however, was not astonishing; one would have sworn that his talents arrived suddenly, like flowers that open at an appointed time. If he was asked how he had learned this or that, he raised his eyes ingenuously, gleaming with a mysterious flame, and smiled, without having appeared to understand the question.

The further he went, the more he seemed hungry for knowledge. Nothing was indifferent to him. Life, books, people, arts and things: he studied them all at the same time. His enormous brain seemed to be marvelously organized. A single reading was sufficient for a work to remain permanently engraved in his memory, classified and judged. At eight years of age he could have passed his baccalaureate.

His parents, who adored him—for he was handsome—lived in apprehension, with a terrible fear of losing him. At the slightest headache they thought about meningitis or typhoid. But no, Victor grew normally, ate heartily, never got drunk, and became witty, unlike the common run of child prodigies. Eventually, he reached puberty on time, neither too early nor too late.

Around his eighteenth year, he committed the follies typical of his age, but, by virtue of an inconceivable faculty, he never ceased for a minute to store new and ever more profound knowledge. To see and to know was, for him, the very formula of life. He learned as others breathe. Perhaps he would have died of starvation if some unknown obstacle had prevented him from assimilating all that the centuries had accumulated up to our own day of scientific, literary and artistic marvels.

A few physicians certainly claimed that Victor Hombre was ill, but everyone laughed at their diagnosis on seeing him formed, growing up, becoming a solid and well-built fellow. At the end of his adolescence, in being transformed, he lost none of his grace and beauty. With his profound, smiling eyes, his sensual mouth and the harmony of his entire being, he became exceedingly seductive—and what is more, he did not skimp on his seduction.

His head, however, had something disquieting about it. The forehead seemed vast, to the point of inspiring fear. The skull was enormous, and prodigiously inflated in the region of the cerebellum. But its contours were so firm and so beautiful that the result of those anomalies was an impression of power and grandeur.

A doctor of law at nineteen, a doctor of medicine, of sciences and letters at twenty, the acquisition of diplomas was child's play for him. In examinations, he was the one who instructed the professors. When he had exhausted scientific knowledge, learned all languages, and, in sum, had violated the secrets of all literatures, he threw himself into the arts. A sculptor, painter, engraver and musician by turns, he discovered a hand as alert as his mind, a taste as reliable as his judgment, a eye as delicate as a virgin's modesty. He signed paintings statues, etchings, and an oratorio as tedious as one could desire. And he marched on, realizing in an absolute fashion the *nil human alienum*.

A day came when Victor Hombre found nothing more in books that he did not know. He could still study people and travel the world. From east to west and north to south, he traversed the continents and crossed the seas. His ever more demanding brain required new aliments, an imperious demand for leaning still growing indefinitely within him. He studied the humblest facts, after having exhausted the enormous.

For ten years he explored all the corners of the globe, scaled mountains and penetrated abyssal depths, after which the Earth, unveiled, appeared to him to be wretchedly narrow and ridiculously limited. Nothing remained for him to discover; he knew everything. Along the way he had searched minds, analyzed brains, sounded loins and hearts. Here and there, virtues had appeared higher than the heavens, and vices more odious than reptiles. Everywhere, governors and the governed had the same weaknesses, the same hypocrisies, the same kinds of cowardice.

Only two sentiments stood up before him eternally young: love and hope. Outside of those, everything was recommencement. Charity proceeded from vanity or fantasy. Courage and honor varied on accordance with climate.

Meanwhile, as his mind had not let go of any fraction of what he had learned, he had become a prodigious being, endowing the world with some new benefit every day.

The elements were almost an obsession for him. The lightning that he harnessed submissively to the progress of society accomplished its unexpected work. Before him, dolor was extinguished. He had the secrets of life. If the desire had come to him to render youth to the aged, he would probably have succeeded. His inventions stupefied the academies, which accepted them without understanding them.

In politics, his views seemed crazy, they were so far above the vulgar span of the most perfect Statesmen. If he had not been an adversary of conquests and battles, the entire world would have become his physical domain in a short time, as it was already his moral and intellectual domain, but he was ignorant of ambition. The honors people wanted to render him awoke his disdain.

Nothing was capable of retaining him, except for what he did not yet know. Driven by an unknown force, the Doctor was always aspiring, always learning. Everything else seemed superfluous to him. Passions and human interests were dead letters to him. Neither money nor glory was capable of moving him, to the extent that he did not even think of spreading his enlightenment around and dazzling humanity. By condensing into an encyclopedia everything that he had read, discovered or divined, he could have filled the second half of an incomparable existence. Unfortunately, he was not one of those who reflected. Impressions remained ineffaceable in him, but he only found appeasement in the ingestion of new knowledge.

In reality, he was a monster: an admirable, unique individual, a genius, almost divine, but by that very token, a monster gnawed away by a cerebral bulimia.

There are people stupidly envied who suffer all their life from a furious insatiability of the heart. Victor Hombre felt pitilessly driven by the insatiability of the mind. Like the Jew whose curse obliged him to walk for century after century, the Doctor seemed condemned to go deeper every day, relentlessly, into the unfamiliar, into the unknown, into the infinite.

And yet, it was inevitable that the depths on which he drew would one day run dry. He wanted to love, he wanted to suffer. And then that too was exhausted. Women, children, dolor, disease, envy, hatred, avarice, play, the ambition of others—he explored them all without being able to satisfy his thirst.

He needed more, but what?

Frightened, he asked himself, while gazing at other people, why he was so made that the repose of the soul was fatally forbidden to him. For the first time, he really suspected causes. His gaze extended beyond this world. His life, his insatiable appetites appeared to him as the spectacle of a perfectly defined torment. Having examined the lives of the great scourges of humanity, Sesostris, Caesar, Attila and Napoléon, he thought he glimpsed that they too had been obedient to an incoercible destiny, perhaps a terrible mission.

And immediately, he felt an immense need to fathom the unknowable. There, in fact, must lie the bottomless mine in which he would find the fuel that would aliment the hearth of his brain.

He therefore plunged into the occult with a veritable frenzy—but what he divined therein was no better or worse than old wives' tales or the dogmas of the founders of religions. He did not retreat, thought. Through the mists of the uncertain he glimpsed consoling, terrible or superb mysteries before and beyond our lives. His thought, in the depths of infinity, divined diversities of miracles from one end of the heavens to the other: every star, every world; every world, every new work of the creator.

As he further penetrated into those immensities, there were profound joys.

"I didn't know anything!" he exclaimed. "Everything that I've heaped up in my head is elementary and vain knowledge. I have no merit in having acquired it when it was within the reach of my hand and my desires. But the beyond! The other side! Up there, in space! God! The soul! That's what it's necessary to discover, to excavate, to reveal, to prove."

Thus, little by little, by dint of seeking to know more, he arrived at the edge of a gulf, over which he leaned passionately.

He tried, therefore, to shake the doors that guard death. That was to collide with the invincible. One cannot pass. But he had gone too far to understand it thus.

"I shall pass," said Victor Hombre. "It's me who will carve out the route by which one can go toward a new world far more curious and far more various than that of Columbus."

Scornful of glory insofar as it alimented earthly things, he regarded it as a radiant and sublime recompense with that new goal for an objective: to unveil the secrets that the spectacle of the world gave grounds to suspect became his obsession.

What he knew about the ascetics of Tibet and the miracles of fakirism served as his point of departure. To evoke spirits and command souls appeared to him, at first, to be simple things. Certain practices of spiritism were familiar to him. He believed that by pushing them to the extreme consequences he would extract dazzling, victorious enlightenment therefrom—but alas, the unbreachable wall that hides the other side from us remained insurmountable. God did not become manifest; the Sinai remained mute. The souls that seemed to communicate with him took on, in moments of doubt, the appearance of deceptive and slightly ridiculous illusions.

The Doctor floated over an ocean of theories, suppositions, divine dreams and cruel discouragements. One day, he flattered himself that he held the truth in his hand, and abandoned himself to the feverish intoxication of triumph. The day after he fell back into doubt, into negation; the proofs that he had admired yesterday appeared miserable and empty today. The presumptuous explorer of the Beyond has decidedly not been able to pass through.

Then a terribly logical idea occurred to him: to go and see. With the haste that he applied to all his projects, he studied the means. Without a more precipitate heartbeat, he sounded the tenebrous depths for the second time, as one advances one's upper body above the void. The hypothesis of his departure did not trouble him. He was only stopped for a moment by the philosophical dread of reasoning falsely. Why, in fact, did he want to know everything? To be in possession of revelations that no human before him had been able to achieve and to collect the honor of his immense discovery on the very planet whose inhabitants would know, thanks to him, the why of their existence.

If, in consequence, he died, adieu to that honor!

But no, was it really so necessary that other people participated in his own knowledge? Did they even merit it? Was it not for himself, for himself alone, that he was tempted to launch himself into the abyss? What did it matter, then, whether he was on a world named Tellus rather than another by the name of Mars of Jupiter? In any case, there was no other means. If there was nothing beyond, well, it would be finished a little sooner. No regrets! But he was not mistaken; if there was something—dazzlements, marvels, miracles—if he were going to put his finger on improbable beings and things, if he were to succeed in understanding the creation of worlds and the life of the Eternal, what could he regret in the infimal, narrow planet that he was proposing to quit?

Thus, he prepared himself. His serenity did not abandon him in the least. Still smiling, he went toward the supreme act with an urgent curiosity. By dint of incubation, his desires and hopes were becoming realities. The ineradicable conviction had come to him that soon, tomorrow, he would known the cause of his existence, and then know more, and more, still learning, still rising, rising incessantly into indefinitely renewed heights, until the end of time.

He had one petty crisis of human respect, through.

Suicide! he thought. *Ridiculous and banal suicide! Well, what does it matter what name my imperfect and limited peers have given to it? What I want is to force the great secret.*

What am I, in this faint candle suspended in the midst of the immensity? And that candle itself, hanging in space? What is it for, really? What is my name in the language of infinity? Am I a being? Am I nothing? Are those we call animals also something more than a body? I'm frightened and thirsty. Shall I know tomorrow the empire of worlds? Shall I travel through space? Shall I discover what is there? How all that moves, and gravity? Shall I attain other planets? I want to see the autochthons of the sun, the bodies elsewhere, the souls that are everywhere. I want to question them; I want to sound them out; I want to lay them bare as I have done for humans. That is the goal; that is the intoxication; that is the glory.

The obsession became more acute every day. A void formed in his unoccupied brain.

"It's necessary," he said, naively. "It's necessary to go out there."

His powerful imagination, aided by his universal knowledge, represented time and space to him in aspects unknown to humankind. He sensed that one ought to be able to live for centuries in five minutes. He divined seconds as long as centuries. He saw himself running from star to star, plunging into the blackness of skies so profoundly that the mere idea engendered sharp frissons in his loins and beneath his hair.

"Let's go!" he said. "What a radiant tomorrow is about to blossom! I shall know everything, everything, everything. God and his justice—who knows?—calling me to their witness stand. If I can judge by my eyes and my human sentiments, I shall be absolved, aided, glorified. And I shall have millions of years to learn, and learn more...

"Let's go! En route!"

Cheerful, lively and happy, Hombre seized his scalpel. His lips smiling, attentive, without a crease in his forehead, his gaze firm, he opened a vein and waited.

The blood ran out, drop by drop. Ecstasy was painted on his face. He fell, murmuring, like Goethe: "Wings! Wings!"

Then, a few seconds later, in the supreme spasm of an ideal agony: "I can see, I can see, I can see..."

Arnould Galopin: *The Man With the Blue Face*
(c.1907)

He went staggering, like a lugubrious child,
Like a madman. The crowd opened in front of him...
Léon Dierx[30]

I

He appeared abruptly at the corner of the street and advanced, seemingly wearily, his chin on his chest and his face hidden by a huge black silk bandana.

A woman who nearly bumped into him uttered a piercing scream and fled, fearfully.

Almost at the same moment, confused exclamations rose up on all sides:

"Him!"

"Him again...!"

"Oh, the horror!"

"The monster!"

There was a long murmur, a moment of recoil, and, instinctively, all the faces turned away.

For a few seconds he remained motionless, fixing on those who surrounded him two yellow eyes, moist and shiny; then he uttered a long sigh and resumed walking, slowly, under the jeers.

As he went past an outbuilding in the process of demolition, someone threw a lump of plaster after him, which shattered at his heels in a cloud of white dust, and a bold street-urchin went to far as to tug on his overcoat.

---

[30] The lines are from Léon Dierx's poem "Lazare" [Lazarus] (1867).

The man turned round and looked at the child, who remained nailed to the spot, terrified, his mouth open and his fingers splayed.

A crowd had gathered, overexcited and tumultuous.

"If we hadn't arrived, he would surely have hit him," said one woman, with a threatening gesture.

"Certainly," said another. "Only the day before yesterday, you know, he ran after my little boy. Even when we got home, the poor kid was shaking. His blood had 'turned.' As they say."

"But why isn't he locked up? They locked up that beggar in the Rue d'Orléans, you know—the one whose face was burned and had two red holes instead of eyes."

"That's true…and he wasn't as ugly as this one, and never moved from the one place…he was always outside the door of the orphanage. Those who didn't want to see him only had to pass by on the other side of the street…while one encounters this individual everywhere."

"Doubtless he lives in the neighborhood?" someone asked.

"Yes, quite near here, next door to the fodder-merchant, in the little house at the corner of the Passage Tenaille."

"We need to get rid of him," growled an old gentlemen afflicted by a tic, punctuating the sentence with a swish of his cane and a wink.

"The Commissaire says that he can't do anything,"

"Oh, we'll see about that! Yes, we'll see. After all, it's scandalous. Truly, it can't go on."

The man was already some way off. His tall, curbed silhouette gradually dissolves into the pale luminosity of the dusk, and for a long time after he had disappeared, the crowd remained grouped on the sidewalk, cursing the unknown man whose brief appearance had disturbed them so strangely.

For the month or so that the man they called "the Horror" had been living in Montrouge, he had been going out regularly at nightfall, like the bats. He went along deserted streets, timidly sticking close to the houses, seeking as far as was possible to hide in the shadows. The first time he had been seen he had provoked a sentiment of anxious curiosity, a kind of indefinable malaise, as if people experienced something strange and abnormal at the sight of him, which frightened and disconcerted them. Then, at length, fear had given way to aversion and aversion to disgust. They were afraid of the man, and they detested him at the same time, because he troubled the quietude of peaceful folk and was obstinate in living as other people did, when he seemed condemned by nature to lead the existence of ancient lepers. For two pins, they would have demanded that he cover his head with a veil and advertise his presence with a rattle.

He had become a kind of public enemy; a dull rage seethed at his approach, and but for the policemen, he might have been lynched, so forceful was the hatred again the man, who could not, however, be reproached for anything but his ugliness. There are physiological miseries that overexcite the nerves and which, after having caused a frisson, end up making hair stand on end. They become an obsession, and at the sight of them, instead of an exclamation of pity, it is a cry of fury that escapes, for modern altruism adapts poorly to certain complications and does not like to be subjected to too rude a proof. It is understood that everyone loves his neighbor, and is sometimes disposed to help him and console him, but only on condition of not forcing hearts to overly heroic devotions.

Darkness had fallen completely when "the Horror" arrived back at his home, a small two-story building with a cracked façade and disjointed shutters, situated almost on the edge of the Avenue de Maine.

The building, which was protected against collapse to the left by worm-eaten beams, backed on to an outbuilding on the right, in which bales of hay and straw were visible, symmetrically stacked. An interior courtyard connected the outbuilding to the meager house, but now that the latter was inhabited, a kind of partition had been hastily erected, formed of disparate and half-rotten planks, linked together at the top by a cross-piece of new fir-wood. Two windows overlooking the court-yard had been blocked by means of brackets, and the black marks of shutters could still be seen on the wall.

The hovel belonged to a neighboring fodder-merchant; it had been abandoned for some time and its owner had decided to demolish it when a man of about fifty, who said he was a physician, had asked to rent it one day, and had signed a three-year lease. "It's for one of my friends," he had said. "A scientist who desires to be tranquil..." The name of Martial Procas had been entered on the receipt for a year's rent paid in advance, and the man had gone away.

Two days later, a large removal van stopped in front of the building, and the movers had not taken long to clutter the sidewalk with broken furniture, packages, bales and a large quantity of bizarre instruments and objects like those seen in laboratories: retorts with curved stems or convoluted rims, bell-jars tapering at the base, spherical or ovoid flasks with narrow necks, pear-shaped aludels made of clay, stacked inside one another. Then there was a profusion of test-tubes—straight, bent and U-shaped—cupels, crucibles, bottles, filter-funnels, eudiometers and siphons.

Passers-by stopped, intrigued by such a mass of mysterious things, and gazed with suspicious eyes at the invasion of glassware.

Finally, the movers took two cupper furnaces out of the vehicle, a small iron bedstead, a Norman dresser, a faded red velvet divan, a few chairs, a large oak table that resembled a work-bench…and that was all.

The men waited for someone to come and tell them where to put it all, and when the tenant did not show himself, they went to install themselves in a wine-shop, after having asked a small boy to come and tell them "as soon as the parishioner arrived."

It was necessary to believe, however, that the "parishioner," as they called him, was in no hurry to occupy his new dwelling, for he did not make his appearance until the moment when the street-lamps were beginning to light up.

Although it was May and quite warm, he arrived in a closed cab—one of those archaic fiacres that one encounters by night in the courtyards of railway stations, driven by rubicund and unkempt sexagenarians. After paying the coachman, he pulled a black felt hat down over his eyes, put a hand over his face and plunged rapidly into the vestibule of the house. One might have thought, on seeing him, that he had suddenly been struck, and, stunned by the blow, was fleeing in order to escape an invisible enemy.

The movers, having been alerted, appeared, grumbling, their tread heavy and unsteady.

"Oh, it's not right," said one.

"The fellow's decidedly making fun of us," said another. "Just wait—we'll sort out his glassware, and properly. If there are breakages, too bad—it won't be our fault, since it's dark."

A dry, slightly nasal voice emerged from the vestibule.

"Don't break anything, my friends, I beg you. There'll be a good tip."

The movers looked at one another, and started laughing stupidly, nudging one another with their elbows.

The chief of the crew, a tall fellow with tattooed arms coiffed in a red bonnet, replied in a drawling faubourgian accent: "Don't worry, Bourgeois, we'll take care of your vessels. As long as there's a good tip, it's okay. Come on, lads! Let's begin with the furniture. We'll see to the glassware later."

And with gestures with which they strove to alleviate their bad manners, the men loaded their shoulders with the meager furniture that was heaped pell-mell in the street.

That took scarcely a quarter or an hour, and then they "attacked" the glassware, getting down to work with a meticulous care that they exaggerated in a ridiculous manner.

Meanwhile, the tenant had not yet shown himself. Hidden in a room on the first floor, he rapidly interrogated every time he heard the stairs creak: "What are you bringing up?"

"The bed."

"Good…on the first…the room to the left."

A few moments later, he asked again; "What are you bringing now?"

"Glass trinkets."

"The room to the right downstairs, on the ground floor."

Sometimes his voice sounded very nearby, sometimes it was slightly muffled, coming from the depths of a room or a corridor, but the movers were never able to see who was speaking to them. When they draw nearer to the place where the singular individual was, they heard a rapid rustle, and saw a shadow that brushed the walls and disappeared behind a door. One of them, who was wearing espadrilles, succeeded in unearthing the "parishioner," but the latter, taken by surprise, abruptly turned his back and stayed in a corner, bending down slightly, as if he were arranging something.

When everything was brought in, set down and fixed, the man asked again: "Where are my microscopes? I can't see them."

"What's he talking about?" asked one of the movers.

"I don't know," his comrade replied. "I think he's asking for his myroscopes."

"They're in a black wooden box," said the invisible man, without emerging from the corner where he was lurking.

"Oh yes! I know what you mean," said the chief of the movers. "We'll bring it up, Bourgeois. The box is downstairs in the hallway. Beg pardon! Sorry—we forgot it."

Coins were then heard clinking, and the tenant announced: "I'm putting your money on the mantelpiece of the room on the right."

The movers came forward rapidly, but when they arrived the man had disappeared.

The chief counted the money, clicked his tongue in satisfaction, and then bowed ironically and said: "It's all there…and generous. Thanks a lot, Boss, and *au revoir*! No, I can't say that, since I haven't seen you…but that's okay, you're very good all the same. Let's go! Until next time!"

There was a sound of hob-nailed boots on the stairs, sonorous stumblings, and then the door slammed shut.

239

The man listened for a few moments, standing still at the top of the stairs. When he was quite sure that the movers had gone, he came down very rapidly, shot the bolt of the main door, and lit a candle. Then he threw himself down on the old red divan that lay in the midst of a frightful mess, put his head in his hands, and started sobbing.

II

Who was that dolorous individual? Where did he come from? Why did people abruptly turn away when he approached? There must, in consequence, be something terrifying and horrifying about him?

Yes. He was ugly: atrociously ugly, with an ugliness that surpassed anything imaginable. Not that his face was ravaged by some kind of lupus, labored by a repulsive tumor, or covered in nasty wounds; he was not subject to any deformity; no accident had contorted his features. What rendered him ignoble and monstrous was simply his color.

It was blue...entirely blue. Not an apoplectic blue extracted from violet dregs of wine, but a raw, violent, almost bright blue, intermediate between Prussian blue and ultramarine.

I have lived in hospitals for a long time. I have seen all the deformities and all the monstrosities that nature is sometimes pleased to heap on poor humanity, but I have never encountered a monster more repulsive than the one whose heart-rending narrative I have undertaken to relate.

Nothing was as impressive at that face, which seemed to be that of a decomposing cadaver, but which, however, was illuminated by two yellow eyes in which the dolor of life gleamed, and the exasperation of no longer being counted among the living. Only the pen of an Edgar Poe could render such a frightful vision. It caused a frisson and a fascination at one and the same time.

And yet, the man had once been handsome! His long curly hair, with tawny reflections and his profound velvety eyes had caused more than one woman's head to turn when he was lecturing at the Sorbonne on the arid subject of bacteriology—for some of them had acquired the habit of going to his lectures as they might go to a five o'clock tea party, and on the tiers of the amphitheater there was a striking contrast between those socialites in sparkling outfits and the hard-working students, paled by late nights, buttoned up in their miserable frock-coats.

Embarrassed by that feminine invasion, Martial Procas' students had ended up grouping together at the back of the auditorium, where they indulged from time to time in indecent practical jokes, the most anodyne of which involved crushing ampoules of sulfur or blowing iodoform powder over the hats and corsages of the beautiful auditors.

Those petty annoyances did not deter Procas' admirers. They were perfectly well aware of being out of place in that intellectual environment, but they came anyway, in ever-increasing numbers, elbowing one another like fish-wives in order to get as close as possible to the young master's podium. A few took notes, for the sake of appearances, and their slender fingers laden with rings could be seen running rapidly over cloth-bound notebooks; others, franker and a trifle cynical, contented themselves with gazing at the professor with eyes like sleepy doves, and swooning extravagantly after some demonstration that would have required preliminary scientific studies to be comprehensible.

Those lectures, mortal for the profane, seemed to delight the young women in the audience—"the tangents," as the student maliciously labeled them, because they had the habit, when the lecture was over, of approaching Procas and brushing him slightly. Nothing put off those "bacteriomaniacs." Procas could have been talking Hebrew or Hindustani, and they would still have been numerous in their presence on his course.

Soon it became a frenzy, and in the evenings, at the salons, no one was talking about anything but the young professor.

"What, my dear, you weren't at Monsieur Procas' last lecture? Oh, what an admirable session you missed! He spoke to us for an hour about pathogenic microthingies. It was delightful! I'd never have thought that one could be interested in microbes in that fashion."

And among those enthusiastic socialites there was soon no topic of conversation but bacilli; some of them even set up little laboratories at home, and bought test-tubes, microscopes and jars—but refrained, of course, from any study. They only talked a great deal about bacteriology, as the young women of our day waxed ecstatic about Nietzsche and found him "exquisite" without ever having read him. They became "microphiles" as they had once become Nietzscheans, without knowing why, out of snobbery.

Nevertheless, something other than snobbery infiltrated the admiration that those women professed with regard to Procas. Unlike the author of *Zarathustra*, he was not a distant figure "burning with the fire of his own thought," someone impassioned with individualistic ethics, a superman intensively cultivating vital energy and striving to found a morality of the will. He was a visible, palpable individual, who would not even have needed to be a scientist to trouble hearts. And women were all the crazier about him because he seemed indifferent to the advances they made to him.

His latest volume on *Phagocyte Cells*—seven hundred pages in Jesus octavo, with colored plates—had the success of a novel of adventure. The first edition sold out in a fortnight and it was necessary to reprint it, to the great amazement of the publisher, who had never see a scientific work take off like that. It then became a matter of good taste to have *Phagocyte Cells* on one's drawing room table, and a portrait of the author on the piano.

If Martial Procas had not been a timid individual, he would have been able to possess the most audacious of his admirers—those who came to find him to ask for a dedication—one after another, because those visits were always preceded by a little letter mauve or lily-pink letter, which left no doubt as to the intentions of the signatory; but Procas, brought up in modest circumstances, the son of a petty optician in the Faubourg Saint-Denis, felt ill-at-ease in the presence of a worldly woman, and always affected a coldness under which, nevertheless, a great intimate emotion was palpitating.

"I must pass for an imbecile in women's eyes," he often said, "but what do you expect? It's stronger than I am. I've ventured into society a little, but I'm still a savage..."

As much as he felt himself a master at the Sorbonne, with a Petri dish in his hand, triumphant and superior, he was hesitant and gauche in his apartment in the Rue Soufflot. He only had to offer his lips to accumulate kisses, but he scarcely dared to offer his hand, and did not even seem to perceive the brutal pressure that slender trembling fingers imprinted thereon.

That timidity, which was mistaken for disdain, did not fail to give rise to critical gossip. Soon, his listeners were all convinced that they had a rival.

If, in the course of his lectures, Procas turned his head more frequently toward one brunette, or smiled as he looked at a blonde, eyes charged with hatred immediately flashed thunderously at the privileged individual, and the quivering bacteriomaniacs murmured "It's her!" between their pretty teeth.

Then, they took stock of the one they believed to be the elect, with ironic smiles wandering over their lips, and when the lecture ended there were whispered conversations in the corridors, punctuated by busts of insolent laughter, expressions of disgust and little fits of significant coughing.

After a few months, all of Procas' listeners had fallen out mortally; each of them believed that they saw in another a preferred rival; but the most enraged of all were the women in decline, those who could not believe in the outrage of the years, who were striving in vain to hide annoying nasty crows'-feet beneath skillful make-up. They were truly intrepid, and abandoned all their occupations—if they had any—in order to play detective.

Unfortunately, as they were unaware of the savant deductive method of Allan Dickson,[31] they could not discover the slightest "flagrante delicto" and were reduced to spying on one another—which gave rise to singular misunderstandings and led to a few minor scandals about which two or three families blushed.

And while this feminine surveillance was exercised around him, Procas calmly continued his research into pathogenic bacilli. Perhaps he would have lived impregnably in his ivory tower if he had not accepted a few invitations.

He went to two or three salons—always the same ones, for nothing weighed upon him so much as a first welcome. Intimacies did not take long to become established; he found some of his admirers there; the flirtations began. Procas was on the fatal slope. From flirtation to love there is only one step to take, and that heart, which had thus far beaten for science alone, finally knew the torment of amour.

The woman who was able to capture that savage was an American named Margaret, who was familiarly nicknamed Lovely Meg. We shall dispense with painting her portrait by employing, in order to depict her, the precious and scholarly terms that always make a heroine the sweetest, most captivating and most ideal of creatures. We shall simply say that Margaret was beautiful. Furthermore, she was knowledgeable, having undertaken challenging studies at the University of Baltimore, and she was certainly the only one of Procas' listeners capable of understanding the professor's scientific explanations.

---

[31] Allan Dickson was a detective invented by Galopin, who appeared in a number of short stories published in the first decade of the century, some of which were subsequently integrated into the portmanteau novels *La Ténébreuse Affaire de Green-Park* (1910) and *L'Homme au complet gris* (1912), the latter of which (to be published by Black Coat Press) included an episode that introduced him to his obvious model, Sherlock Holmes.

She really was the woman of whom he had always dreamed, the companion who might be a collaborator as well as a lover, with whom one could still talk when one has finished laughing. It did not take him long to fall madly in love and, for fear that someone else might take her, he married her. Poor innocent, who thought that a "yes" might be sufficient to enchain a woman's heart!

For a month, there was a triumph of love, a folly of caresses, an intoxication. Procas no longer lived except for Meg, and his passion was all the keener for having been so long contained. Like all true lovers, he was ferociously jealous. He made a luxurious nest for her, in which he intended to keep her for himself alone, far from the tumult of society and the gazes of the crowd.

At first, Meg accepted that role of captive goddess, which flattered her romantic temperament. A skeptic by atavism, like all American women, she did not imagine that there really could be men as tender as the heroes of fiction. It seemed amusing to be pampered and coddled like a little girl, but at length she wearied of that claustral life and of the poor lover who was always kneeling before her. She even reached the point of finding him perfectly ridiculous, and made him understand one fine morning that she would like to replace the honeymoon with a little sunlight.

Procas resigned himself to it, with death in his soul. He was obliged to go out, to show himself in society again. Then his wife demanded that he resume his bacteriological research, doubtless to put an end to an intimacy that was becoming troublesome.

We shall not undertake to recount here how Meg, who had an incessant need for money and for whom her husband's resources were no longer sufficient, went about augmenting her luxury. The woman is only due to play an episodic role in our story; she is no more, in sum, than a shadow, a figure who passes by and must soon fade into darkness.

One day, Procas, who was still very smitten and whose mind had never even been brushed by suspicion, learned abruptly of Meg's infamy. The proofs were there, cynical and overwhelming. The woman who was his entire life, to whom he had sacrificed his ambitions as a scientist, his dearest dreams, had deceived him odiously. Letters forgotten in a writing-desk whose drawer had been left ajar had told him of the atrocity, the frightful truth.

A dull rage rose within him.

Suddenly, he became motionless, his pupils dilated, his gaze fixed. His lips moved, but nothing came out except a vague whimper, inarticulate sounds that resembled the wailing of a tiny baby. He put his hands to his breast; his breath was short and staccato; his face, pale at first, colored abruptly; it became red, almost purple; the whites of her eyes were blood-shot; one might have thought that the blood impelled toward the face by a violent pressure was about to spring forth of all the pores in its skin. Pink foam trickled from his mouth. Then, vacillating like a tree shaken by the wind and felled, he suffered one last shudder and collapsed backwards, his gaze anguished, uttering a sinister cry that resembled the gurgle of a man whose throat has been cut.

III

At the noise he had made when he fell, a domestic came running. He lifted Procas up and carried him to his bed.

Soon, the whole house was in turmoil, and a physician, alerted by telephone, arrived in a matter of minutes. He was a blond young man, very myopic, newly established in the neighborhood. He approached Procas and examined him rapidly. The unfortunate was still unconscious, and his violet-tinted face was a horrible dark stain upon the whiteness of the pillow.

Assisted by the valet, the doctor lifted the patient up slightly and removed his clothing. Procas' body appeared in all its nudity, with large blue patches on the skin. Cavernous laughter escaped from his throat.

That's singular! the young practitioner reflected. *Cyanide poisoning? Asphyxia by lighting gas? No, it's impossible. In the former case he'd have been dead for a long time, in the latter, there'd be an odor in the air that would leave no doubt. It's more likely an attack of apoplexy, although...in sum, I believe I ought to bleed him...*

And, approaching the domestic, who was looking at him with frightened eyes, he said: "Quickly! A strap and a basin."

When he had what he had requested he washed Procas' arm carefully. The patient hiccupped, and then vomited.

"How cold he is!" said the domestic.

"Yes," murmured the physician, "and that's strange...for in these sorts of attacks, the temperature always goes up, not down."

"Perhaps he's going to die?"

The doctor continued washing the sick man's arm. When the skin seemed sufficiently clean, he coiled the strap around it, above the elbow, in order to make the veins of the forearm stand out. They seemed enormous, intensely blue. Then he passed his lancet through a flame and was preparing to plunge it into the flesh when someone put a hand on his shoulder.

He turned round, and found himself face to face with a tall old man with a cool, calm gaze.

"Professor Viardot!"

"Yes...I was passing. Someone told me what had happened to my poor friend, and I came up. With your permission?"

And the illustrious master approached the invalid.

"It's an attack of apoplexy, isn't it?" asked the your physician.

"You think so?"

"Indeed!"

"You're in error, my friend...and you can put your lancet away. Have you noticed these blue patches?"

"Yes...and I confess that they surprised me."

"Were they as large as they are now when you arrived?"

"No...at the most, they had the diameter of a five centime coin, and were fairly scarce."

"Ah! Look, now they're less spaced out; they're getting larger and closer together; they're even showing a tendency to join up and fuse...within an hour, they'll have invaded the entire cutaneous surface, and the poor fellow's body will be uniformly tinted with a very characteristic blue coloration. Now let's check the mucous membranes..."

Dr. Viardot asked for a spoon, and opened Procas' lips and teeth. The patient was still inert.

"Look," said Viardot to his colleague.

"The interior of the mouth is an intense blue."

"As well as the tongue and the pharynx! The eyelids are also becoming colored. Do you have your thermometer?"

"Here it is."

"Good. Take his temperature."

There was a long silence, during which the two men did not take their eyes off the invalid for an instant. Then, at a sign from Dr. Viardot, the young physician looked at his thermometer.

"Thirty point four degrees," he said.

"I was sure of it. When Procas recovers consciousness, his temperature will probably go back up to thirty-five or thirty-six degrees, but never to thirty-seven. Poor fellow! If he escapes, he'll only be a shadow of his former self. He might still hang on for a year or two, perhaps three, but he'll remain hideously repulsive, and he'll often be in pain. At the slightest abrupt movement or the slightest effort, the choking sensation will take hold of him again. The slightest exercise will give him vertigo. He won't be able to run or walk rapidly without experiencing a frightful oppression, accompanied by palpitations and anguish."

"Yes...yes, I'm beginning to understand."

"Look at the lips now. They're deep blue, as are the nostrils and the ear-lobes. Examine the hands; notice that deformity of the fingertips. Is it sufficiently evident? The last phalanx is swollen, rounded, as if displayed; the nails are thick, broad and curved back."

"Indeed. Why didn't I notice all that sooner?"

"These cases of cyanosis are extremely rare, my friend, and young practitioners can be excused for not recognizing one. In general, it's a matter of congenital affliction, and the individuals afflicted usually die very young. Very few reach thirty. On the other hand, if the contraction of the pulmonary artery in acquired—which is to say, as a consequence of an adult malady, as in his case—the illness can reveal itself at any age in life. I've had occasion to treat Procas for acute rheumatism; in that era, his heart was affected; an endarteritis of the pulmonary artery had contracted the opening of the vessel. I often said to him: 'Be very careful, my friend, or your heart will do you a bad turn.' Unfortunately, I wasn't mistaken. Since then, the contraction has only got worse. All these symptoms: the blue coloration, the dyspnea, the apathy and the cooling that we now observe in him, are explained by the fact that from now on, he'll have too much venous blood and not enough arterial blood; too much carbon dioxide and not enough oxygen. It will be an eternal asphyxia."

"But how have these accidents been provoked today?"

"Undoubtedly, they could have burst forth yesterday, or not until tomorrow. It's surely some emotion that brought on this crisis…a very violent emotion."

And Professor Viardot, who was doubtless up to date with certain details of Procas' life, slowly shook his head as he looked down at the invalid, with a sad expression.

Then, as he got ready to leave, the young physician said: "What must I do, Master?"

"Nothing. Wait until he recovers consciousness. Then, on my behalf, recommend that he rest: absolute tranquility of the body and the mind. Let's go! *Au revoir*…I'll be back soon."

Procas finally came round. He did not remember anything, however. He knew that something had happened to him—but what?

He looked at the physician with a bewildered expression, raked the sheets with his fingernails, and then, suddenly, his bloodshot eyes fell upon Meg, whom a chambermaid, fully informed about her mistress' life, had gone by auto to fetch from the depths of Passy. A long sigh escaped his breast; he shuddered, and tried to get up, but fell back heavily, grinding his teeth.

Meg, who had leaned over him, straightened up almost immediately, chilled by fright. Procas' eyes were fixed upon her, but in such a strange fashion; there was such a surge of hatred in that gaze, at the same time as a profound distress, that she divined immediately what had happened. Her husband knew everything!

Then, slowly, as if hypnotized, she retreated to the door, opened it abruptly, and fled like a madwoman from the bedroom into which she had once brought love, and where she now left behind nothing behind but despair and shame.

For a week, the physicians were unable to pronounce judgment on Procas' fate, for his malady followed a strange, disconcerting route. Sometimes the invalid seemed to be on the mend; sometimes he fell back into a disquieting immobility akin to coma. Finally, his condition seemed to ameliorate, but the frightful blue tint, instead of diminishing, became, on the contrary, deeper and deeper. It finished up reaching the entire body, but it was the face that was the worst afflicted. Frequently, he felt an intense internal cold and his body temperature immediately dropped in an alarming fashion. He also had frequent hemorrhages and sometimes vomited blood. Then he experienced atrocious palpitations, which almost always terminated in generalized convulsions with a considerable analogy to veritable epileptic crises.

Dr. Viardot, who came to see him twice a day, strove in vain to make him feel better, but Procas, increasingly obsessed by the memory of Meg as soon as he could collect his ideas, remained deaf to any exhortation. He was, moreover, convinced that he was going to die, and was even anticipating with a kind of impatience the fatal moment when his eyes would close forever, and when his incessantly laboring thought would finally fade away into gentle nothingness.

Poor Procas! It is necessary to believe that he had not yet suffered enough and that his dolorous existence would not stop there. His ordeal, alas, was only just beginning.

One evening, when he could hear the regular snoring of the domestic charged with watching over him, coming from the next room, he slipped quietly out of bed and groped his way to Meg's room. Once inside, he turned the commutator, and headed toward the little writing-desk where he had found the accursed letters.

They had disappeared.

Procas stood there, bewildered, wondering whether he had not had a frightful dream, and whether his poor, sick imagination might have created that lamentable history of treason in its entirety.

But no…he was certain that he had held them, those letters. He could still see one of them, among others, which began with the words: *Sweet Meg, darling of my heart*… He remembered that it had been a trifle crumpled, and that it bore a figure in relief in one corner, with interlaced initials. There had also been a telegram with an address in the Avenue Friedland, where there was mention of a missed rendezvous, and another love-letter signed *Robert*, in a ridiculous and pretentious style.

He had wanted to find those letters again, in order to screw them up, tear them apart, trample them underfoot and, in sum, take out on them all the rage that was biting his flesh.

He started searching all the items of furniture, emptying out the contents of drawers pell-mell on the carpet, furiously breaking open boxes and caskets.

Woken up, the domestic immediately came running. Perceiving him, Procas uttered a howl like a wild beast, and gestured at him to go away. And in his gesture there was something so menacing that the servant fled, prey to a mad terror, absolutely convinced that his master had lost his reason.

Soon, the news spread like a burning fuse: *Monsieur is mad...furiously mad...he's certainly going to do something terrible...*

In a trice, the house was deserted; those domestics who had not fled locked themselves in their rooms and barricaded the doors.

When Procas could no longer hear any sound, he started pacing back and forth, sometimes stumbling over the debris strewn over the floor, holding on to the furniture as soon as his legs buckled under him.

Suddenly, he stopped. A portrait of Meg hanging on the wall was gazing at him with wide, astonished eyes. He contemplated it for a few moments, and then slowly kissed the head, compressing with his two hands the disorderly beating of his heart. Now that his fury had calmed, and his hatred had given way to a great depression, he felt that he was becoming weak, and if Meg had come back at that moment, he would probably have thrown himself at her feet like a guilty man.

He looked at the portrait again, his breast shaken by little convulsive sobs, and then went into the drawing room, which lit up as soon as he opened the door. The piano was still open, and still displayed on the lectern was a lullaby by Grieg that he loved to hear and often played with Meg, because he found a sweet and melancholy charm in the melody, by which his lover's heart was strangely troubled.

On a sideboard, in a crystal vase, flowers were finishing dying. He took one and raised it to his lips.

At that moment, the clock on the mantelpiece suddenly stopped ticking. One might have thought that a heart had suddenly ceased beating, and a lugubrious silence filed the room.

Procas shivered.

His gaze fell upon the mirror in which two electric bulbs were reflected. He approached it mechanically, clutching the poor crumpled flower in his trembling hand, but stopped, terrified, like a man who perceives a phantom before him.

It was the first time he had seen himself since the terrible crisis had struck him, and he thought he was the victim of a nightmare. It seemed impossible that it could be him, that blue monster, ridiculous and sinister, more hideous than a Japanese mask. He closed his eyes, and then reopened them after a few seconds. The frightful head was still before him, grimacing and malevolent.

He pinched himself violently in order to assure himself that he was really awake, and pronounced a few inconsequential words. The mirror sent back the movements of his arm and his lips.

Then he was afraid.

With a hesitant gesture, he pressed an electric button and waited, anguished, no longer daring to look into the mirror.

No one responded.

He opened a door and called. His dry, hoarse voice was lost in the darkness. Nevertheless, he repeated his appeal, even striking the floor with a chair. Nothing stirred within the house.

"My God!" he stammered, trembling. "My God!"

And he crouched down in a corner, folding himself up and gripping his head with both hands.

Now he took account of everything. Words pronounced at his bedside came back to mind: "Blue coloration…he'll remain frightful…terrifying... Poor fellow!"

Yes, people had said that. Everything was now precise in his bruised brain. He guessed why the domestics had not responded to his appeal.

"I frighten them," he murmured. "They too have abandoned me!"

He understood then that he was no longer anything but a human wreck, a horrible and repulsive thing. And in the heavy atmosphere of the silent room, he dreamed dolorously, his gaze bleak and vague.

IV

The next day, when Dr. Viardot came to visit Procas, the concierge brought him up to date. "Monsieur went mad yesterday. He tried to kill his people."

"That's impossible!"

"I assure you..."

"Do you have the keys to the apartment?"

"Here they are...but be careful, Monsieur. It might be better to call the police."

"There's no need."

"Oh, Monsieur! Be careful...it seems that he's in a state of terrible excitement. He was heard knocking over furniture all night."

Professor Viardot went upstairs on his own, and went into the apartment. At first he could not find his patient, but he eventually discovered him. He was crouching in a corner and seemed to be asleep. At regular intervals his shoulders rose and fell convulsively, and his teeth could be heard chattering.

The doctor touched him lightly.

Procas started like a surprised animal, uttered a groan and looked up. On recognizing his old friend he tried to get up, and braced himself with his hands on the floor—but he was so weak that he fell back, whimpering.

The physician picked him up and carried him back to his room, and then put him to bed, as he would have done for a small child.

Procas looked at him with wide, troubled eyes.

"It's madness, my friend. Were you trying to kill yourself?"

The invalid did not reply. He clutched the doctor's hand and burst into sobs.

"Come on! Courage!"

But Procas could no longer hear him. His poor head was reeling, his mind adrift, and he pronounced incoherent words.

"Meg...Meg! She will always be thus...there...close to me...even closer...always closer... Meg! Meg! Oh, how cold your little hands are! Look at me! Answer! It's me…you know full well…. Meg! My lovely Meg! The sun…how beautiful it is…flowers! Flowers, Meg! I want them…why are you hiding them? No…no…I don't want them any longer…I no longer want…oh, that portrait! Those letters…your lying eyes…they lie…they always lie…is it you that I see in that mirror? Meg! Meg! Are you dead? Speak to me…I want to hear your voice…oh, I'm afraid! I'm afraid!"

He tried to get out of bed, but the doctor was holding him solidly.

Exhausted by the effort, Procas remained immobile, his lips quivering. Then the divagations continued, confused and oppressive.

"My queen…my little queen…look at me…smile again…don't run away. Why are you leaving me, Meg? Oh, those letters again! And there, in the mirror…that frightful man! Get rid of him, Meg! Get rid of him! Play…quickly, play our pretty lullaby…always play…oh, that's it…keep playing…tra la la la, la la la…tra la la…la la…la…la…!"

That song, which resembled a death-rattle, died slowly on his lips. Then he became drowsy, his frightful blue face swaying to the right and the left.

Professor Viardot was sitting beside the bed, holding his friend's hand in his own. At times, Procas shivered; his lips parted and little shrill groans escaped, which resembled the whimpering of a puppy.

That drowsiness was of short duration, however. The sick man did not take long to open his eyes, and seemed quite astonished to find someone beside him.

"Are you feeling better?" the physician asked.

"Yes. Why, it's you! Thank you—you're very kind."

"Do you want anything?"

Procas made a vague gesture. What could he want?

"You can't stay here on your own."

"That's true…I remember…I'm alone. They've all gone…they're afraid of me."

"I'm going to take you away."

"Ah! Take me away?"

"Yes, to a house where I have friends. They'll look after you."

"I'll scare them too. I scare everyone, even myself!"

"Come on, calm down. Will you promise me not to budge from your bed while I'm away?"

Procas nodded his head. "I promise."

"Good. Try not to think about anything. Try to sleep. Only sleep can calm you down, heal you."

"Heal! What's the point?"

"Oh, now you're starting again!"

"No, no. I'll listen to you. I'll try to sleep."

The doctor went to fetch a little water in a glass, and let a few drops fall into it from a little bottle that he took from his pocket.

"Drink," he said. "It will calm you down."

Procas drank meekly, grimaced a smile, and then closed his eyes, allowing his head to fall back. A few minutes later, he was asleep.

Then Professor Viardot went out silently, closed the door and went rapidly back downstairs. Once in the street, he looked at his watch.

It was half past eleven. He had missed his lecture. It was the first time that had ever happened to him.

At midday a motorized ambulance took the patient to the Rue Oudinot, to a sanitarium where the doctor had reserved a room.

I shall not describe Procas' convalescence. It was long, dolorous and interrupted by frequent relapses, which often gave rise to fears of an abrupt denouement.

Procas recovered his strength, however, and one morning. Dr. Viardot came to tell him that he could go out.

In that poor empty head, the fire of which had finally been eased by rest, there was then a complete reversal. The past seemed entirely obscure, the intellect that had vacillated momentarily became once again what it had been before "the event." The man who could no longer live among humans had renounced dying.

He set forth, his heart somewhat settled once again, his head full of projects—but the tide did not take long to send the wreck back, and Procas, more discouraged than ever, ran aground in his old friend's house, threw himself into his arms and murmured, in a broken voice:

"Oh, you'd have done better to let me die! Death is a hundred times preferable to the atrocious existence I'm leading. I'm an object of disgust. People pursue me in the street like a malevolent beast. I've had enough; I want to put an end to it."

Professor Viardot took his hands. "My poor Procas, I know how you must be suffering and what tortures you must be undergoing every day. To someone else, perhaps I'd advise suicide, but I order you to live. You must." And as Procas made a gesture of protest, the doctor continued in a vibrant voice: "Yes, I order you to live, you understand, because, in the midst of your distress you have one friend that will never abandon you, which will be sustain you by itself—and that friend is Science. You have already endowed your country with precious discoveries; you have, in large measure, augmented humanity. A man like you cannot disappear; he owes it to his country. Live in isolation, but live within your mind. Work enables one to forget life. Install a laboratory for yourself in some remote corner, far from the indiscreet gaze of the crowd; search, investigate—become, in a word, what you were a few months ago.

"Tomorrow, I'll go find you a little house where you can live quietly. I'll have all your apparatus and glassware transported there, and you'll see that you won't take long to be reclaimed by your former mistress, the one who never betrays us. I'll come to see you from time to time, and you can tell me about your research. I'll renew your courage, restimulate your energy, and I'm certain that, before long, you won't regret having followed my advice.

"One doesn't disappear like this, damn it, when one can do great things, when one senses in one's heart that sacred spark that can turn worlds upside down by hastening he march of progress. As long as one has a task to fulfill down here, one doesn't desert one's post—that would be cowardice!

"Listen to me carefully, Procas, you know that I love you like a son, that I was at one time the only one to support you against certain colleagues who were criticizing your methods. If I've broken lances for you, if I've been attracted to terrible intimacies, it's because I divined in you a man capable of taking a giant step forward in science. Well, today, in memory of our old struggles, I'm begging you...imploring you...to go back to work and continue to march forward.

"Instead of marching in bright sunlight, you'll be advancing in the shadows, but what does it matter, since it's only the result for which we're searching? Life is nothing in itself, my poor friend; it's a phase that it almost always dolorous, but it's necessary to know how to employ it usefully, to extract from it all that it can yield to us, and it's on that condition alone that it's worth the trouble of being lived. Do you think that I place much value on my own life? No—not in the least, but I try to prolong it as much as possible, because I believe that I'm useful, and might become even more so."

As he spoke, Dr. Viardot embraced Procas with the affection of an older sibling sending his younger brother into combat.

V

Procas had taken refuge in the little house in the Avenue de Maine. He spent his days behind the windows, gazing out. Although he strove to react, to master himself, he felt a great sadness invading him. The past—the entire past—came back to his mind.

Can one accustom oneself to forgetting between one day and the next? A long time after a stone has fallen into a lake, it leaves traces of its fall. A life that has collapsed is like that stone. It was more than three weeks before Procas was able to resume his work.

Finally, one day, he reinstalled his laboratory as best he could. He took his microscope out of its box: an excellent instrument with a revolving objective-carrier capable of enlarging to two thousand diameters, and installed it before a window, which, thanks to a white wall situated directly opposite, received an intense and very even light. For his nocturnal labors—if he ever had the courage to work by night, as he had before—he made use of a Ranvier albo-carbon lamp.[32]

He also set up a Chamberland autoclave[33] with a small cylindrical heater, which could produce a temperature between a hundred and twenty and a hundred and twenty-five degrees. In order to be able to maintain his cultures at a desired temperature favorable to their development, he prepared an incubator. It was a metallic box protected against external variations in temperature by an envelope of felt and warmed by a burner.

Then he arranged a quantity of test-tubes on the worktop, large Erlenmeyer flasks, Pasteur matrasses, a few scalpels, pairs of scissors, forceps, separators and Roux syringes—in brief, all the apparatus necessary to prepare culture media.[34]

---

[32] Louis-Antoine Ranvier (1835-1922) was a pathologist and histologist. He had nothing to do with the invention of the intense albo-carbon lamp patented by James Livesey, but he did recommend its use in microscopy in the journal he co-founded with Edouard Balbiani, *Archives d'anatomie microscopique*.

[33] The high-pressure steam autoclave for sterilizing surgical and experimental equipment was invented by Louis Pasteur's collaborator Charles Chamberland (1851-1908) in 1879.

[34] Conical flat-bottomed flasks were named after Emil Erlenmeyer (1825-1909), who popularized the design in the 1860s. A matrass is a round-bottomed flask with a long, narrow neck; Louis Pasteur used them to seal in culture media to prevent airborne contamination. A Roux syringe is a large injector

After that, he had Dr. Viardot send him a provision of peptones, gelatin and tubes of the gelose known as agar-agar—the exotic product that, as everyone knows, comes from an alga from the Indian Ocean.

However, he no longer had the sacred fire. What had once enthused him left him almost cold today. He went back and forth in the room indecisively, hesitating to light his autoclave. A few lines discovered in a German work occupied him for a week, because it was a matter of a rather curious discovery, but he soon fell back into his habitual apathy. He became more and more absorbed in reverie. He thought about the woman who had caused his misfortune, and wondered whether he might have been guilty in her regard.

He even reached the point of imagining that he had been a detestable husband, since he had not been able to retain the woman he has wanted for his companion. Gradually, that idea took form in his mind with ever-greater precision...and he accused himself of having neglected Meg too much. If he had been able to understand her, perhaps the catastrophe would not have occurred and he would have continued to live happily with her. But he had not known! And that was why that chapter of his life had come to an end, abruptly, without consequence, without anything!

He sensed that he was now a poor, impotent, pitiful individual, and at times he was haunted by the idea of suicide. On the mantelpiece of his laboratory he had a small bottle of potassium cyanide, and he often looked at it. Once, he picked it up and took out the stopper, but the memory of his former master came back to mind. He had promised to work, and he could not break his word. He put the bottle back and masked it with another, in order not to have it constantly in view any

---

used for repeated dosing; modern versions are semi-automatic, but the primitive model developed by Émile Roux (1853-1933) of the Pasteur Institute simply had an internal scale for measuring doses and was easily dismantled so that the parts could be conveniently sterilized.

longer—but he often thought about it, especially at night, when he could not sleep and felt the pain of living exasperating, with the agony of a wound that no balm could soothe.

There were weeks when he spent entire days lying on his divan, his eyes half-closed, listening to the noises in the street and the mechanical chiming of the hours. When darkness fell, he put on his overcoat, turning up the collar in order to hide his face, and a felt hat with the brim pulled down, and went out to buy his dinner, for he no longer dared go into a restaurant, since the day when he had been refused service in a frightful cheap eatery in the Rue des Plantes. He had gone in timidly and sat down, but when the owner had turned up the gaslight and perceived him, he had gestured to him to get out, without a word. And Procas had gone, chased away like a mangy dog.

Now, therefore, he waited until it was dark in order to slip out, hugging the walls as far as the corner of the Rue Gassendi. There was a little shop there where an old woman that everyone called Maman Mélie sold fried potatoes, sausages and fish, all cooked in the same fat. The first time she had seen Procas, in the dim light, she had mistaken him for a negro. "There you are, my old Sidi—that's fifteen sous." And squinting, she had tipped hot sausages into a yellow paper cornet. Procas had paid without saying a word, and since then he had gone back every night in search of his meager pittance.

Maman Mélie, who was a good woman, had taken pity on him, and always served him copiously. Nevertheless, she confessed to her clients that the "Sidi" frightened her, and that she dared not look at him. "I've never seen such a monster," she said. "A face like that surely isn't natural. It would be better to be dead!"

And everyone shared her opinion. Yes, the man was truly too repulsive.

Soon, curiosity-seekers were drawn to Procas, and the scenes that he had taken so much trouble to avoid recommenced. They lay in wait for him, and when he made his appearance there were gibes and insults. Often, the poor man was obliged to go home without bringing back his meager meal.

One evening, he tried to talk to the crowd, to implore its pity. His words were greeted with bursts of laughter and he was obliged to flee, ashamed and discouraged.

Having returned home, he sat down at his table and burst into tears. He understood that he would never be able to turn back the tide, and that his life would be a perpetual dolor. Perhaps, among those who jeered at him, there might have been a few who were accessible to a generous impulse, but they allowed themselves to be dominated by the others. Crowds are easily influenced; one man is sufficient to draw them toward good or evil.

One evening, however, more irritated than ever, Procas tried to stand up to the malevolent people, and was nearly lynched. After that, he passed for a furious madman, and timorous citizens demanded his internment.

He had hopes that things around him might ease off eventually, but he realized then that his enemies would not lay down their arms any time soon.

From time to time he received a visit from Professor Viardot, who interrogated him about his work, suggested ideas to him and kept him up to date with recent communications made to the Académie de Médecine.

Those conversations comforted poor Procas somewhat. He emerged from his lethargy, and promised to get back to work, but when he found himself alone again in his cold house, discouragement took hold of him, and he felt more disillusioned than ever.

If he had still had someone with him, a living being that he could have heard coming and going, to whom he could address a few words, perhaps he would have recovered a taste for living, but thus far, no one had consented to enter his service. A housekeeper sent by Maman Mélie had come for a week, but then she had collected her wages and never come back. To those who interrogated her she invariably replied:

"Perhaps he's not a bad man, but he frightens me. Just the sight of his yellow eyes made my shiver."

Then he had remembered a laboratory assistant he had once employed, and had written to him. Aristide—that was the assistant's name—had presented himself one morning and had consented to remain with Procas, but Aristide was an inveterate alcoholic. When he was drunk, he upset everything in the house, breaking retorts and flasks and insulting his master. Procas had to sack him. There was a fuss; a policeman was obliged to intervene, and the rumor ran round the neighborhood that the man with the blue face had tried to kill his domestic.

Procas was reduced once again to living alone. Then a veritable apathy, a gradual exhaustion of his person, and frequent crises overwhelmed him, and he went into a visible decline.

Professor Viardot tried, however, to revive his courage.

"Come on, Procas, get back to work..."

"What's the point?"

"You must...I want you to...I want it, you understand?"

In response to that imperious tone, the invalid seemed reanimated; he promised, and swore that he would relight his autoclave—but as soon as the professor had left, he fell back into bleak depression.

Nothing interested him. An indifference to everything concerning matters of life was definitely anchored within him. The external world no longer existed; he now experienced a profound disgust for humankind, and only desired one thing: the moment of supreme serenity.

In the neighborhood, meanwhile, at length, people no longer paid attention to him. People almost got used to seeing him, and two or three people even began speaking to him. In the evening, he was able to go out in search of nourishment without being abused as before.

The appeasement was taking place. Doubtless people had understood how cruel it was to persecute a poor inoffensive individual. Crowds have their mood-changes, and sometimes feel sorry for their victims.

At first, Procas was surprised. He was momentarily bewildered, like a man who, after having lived in darkness for a long time, suddenly returns to the light. Then he gradually recovered his confidence.

A visit from Professor Viardot completed the restoration; the fog in the midst of which he had been living for months finally dissipated; he saw things more clearly again, put his laboratory in order again, re-examined his test-tubes, cleaned the lenses of his microscopes, and prepared his incubator.

The bacteriologist was reborn...and when his former master came to see him again, he found him poring over gelatine plaques.

VI

Procas had returned to work. He had almost forgotten that he was a poor man condemned to live alone, like a leper, and in the little room where an odor of gas and collodion floated, he "sowed" his bacilli.

The days that had once seemed interminable now flowed so rapidly that he sometimes forgot to go to the Rue Gassendi. He contented himself then with chewing a crust of bread and installing himself again in front of his work-table.

Riffling through an old manuscript that contained an account of one of his voyages to India, he had found a study of the plague bacillus, and had resumed his interrupted work ardently.

Professor Viardot, astonished to see him so active after a long period of depression, aided him with his advice, and now came almost every day. Then they entered into long discussions; Procas became as animated as he once had been at the Sorbonne, sustaining some theory or other, citing texts—and his former master listened to him, delighted to have rediscovered the man he had known before.

While Procas recovered his appetite for work, however, events were in preparation that were once again about to turn his life upside down. It is often at the moment when one begins to hope again that catastrophes occur.

One morning, he received a visit from the Commissaire de Police, accompanied by his secretary. The magistrate had a severe expression, and seemed embarrassed. He looked at Procas, cast a glance around the room, and said: "Monsieur, complaints have been received from several sources..."

"Complaints?"

"Yes...and my duty is to conduct an investigation."

"What is it about, Monsieur? I'm wondering what reproach anyone can make to me." Procas pointed to the door of his laboratory, where his autoclave was humming. "As you can see," he said, "I devote myself to research. I'm occupied with bacteriology. Being unable to frequent society any longer, because of my illness...I try to forget...by working..."

"You once taught at the Sorbonne?"

"Yes."

"You never receive visitors?"

"I only see Dr. Viardot, my master. I was discouraged, and thought about escaping existence. He has helped me to recover, gave me new energy, and, as you can see, I've resumed work."

The Commissaire looked in all directions. His eyes paused on the autoclave, the incubator and the large worktable crowded with small items of glassware.

"You never go out?"

"Never, Monsieur...except to go and buy a few provisions in the vicinity. But I never go very far..."

While Procas was speaking, the Commissaire's secretary had opened a cupboard and inspected its shelves. He also opened a large wooden chest in which the scientist kept his manuscripts.

"Come on, Monsieur," Procas murmured. "Of what am I accused?"

The Commissaire did not answer the question. He contented himself with asking: "You have several rooms?"

"Yes, four. The one I use as a study, the kitchen that I've converted into a laboratory, and two bedrooms on the first floor."

"Good. Let's go upstairs."

"It's a search, then?"

"Yes, Monsieur, and I'm acting in accordance with a warrant from the public prosecutor."

"Inspect everything, Monsieur," said Procas, whose voice was tremulous, "but I confess that your visit surprises me. For what can I be reproached? My life is simple. If someone had made a complaint against me, it can only have come from enemies, for I have enemies. I'm an object of horror, and perhaps someone in the neighborhood wants to get rid of me—but I do not harm to anyone: I'm an unfortunate man disfigured by a frightful malady. Instead of feeling pity for me they hate me, because I scare children. But I've already told you that I only go out at night and I hide my face as much as I can."

That had been said in such a sad tone that the Commissaire felt sorry for the man with the dolorous mask, lamentable in the old black suit that had become too large for his meager frame.

"If I need a character witness," Procas continued, "you can interrogate Professor Viardot, 12 Rue de Sèvres. He'll tell you who I am, because he knows me. He knows what my life has been, since the day when I was obliged to isolate myself in this house. I have an entirely honorable past behind me, Monsieur. My former colleagues can testify to that, if necessary..."

"I'm convinced. Excuse me, but I was obliged to carry out the step I've just taken. Believe me, I shall address a report to my superiors in which I shall demonstrate the inanity of the accusation made against you."

"But may one know what that accusation might be, Monsieur?"

"In these sorts of cases, there's always a great deal of exaggeration, and we're accustomed only to attach a mediocre importance to the denunciations that reach us every day. Most of the time we ignore them, but there are instances in which we're obliged to follow them up, if only to give satisfaction to public opinion. Don't worry; it will stop here and you'll be left in peace. Continue your research. I understand that only work can make you forget everything, and I apologize for having come to disturb you—but we sometimes have to carry out painful missions."

And so saying, the compassionate magistrate shook Procas' hand. It was the first time in a long while that anyone had shaken the hand in question—a stranger, that is—and he experienced a singular emotion at that contact. He thought that it was a return to normal life, and forgot his dolor momentarily. He escorted the Commissaire and his secretary to the door, and such was his disturbance that he neglected to ask the question that was still burning his lips for a third time.

When his visitors had gone he stood motionless at the window, wondering what it was of which he could have been accused. He could see people in the street engaged in animated discussion, who were turning to look in the direction of his house from time to time.

He let the curtain that he had lifted fall back, and went into his laboratory.

Although the Commissaire's words had reassured him momentarily, now that he was alone, left to his own thoughts, he felt invaded by a strange anxiety. The accusation must, after all, have been serious, since they had come to search his house, like the house of a malefactor. Had his enemies not laid down their arms, then? He had thought he was s tranquil now...

Perhaps I've been accused of being a forger? he thought. And a pale smile brushed his lips.

In the afternoon, he waited in vain for Professor Viardot, who had been coming almost every day for a week to follow the progress of his work. In the evening, he received a telegram informing him that his former master was ill. Briefly, he thought about going to the Rue de Sèvres, but he decided to wait. Perhaps it was only a slight indisposition. Then again, to tell the truth, he dared not present himself at the house where he had once been received, when he had been a man like any other. He understood that now, whatever happened, he could no longer quit his lair.

There are unfortunate individuals who, at length, end up forgetting their infirmities, but Procas was well aware of his condition. His life had to end there, in that wretched building, far from society, far from everything that had once been dear to him. Once, however, he had had a nostalgic desire to see one again the quarters where he had lived happily, full of dreams and illusions, and he had taken a taxi at nightfall and had gone to the Rue des Écoles, opposite the Collège de France, and then the Rue Soufflot, in front of his former dwelling. The second-floor apartment that he had once occupied was let now. The four windows overlooking the street were illuminated. Shadows were moving back and forth behind the tulle curtains. Then, all the past rose up within him, and he dissolved in tears.

He spent a frightful night, and took a long time to recover from the emotion he had experienced.

There are memories that it is necessary not to retain within oneself, for, like a wound that is beginning to scar over, they become more painful if the bandage of forgetfulness that covers them is removed.

VII

He still did not know why the Commissaire had come to his house. While working, he thought about that visit, and reproached himself for not having demanded an explanation.

The poor fellow had no suspicion that just when he thought that peace had finally returned, a dull rumor had rumbled in the neighborhood. Groups formed here and there; discussions had been held on doorsteps; and there was a concert of maledictions against the man that they called "the monster."

For about a month, people had stopped paying attention to him when he went out to go to Maman Mélie's shop in the Rue Gassendi. People had even become accustomed to rubbing shoulders with the repulsive being who emerged at dusk like some horrible phantom, timidly shirting the houses in search of shadowy corners, quickening his pace when he passed under the light of a street-lamp. The sentiment of horror and disgust that he had inspired at first had gradually attenuated, and he sometimes overheard a few words of pity as he passed by.

People were beginning to feel sorry for him when something happened that suddenly disturbed minds. The son of a haberdasher in the Rue Liancourt, a ten-year-old boy, had suddenly disappeared. A week later, in spite of assiduous searching, he remained undiscoverable. It was thought at first that he had run away, the child having a vagabond humor, but with the aid of gossips, the word "murder" had been pronounced. The last time the child had been seen, he was playing at dusk at the corner of the Passage Tenaille and the Avenue du Maine, just outside the house of the "monster."

Suspicions were immediately directed at Procas. People playing detective had posted themselves outside his windows in the evenings, listening to what was happening inside. Through the crack in a shutter a strange apparatus had been perceived, like some sort of boiler, from which a muted hum could be heard. A sinister blue flame flickered beneath that boiler, over which the meager silhouette of Procas sometimes leaned.

What mysterious work was he doing? What purpose could that receptacle resembling a percolator serve?

The curious also distinguished a large wooden table on which bizarre implements were arranged, gleaming like knives. Someone even affirmed that they had seen blood on the floor.

That was more than was necessary to overexcite the imagination of simple folk, and the rumor spread with the rapidity of a gunpowder fuse that "the monster" had abducted the child, butchered him and then burned him in his boiler. Denunciations flowed into the Commissariat in the Rue Sarrette, and people came to give evidence under oath, with the exaggeration that people addressing themselves to the law always put into their testimony. It was then that the Commissaire, in order to give satisfaction to public opinion, had obtained a search warrant from the Court.

While he was in Procas' house, the crowd gathered on the sidewalk had waited anxiously for the result of the search. They were convinced that "the monster" was going to be arrested, so they were disappointed when the magistrate and his secretary reappeared alone. Some risked interrogating them before they got back into their vehicle, but only obtained vague responses, which they immediately interpreted in favor of their thesis.

What was surprising, however, was to see that no official surveillance was established in the vicinity of the house in the Passage Tenaille. Neighbors promised to spy on the monster, and did not fail to do so. When he went out, he was followed by the butcher's son, a thickset brute, drunk most of the time, who was nicknamed "Bat d'Af"[35] by the local cobbler. He repeated to all-comers: "Have no fear; if he tries it again, I'll be down on his neck, and how!"

Procas wondered, anxiously, why those people, who had ended up no longer paying attention to him, were now looking at him with the eyes of wild beasts. He would have liked to talk to them, but fear held him back. Besides which, what would he have said to them? Then again, having lived for so

---

[35] A conventional contraction of "Bataillons d'Infanterie Légère d'Afrique" [African Light Infantry Batallions], which were penal units formed from convicts who had not yet done their military service, and soldiers subjected to disciplinary punishment.

long in solitude, he had lost the habit of speech. Furthermore, with his illness, his voice had become weak and toneless; when he spoke he ran out of breath, and was obliged to start over twice to finish a sentence he had begun. Under the empire of emotion, he choked and had coughing fits, sometimes followed by epileptiform crises. He sometimes lay prostrate on his divan for hours, breathless, almost suffocating, laid low by dyspnea.

He did not hide it from himself that one of those crises would eventually kill him, but that did not frighten him, for he had got used to the idea of death. There were, however, days when he wanted to live for a few more months in order to complete a study on the saprophytic microbes on which he had been working before the misfortune that had turned his life upside down, and which he had resumed on the advice of his friend, Professor Viardot.

A Danish scientist had recently published a paper of saprophytes, but the work was incomplete, the conclusions too uncertain, and Procas intended to demonstrate that his foreign colleague had only taken up again, while amplifying them, the theories of Schlumberger falsified by Dujardin-Beaumetz.[36] He, Procas, was on the road to a discovery: a discovery to which he would bequeath his name, and from which science would profit. It was not vanity that guided him, but only the desire to do useful work. Every day, he put inseminated test-tubes in his incubator, inseminated them again and gradually obtained different results.

---

[36] The first reference might be to the marine engineer Charles Schlumberger, who published a number of studies of miscoscopic species in the 1890s, although I cannot locate one on any kind of bacteria. Édouard Dujardin-Beaumetz (1868-1947) studied the plague bacillus at the Pasteur Institute throughout the first four decades of the 20th century. The use of the term "saprophyte" in this paragraph and elsewhere is, however, puzzling, as it refers to species that live on dead or decomposing matter.

He had wanted to bring his former master up to date with his research, but Professor Viardot was still ill. Procas had received two letters from him, and then nothing more. He had wanted to telephone, but at the Post Office where he had presented himself he had been greeted in such a fashion that he had been obliged to withdraw.

Then, one evening, he took a taxi and went to the Rue de Sèvres. Not daring to go into the concierge's lodge, he sent the driver to ask for news.

A few minutes later, the man came back. "The doctor died four days ago. He was buried yesterday."

Procas gave his address in a tremulous voice, and dissolved in tears. When he got home, he let himself fall on to the divan, overwhelmed by grief. So, now he was alone in the world, with no friend to whom he could confide his pain. Solitude; cold solitude! What reason to live did he have now?

For two days and two nights he was, so to speak, no longer conscious of what was happening around him.

Finally, the animal got the upper hand again, and he perceived that he was hungry. It was dark. He went out.

People were assembled outside his door. When he appeared, he was greeted with cries of hatred; a great murmur rose up.

Procas looked around

"Come on, my friends," he said. "What have I done?"

"Murderer!" shouted a woman, advancing toward him, brandishing her fist.

"Wretch!" growled a man. "Oh, you're asking what you've done?"

"He's got a nerve!" said another.

The crowd swelled.

Understanding that it was impossible to make the furious mob listen to reason, Procas shrugged his shoulders and started walking, hastening his steps. Threats and maledictions rained upon him from behind. It was the women who were the most excited.

Procas continued on his way, sticking close to the walls. When he had bought his modest meal, he returned precipitately, but at the corner of the Rue Liancourt, people threw themselves upon him.

In spite of his malady, Procas had remained fairly vigorous; he struggled furiously, succeeded in freeing himself, and fled, pursued by a howling mob. Having arrived at his door he took out his key, and tried to insert it in the lock, groping.

Just as he was about to open it, two eyes were fixed upon him—two eyes in which there was astonishment, and goodwill. It was a dog: a poor dog, filthy, pitiful and shivering, which seemed to be saying to him, like Baudelaire's dog: "Take me with you, and of our two miseries, we might perhaps make a kind of happiness."[37]

Procas was moved by that gaze, which was doubtless the reflection of an inferior soul, but a gentle and benevolent soul, ignorant of human hypocrisies. He let the animal in. Numb with cold and shivering, it licked his hand, and went to lie down in the laboratory, in front of the autoclave, which was filling the room with a gentle warmth.

Outside, the cries redoubled. Stones began to hit the shutters. Procas was wondering, anxiously, whether they might be about to break down the door and invade the house, when a loud voice, the authoritarian voice of a policeman, launched a resounding "Move on!" There were protestations, and an argument began, but then the noise died away in the distance.

Then, after making sure that the windows were firmly shut, Procas went to sit at a little table, set out his modest dinner, and then whistled to the dog, which came to lie down, quivering, at his feet.

---

[37] The quotation is the last line of the prose-poem "Les Bons chiens" (1869).

VIII

Sometimes, in life, there are encounters that encourage and reanimate. One dog now replaced, for Procas, the entire human race. The soul of a man and that of a beast fused in a reciprocal affection. That man, pursued by the hated of the crowd, needed friendship; hazard had sent him a dog.

Procas remembered then that he had once been a grim vivisectionist, who had killed a number of dogs in order to try to obtain the mysteries of life from their poor quivering bodies, in order to combat his neighbor's ills. He saw once again, as if he had only quit it the day before, the large room with white walls, in which the poor animals sent by the pound had agonized, tied to boards or easels, skinned, bloody, uttering plaintive little yaps or howls of pain. That rent his heart. It seemed to him impossible that he had been able, coldly, to cut up living animals, which were incapable of feeling, according to Malebranche.

His mind went back, reluctantly, to one poor little dog that he had tortured or nearly a fortnight. He saw once again the supplicant gaze of the animal, which death did not want, and from which he had removed scraps of flesh, muscles and tendons on a daily basis, with a cold impassivity. He had also removed an eye, which had left the poor animal with a big red hole in its head, through which bone was visible.

He also remembered another dog, which he had kept pinned to a table, its paws splayed, after having made a large incision in its side, in which he had placed a silver tap. He had been a torturer of animals, an executioner, almost without necessity, a little by habit, and because he believed that vivisection was a convenient means of investigating certain physiological phenomena, refuting some argument or other, or proving some item of knowledge that no one contested.

For the so-called good of humanity, he had sacrificed poor creatures, and that humanity, which he had then loved more than anything else, was the same one that now threatened to put him to death, slowly but surely, while the animal, a sibling of those he had once sacrificed, was consoling him in his solitude for the injustice of men.

After having dissected the dead, he had dissected the living, in order to lay bare and observe the functioning of the hidden parts of the poor organisms. Without vivisection, he had accustomed himself to repeating—perhaps to excuse himself—no physiology, no scientific medicine, would be possible, and he considered, in the words of Claude Bernard, that it was "necessary to see a large number of animals die because the mechanisms of life could only be unveiled and proven, by means of a knowledge of the mechanisms of death."

And he killed without keeping count, convinced that one could extrapolate from the animal to the human, even though, in a number of cases—as has been demonstrated—the effects of certain poisons of a psychic order, such as morphine, cocaine and atropine did not produce the same effects on animals as on human beings.

And it was all of that that he thought about now, in looking into the benevolent eyes of the animal he had taken in. The intelligence of animals had not preoccupied him much before; he had considered them primarily as animate machines, automata with well-regulated movements but only able to take vague account of their actions. Now he recognized his error and even became indignant about the cruelty of Malebranche.

What? he said to himself, *that philosopher was able to claim that animals don't feel? Is an animal not organized in the same way as a human being? Does it not have the same senses, the same nervous system? Does it not give the same signs of receiving impressions? Why should the cry of an animal not express pain in the same way as the cry of a child? When humans are not perverted by habit and by cruelty, they cannot see animals suffering without suffering themselves; is that not manifest proof that there is something in common between them and us? For sympathy is always an effect of similarity.*

Procas was ashamed of what he had once been. And he stroked the dog, lavished affectionate words upon it, as if he wanted it to forgive him for his laboratory crimes.

The animal that he had made his companion belonged to the race of barbets. Its grey pelt had the dull coloration of animals that are not well cared for. One of its forepaws, the right, was deformed, slightly twisted inwards. A long scar was visible on its back, the result of some recent blow with a stick.

It had once had a collar, for the fur on its neck had retained the trace of it, but it had doubtless been removed in order that no charitable passer-by would be able to return it to its owner. And the poor animal had been obliged to wander the streets for a long time, to judge by the mud with which its belly and paws were stained. Chased, harassed, stoned, it must have traveled straight ahead for a long time, avoiding human beings, its torturers, only finding a little tranquility when dusk fell, and moving on again as soon as the street-sweepers came to remove the rubbish in which it sought its life.

What instinct had guided it to Procas? How had that dog, rendered half-feral by the malevolence of humans, been bold enough to implore the aid of a stranger who, like everyone else, might have greeted it with kicks, accompanied by the utterance that it had heard so many times: "Get away, filthy beast!" Whence came the confidence of the abandoned animal in a human being as unfortunate as itself? Is there a mysterious affinity between creatures that are suffering?

Procas, who had stopped speaking months ago, spoke now to his dog, as if he were confronted by a confidant capable of understanding him. He had given him a name; he called him Mami—a simple diminutive of "mon ami"—and it really was a friend that he now had beside him.

Gradually, Mami was transformed; his fur, which had once hung down in long dirty hanks, became neat and shiny. In his great sad eyes, truly human eyes, a little flame now gleamed. At the sound of Procas' voice, he rolled over on to its back and yapped softly. In the early days, however, he remained a little apprehensive; every caress surprised him; but gradually, he became accustomed to his new master.

Procas had made him a bed with old blankets, in a corner near the incubator. It was warm there, and Mami lay there blissfully while the poor scientist worked, bent over his table, where large volumes were piled up and glass slides were protected by wooden boxes.

The worthy dog undoubtedly dreamed, because he was agitated occasionally by an abrupt start, raised his head and let it fall back again with a little growl of satisfaction. Perhaps he was reliving, while asleep, the dolorous hours of his existence as a stray, when he fled with its tail between his legs, peppered by stones thrown by children, in search of a place where he could licks his wounds, far from his enemies, in the protective shadow of night.

He only closed one eye when he slept, though. As soon as Procas made a movement, he looked at him, and only dropped off again when he saw him poring over his books.

Procas was now absorbed by a new discovery, and often forgot meal-times. Thanks to the sobriety acquired in the course of long days of wandering and starvation, Mami did not eat much. A crust of bread, a bone to gnaw and a few meager scraps of nourishment, and he was satisfied. In any case, what more could he want? He had a name, and he belonged to a master who did not beat him. Was that not sufficient for the happiness of a dog?

He would have liked to remain perpetually huddled in his corner, in the mild warmth of the incubator, so when Procas got ready to go out he became anxious. The street frightened him. Once outside, he walked apprehensively at Procas' heels, his ears lowered, his muzzle at ground level, darting fearful glances to either side, as if he expected his old enemies to surge forth at any moment. Children, especially, frightened him, and if he perceived one he stuck close to his master. He was never happier than when they resumed the homeward route. As soon as Procas had opened the door, he plunged into the vestibule rapidly and started jumping and yapping, as if to say: *Now I'm tranquil; the evil people who made me suffer so much can't get to me here.*

For Mami, every passer-by was an enemy. If he heard a noise in the street he growled dully until Procas had reassured him. Then he licked his hand, shivered and went to lie down near the incubator, his muzzle on its paws, his eyes half-closed, attentive to the slightest movement of his great friend, who talked to him from time to time in a soft voice, as one speaks to a little child.

IX

The poor scientist had found a little tranquility again. He was beginning to get reaccustomed to life. While working, he held long conversations with his dog.

He no longer felt so alone; a living being was coming and going around him, animating the house. When he had inseminated his culture broths and disposed them in his incubator, he sat down on his divan and read.

He received scientific journals regularly, which he never failed to scan. In general they were not very interesting; he only found banal communications therein or embryonic studies of subjects that were often a trifle fantastic. Now and again, however, his attention was retained by the announcement of a discovery or a laboratory experiment carried out by a foreign scientist, who only gave incomplete details of his work, exempt from formulae and precisions.

One day, while reading one of those communications, he felt a surge of anger. In a long article, an English bacteriologist attributed to himself all the merit of a discovery regarding *Proteus vulgaris*.[38] Now, it was Procas who had first demonstrated the harmful potential of that bacillus, which he had cultivated successfully two years earlier. It had even been the

---

[38] A rod-shaped bacterium that inhabits the intestines of animals and humans, sometimes infecting wounds. It was first described in 1885 by Gustav Hauser.

278

object of one of his lectures at the Sorbonne, and Dr. Roux had congratulated him warmly at the time. The plagiarism was flagrant, and Procas, under the spur of indignation, immediately set about writing a protest, in which he took the man who had had the impudence to appropriate his work violently to task. He covered ten large sheets of paper with his compact handwriting, but, as he was about to send his protest off, he said to himself: *What's the point?*

Would it be useful, then, to call attention to himself, to reveal the jealousies of his colleagues that were still smoldering under the ashes? He recalled the words of his former master, Professor Viardot: "Work in the shadows, without caring about the external world. Our lives, as scientists, do not belong to us but to humanity."

Procas' excitement faded away abruptly. He smiled in disenchantment, and threw his letter in the fire. Nevertheless, although he had renounced the glory that he could no longer accumulate while alive, he experienced a bitter sadness at the thought that someone else might benefit from his own work. Oh, if he had been as he once was, if he had been able to show himself, to speak in public, with what joy he would have sent that unscrupulous English scientist, that shameless bandit who pillaged modest workers, to the pillory!

To discharge his bile, he spoke, while pacing back and forth, his face turned toward an invisible audience, sowing his futile words in the void, becoming excited, raising his voice— to the great alarm of poor Mami, who doubtless imagined that the imprecations were addressed to him; he looked at Procas with wide frightened eyes, not daring to budge, perhaps expecting to be expelled from the house where he was so comfortable, after so many days of misery. He was only completely reassured when his master leaned over to stroke him.

There was calm thereafter. Procas resumed work—but it was written that the unfortunate fellow was not to live in peace in his hermitage. The hatred of his neighbors, still brooding since the mysterious affair of the child's disappearance, was suddenly reawakened, more forcefully.

After the Commissaire's visit, people had kept quiet for a few days, but in the shops and workshops, the commentaries continued. Everyone was convinced that little Maurice, the haberdasher's son, had been kidnapped by the monster, and that the latter, having slaked some bestial passion on the poor child, had cut him into little pieces and burned them in his "cooker." As always happens in such cases, the number of his accusers increased by the day. Some claimed to have seen little Maurice, shortly before his disappearance, playing outside Procas' door. Others affirmed that the following day they had smelled an odor of roasted flesh emerging from the house in the Passage Tenaille. Imaginations became heated. Some people were already talking about breaking into the monster's home and "setting his account."

One morning, fat Nestor,[39] the son of the butcher whose house was next door to Procas', went to see the Commissaire in the company of two shopkeepers who were reputed to be sober individuals and who belonged to the electoral committee of Monsieur Jacassot, the local député. Immediately received by the Commissaire, they sat down gravely in his office, and Barouillet, one of the shopkeepers, in his capacity and an orator at public meetings, took the floor.

"My name is doubtless known to you, Monsieur le Commissaire, and you must know that I have the reputation of being a serious man."

The Commissaire nodded his head indulgently.

"If I have decided to come to you with these gentlemen, it is because I thought it my duty as a citizen to make you aware of certain facts that are causing a disturbance in our neighborhood. Now, you know as well as I do that the first

---

[39] The butcher's son is invariably named as "gros Nestor," which implies coarseness and brutality as well as a mere excess of weight, but there is no English adjective covering the full range of implication that would be applied as a commonplace epithet in the same way.

concern of the law is to maintain surveillance of the actions of suspect individuals."

"Get to the point, please," said the Commissaire, irritated by that preamble.

"I'm getting there, Monsieur, I'm getting there. A child has disappeared, little Maurice Pinchon, and in spite of all research, he had so far remained undiscoverable."

"Yes, I understand. Is it the man in the Passage Tenaille that you're accusing again?"

"Because everything is against him. He's some sort of madman, a maniac capable of anything, on whose account one has the worst information..."

"What is this information?"

"First of all, he took up residence in the Passage Tenaille, so to speak, clandestinely. One evening, individuals of villainous appearance brought a heap of bizarre objects, among which was a kind of stove, or oven, of an unusual form. Then again, he has implements that are not seen any-where else: all kinds of pincers and curved knives—I brief, devices that are not Catholic. Once installed, the man shut himself up and only came out at nightfall, like a malefactor in fear of being recognized. Do you find that natural, Monsieur le Commissaire? Come on, is there no reason to suspect that in-dividual? He's more than suspicious, and if the police don't decide to take action, I fear that the people who have risen up against him might do something drastic..."

"The man is an unfortunate fellow disfigured by a fright-ful malady. That explains why he shows himself in public as little as possible."

"He's a madman, a maniac, and you know as well as I do, Monsieur le Commissaire, of what those sick individuals are capable. There are inoffensive madmen, but this one is dangerous."

""Reassure yourselves; if he were dangerous I would not have hesitated to have him imprisoned. I've searched his house. I've interrogated him at length, and I've been able to convince myself that he's harmless. He's a scientist, a bacteriologist, whose name was once celebrated."

Fat Nestor thought that he could risk a remark. "Scientists, when they become criminals, are more dangerous than the others."

"Certainly," Barouillet approved. "We've often had the proof of it. And look, Monsieur le Commissaire, if you'll be good enough to listen to me for a moment longer, I'll tell you something that might make you reflect. Do you recall the date when the 'man' took up residence in the Passage Tenaille?"

"In truth, no. I believe it was about six months ago..."

"Five months and fourteen days exactly. It was the evening of the twenty-third of May."

"The date hardly matters."

"I beg your pardon; on the contrary, it's very important. If I say that it's because I too have carried out an investigation with Parizot, the paint merchant in the Avenue du Maine, and we've made a discovery that you shouldn't neglect."

"I'm not in the habit of neglecting anything," replied the Commissaire, dryly, "when it's a matter of enlightening the law."

"Oh, I know, I know! You misunderstood me. I simply wanted to inform you of a fact that might be of interest. Notice that I'm affirming nothing. No, far from it; I'm only pointing out a coincidence to you. Yes, that's the word: a coincidence...which struck Parizot and me. Exactly eleven days after the installation in the Passage Tenaille of the man you call a scientist, the cadaver of a little girl was discovered underneath the projectionist's booth at the Carillo Cinema—the little Soubiroux, whom the murderer had cut into pieces. You remember the affair. The arms, the legs and the trunk of the poor little girl had been stacked up carefully on top of one another, and the head placed on top of the bloody assemblage. Only a madman could have committed such a crime—a sadistic madman—for the physician certified that the little girl had been raped with an unusual brutality..."

"I know all that, but I don't see what it has to do with..."

"Of course, Monsieur le Commissaire, but the most seri-ous thing is that our individual was seen in the vicinity of the Carillo Cinema on the evening of the crime."

"By whom?"

"Oh, several people."

"Give me their names and I'll summon them to my of-fice."

"Their names I don't know. One hears something said, you understand, but one doesn't think of asking people what their names are. All that is certain is that I've heard more than ten people affirm the same thing. It's rather troubling, isn't it? Juxtapose that with the disappearance of little Maurice, and you'll admit that there's god reason to be disturbed. Two crimes, almost blow for blow—and what crimes! It makes one think. And then, you said yourself that the man in the Passage Tenaille is a scientist, a bacteriologist—one might as well say a physician…and only a physician can cut up a body so skill-fully…"

"Or a butcher."

Fat Nestor protested, indignantly. "Oh, I know," he said, "whenever a murderer cuts up a body properly, people imme-diately say that it's a butcher who did it—but that's stupid, yes, utterly stupid. Just because one knows how to cut up a sheep or a calf, that's no reason why one should be capable of butchering a human being. Butchers have broad backs, of course, but you tell me whether anyone thinks that they're more criminal than anyone else. Me, I confess that I'd be very embarrassed if I had to slice, section and carve the flesh of a Christian. That's the business of medical students. Everyone to his trade."

The Commissaire, who wanted to get rid of those visi-tors, as prolix as all people are when they enter into the details of some story, as quickly as possible, promised to mount a narrow surveillance on the little house in the Passage Tenaille.

"That's right," said Barouillet. "Keep an eye on the indi-vidual, and you'll see that you'll learn something new before long. For our part, Nestor and I are going to keep watch. No

283

matter how clever he is, we'll succeed in catching him in the act. When he thinks he's quite safe, he'll doubtless attempt something else, but we'll be there, and I guarantee that we won't hesitate to grab him and bring him here."

"No imprudence," advised the Commissaire. "Warn me before doing anything whatsoever, because an error could cost you dear, you know."

X

For several days, Procas had not been feeling well. He usually had atrocious crises at night, which left him so exhausted that it was impossible to get up in the morning. It began with a sudden frisson and a sharp pain below the ribs. The heat of the skin, the rapidity of the pulse, anorexia, thirst and an intense cephalgia always presaged the crisis. His respiration was short, anxious and frequent. Soon, he had a little dry cough, felt a salty taste on his tongue, and was then obliged to get up, for he knew that those symptoms always led to hemophthisis. At that moment he experienced the need to breathe deeply, and went into the little courtyard situated behind his house. It did not take long for his blood to return, and the suffering that he experienced then caused him to utter stifled groans.

He feared those crises, of which he always had warning, and these days made arrangements so as not to have to go outside. He remained confined in his laboratory, his legs swathed in a woolen blanket, reduced to almost complete immobility. His poor dog, who did not understand any of it, came from time to time to lick his hand, and Procas spoke to him gently, in a toneless voice—a voice that seemed to emerge from a box filled with cotton wool. In order to warm up again, he sat by his autoclave, and got up from time to time, supporting himself on his table, to look at the glass slides that he had placed in a small shelf-unit. For he continued to work, although he was under no illusion regarding the ultimate outcome of his malady.

He knew full well that one of those crises would kill him one day, that it would be abrupt and devastating. His heart would stop dead, and he would drop as if he had been shot. Death did not frighten him; he had been prepared for it for a long time. A few weeks before, he had even wanted it, but today he was haunted by an anxiety.

What would become of poor Mami when he was no longer there? At that thought, a great sadness took hold of him, and he almost regretted having taken the animal in.

Then he remembered a lady named Romieu, a fervent antivivisectonist who had waited at the door of his laboratory one day and had broken her umbrella on his back, calling him: "murderer!" Who could be more interested in a poor dog commended to her than that furious friend of animals?

Procas knew that Madame Romieu was the president of the League Against Vivisection, and he remembered the address of the League, whose members had so often expressed their views in newspapers and journals. He therefore wrote a long letter to that former enemy, which could not fail to move her, but he dared not give his real name; he altered it slightly and signed himself Procas.

At the same time he wrote to a notary with whom he still had some funds deposited, asking him to be kind enough to call on him.

It was nearly two years since the two men had seen one another. When they found themselves in one another's presence in the little house in the Passage Tenaille, they shook hands, but the notary's grip was rather soft. Procas evidently inspired an invincible repugnance in him. Perhaps he also feared that the disease might be contagious, for he only remained with his client for a few minutes.

In any case, Procas had very little to say to him. He enquired briefly about the sum he had on deposit at the office—a sum that served his interests, providing for his living expenses—and handed the notary a sealed envelope, saying: "When you learn of my death, you should immediately inform the person whose name you'll find in this letter, whom I institute as my sole heir."

"That will be done."

"Good—but it's necessary to hasten to warn her, because I charge her in my testament with…in sum, a grave and urgent responsibility."

"You can count on me. But let's hope that I occupy myself with that affair as late as possible."

Procas made a vague gesture, and the notary, who had refused to sit down, went away rapidly, like a man who fears being contaminated.

When he had gone, Procas shrugged his shoulders.

"You see, my poor Mami," he said. "People flee from me like the plague. For them, I'm an object of horror. There's only you, my good dog, who has any amity for me."

Mami came to lick his master's hand.

"Yes, you're good, you…and perhaps you understand that I'm unhappy; but it will soon be necessary for us to part, Mami. I sense that I don't have much longer, that the end is nigh. The days I'm living at this moment are days of grace; every hour that goes by warns me that I'm heading for the tomb. Oh, life! She was very beautiful, though, and I fell in love with her. I was too happy; I thought it would last forever! How stupid it is to have such ideas!"

A fit of coughing cut off his speech, and a trickle of blood stained his lips. He got up, took a few steps across the room, and let himself fall on to the old divan that now served him as a bed, because he no longer had the strength to go upstairs to the bedroom on the first floor. The slightest effort left him breathless and anguished. Asphyxia was lying in wait for him, and he was well aware of it, for he had studied his malady now. Among the studies made of cyanosis he had procured those of Doctors Debove and Vaquez, Constantin Paul and

Variot.[40] He even experienced a scientific curiosity in following the progress of his own illness.

However, the crises began to become rarer; his heart resumed functioning in an almost normal fashion, and he was finally able to obtain a little rest.

Like an invalid entering into convalescence, he recovered a taste for life, and resumed is interrupted work. Soon, bent over his work-table, with his dog at his feet, he was inseminating his cultures. Science had him in its grip again. Someone could have knocked on his door and introduced themselves into his house then, without him hearing anything—but he sometimes fell back into his habitual apathy and spent days lying on his divan, his mind lost in a vague reverie.

At those times, the entire past flowed back into his mind. He saw the great hall of the Sorbonne again, where the women crowded to hear his lectures; he remembered the slightest details of his debut as a lecturer; and then his idyll with Meg, the first words they had exchanged, the confession that he had dared to make one day, came back to his memory.

He experienced a kind of dolorous pleasure in evoking those too-brief moments, in ruminating his defunct happiness, like those old men who revive in memory the happy days of their youth. Sometimes, he wondered what had become of Meg. He had kept her portrait, and looked at it often; he forgot the harm that the woman had done him, and wanted to see her

---

[40] The pathologist Georges Maurice Debove (1845-1920) collaborated with numerous other workers, including the cardiologist H. Vaquez, whose explanatory description of the symptoms of cyanosis, as quoted in Debove's *Manuel de diagnostic medical* (1900), apparently forms the basis of Viardot's (somewhat exaggerated) description of Procas' condition. The physician Constantin Paul had described numerous relatively mild cases, going back to the 1870s, and was routinely cited in all the reference books of the period. Jean Variot also recorded cases in the same way, and offered hypotheses to account for the phenomenon similar to those of Vaquez.

again—but without her seeing him, for he understood fully that he could no longer show himself to her. A tenderness gripped him, in which he lingered for long hours—and then, abruptly, he put the portrait back in a cupboard and strove no longer to think about the vanished woman. But a first love cannot be uprooted from a heart so easily.

A fortunate man can laugh at the women who have occupied his life, but Procas had only loved once, and his entire being still vibrated when he remembered the happy hours, too brief, that he had lived with Meg. He was a sentimental rather than a sensual person, and it is well known how unfortunate men are who love primarily by heart...

One day, he had the idea of writing to Meg. He did not know her address, but was sure that if he sent the letter to Mrs. Reading, her confidante, it would be handed on to her. He had no hope of attracting his former wife to his home, but it would have been pleasant to confide his distress to her, to obtain a response and to correspond with her as if with an invisible friend who shares your troubles and consoles you with kind words, which are perhaps nothing but literature, but whose softness is a delightful balm for a suffering soul.

He drafted a long letter, in which he carefully refrained from making any allusion to the past. He simply spoke about his misfortune, and gave an account of his life and his work since the malady had forced him to isolate himself from society.

He reflected, however, Meg, yielding to an impulse of pity, was quite capable of seeking information, discovering his address—and then she might come, might see him.

No, no, that was not possible.

He tore up the letter and went back to work. He wanted to take advantage of the respite that the malady was giving him to bring to a conclusion the research that, in spite of everything, impassioned him and made him forget his suffering for a time.

He had noticed that certain bacilli that had previously been thought to be inoffensive were, in fact, very dangerous when isolated. They developed rapidly then and did not take long to produce thousands of colonies. He was able to combat them by causing them to be absorbed by other saprophytic microbes much better adapted to their nutritive environment.

The assiduous work to which he devoted himself, however, fatigued him greatly, and from time to time he experienced the need to get some air. He waited for nightfall, and left the house, accompanied by Mami. He went along the Avenue de Maine, the Rue Gassendi and then the Rue Froidevaux, which runs alongside Montparnasse cemetery and is almost always deserted at night. Then he went back home, after having obtained a few provisions from the vendors where he still bought food, but who had been displaying an increasing hostility toward him for some days. Instead of serving him quickly, as before, they left him standing in the shop, and were no longer embarrassed by treating him harshly. Although he paid very dearly, they only gave him the worst gods, and one day, when he hazarded a timid observation, he was rudely rebuked.

More recently, he had begun obtaining his provisions from a small shopkeeper in the Rue de Lunain who had consented to come to his domicile; he brought provisions for a week on Monday and deposited the parcel in the antechamber.

"How much?" Procas asked.

The delivery man passed his bill under the door, and Procas paid, without showing himself, by expending his arm through a narrow gap. He always gave a generous tip.

One day, however, the delivery man no longer came.

He went to make enquiries, and the proprietor informed him that he did not want to serve "people like him."

XI

Procas had thought that he would eventually be forgotten, but now, suddenly, he sensed hatred growling once again around his dwelling.

In the evening, if he opened a window, he saw people stationed outside his door. If he went out, he perceived shadows gliding along behind him, keeping close to the houses. He heard bizarre noises in the courtyard behind his laboratory, and one night, he thought he saw a man climbing over the wooden fence separating it from the Passage. Truly, that life was no longer tenable, and the poor man, always apprehensive, wondered continually whether his house was about to be attacked. He thought about moving, of going to live elsewhere, in some remote corner of the suburbs, but who would want him? All doors closed as soon as he was perceived. Then again, even if he found a residence, would he be able to install his autoclave, there, his incubator, and all the apparatus garnishing his laboratory?

For the first time, a sentiment of revolt took possession of him. The intense meditation of that gentle and resigned soul was succeeded by a muted anger against those people he did not know, and who were taking a ferocious joy I torturing him.

To think, he said to himself, *that no one will have pity on me! If they only knew how I'm suffering!*

One night, when sleep fled him, he had opened the window overlooking the avenue, for one of his crises of choking had taken hold of him. Leaning on the sill, he allowed his gaze to wander over the glistening roadway, where automobiles were gliding by rapidly, projecting long conical beams in front of them. A few belated passers-by were hurrying home. A drunkard sitting on a bench was talking to himself. The twelve strokes of midnight took flight from the church of Saint-Pierre de Montrouge, and Procas was just about to close his window again when a man loomed up on the sidewalk lighted by a gas-lamp and advanced, his fist clenched, shouting: "Murderer! Murderer!"

Procas thought at first that it was the drunkard coming toward him, but it did not take him long to recognize his neighbor, the butcher's son.

"Yes, murderer! If the police protect you, we'll do justice ourselves!"

"Come on, my friend," said Procas. "Is it really me that...?"

"Yes, yes, it's really you, blackguard. Oh, I don't know what's stopping me from bashing your vile face in!"

And so saying, fat Nestor tried to reach the window-sill.

Procas, understanding that there was no reasoning with the fanatic, swiftly closed the shutters and engaged the latch.

The butcher, who had been drinking, did not cease vociferating, but someone must have taken him away, for there was a brief discussion, and Procas heard no more. He went to bed, but took a long time going to sleep.

The fellow was drunk, he said to himself, *but he called me murderer—me!*

He was anxious. The scene had disturbed him. He remembered the visit that of Commissaire had made, the search of his house that had been carried out, and a host of thoughts assailed him. He still did not know about the disappearance of the haberdasher's child; otherwise, he would have understood. He stopped at the idea that his ugliness alone was the cause of everything, and wondered, momentarily, whether they might be trying to frighten him in order to rid the neighborhood of his presence.

He would have liked nothing better, but where could he go?

"Bah!" he murmured. "They'll end up calming down. Anyway, they see so little of me; I'll go out as little as possible."

The next day, when he woke up, he heard people talking outside his door.

"There's evidence now," said a voice he recognized as that of the young butcher. "Yes, there's evidence. They'll soon see that we're not mistaken."

Procas quietly opened the door slightly, but the group had drawn away, and he only caught a few scraps of phrases, which signified nothing to him.

Poor Procas—if he had been able to hear what they were saying, he would have been terrified!

In fact since their visit to the Commissaire de Police, fat Nestor and Barouillet, assisted by a former enquiry agent who undertook amateur police work, had been spying covertly on Procas. Every evening, the three men met in a little café situated at the corner of the Rue Liancourt and the Avenue du Maine, and exchanged the information that each of them had been able to gather.

Bezombes, as the enquiry agent was named, brought to that collaboration the acquisition of twenty years of private police work and was well able to apprehend "criminals" because, he said, he had undertaken many difficult investigations. In reality, Bezombes was a poseur, a man of limited intellect who had read a lot of crime fiction and fancied that he had the talents of a detective.

One evening, when Nestor and Barouillet displayed a certain skepticism about the results of his investigations, he told them, in a confident tone: "there'll be something new tomorrow."

And, indeed, the next day, he went to find them at the café.

"We wanted proof," he said to them. "Well, I have it. You can trust an old sleuth like me to follow a trail. Following a trail is the infancy of the art, but it's necessary never to let go of it. Often, it doesn't lead anywhere; it's then that what is commonly called flair, and what I call deduction, intervenes. One starts on a road, one thinks it's good, and suddenly, one reaches a crossroads where there are several roads. Which to choose? It's often necessary to review the whole investigation, to proceed, so to speak, mathematically, to extract the unknown, and their likes the difficulty. Ordinary policemen, when they come to arrest a malefactor, are mostly assisted by benevolent informers, but me, I scorn those often-interested denunciations, which often have no other result than confusing everything. I go straight to the point, armed solely with information that I've collected, and I almost always obtain a clue.

Perhaps you're going to say that it's a matter of luck? No—luck is a word devoid of meaning. For me, it's the logical consequence of a long meditation and a series of deductions."

At this point, Bezombes interrupted himself in order to sip his aperitif. Fat Nestor and Barouillet looked at him, surprised. They did not know yet what he was going to reveal to them, but they were anticipating a *coup de théâtre*.

"From deduction to deduction," Bezombes continued, stroking his graying beard, "I've arrived at the conclusion—which is to say, the proof. Until now we've only had presumptions—grave, it's true, but insufficient to motivate the arrest of the guilty party. Today, I have certainty."

"Ah! Finally!" said fat Nestor. "So we can prove to the Commissaire that we're not imbeciles."

"Thanks to me," said Bezombes, modestly.

"Oh, certainly, thanks to you."

"And this certainty?" asked Barouillet, slightly vexed by no longer being able the principal role in the investigation.

"I can let you put your finger on it," Bezombes replied emphatically, "if you wish."

"Go on, then!" cried Nestor, without asking how it is possible to put one's finger on a certainty.

"Well, come with me!"

"Where to? Is it far?"

"You'll see."

All three of them got up, and Nestor paid the bill. It was always him who paid, but he did not regret his money, so glad was he to be mixed up in a sensational affair.

The owner of the café stopped Bezombes on the doorstep. He had not dared to join in the three men's conversation, but while lending an ear to it, he had heard a few words that had intrigued him.

He winked interrogatively at the enquiry agent.

"All right," replied Bezombes. "Very well, in fact."

"You've got him?"

"Of course."

"It's not too soon. Ah! Good for Monsieur Bezombes! Murderers have to watch out for him."

"Bah! It's just a matter of having been in the business for twenty years."

"Oh, that's not a reason. There are men who's been in the police as long as that and never pinched a criminal. Our Commissaire, Monsieur Morisseau, for example."

"We'll give Monsieur Morisseau a surprise!" said Nestor.

They went out. Bezombes marched on ahead, as befits a leader, but Nestor and Barouillet soon fell into step to either side of him, in order to reestablish equality.

A few moments later they went into the yard of the forage-merchant whose house was next door to Procas'.

The merchant, a stout Auvergnat who was known in the neighborhood as "Grinchu," was in the little shed that served as his office. On recognizing Bezombes he could not suppress a surge of ill-humor.

"You again!" he said.

"Yes, Monsieur, me again. I regret disturbing you, but in the interests of justice..."

"All right, all right—what do you want? Do you want to get into my neighbor's yard again? Leave the poor evil alone—he's unhappy enough as it is."

"You don't know what your tenant is, Monsieur, and if you did..."

"I know that he's a poor fellow, that's all, and that it's necessary to have no heart to harass an offensive individual this way."

"Inoffensive? You believe that?"

"Of course I believe it."

"You won't think so for long—and when he's arrested, when the newspapers reveal what he's done, you won't use the same language."

"Don't you know what he's accused of?" hazarded Barouillet.

"It's always easy to make accusations."

"Today, we'll have proof."

The forage-merchant shrugged his shoulders. "Ah, leave me alone with your stories. Have you been sent by the Commissaire de Police? No, you haven't. Well then, get out."

"But, Monsieur…!" said Bezombes.

"Don't Monsieur me."

"You're refusing to let us go into your tenant's yard?"

"What do you want to do there? You saw it yesterday, didn't you? Well, that's enough."

"I want to show these Messieurs."

"These Messieurs aren't the police, I suppose?"

"No, but they have an interest, as I have, in discovering and catching a murderer."

"A murderer! Don't make me laugh. I think you're all mad. Go home—that's better than…"

"You're refusing, then?"

"Yes."

"You don't have the right, when it's a matter…"

"No right? No right? What are you telling me? Am I the master in my own home or not?"

"Yesterday, though, you consented to let me…"

"Possibly, but today I don't want to. Is that understood? It'll turn into a procession in the end."

"Monsieur," said Barouillet, in a nobly paternal tone, "the superior interests of justice, security…"

"You, go bray at your public meetings and leave me in peace."

There was nothing to be done. Père Grinchu was one of those stubborn and bad-tempered old men who have no fear, if need be, of throwing a punch—and the Auvergnat was solidly built. He was beginning to lose patience, and turning as purple as an aubergine. Bezombes and his two friends thought it prudent to beat a retreat.

"What a brute!" said Barouillet, when they were in the street.

"I wanted to lay him out," growled Nestor, who was always talking about beating people up but was, fundamentally, as cowardly as a hare.

XII

The most vexed of the three was certainly Bezombes, who had not expected such a reception. He had thought that he was going to astonish his friends, and had received a slap in the face. How could he have suspected that that animal Grinchu, who had been almost amiable the previous evening, would behave so boorishly the next day?

They went back to the little café in the Avenue du Maine, and held a conference there. Nestor and Barouillet still did not know what Bezombes had discovered in Procas' yard, for the enquiry agent had not yet said anything that might clarify the mystery. Bezombes, like all pretentious and hollow individuals, liked to hold back his effects before pressing the spring that caused the jack-in-the-box to spring forth.

"What are we going to do now?" asked Nestor.

Bezombes, his elbows on the table, and frowning, seemed to be plunged in laborious meditation. He only emerged from his reverie to raise the Lemon St. Raphael that Nestor had ordered to his lips. He drained his glass in a single draught, wiped his lips with the back of his hand and finally consented to reply.

"What are we going to do? Well, obviously, we're going to ask the Commissaire to accompany us to Grinchu's."

"Oh, the Commissaire!" said Barouillet. "We can hardly count on him. He'll tell us once again that he'll investigate, and that will be all. He'll let the affair drop. What we can tell him won't convince him. His mind is made up. I saw that when I went to see him with Nestor. He made us welcome, I admit, but he didn't seem to take what we were saying seriously. Those people don't like ordinary citizens to interfere with the police. They always have a tendency to believe that witnesses are lying or exaggerating."

"When one brings them evidence, however…," said Bezombes.

"Yes, I don't deny it—but have you really got any?"

Bezombes gave a slight shrug, and took his time before replying: "I have it."

Nestor and Barouillet looked at him. Fundamentally, they were unconvinced, even though they trusted their friend.

"I have it," Bezombes repeated, gazing with an astonished expression at his empty glass. "I wanted to show it to you on the spot, but since that boor Grinchu didn't want to let us into the yard, I'll tell you everything. Listen to me, and you'll see whether I'm not supported by seeming proofs. I'm not one of those fantastic detectives like Sherlock Holmes, who build suppositions on suppositions and emit hypotheses, one of which must fatally lead to the discovery of the murderer. Me, I'm a precise, methodical man. I only believe what I see. Now, I've seen."

At that point Bezombes stopped, in order to enjoy the effect that his affirmation produced. His two listeners, conquered by his assurance, waited anxiously, leaving toward him, eager to catch the words that were about to fall from his lips.

"Yes, I've seen, that which there is to be seen. First, you need to know what I did to arrive at my conclusion. The affair was delicate. A child had disappeared, suspicions fell on the man in the Passage Tenaille, but that was all. There was no proof that the poor kid had been murdered. Some vagabond might have taken him away. According to what I've heard, the child wasn't very intelligent; his mother says herself that he was naïve and trusting, very easy to influence. The last time he was seen he was playing on his own at the corner of the Avenue du Maine, almost directly opposite our man's house. All that was very vague, and nothing had come along to focus my suspicions, when Barouillet reminded me about the murder of little Soubiroux, which happened a few days after the monster moved into the neighborhood. On the other hand, the information I'd collected soon shored up my conviction. Twice, the ignoble individual from the Passage Tenaille had been seen following children in the Rue Gassendi."

"That's true, said Nestor. "Last week, little Cheiret, the son of the concierge at number 44, came home frightened, saying that a man had followed him all the way to the corner of the Rue Liancourt."

"So you see," said Bezombes, "my information is correct. You understand that, before accusing the recluse of the Passage Tenaille, it was necessary to obtain information about him. When I had sufficient, I started following him, and I noticed that he did indeed look at children with a strange expression, especially the little girls coming out of the school at dusk. He stood in a doorway in a bizarre fashion. To be brief, I'll pass over certain details. Our individual must be a satyr, and he was doubtless in search of some new victim. From there, I followed this reasoning: Since the haberdasher's child disappeared when he was opposite the house in the Passage Tenaille, he must have been attracted into the house, and as he hasn't reappeared, he must have been murdered. You see how everything fits together marvelously."

"Indeed," conceded Barouillet. "But you'll see that our imbecile of a Commissaire won't allow himself to be convinced."

"Wait—all that's just the *hors-d'oeuvre*. I'm arriving at the main course. Since little Maurice had gone into the recluse's house and hadn't come out again, his body must be somewhere. Now, the testimony of serious people had told me that, the day after the disappearance, smoke had been seen coming out of our individual's chimney. Why, in that rather mild weather, had he lit a fire, if not to incinerate his victim? Several passers-by also smelled an odor of burned rubber that day, such as is emitted by human bodies when they're roasted over a fire."

"Exactly," said Nestor. "I smelled that odor myself, and I even said to my father: 'What's burning? It's jolly sharp.'"

"That, it seems to me," Bezombes continued, raising his voice—for he had noticed that the customers were listening—

"is a commencement of proof. An ordinary detective would be content with that, but it wasn't sufficient for me. I needed visible proof, something that confirmed my conviction and would permit me to say to the law: 'You're looking for the guilty party, well, I, whom am neither a Commissaire nor an Inspector, have found him.' So, I pursued my investigation. A murderer, no matter how skillful he is, can't cut a body into pieces without that dire operation leaving traces. Twice, by climbing over the fence, I got into the little yard that you know, and, equipped with a hooded lantern, I carefully examined the wall, the door and the flagstones lining the ground. And it was on the flagstones that I found what I can call 'the crucial piece of evidence.'"

All the listeners were breathless, looking at Bezombes admiringly.

"It's that crucial piece of evidence that I wanted to show you, and which you would have seen, like me, in the satyr's yard, if that idiot Grinchu hadn't refused to let us into his house."

"But what was that crucial piece of evidence?" someone asked, timidly.

"Those pieces, I should have said," Bezombes went on, "for there were several—yes, several. Large bloodstains, still quite visible, as big as hundred-sou pieces, and even bigger. Doubt is no longer possible. It's definitely in that yard that the wretch cut up his victim."

The customers had gradually drawn nearer in order to listen to Bezombes, who had gradually raised his voice as he saw his audience growing. They were all unanimous in recognizing that the enquiry agent had the soul of a great policeman.

While savoring those eulogies, Bezombes replied in a modest fashion to those who congratulated him: "No, no, you're exaggerating. It was sufficient, to bring the investigation to a conclusion, to have a little judgment; the rest is a matter of routine. With the elements I had in hand, I had to succeed. It was all a matter of not letting go for an instant of the thread that I held, and above all of not allowing myself to be influenced by anyone's opinion. Straight to the goal—that's my method. I hesitate at first; I throw out probes here and there, and then, when I sense that the ground beneath my feet is firm enough, I advance boldly."

Nestor never ceased repeating, while widening his great bovine eyes: "That's marvelous! Marvelous!"

Barouillet, a little put out by not having discovered anything, was more reserved, contenting himself with slowly nodding his head s a sign of approval. The most enthusiastic of all, however, was a local rentier, Père Corbineau, a man with a nutcracker chin and eyes like a white rabbit, who howled in a thin, broken voice: "Three cheers for Bezombes! Three cheers for Bezombes!" They had all the difficulty in the world making him understand that it was not a matter of a celebration but a matter that, until further notice, must be kept absolutely secret.

Everyone promised not to say anything, but an hour later, from the Lion de Belfort to the Rue de la Gâité, no one was any longer greeting anyone except with the words: "Well, there it is, eh? It seems that he's pinched!"

XIII

The next day, early in the morning, Nestor and Barouillet rang Bezombes' doorbell. He lived in a modest ground floor apartment in the Rue Boulard, at the back of a courtyard. On a glazed door, a placard could be seen bearing the boldly-traced words: *Marius Bezombes, Legal Adviser, Defender in the Magistrate's Court. Divorce Enquiries, Family Research, etc.*

Bezombes was waiting for them. He was sitting at a little table cluttered with dusty files. On the black marble mantelpiece, between an alarm clock and a carafe, a plaster bust representing Justice was enthroned, one of whose scales was broken. There was a mahogany chest of drawers in a corner, which had been transformed into a filing-cabinet.

"Oh, there you are," said Bezombes. "Give me a minute. Sit down. Just time to sign a few documents, and I'm all yours."

Barouillet let himself fall into an old armchair upholstered in red rep, from which a cloud of dust emerged. As for fat Nestor, he brought forward a chair, the only one in the room, but, realizing that if he sat down on it, it would collapse under his eight, he remained standing, leaning against the wall, admiring himself from afar in the mirror above the mantelpiece.

"Ah!" said Bezombes, finally, taking off his large celluloid spectacles. "I've finished. Let's talk about out affair." And, pivoting in his seat, which yielded a dull grating sound, he turned to face his visitors. "Today," he said, "We enter into the period of action, the decisive period. It's necessary that this evening, tomorrow at the latest, our individual is behind bars."

"It's a pity we can't arrest him ourselves," growled Nestor. "I'd have had great pleasure getting me hands on that villain."

"That's the business of the police," said Bezombes. "Our role is limited to delivering the murderer."

"Will it at least be known that it's us— pardon me you— who have discovered him?"

"Perhaps. But it's necessary not to count on it too much, for the police have a habit of always claiming the credit for themselves. The moment one isn't in the club, one doesn't count. You'll see that the Commissaire won't even congratulate us."

"The Commissaire," said Barouillet, shrugging his shoulders, "is capable of not taking our visit seriously. When Nestor and I went to see him, he scarcely listened to us. In your place, Bezombes, it isn't the Commissaire to whom I'd address myself."

"The head of the Sûreté, then?"

"Perhaps—but there's something even better."

"Oh? What's that?"

"That would be to go to a newspaper. If the press gets involved in the affair..."

"My word, perhaps you're right. That way, the police wouldn't be able to attribute all the merit for the investigation to themselves, and there'd be some mention of us. It's not that I want the renown...no, I'm a modest man, and if I'd wanted to carry on like some people...well, in sum, your idea isn't bad. Do you know someone at a newspaper?"

"Yes, a reporter for the *Égalité*, who has come to our meetings several times during electoral campaigns. He's also a friend of Monsieur Jacassot, our député."

"Well, let's go see him. We'll explain the affair to him, and if he's an intelligent fellow, he'll be able to make a sensational article out of our information. I can already see the headline: *The satyr of Montrouge...Horrible details*. It'll be one in the eye for the Commissaire."

"Oh, steady on, Bezombes. Don't imagine that journalists move as fast as that. And the legal investigation—you're not thinking about that."

"That's true, but there's no need for an examining magistrate here. Haven't we got proof?"

"Obviously...nevertheless, it's better to act prudently. Let's go visit my friend and see what he says. Journalists are clever, and they often find means of saying a lot without saying anything at all."

As Bezombes did not appear to understand, he explained: "Yes, when one can't put forward a fact, for fear of compromising oneself, one proceeds by insinuations, by implication. You'll see. Oscar Phinot understands those sorts of articles. It's by means of insinuations and implications that he demolished Taupin, our député's opponent."

"Oh! Your journalist is called Phinot? I've seen that name before somewhere."

"Possibly. He writes a great deal, and is beginning to acquire a certain reputation. Let's go find him. If the affair doesn't interest him, we'll fall back on the Head of the Sûreté."

"When can we see him?"

"In the afternoon, generally. In any case, I'll telephone him to announce our visit."

"That's good. To do well, it will be necessary for the article to appear tomorrow morning. I'll jot down a few notes on paper, which might be useful to him. I'll wait for you here—come and pick me up as soon as you've obtained a meeting. But wait, I've just thought of something. It's necessary not to let our man slip away, isn't it? What if, when they come to arrest him, the house is empty?"

"No danger," the butcher's apprentice replied. "I'll keep an eye on him."

Nestor and Barouillet shook hands with Bezombes, and withdrew.

To the people they met and who interrogated them with a little movement of the head, they replied, with an enigmatic smile. "There'll be some news before long."

Groups were already beginning to form outside the little house in the Passage Tenaille, and Barouillet was annoyed.

"Do you want to ruin everything?" he said. "If you stand there planted like pickets, he'll suspect something, and slip through our hands. Go home and wait. We'll be rid of that individual within twenty-four hours."

"Yes…people have been saying that for a long time," murmured a little man afflicted with a red birthmark on his right cheek, "but he's still there!"

It was at that moment that Procas had lifted the curtain at his window.

"Look, you can see that he's listening to us," said Barouillet. "You're definitely going to compromise everything. It'll have been well worth the trouble of going to such lengths."

The curiosity-seekers dispersed slowly, while Procas wondered, anxiously: "But what's the matter with them? What do they want? I don't understand what's happening at all."

XIV

When the crowd is in league against a man, the man must necessarily succumb, unless he can impose himself upon it by audacity and violence. Now, poor Procas did not have what was necessary to stand up to the unchained mob that was growing by the day. While he sought in vain for the reasons for the muted war that had been declared upon him, the leaders were collecting evidence against him—or seeming evidence—that was having a snowball effect and was being deformed by imagination with the customary exaggeration of the common people.

Bezombes continued to draw up what he called his "plan of campaign," and everyone in the neighborhood, with was now in ferment, was waiting for a *coup de théâtre*.

Accompanied by fat Nestor and the solemn Barouillet, he had gone to the offices of the *Égalité* in the Boulevard Montmartre. Received by Phinot, whom Barouillet had alerted by telephone, he had, with his Southern verve, explained to the reporter the "reasons" on which he supported his accusation of Procas. Those reasons seemed plausible, and Phinot, who was searching for a subject for a sensational article in order to get back into the good graces of his editor, who had reproached him for certain "duds," had welcomed Bezombes' revelations enthusiastically. Nevertheless, rendered prudent by a recent gaffe, which had earned the director of the *Égalité* a rather stiff fine and two months in prison, he did not launch himself wholeheartedly into the affair. He contented himself with testing the waters. In a front page article only transparent to initiates, he skillfully primed the pump of scandal.

The next day, people were snatching copies of the *Égalité* all over Montrouge. The fire had taken hold. Those who still doubted the culpability of the "man of the Passage Tenaille" considered him from then on as a frightful criminal, and were astonished that the police had not yet arrested him. Bezombes, flanked by Nestor and Barouillet, stopped off in numerous cafés, where he held forth untiringly, explaining for the hundredth time how he had been able to discover the guilty party.

That evening, when Procas went out at dusk in search of his dinner, he was followed by a dozen individuals, whose number was gradually augmented, and when he returned home, a sinister, menacing clamor went up: "Death! Death!"

Frightened, he plunged into the vestibule with his dog, slammed the door shut and started listening behind a shutter, wondering whether the fanatics were not about to break in. He still did not understand what had unleashed their anger, but he realized now that life was no longer tenable, and that he would probably be obliged to flee the neighborhood where his appearance provoked such hatred.

He perceived a few fragmentary phrases, which only augmented his anxiety, without enlightening him as to the motive for the abrupt change of mood. He finally realized that his ugliness could not be its sole cause, and that there must be something else, but the poor fellow was far from suspecting the terrible accusation that was weighing upon him.

For a moment, he had the idea of writing to the Commissaire and asking for police protection, but he renounced the idea, hoping that the fury of the crowd would eventually dic down, as it had died down a few months earlier.

The mob, harangued by Bezombes, who had become the man of the moment, abstained from any manifestation for a week.

"It's up to the law to take action," Bezombes never ceased repeating. "Let's wait; it's impossible that the wretch can enjoy impunity for much longer. An investigation has been opened, I know. We'll soon see the murderer arrested."

Bezombes was mistaken. An investigation had, indeed, been opened, but had the result of having him summoned to see the Commissaire, who had demanded, in rather hot terms what he was playing at. Bezombes had tried to get the upper hand, but he was reminded of an affair of loans taken out on bonds, which had never been fully clarified, and it which he had played a role that was more than shady. He was even advised, in his own interest, to keep quiet in future, and not to trespass on the prerogatives of the police.

Bezombes went out utterly crestfallen. That evening, he met Nestor and Barouillet at the café, but carefully refrained from telling them how he had been received by the Commissaire.

"It's always dangerous to get mixed up in these affairs, you see," he told them. "The police don't like people saying that they've made a mess of things. They'd rather let a guilty man escape than frankly admit their incompetence. Me, I've seen it; I've done all that I can do, in the interests of our neighborhood. I tried to unmask an evil-doer, and it seems to me that I've succeeded, but the police take a dim view of all that. Soon, if this goes on, it'll be the accusers who are the guilty parties. I renounce any further part in the affair. Others can replace me, but personally, I'm sick of it."

Nestor protested. "What, Monsieur Bezombes, you're talking like a coward? No, you mustn't do that."

"I have spoken," said Bezombes, in a peremptory tone.

Barouillet intervened. "Come, come, you're not going to throw the towel in just like that. Ought we to worry about the police? Duty commands us to remain in the breach. Is it at the moment when we hold all the trumps that we're going to abandon the game? What will people think of us? Since our Commissaire is incapable, it's up to us the take action. I'm going to go find Phinot, and he'll show the Commissaire something."

"No, no," protested Bezombes. "Let's not get into a fight with the Commissaire. We wouldn't win. It's would be the earthenware pot fighting the iron pot. These policemen are diabolically vindictive, and capable of all kinds of rascality."

"What do we have to fear?" Barouillet retorted. "Our conscience has nothing for which to reproach us has it? One can search our lives. Me, I don't give a f about the Commissaire, and if he persists in turns a deaf ear and protecting the murderer, well, I'll have him sacked…yes, sacked, you hear. I'm going to address myself, no later than tomorrow, to

Monsieur Jacassot, our député. He'll go to the Prefect of Police if he has to, and you'll see that he'll make your Commissaire dance. He'll have to take action, or explain himself."

Bezombes did not feel tranquil, because of the old affair of the loans that threatened to surface again. This, he showed himself opposed to "direct action." He could not, however, renounce everything without appearing to be a coward. He got out of it rather cleverly.

"Unfortunately," he said, "I don't have enough connections to go to war against people who dispose of secret influences and belong to the police freemasonry, which is as powerful as the Jesuits. But you, Barouillet, who are on the best of terms with our député, Monsieur Jacassot, and have friends at the *Égalité*, can achieve a result. Me, I've carried out an investigation; that ended with the discovery of the murderer, but the police refuse to act. It's necessary to force them, and you alone can do that."

Barouillet was deeply touched. He swelled up with pride, frowned, struck a pose as if he needed to be begged, and then, very gravely, uttered these words;

"Since it's necessary, I'll take action, even though I don't like to put myself forward."

"Remember that you're working in the interests of everyone, and the mothers of families will be grateful to you for having rid them of an individual who is an object of horror and dread for them, who has become a public danger."

"But you'll continue to assist me with your advice, Bezombes, I suppose?"

"Can you doubt it?"

Barouillet brought a round of drinks, and fat Nestor another; then they parted, arranging to meet again the next day.

Now Bezombes was almost tranquil; the affair was following its course, but he was no longer involved. It would be the excessive Barouillet who would shoulder all the responsibility, in company with fat Nestor.

If Bezombes remained in the shadows, however, he continued nevertheless to lead a clandestine campaign.

Barouillet, glad to be no longer under the tutelage of the inquiry agent, talked loudly, telling anyone who cared to listen that he would "soon force the hand of the police." When he passed by, the shopkeepers called out to him, bombarding him with questions, and his response was always the same: "I've made a round of the newspapers. You'll see what a fine scandal is going to burst out."

People listened delightedly, and drank in his words; he was congratulated.

Meanwhile, the man of the Passage Tenaille—the "satyr," as people called him—continued to come and go at nightfall, followed by a mob who abused him in a cowardly fashion and accompanied him as far as his door. Fat Nestor was always part of that mob, because, in accord with Barouillet, he had instituted the "surveillance" of Procas, whose abrupt disappearance was feared. Street urchins joined in with the cortege, and one of them, having wanted to get too close to the "satyr" one evening, was forced to beat a prompt retreat by the menacing fangs of Mami, whom the shouts of the children rendered furious.

"That filthy cur," said fat Nestor. "I'll have its blood it before long, you'll see. While we're waiting to get rid of the man, I can always take away the pooch's appetite for bread."

XV

Everyone in Montrouge was expecting the famous *coup de théâtre* any day, but it was a long time coming. A fortnight had passed since Bezombes had "passed the baton" to Barouillet—a fortnight during which increasingly overexcited minds had gradually arrived at such a state of exasperation that anything was to be feared.

Prudently, Barouillet, who had not succeeded in his measures, remained shut up at home, prey to an illness that was probably simulated. As for Bezombes, he no longer showed himself in the little café in the Rue Liancourt. Only fat Nestor, with his brutal tenacity, continued to spy on Procas, and whenever the poor fellow went out, he abandoned his stall and followed the "satyr." Idlers and people out of work, as well as a few harpies, joined him in dogging the steps of the poor man.

To escape the enemies who were massing behind him, Procas sometimes turned a street-corner swiftly and huddled in some doorway, but he was always denounced by Mami's growling. Then the crowd surrounded him, menacingly, and he fled, shaving the walls. As soon as he went into a shop to buy bread or a little meat, a gang formed outside the door and irritated voices peppered him with a strong of insults. Some shopkeepers refused to serve him, and he was soon obliged to go beyond the Rue de la Tombe-Issoire to procure a few meager provisions.

One evening, near the Reservoir Montsouris, at the corner of the Avenue Reille, he was set upon by a group that included fat Nestor. They took hold of him brutally, tore off his clothes, and would probably have lynched him if the police had not arrived.

Half-mad, Procas ran home, but when he reached his door he could not see Mami. He whistled and called, but the dog did not appear. Procas called again, and, seized by a sinister presentiment, he started searching.

He retraced the route that he had already followed, still whistling, fearing disaster. The dog remained undiscoverable. Procas thought that the animal, maddened by the scene that had occurred, or pursued by stones thrown by the children, might have fled in the direction of Montsouris. All night long he searched the neighborhood, returning ten times over to his door in the hope that Mami might have come back.

In the morning, at daybreak, he was sadly going home, still conserving a faint hope of finding his dear companion, when, at the corner of the Rue Saint-Yves, he saw a large grey mass in the gutter. He approached it, bent down, and recognized his dog, his poor Mami, his head crushed, in a pool of blood.

Procas uttered a heart-rending cry, his fist extended into the air in a threatening gesture. Then he picked up the animal and carried him away in his arms. Those who saw that horrible man with the cadaver of the dog that he was carrying like a child stood there astonished, and a few permitted themselves to laugh, but Procas looked at them with such a terrible expression that they recoiled, paralyzed by the yellow eyes, which seemed to be those of a demon.

Having returned home, Procas deposited Mami's cadaver on the table in his laboratory, and burst into tears.

So, he was now alone, completely alone. He had only had one friend any longer, and they had killed him.

Why?

Was he responsible, the poor animal? Was he also the enemy of those brutes? He did not bother anyone, though. He was a poor dog, very gentle, very fearful, and if he sometimes showed his teeth, it was to defend himself rather than to attack. The street-urchins had often teased him and harassed him, and he had never bitten any of them. He seemed, like his master, resigned to suffer. He only asked for a little pity, that was all. And they had killed him, without any motive...except, perhaps, because he was his dog, the accursed Procas' dog. Why had they not attacked the man, instead of killing an inoffensive animal?

And Procas sobbed, holding poor Mami's cold paw in his hand.

For a long time he remained beside that blood-spattered cadaver, whose sad eyes, veiled by death, still conserved an infinite tenderness, and in which there was an almost-human expression.

Suddenly, there was a sound of voices outside that made him shiver. Returned to a sentiment of reality, he raised his head, looked toward the window, and distinguished moving shows between the poorly-drawn curtains, which were magnified immeasurably by the light of a street-lamp. Inertia and torpor were abruptly succeeded in Procas by a dull wrath. He went to the window, opened it, and shouted in a terrible voice: "Go away! Go away, wretches!"

A volley of insults greeted him, but he stood up to the storm. He was no longer the poor, retiring, fearful individual who ought to pass unperceived in the street. He was now a resolute man, ready to attack, a man crazed by despair and wrath, rendered capable of anything. Under the raw light of the gas-lamp, which struck him full in the face, there was something so terrifying about him that the voices insulting him fell silent.

"Wretches! Wretches!" he howled, showing them his fist.

But an oppression seized him, and blood rose into his throat. He scarcely had the strength to close the window, and he collapsed, breathless and suffocating, struck down by a fainting fit.

When he came round, the sunlight was illuminating his room, where a fine golden dust was dancing in a conical sunbeam, like a swarm of minuscule insects. Still lying on the floor, he experienced a sharp sensation of cold. He was shivering, his teeth chattering. He looked around, astonished, but the idea of getting up did not even come into his mind. He remained recumbent, still shivering, his throat dry and his limbs so weary that he did not feel the courage to make any movement. The noises from the street reached him, attenuated, scarcely perceptible, there was such a buzz in his ears. Everything in his mind was vague.

He thought for a moment that during his crisis he had had a frightful nightmare, as often happened, but a frightful doubt gripped him. He forced himself up painfully, bracing himself on his elbows and knees. The first thing he saw was the table on which his dog was lying, and then he remembered everything. He moved closer, staggering like a drunken man, and passed his hand over the dull coat of the animal.

He stood there motionless, his forehead furrowed, his eyes staring. He appeared very calm; it was discernible that he was pursuing an idea that was gradually taking form in his mind. Suddenly, his face lit up; he turned toward the window with a defiant expression, as if to threaten invisible beings, and then uttered these words:

"Poor Mami, they've killed you, but you'll be avenged before long...and it's you that will serve for my vengeance."

XVI

The following day, in the little café in the Rue Liancourt, fat Nestor and Barouillet were talking in low voices. Something had happened that they could not help finding slightly troubling.

Bezombes had disappeared, without warning.

"It's decidedly incomprehensible," said Barouillet. "Bezombes would have told us if he had to go away. I've noticed that he seemed very preoccupied, but I didn't expect that he'd just disappear."

"Perhaps he's gone to the provinces on business," Nestor suggested.

"No, it must be something else."

"What?"

"That's the question!"

"What if he's been murdered? The man of the Passage Tenaille might have found out that Bezombes had unmasked him. How can we know? That horrible individual is capable of anything. He never showed himself before, but now he's opening his window, looking at people, letting himself be seen, and continually insulting them verbally. The other evening, he called us wretches and showed us his fist. I can guarantee that if he's been able to get hold of one of us, he'd have spent a bad quarter of an hour. He's like a furious madman."

"It's the death of his dog that's put him into that state."

"He'll see many others, then, for as long as they don't arrest him, we're going to give him an escort every time he goes out. Come on, Monsieur Barouillet, why isn't the fellow locked up?"

"I don't understand it."

"You've taken a grip on the affair, though, with influential individuals?"

"Yes, our député has been to see the Commissaire, but he got the same response as us. According to him, the man of the Passage Tenaille isn't dangerous."

"But what about the evidence Bezombes collected?"

"The Commissaire says it's childishness."

"Oh, of course! What does he need, then?"

"Me, I'm giving up on the affair. I'm wasting my time on it, and not getting anywhere."

"What about the newspapers?"

"The editor of the *Égalité* now says the same as the Commissaire."

"That's too much! Well, I'm not abandoning the game, and we'll see whether they don't decide to arrest the satyr soon. It's all very well to say that he isn't dangerous, but in the meantime, the haberdasher's kid hasn't turned up, and they haven't found the murderer of the girl in the cinema. Now, to complicate things, Monsieur Bezombes had disappeared too. You can say what you like, but all that isn't natural. Oh, if I could just get inside the house in the Passage Tenaille for five minutes, I can guarantee you..."

And fat Nestor nodded his head in a significant manner.

Barouillet sipped his vermouth-cassis pensively. He did not understand any of it either. He had launched himself full tilt into the wretched affair, but he now took account of the fact that the influence he enjoyed in the neighborhood, in his capacity as electoral agent, did not match that of the Commissaire. Where Jacassot had failed, he could not help but fail too. It was better to abandon the game, but discreetly, skillfully, for he feared becoming suspect to those he had drawn in his wake.

Nestor, more combative, was, as he delighted in repeating, determined to "get to the bottom of it." His conviction

313

was firm. The police were protecting a murderer, but he would be able to disentangle the truth.

"Another round, Monsieur Barouillet?"

"No thanks—another time."

"It's all right, you know. Go on, another little apero—it can't do any harm."

Barouillet allowed his arm to be twisted.

"Fill them up, Père Chevassu," ordered Nestor, pointing to the empty glasses.

The proprietor, a fat, pale bald man with an ebony black moustache, immediately arrived with two bottles. While pouring, he smiled. It was obvious that a question was burning his lips.

Finally, he asked: "And Monsieur Bezombes? We don't see him any more..."

"He's disappeared," Nestor replied.

"You doubtless mean that he's traveling?"

"Disappeared, I tell you. No one knows what's become of him. Mysterious things have been happening in this neighborhood for some time."

Père Chevassu became thoughtful. "Truly, he said, no one knows what's become of him?"

"How many times do I have to repeat it?"

"Damn! Damn! That's annoying. Yes, very annoying...it's just that...it's not my business...not at all...I trusted him, you see, and..."

"Does he owe you money?"

"Exactly."

"A lot?"

"I think so...fifteen hundred bullets."

"Impossible!"

"It's the truth."

"And he borrowed it all in one go?"

"No...in three lots...it as for business, you understand, and...I didn't think I could refuse him, inasmuch as he was recommended by you."

314

"Oh, that's too much!!" exclaimed Barouillet. "He never said a word to us about that."

"He came to see me several times…he seemed very agitated…the affair was preoccupying him greatly, and he was, it seems, obliged to make certain payments in order to obtain information. In brief, I let him have fifteen hundred francs. If he doesn't come back, I'm cooked."

"Bah! He'll come back. Bezombes is, I believe, an honest man..."

"But if he were an honest man, he wouldn't have said that he was recommended by you. That's a lesson. I won't be taken in again…"

And Père Chevassu, whose wife had just called him, headed back to his counter.

"That's shady, that story," said Nestor.

"Yes, rather," murmured Barouillet.

There was a silence.

"Do you want to know what I think?" said the apprentice butcher, eventually. "Well, I was always suspicious of Bezombes. What does he live on, anyway? No one ever comes to his office. And when he was occupied with our affair, he was always in the café. He talked, that's all. Anyway, whether he comes back or not, that doesn't prevent us from continuing what we've begun, does it?"

"Oh, I've already told you that I'm giving up on it."

"Seriously?"

"Seriously."

"Oh, that's not good, what you're doing there, Monsieur Barouillet. Leaving your friends like that, no, it's not good. What will people think in the neighborhood? We'll look like clowns."

"But what do you want me to do, my friend? You can see that we've run into insurmountable difficulties. We have the police against us; they don't want it to be said that we were cleverer than them...and you know, when one attacks the police, no good comes of it."

"Bah! You and I have nothing to fear, do we? They won't lock us up because we want to get rid of a dangerous individual. I'd like to see the Commissaire say something to me—I'd give him a fine welcome. I'm an honest man, me; I have nothing to reproach myself for, so I'm tranquil. Since everybody's quitting me, I'll work alone, and I'll give my head to be cut off if I haven't succeeded in getting the individual from the Passage Tenaille pinched within a fortnight. Besides, it's quite simple...if they don't arrest him, the local people will kill him, one evening, just as we killed his dog. They've had too much of him, and I know lads who won't hesitate to do him in."

"Oh, not that, eh?" said Barouillet. "That would be serious, and might cost you dear."

Fat Nestor shrugged his shoulders. "There are things that sort themselves out. Everyone has it in for that man, and sooner or later, he'll end up copping it."

XVII

Procas kept the corpse of his dog for twenty-four hours, during which he removed several morsels of flesh; we shall see why in due course. Then, one evening, he buried him under the bank of the fortifications.

From that day on, he was no longer the same man. He surrendered himself, reluctantly, to criminal meditations. In vain he tried to chase away the atrocious thoughts that assailed him, but he could not succeed in doing so. The idea of vengeance ended up crystallizing in his brain.

Ordinarily, under the influence of a violent anger, a man dreams of a thousand projects of vengeance, and then gradually resumes possession of himself. A thunderbolt has turned his entire being upside down, but once the commotion dies down, he recovers his calm of mind.

In Procas, a sequence of commotions—for he had to face the fury of the crowd every day—gradually led to a subjective, almost hypnotic psychic depression destructive of all morality.

He was not yet mad, since he was acting deliberately, but his brain was no longer that of a sane man. Under the effect of grief, his self was transformed, and he arrived at the most monstrous conceptions. A kind of momentum drew him into crime without him making any attempt to restrain himself.

That state of mind might appear explicable in a primitive individual, but in an intellectual like Procas it seems a monstrosity. In order to be enlightened as to the psychology of the unfortunate, to descend into the darkness of his soul, it is necessary to go back to the genesis of the evil. Procas is a neuropath with overstimulated meninges; he has anatomical lesions. His sensations are now reaching the paroxysm of violence. Their intensity has ended up stifling the voice of conscience. He is no longer rational. His actions are prey to an obsession. All his mental forces are concentrated on a single objective: vengeance. He no longer sees anything but that, and in his solitude, he ruminates the most terrible things.

Such an individual requires calm, but the hostile crowd that he sensed around him, and the cries of hatred that reached him every day, through the walls, all exasperated him more and more.

He reinstalled himself in his laboratory and went back to work—but this time, it was no longer to endow humankind with a discovery; it was to sow death among his fellows.

And it would be the tissue that he had removed from his dog that the poison would be hidden. He remember that, in the course of his previous endeavors, he had carried out a number of experiments culturing microbes in milieux containing substances extracted from the spinal cord and the brain-tissue of dogs. He had even extracted a material that he called "medullose," which, added in minimal doses to nutritive milieux, had the property of augmenting considerably the virulence of pathogenic microbes. But it was necessary for him to select, among the latter, the one that could cause death most readily. He remembered then all the infectious maladies that he had once studied, and consulted reference-books on bacteriology, but did not find what he wanted.

For reasons that will soon be understood, it was via water that he wanted to propagate the microbe. The virus of bubonic plague, which he considered momentarily, is undeniably one of the most active, but have not recent experiments shown that water only plays a secondary role in its propagation?[41] In order to provoke an epidemic, it was necessary to find a new, redoubtable poison. Where could he find the unknown germ, the tiny invisible creature that would slyly penetrate the entrails and kill more surely than a revolver bullet?

Procas was prey to a dull rage. He would never be able to avenge himself on those who had made him suffer so much, and continued to torture him every day.

While riffling through an old manuscript, however, he was struck by the notes he had made in India regarding a certain epizoon of rats. He had noticed that thousands of those rodents perished in twenty-four hours, and that at the same time, the inhabitants of a small village near Madura were afflicted by a hitherto-unknown disease.

He had devoted himself to scrupulous research, had isolated and cultivated an extremely tenuous bacillus, difficult to stain, and which, inoculated into rats and mice, brought about the same ravages as those produced by the mysterious epizoon. For a long time, after his return to France, he had studied that question, and had written a detailed report of his discovery, but had never determined to publish the work, to which he had given the title "Researches on *Bacillus murinus*."

Later, in Marseilles, where he had been sent by the Minister of the Interior in order to study the prophylactic measures to be taken against the plague, which had claimed a few vic-

---

[41] The reference is to the experiments carried out by Kitastao and Yersin in Hong Kong in 1894, which apparently confirmed the suspicion that rats played a significant role in the plague, although they did not reveal the vital role of fleas.

tims, he had, while dissecting a cadaver, collected and isolated the same *Bacillus murinus* that he had discovered in India.

Now that he remembered all the details, he had a sudden idea. He searched his collection of microbes and found a test-tube containing a culture of the bacillus in question, but it was almost dried out. Its virulence—which is to say, its aptitude to develop in an animal body and secrete bacterial poisons there—must now be ineffective. It was therefore necessary to rediscover the bacillus, isolate it, and cultivate it again.

From that day on, he could be seen every night removing a plank from the palisade that separated his dwelling from the forage shed. With a little lantern in his hand, he set out traps, and then searched the ground, in the hope of discovering a dead rat. There were a great many rats in the hangar, and he did not despair of finding what he was looking for.

In a week, he captured a dozen rodents, but one night he found two that were dad. He immediately proceeded with their autopsy, and took blood from the heart, after having first burned the surface of the viscera in question, in order to avoid any possible contagion. Then he distributed the blood in nutritive milieux prepared in advance, and after twenty-four hours, obtained different cultures.

In the majority of those cultures he found the well-known Danysz bacillus,[42] which produces a disease in rats very similar to human typhoid fever. A few days passed in feverish work. With minute patience, Procas dissected the

---

[42] Jean Danysz (1860-1928), a Polish microbiologist specializing in the development of methods for the destruction of agricultural parasites and pests, joined the Pasteur Institute in 1893, bringing with him a bacillus, *Salmonella enteritidis*, which became known as the "Danysz virus" when he promoted it enthusiastically as a possible means of killing rodents. At that time, the term "virus" did not have the specific meaning that it later acquired, but was simply a generalized term for a virulent agent.

cadavers of rats one by one, injecting test tubes with a quantity of their blood, but the *Bacillus murinus* still did not appear.

One night, however, he found more dead rats than usual in the forage store. He collected five.

There was no doubt about it; an epizoon had manifested itself—and what confirmed it was that the traps he set every night were now empty. It is well-known that when an epidemic breaks out, the rats, which are no less intelligent than other animals, flee from the nucleus of infection and emigrate to other locations.

Procas was overjoyed when he recognized lesions on the dead rats he had just found exactly similar to those he had observed in India. He removed various blood samples from the animals, and, twenty-four hours later, he was able to observe a white streak on the gelose with characteristic lateral ramifications.

No doubt was any longer possible; he finally had his *Bacillus murinus*.

Then he took a glass slide, deposited a drop of the culture on it, spread it out with the tip of a pipette, stained the preparation with a compound he had made, and then examined it under the microscope. In the field of the apparatus he observed the presence of short, slender bacilli.

It really was the bacillus he sought; he recognized it perfectly. It only remained for him to carry out what is known as the "Koch triad," which consists of inoculating receptive animals with the microbe.[43] He injected the virus under the skin of three living animals; he introduced it into the intestines of three others in the form of food pellets.

---

[43] The pioneering bacteriologist Robert Koch (1843-1910) identified the agents responsible for tuberculoisis, cholera and anthrax, and standardized a methodology for such detective work, based on the logical extrapolation of "Koch's postulates." The "triads" to which the text refers are an aspect of that methodology,

The first three succumbed in twenty-six hours; the other three only died after four days. The virus already seemed sufficiently violent, but it was weak, of it were compared with the one found in the rats of the Indian village. Procas was not discouraged, however. He knew that, thanks to the procedures of modern bacteriology, one can increase the virulence of microbial pathogens considerably and transform a microbe that is almost inoffensive for a particular species into a virus mortal for that species.

In this case, his dog, his poor Mami, would render him one last service. The medullose would enter into play and collaborate with the augmentation of the toxicity of *Bacillus murinus*.

From then on he employed a very effective method invented by Metchnikoff, Roux and Salimbent during their scientific research on the cholera toxin.[44] He introduced little capsules of collodion filled with culture broth and medullose inseminated with *Bacillus murinus* into the peritoneum of rats.

He operated with all aseptic precautions in order to avoid infection of the peritoneum, which might have distorted the results of the experiment. Two or three days later, he sacrificed the animal and removed the capsule in order to inseminate the culture in a new collodion capsule and then introduce it into the peritoneum of another rat. When the virus had passed alternately through the organisms of several rodents it became much more active.

Soon, he succeeded in killing rats in three or four hours. Finally, by multiplying the passage of cultures through several rats, Procas obtained an exceedingly toxic virus.

---

[44] The Russian biologist Élie [Ilya] Metchnikoff (1845-1916) became one of the leading lights of the Pasteur Institute and received the Nobel Prize for Medicine in 1908 for his work on phagocytosis. Dr. Dalimbent, another employee of the Institute, most commonly cited with reference to his work on malaria, remained far more obscure

XVIII

He was at that point in his research when another crisis laid him low. One evening, when he had worked very late, he was suddenly dazzled; a red light passed before his eyes and he collapsed on the table in his laboratory.

When he recovered his awareness of things it was broad daylight. So far as he could tell, it must be nearly midday. The circulation on the sidewalks was more active, and in the restaurant situated not far from his dwelling he could hear the sound of plates and glasses clinking.

He tried to go as far as the window in order to pull the curtains and block a ray of sunlight that was blinding him, but he was incapable of taking a step. He fell to his knees, and it required all his strength to drag himself as far as the divan, on which he stretched himself out, with great difficulty.

It was impossible for him to remain lying down, however, and he had to sit up. His heart seemed to be about to stop at any moment, and Procas compressed his chest with his cold hands. His head was empty of thought; he was conscious of nothing except his illness, the phases of which he followed with anguish.

He remained doubled up for a long time, his gaze fixed, like a man fearful of a catastrophe; then he experienced a strange sensation. His vision became obscured, his ideas became imprecise; it seemed to him that he had suddenly been transported into an unreal world, far from conscious life. He had the impression that his spiritual being had deserted his body, that he was floating in space, and he wondered if this might be death—but no, for when he touched one of his limbs, which he pinched, he was conscious of the pain.

He was still there some time later, nailed to his divan, motionless, and as cold as a man of wax. When he thought he was a little better, he formed the project of going to the window and opening it in order to breathe in a draught of fresh air, but he was apprehensive of the moment when he stood up, because he was well aware that the slightest effort might provoke a further crisis. If only he had, at least, been able to sleep!

At the price of dolorous efforts he had succeeded in leaning backwards and supporting his head against the wall. At first he experienced some relief, and closed his eyes. A relative wellbeing followed, which did not last long, for the new position he had adopted put too much strain on his thoracic muscles and compressed his respiration. He was obliged to lean forward again, with his elbows on his knees, and to stay like that, without making a movement.

An ardent thirst was burning his throat. He was shivering, his teeth were chattering and he felt the cold overtaking his extremities, running along his arms and legs, and rising toward has breast.

Is this the end? he thought.

That prospect did not frighten him. On the contrary, he envisaged it with serenity, astonished still to be alive. The noises of the street reached him, mutedly, and he almost wished that he could no longer hear anything, that he could flee forever the world where he had encountered no pity, the people whose footsteps he could hear on the sidewalk, the hoarse voices, and the bursts of laughter, which were all tortures for him.

After a further crisis, less violent than the others, which held him prostrate on his divan, he recovered a little physical tranquility and was able to take a few steps across the room. He drank a large glass of water, but as his legs were buckling, he was obliged to sit down. It was three days since he had eaten anything, but, still prey to fever, he was not hungry…a little water was sufficient.

The shock that he had experienced had brought a certain relaxation to his mind. He was no longer thinking about anything, but as life took hold of him again, the memory returned of everything that had happened. An insurmountable agitation gradually penetrated him, and even if he had wanted to forget, it would have been impossible for him to do so.

When he was finally able to go out to get his provisions, he found the same hostile crowd in front of him, and the desire for vengeance that was slumbering in his heart was reawakened, more violently than ever.

Fat Nestor, who had not laid down his arms, was more determined than ever. He had taken on more importance since the defection of Bezombes and Barouillet, and it was now him that was "leading the dance."

He had turned improvised detective. In the evening, he stationed himself at a small window overlooking the house in the Passage Tenaille and the fodder-shed. With a patience that never weakened, he lay in wait for the man he called "the satyr" for hours on end. He imagined that the latter was preparing to flee.

What maintained that idea in him was that he had not failed to remark Procas' comings and goings with his little hooded lantern, while hunting rats. Nestor had concluded that he had packed his trunks and was looking for wood with which to make crates in which to lodge all his equipment.

He had even thought that it was his duty to warn the proprietor, Père Grinchu, who had shrugged his shoulders and shut the door in his face. Furious, Nestor had begun spreading calumnies on the fodder-merchant's account the following day, accusing him of being "in cahoots" with "the murderer."

The affair was visibly taking on new proportions, and the crowd, so easy to convince, was now in tow to fat Nestor, who, the produce of the role of administrator or justice that he believed he was playing, stoked up the hatred on his partisans every day. He made speeches in the street, and people listened to him complaisantly, for what he said corresponded exactly with what a number of local people thought.

It is well-known that common people have an unfortunate tendency to see mystery everywhere, and to imagine that certain privileged people have a special grace. They have an iron conviction that the law is pitiless for the humble, while it reserves all its indulgence for those who belong to a certain social category.

The whisper had gone around that "the man of the Passage Tenaille" must once have played a political role that had made him party to certain secrets, and that it was for that reason that the police were protecting him.

"If he was a poor devil like us," Nestor never ceased repeating, "he'd have been locked up long ago."

Every day, in the workshops, on the doorsteps and in the shops there were mysterious conversations; everyone wanted to seem well-informed; some old gossips, who did not lack imagination, competed in embroidering the rumors, and some of them had turned the head of mother of the missing child that the poor woman, convinced that Procas had murdered her son, was among the demonstrators every evening when "the satyr" emerged furtively from his dwelling.

Where would it all end?

Nestor was convinced that the police, faced with that popular movement, which was becoming more important every day, would eventually take action.

But Procas' hatred grew along with that of the fanatics, and one evening, when, pursued by a howling band, he had once again been insulted, molested and struck, he reached home in such a state of exasperation that the idea of vengeance brooding within him, but which had perhaps been attenuated, was revived more fervently than ever.

"They'll have brought it on themselves!" he cried, in a hoarse voice.

And the following day, he resumed his frightful task.

XIX

He was not yet sure that the virus he had discovered would be able to act as effectively on a human being, but he had an intuition of it. The experiments he had carried out seemed conclusive. He was not at the end of his project, however. Although he had succeeded in isolating an exceedingly violent infectious agent, which ought to produce terrible effects, it was necessary that the virus would be able to propagate in water, in order that the toxic germs could multiply therein. That was an essential condition to obtain an epidemic that would not be limited to a few isolated cases.

There, a difficulty emerged.

Water, as everyone knows, is not ordinarily sterile. It always contains a fairly considerable quantity of bacteria, which do not develop in living organisms but develop at the expense of dead matter—which is to say, saprophytic bacteria. And that quantity depends on the very variable conditions of climate and proximity to some source of contamination.

Have not 415,000 microbes been found in a cubic centimeter of water from the Seine? And as many as 6,680 in the water that aliments Paris? It follows that the purest water conceals a microbial fauna, and enough organic material to nourish thousand of bacteria for a certain length of time.

In sterilized water microbes propagate even more. Water massively invaded by bacteria does not permit the facile development of the bacilli that live in it, and in the same way, does not permit the evolution of a new microbe, unless it is much more robust than the first inhabitants of the element. It is the eternal law of the struggle for existence that governs relations between those invisible beings, as it governs the relations of humans: the strong eat the weak.

Based on that fact, some scientists have put forward the opinion that the purest water, from the bacteriological point of view, is often the most dangerous, when it is impossible to protect it against contamination by some local nucleus of infection.

We beg pardon for these few scientific details, but they are necessary to the comprehension of what will follow, and serve to explain the terrible drama that is about to be played out.

Most pathogenic microbes develop quite easily in sterilized water, but when put in the presence of other saprophytic microbes that are much better adapted to that nutritive environment, it is necessary for them to sustain a fierce struggle for existence, and most of the time, they end up being vanquished.

The life of pathogenic microbes in the liquid element depends on numerous factors. First of all, there is the chemical composition of the water, principally its richness in organic matter; in addition, there is the elevation or depression of temperature, the presence or absence of light and movement. Finally, there are other conditions that depend on the microbes themselves: their vitality and resistance in the battle with their enemies.

When the pathogenic microbe begins to get the upper hand in that struggle for existence, and the others perish, there is than an increase in the nutritive matter in the water, at the expense of the cadavers, and the victorious microbe can develop much more abundantly.

Procas had taken water from the city supply and submitted it to the Koch method. After heating tubes containing gelatin impregnated with meat broth to a temperature of forty degrees, he added a certain quantity of water. The dissolved gelatin was then poured into glass vessels known as Petri dishes.

Ordinarily, the colonies of microbes appear after twenty-four or thirty-six hours in the form of little white dots, and the numeration of those colonies gives the total number of microbes in the quantity of water used for the insemination.

The city water analyzed by Procas was not rich in microbes; their number did not exceed eighteen hundred per cubic centimeter. It was evident that the water in question could offer a favorable environment to *Bacillus murinus*; the struggle for existence would not be very difficult. To verify that fact, Procas inseminated a cubic centimeter of *Bacillus murinus* in a five-liter flask filed with city water. Every six hours, he spread specimens of that water on the gelatin and counted the number of colonies that appeared after twenty-four hours in the incubator.

The second experiment revealed a notable diminution of colonies of the bacillus and in thirty hours they had almost completely disappeared. The rat bacillus, which was so potent and so tenacious in the animal organism, was vanquished by the invisible creatures.

But Procas was not discouraged. On the contrary, the difficulty stimulated him. He knew full well that one can habituate any bacterium to new conditions of life by changing those conditions gradually. He inseminated his *Bacillus murinus* in a flask containing less meat and more sterilized water, and produced a series of cultures, gradually diminishing the quantity of organic material, However, the bacilli introduced into unsterilized water disappeared after a time. On the other hand, the inoculation of that culture into rats demonstrated that its virulence was noticeably attenuated, and eventually lost its potency altogether.

This time, Procas was utterly discouraged, and might perhaps have renounced continuing his experiments if the hostile cries he heard from outside had not stimulated his energy and maintained his idea of vengeance.

He continued his research, and began to wonder whether, in consequence of a cooperation between two or more microbial species, he might be able to achieve a kind of bacillary union.

Science furnishes several examples of that "symbiosis," an association of microbes that appears to be useful, and even necessary, to the life of a determined type. Has not Metchnikoff observed that the combination of the cholera vibrion with a few other species, such as, for example, *Sarcina*, an inoffensive parasite of the human intestine, is one of the most virulent?

It was necessary to find a microbial type that was able to increase the resistance of the *Bacillus murinus*. He carried out a number of trials, but the results were always the same. The bacillus was attenuated in the water and its virulence disappeared there almost completely.

Would he, then, be forced to renounce his vengeance? Would science be impotent to procure him the poison that would annihilate hundreds of human lives?

Every day he became angrier; he became more deeply absorbed in his idea of vengeance; eventually, he thought about nothing else. He was exasperated, half-mad.

When the shouts and insults of the people massed outside his door reached his ears, instead of frightening him, as before, he laughed in a sinister fashion, gently lifted his curtain, stared at all the individuals who were insulting him and thought that if he succeeded in isolating and multiplying the bacillus for which he was searching, the specter would soon reappear of the Black Death that had traveled through the valleys of Europe centuries before, sowing terror and ruination in its path...

He rejoiced in that thought that, for all those individuals who were making him suffer, there would soon be the darkness of the tomb. No regret or pity found a place in his soul. Coldly, he envisaged the consequences of his action, and awaited with impatience the day when he would be able to suppress his enemies with a simple gesture.

In his laboratory, by the light of a flickering gas-lamp, long into the night, he carried out his deadly work with the fever of a scientist working solely for the sake of science.

XX

Thus far, none of his trials had succeeded; he always ran into the same difficulties, and the microbes he disseminated lost their virulence once they were plunged into the water.

One day, he had the idea of drawing water from an old, very deep well that was in his yard. He was not expecting anything good from the new experiment when, to his great surprise, he discovered that the *Bacillus murinus* developed very abundantly in that unsterilized water.

After twenty-four hours, the number of microbes contained in the liquid diminished, while his bacillus developed increasingly. There was no doubt about it; the initial cause of that augmentation of virulence was due to one of the microbes inhabiting the well, and the same results could be obtained with the pure culture of those microbes in sterilized water. He isolated them, cultivated them separately, and then developed them with the *murinus* adapted to life in the well water and the city water.

The problem was solved! Procas was finally holding his vengeance: two microbes, which, cooperating with one another, became extremely virulent. He carefully prepared a culture of the two bacilli in a two-liter flask, and then let himself fall upon his divan, uttering a profound sigh.

It only remained to accomplish the decisive act: the one that he has been ruminating for such a long time.

Everything was ready—and yet, he hesitated. For long hours he remained motionless, his head in his hands.

Come on, he said to himself internally, *it's necessary to decide. Have they had any pity on me?*

He stood up, approached the vessel, put it under his arm as if he were ready to take it away, and took a few steps across the room. A frightful struggle began within him. He put the flask down again, went to sit down, and became pensive again...

He recalled all his days of misery, the tortures that the savage crowd, which never gave him a moment's respite, had forced him to endure. He started pacing again, suddenly opened the window, and took a deep breath, plunging his gaze into the darkness.

The hour sounded at Saint-Pierre-de-Montrouge, grave and tremulous. It was raining. Clouds were racing across the sky with large wan patches in places. He shook his fist at the street.

Swiftly, he put on his overcoat and hat, and, hiding the flask under his left arm, he opened his door and went out.

In the houses, his enemies were asleep, tranquil and confidant.

Procas went up the Avenue du Maine as far as the church of Montrouge, took the Rue d'Alésia, turned right into the Rue Tombe-Issoire and reached the Rue Saint-Yves. Having arrived at the place where he had discovered the cadaver of his poor Mami a few weeks earlier, he stopped, out of breath, be-

cause he had been walking rapidly and was sweating copiously. Recalling the tragic evening when they had tried to lynch
him, he saw his dog once again, huddling against him and
growling. Then everything was effaced in his mind; he no
longer retained anything but the memory of the anguish that
he had experienced thereafter, when he had run around searching for Mami, and had found him, at daybreak, lying in the
gutter.

"The wretches! The wretches!" he never ceased repeating, prey to a dull anger that was gradually accentuating. At
that moment, everything in him was exasperated. He was no
longer reasoning, and was only thinking about one thing:
vengeance.

He started walking again, advancing furtively, like a
malefactor who senses that he is being watched. He was almost certain that no one had seen him, but he was trembling,
and sought convulsively to make himself small.

The rain was still falling with a weary noise. The lights
of Paris formed a great vacillating mist in the distance, above
the houses.

Having reached the corner of the Avenue Reille and the
Rue Saint-Yves, he got his bearings. In front of him, the reservoir of Montsouris had the appearance of an enormous tumulus covered with a thick lawn, like one of those gigantic sepul-
chers that one sees in some Asian cities. On one of its side,
little glazed edicules rose up, and in the north-west corner,
there was a stone construction surmounted by a metallic kiosk,
which was reminiscent of the bridge of a steamship.

He remembered having come here a few years before,
with a delegation of municipal councilors and chemists, to
examine that were known as the "arrival tanks" into which the
siphons of the Vanne, the Lunain and the Loing discharged. It
had been a matter of a Hygiene Committee investigation. In
his capacity as a bacteriologist, Procas had been appointed to
study on location the dangers of the contamination of the water by the dust that the wind might blow into the adduction
vessels, and he had been struck by the ease with which some-

one could penetrate into the reservoir at that time, which was now protected by solid barriers.

He went along the Avenue Reille and then the Rue de la Tombe-Issoire and the Rue Saint-Yves, which framed the two sides of the great grassy tumulus, and understood that he would never succeed in scaling the walls.

He tried to open a little door framed in the stone, but could not do it. It would have been necessary to force the lock. Procas would not have hesitated to do that, but all that he had on him was a little knife, the blade of which would have snapped at the slightest effort.

While he was reflecting in a shadowy corner, the silhouette of a policeman appeared, moving along the neighboring houses. He waited until the silhouette had disappeared, and then made a second tour of the reservoir. It was as well-defended as a fortress.

With rage in his heart, he took the road back to his dwelling.

The rain had stopped, and a brisk wind was causing the glass of the street-lamps to rattle. Large clouds, like cotton wool peppered with soot, were filing across the sky, illuminated from time to time by a ray of moonlight.

Procas was so troubled that he went astray. Instead of turning left to rejoin the Rue d'Alésia via the Avenue Parc-de-Monsouris, he turned right and found himself in the Rue de la Glacière.

After a long hesitation, he finally recognized his route, but he was so exhausted that he had to sit down on a bench. He was invaded by a torpor, and would probably have let himself fall asleep if a policeman had not called to him rudely: "Don't you have a home to go to?"

"Yes, Monsieur," Procas replied, startled, like a man emerging from a dream.

"Go to bed, then. One doesn't sleep on benches."

Procas stood up. He drew away, his tread heavy, under the suspicious gaze of the policeman.

When he got home, he saw a piece of paper stuck to his door. He tried to read it but, not being able to do so, detached it. He went into his laboratory, switched on the light, and words traced in large letters by a maladroit hand appeared in the lamplight.

Villain! Murderer! Since the police won't arrest you, we'll settle your hash before long.

Procas did not even become indignant. He shrugged his shoulders, crumpled up the piece of paper and threw it into a corner.

He knew full well, of course, that he had nothing good to expect from that overexcited populace whose hatred was growling around him. Threats scarcely moved him.

His flask, placed in front of him on the table, scintillated in the light. *It's me who'll settle your hash, you wretches*, he thought, *and you'll have brought it on yourselves*.

He undressed slowly and lay down on his divan, which he had now converted into a bed—a bed without sheets, with two coarse military blankets. He had left the lamp lit, because for some time, darkness had frightened him. Outside, the rain had started falling again. Procas was drowsy, exhausted by fatigue, and ended up falling asleep.

When he woke up, it was broad daylight. His lamp was burning low, spreading a wisp of black smoke through the room, but he did not have the strength to get up. The prospect of having to live another day sickened him. His failure of the previous evening had discouraged him, but he had not renounced his project of vengeance. The idea was anchored in his mind with such force that he regarded it as something necessary, a kind of obligation that he could not avoid.

He let himself slide out of bed, put on his clothes, which were still damp, and headed for the kitchen, where he had installed his autoclave.

There, he opened the drawer of an old table, rummaged among the objects within, and pulled out a metal stem terminated at its extremity by a double hook, It was the implement he used to withdraw red-hot tubes from the fire that he had heated in order to sterilize them. He searched for a file, which he eventually discovered on a shelf, and, returning to his laboratory, started filing the piece of metal carefully.

That work took him nearly three hours, and when he had finished, Procas threw himself down on his divan again.

He seemed quite tranquil, and at times, a smile creased his hideous face.

XXI

That morning, fat Nestor, contrary to his habit, neglected to knock on Procas' door proffering threats. He had received a visit from Barouillet, who had given him some serious news.

Bezombes had been arrested and taken to the Commissariat in the Rue Sarrette.

"It's the police taking their revenge," growled Nestor.

"Perhaps," said Barouillet, but what's certain is that Bezombes has been accused of fraud."

"Père Chevassu has lodged a complaint?"

"Oh, there are several complaints, it's said. That Bezombes isn't worth much..."

"Possibly, but even so, he rendered us a valuable service."

Barouillet made a vague gesture.

"Yes, all the same, he furnished us with the proofs that we lacked."

"Who can tell?"

"What, you doubt it?"

"Bezombes exaggerated everything. He's a narcissist who only seeks to make himself look good. In any case, whether he exaggerated or not, what's certain is that he's a dishonest man, and he took advantage of the affair to cheat several of the local merchants, and it's very regrettable that we associated with him, because, after all, we were his friends. They only saw him with us...if they were to suppose..."

"Come on, Monsieur Barouillet, everyone in Montrouge knows us. We have businesses, status. We don't owe anyone anything. When the bank employees come to see us, they never leave pieces of paper..."

"I don't deny it—but people are so malevolent..."

"Bah! It's nothing to do with us. Let Bezombes get himself out of it."

"We'll probably be summoned as witnesses."

"Well, we'll tell them what we know. They can't lock us up just because we've been in the company of a crook. These things happen. One makes the acquaintance of a man; one thinks he's honest; if one finds out later that he's a rogue, one isn't compromised for that. Bezombes deceived us, that's all, but that doesn't stop me thinking that he was sincere when he was on the trail of the satyr..."

"How did it get us any further forward?"

"Oh, Monsieur Barouillet, with all due respect, you abandoned us, and you were wrong..."

"No, my friend, I wasn't wrong. I understood that there was nothing more to be done. Our man, for reasons I don't know, undoubtedly disposes of great protection, since, in spite of all the evidence accumulated against him, he's still at liberty. My opinion—have I any need to say it?—hasn't varied. I think he's guilty of a crime, perhaps several, but so long as he isn't caught in the act..."

"To catch him in the act, it's necessary to keep him under surveillance, to spy on him…and that's what I do, every day…or rather, every evening. Ordinarily, he only goes out to fetch his dinner, and once he comes back he doesn't set foot outside again. Well, last night, he went out at about midnight. I heard him open his door. I went to the window and I saw him heading in the direction of Montrouge church. But when I got downstairs he was already far away..."

"You're sure you saw him go out?"

"As sure as I am that you're standing in front of me. I've been watching him...because I have patience, and when I occupy myself with an affair, I see it through to the end. Yes, I watched for him and I saw him come back. It might have been about two o'clock in the morning. Do you think it's natural, going out like that? One of these days, we're going to hear that someone's been murdered, and no more will be said about it. Oh, damn it! I'll pinch the satyr or may I lose my name. From tonight onwards, I'll be on sentry duty again."

"But you can't stay up every night..."

"I'll sleep during the day. My father will take my place on the stall—but it's necessary that I finish it."

"I admire your energy, and most of all your persistence, but I think you'll be wasting your time."

"We'll see, Monsieur Barouillet, we'll see. Until now we didn't know that the satyr went out at night. Now we'll try to find out what he does with his time. Nothing honest, that's for sure..."

"I wish you luck. In any case, don't forget that you can always count on me."

Nestor burst out laughing. "Ah," he said, clapping Barouillet on the shoulder in a familiar fashion, "you've changed your mind...we can arrange to share the work, then. We'll take turns to follow the individual."

""I'd do it with pleasure, but he municipal elections are coming up, and all my evenings are taken, you understand. I'm campaigning for Malavaux, and..."

"What? I thought you supported the sitting councilor?"

"No, Bellerive hasn't kept his promises. He's taken things too easily with the electors. We need a man who'll occupy himself actively with the neighborhood. Oh, if it had been any other time, I'd have been glad to help you, but it's impossible, you see..."

"I'll work alone, then, and do my best to succeed. It will happen, perhaps sooner than you think...and I'll be able to say that I, too, have acted in the interests of the neighborhood."

"People will be grateful to you."

The two men shook hands and parted. Nestor emerged on to his doorstep, where he stood motionless, imposing and superb. To those who passed by, he nodded his head slightly or saluted them with a gesture of his hand.

The role that he had assumed placed him in the Avenue du Maine, and like Bezombes, he assumed a mysterious expression when anyone spoke to him about "the affair."

Everyone was convinced that he knew something but did not want to say anything yet. At aperitif time, however, in the little café in the Rue Liancourt, he imparted a few confidences to two or three friends, who hastened to repeat everywhere that Nestor was about to astonish everyone, and those who has thus far considered him to be an utter imbecile would begin to take him seriously.

It was him, in sum, who was maintaining the hatred of everyone in the neighborhood against Procas—a hatred that would probably have attenuated otherwise, and then died down, as every popular fury tends to do. People continued to spy on the unfortunate scientist, and to "escort" him when he went in search of a few meager provisions, which he did not lays obtain, because the majority of the shopkeepers had made an alliance with the crowd. He was often obliged to go as far as the Rue de la Gaîté and the Rue d'Odessa, where he inevitably found new enemies, who joined in chorus with the others.

It is only just to recognize that, for several days, Procas, who was sure of avenging himself on everyone, had adopted a provocative attitude. Once, he had fled like a poor beast, pursued by thrown stones, but now he stood up to the howling band that escorted him. Often, he stopped, folded his arms and stared at the mob. It is certain that that would end badly one day; he was repeatedly attacked, because he was becoming increasingly odious.

The day before, a piece of paper had been nailed to his door; that evening he found another, on which a guillotine had been drawn, with the words: *Deibler is waiting for you.*[45]

He smiled and went in. He seemed quite calm. He ate a crust of bread and a little roasted meat, and threw himself

---

[45] Anatole Deibler was the Republic's chief executioner from 1899 until he dropped dead in a Metro station in 1939.

down on the divan filly dressed, after having set his alarm clock for midnight.

When the little bell began to vibrate, Procas got up. He took a few steps across the room, toward the window, and listened. Then, putting on his coat, he stood still for a few moments. Finally, he put his hat on, pulling down the brim, picked up his flask, and went out quietly, after having extinguished his lamp.

Scarcely was he outside than he heard footsteps behind him. He turned round and saw a shadow, hugging the walls. By the light of a street-lamp he recognized his enemy and started thinking about ways to put him off the track.

Instead of following the Avenue du Maine he went into the Passage de la Tour-de-Vanves, where the darkness was almost complete, turned rapidly into the Rue Asseline, and hid in a doorway.

Fat Nestor stopped, indecisively, and then, not seeing anyone, continued along the entire length of the street. He went past Procas without perceiving him, came back into the Passage and went all the way back to the Avenue—but Procas had already reached the Rue d'Alésia via the Rue Didot, and then followed the Avenue d'Orléans and the Rue Beaunier, which opened opposite the main entrance of the Montsouris reservoir..

He immediately turned into the Avenue Reille, and stopped outside a little iron door framed in the wall.

The night was dark and slightly foggy. The glow of the street-lamps seemed to be shimmering in troubled water. Putting his flask on the ground, Procas, by means of the hook that he had fashioned the previous evening, started foraging gently in the lock. He finally heard a little click, and the door opened soundlessly.

He was inside.

A frightening tranquility reigned all around. He went up a few steps and reached the large grassy platform that covered the reservoir. Kneeling down on the damp grass, he listened momentarily, then got up again and, bending down, slid toward the glazed edicule that he could perceive vaguely in front of him.

He was trembling in every limb, and felt his heart beating precipitately in his breast. The horrible resolution that he had made was weakening by the minute, and he might have been on the point of turning round when the distant barking of a dog caused him to shiver.

That was the fashion in which poor Mami had barked when he sensed the hostile crowd behind him in pursuit of his master. That barking had something plaintive about it, and it rose into the night at regular intervals.

Procas shuddered. In a matter of seconds, his memories succeeded one another. He saw once again the howling mob of his enemies, their savage faces, their threatening gestures. He thought he could feel the brutal hand of the butcher boy on his shoulder, and hear Mami growling at his side—Mami, whose bloody remains he would soon find lying in the gutter...

And that stifled his dream of forgiveness. At a furtive pace, he continued to advance, hugging his flask to his chest

Why should I have pity on them? he thought.

He had arrived at the kiosk where the double siphons of the Vanne and the Loing opened. He only had to pick the lock of a glass door, which yielded easily. Having reached an iron ramp, he saw a black hole into which the water poured, seething.

His hands, which were holding the flask, had become chilled, and, as he was about to accomplish the fatal gesture that would sow death, his legs vacillated. He pulled himself together, though, stretched out his arm, hesitated again—and then, with an abrupt gesture, poured out the poison.

There was a slight noise. Something like a slight rustle of foliage…and that was all.

Procas was avenged. The irreparable deed had been done.

A frisson of dolor and voluptuousness ran through his entire body, and he fled, prey to a mad terror, thinking that he could see people all around him with fleshless arms, pitiful and supplicant.

He had difficulty finding the little door through which he had entered, but closed it silently, and launched himself into the dark streets, walking with an uneven, heavy tread. He had kept the flask. He threw it on to a patch of waste ground, where it shattered.

All night long he wandered like a lost dog, and only got home at dawn. As he put his key into the lock, a man suddenly surged forth.

"Ah! We'll have your hide, scoundrel!"

Procas turned round and recognized the apprentice butcher. He stared at him, smiled ironically, and closed his door.

XXII

The neighborhood woke up. Procas, who had no desire to sleep, in spite of his weariness, was sitting on his divan, his head in his hands. Now that a little clarity had returned to his mind, he was thinking.

What he had done was horrible, he realized. Tomorrow or the day after tomorrow at the latest, the urban ambulances would be speeding through the streets; the hospitals would be filling up with the dying; all the people who were now going cheerfully to work would soon be struck down by a strange illness, the cause of which would be sought in vain. Death would surprise men, women and children...

Children!

At that thought, Procas felt a constriction in his heart. In order to avenge himself, he would kill innocents, poor little creatures who did not know and did not yet understand anything of human suffering. And yet, had they not tortured him too? Had they not uttered cries of hatred as he passed by, and wild clamors? Were they not part of the barbaric multitude that harassed him every day? Had any one of them ever made the slightest gesture or uttered a single word of pity for him?

Procas, it is evident, by dint of meditating his vengeance, of satisfying it, had arrived at finding it just, almost natural. It is true that the suffering, and the persecution of which he had been the object, had, as we have explained, gradually disturbed his conscience. He was no longer a normal individual.

For the moment, he could only see one thing: he was about to read in faces, in his turn, dolor and anguish. When he sensed a sentiment of pity invading him, he immediately recalled everything that had been done to him, and the anger concentrated in his heart began boiling once again. He maintained around himself an ambience of memories, and avoided interrogating himself, for fear that he might condemn himself.

When dusk fell, he went out. As usual, the same unchained, mocking and evil mob gathered around him. He seemed insensible to the insults; he was no longer an irritable and furious man, as before, but an unconscious individual, as if in a state of hypnosis, for whom the external world no longer existed.

"He's jolly good this evening!" shouted one woman, who was following the crowd leading her child by the hand.

"Oh, you'd better watch out," said another. "Don't get too close. Beware!"

The new attitude of the man with the blue face astonished them, however, and they wondered whether that calmness was natural. Some of them wanted to see him baulk, and aggravated him, even jostling him, like animal-tamers whipping a wild beast to make it roar.

Procas was still impassive.

What's the point? he said to himself. *Tomorrow, they'll no longer be occupied with me...because they'll have another enemy, far more redoubtable.*

And with that thought, a malevolent gleam came into his eyes.

He was able to buy a few provisions that evening. When he went home, he noticed that his escort was still as numerous. He locked himself in, ate slowly, by the light of his little oil lamp, and then, as he sensed clearly that he would not be able to sleep, he picked up a book on bacteriology, and absorbed himself in reading a chapter selected at random.

From time to time, the rumble of a vehicle, the sound of hurried footsteps or a murmur of voices made him shiver. He listened momentarily, and then plunged back into his book, muttering: "No, not yet…it's too soon."

He calculated that the water in the reservoir would not yet have spread into the supply-pipes; it would take at least forty-eight hours for the contamination to be complete. And he followed in his imagination the development of his bacilli, whose colonies must be multiplying infinitely. He represented them as if he were looking at them through a microscope, swarming on a slide.

Suddenly, his head slumped forwards; he was asleep. Then his mind, transformed, denatured and amplified by the dream, showed him the bacilli enormously magnified, with gigantic antennae, the tentacles of octopodes and scintillating eyes. All of them were moving, twisting in slow convulsions, and he sensed the sticky monsters sliding over his body, gradually tightening around him, compressing his chest, choking him…

He uttered a cry and woke up.

He went to open the window. A man was standing outside his door. It was fat Nestor, lying in wait for him. Procas recognized him and, instead of closing the window again, stayed here, leaning on the sill. The apprentice butcher moved off, and went to hide some distance away. Perhaps he thought that his enemy was about to emerge, and was casting an eye over the street before leaving the house.

If there's any justice, Procas thought, *he'll be the first one to be struck down.*

He started pacing back and forth, because he was afraid of going to sleep and having another frightful nightmare.

Fatigue, however, ended up wearing him out, and he collapsed on his divan, where a brutal slumber was not long delayed in taking possession of him.

In the morning he woke up with a frightful headache; he bathed his forehead over a basin, and as the water trickled down his face he wiped it away carefully, fearing that it might already be contaminated. Now he no longer dared drink. Was it not necessary that he enjoy his triumph, and see those who had driven him to do what he had done suffering?

Ordinarily, he never went out in the morning, but today he went to buy the newspapers. A gang of street-urchins assailed him as soon as he set foot in the street, and the housewives chatting on the doorsteps heaped insults upon him, but Procas walked straight ahead, his head tilted forward, his eyes half-closed, like a man in a dream. That persistent calm, contrasting with his habitual state of fury, did not fail to cause surprise. People concluded that his conscience was not tranquil, and that he was doubtless expecting to be arrested soon. While they observed him slyly, he came back, reading a newspaper, which seemed singular.

What could he be looking for in the papers?

Those who had not yet had time to cast an eye over the morning papers hastened to the nearest newsstand and immediately started scanning the columns of the first, second and third pages, hoping to discover a clue there, but it was a waste of effort. However, one decorated old rentier who was mingling with the crowd called their attention to a news item that had not struck the minds of the curiosity-seekers. The item concerned a woman who had been strangled the previous evening in a sleazy hotel in the Rue de la Tombe-Issoire. She had come in at about midnight in the company of an individual who tried to hide his face, and who had disappeared before dawn.

Then, for the people gathered around the newsstand, it was as if a veil had been torn away from their eyes.

"Of course!" said someone. "That's what he was looking for in the paper!"

"For sure," said another. "It's him, and no mistake. For several days he's been going out at night. Where did he go?"

"You'll see," said the old rentier, proud of having given proof of his sagacity. "You'll see that this crime will go unpunished, like the others. Oh, he's clever, that fellow. He's not on his trial run..."

All day long, the murder in the Rue de la Tombe-Issoire was the object of conversations. Fat Nestor was fuming with rage.

"I lost him last night," he said. "I followed him, but he gave me the slip. If I'd been able to stay on his heels, that would have been it—I'd have had him. It must he him who did it!"

No one doubted it, until the evening papers cast light on the affair. The murderer had been arrested. It was someone named Mohamed Ben Agha, a manual worker in a factory on the Boulevard de la Gare. His victim's bracelet-watch had been found on him, and he had confessed.

There was general consternation, but everyone remained convinced nevertheless that "the satyr" was no better than that Mohammed, and that one day or other he would end up being caught *in flagrante delicto*.

XXIII

Procas was still waiting. He no longer cared about the crowd that growled as he passé by. One idea obsessed him: might the bacillus on which he had counted, whose toxicity had appeared evident to him, have lost its properties when it came into contact with an immense expanse of water? The reservoir, he knew, contained about two hundred thousand cubic meters. Might that mass have contained an element that he had not foreseen? No, though—his bacillus ought to annihilate all the others, for the experiments he had carried out on five or six liters of water had sufficiently proved the virulence and combativeness of his colonies. They must be in the process of developing, but had not yet reached the supply-pipes.

Sometimes, remorse took hold of him and he almost wanted to see his attempt fail, but when he found himself con-

344

fronted by the hate-filled gazes of his enemies, and heard their imprecations and their insults, he felt his compassion evaporate.

Certainly, he did not intend to enjoy his triumph for long, because life was weighing upon him like a burden. Once his vengeance was accomplished, he would disappear.

In the afternoon, he went out. He noticed that people were looking at him, but without anger, and he thought that he even read a sort of compassion on some faces.

On the Avenue du Maine, at the corner of the Passage de la Tour-de-Vannes, people were conversing with an air of mystery. When he went by they did not greet him with the habitual clamors that had once rendered him madly furious. He would have liked someone to insult him, though, or even to hit him, because that would have maintained the anger in his heart, which he sensed gradually dying down.

He went home, opened his window and looked out at the avenue.

Usually, as soon as he appeared, there were savage cries and threatening gestures, but today, there was nothing.

Silence.

All day long he remained prostrate at his work table, play to a black depression. Thus, at the very moment when he had condemned it to death, the crowd was humanizing. And he sought in vain for the cause of that appeasement.

He ended up persuading himself that the calm was only apparent, and that they were plotting against him again. That had happened before; he had often thought that he was recovering a measure of tranquility, but the next day he had been assailed by a furious mob once again.

Night had fallen, but he remained at his table, without even thinking of lighting his lamp. Someone knocked on the door, and he shivered. Who could be coming to his home? He hesitated momentarily, and then lit the lamp.

Someone was calling now: "Monsieur! Monsieur!"

He decided to go and open the door, and fund himself face to face with two men—but recoiled on recognizing one of them as the apprentice butcher who had been his torturer, his executioner.

"What do you want with me?" he cried. "What do you want?"

"Monsieur," fat Nestor replied, "We'd like to talk to you."

"Talk to me? What do you have to say to me? You've probably come to murder me, wretch!"

"Calm down," said the second visitor, who was none other than Barouillet. "We've come to clear up a misunderstanding."

The phrase was perhaps poorly chosen, but Barouillet's head was stuffed with electoral clichés, lavishly employed in public meetings.

"Yes," he went on. "A misunderstanding...a regrettable misunderstanding."

Procas had stepped back. "Come in," he said, understanding that he might not have to fight the two men. He went into his laboratory. They followed him.

"Monsieur," said Barouillet, "we owe you an apology."

"Yes...exactly...apologies," agreed Nestor, bowing awkwardly. "Anyone can make a mistake, can't they?"

"And we've been mistaken, grossly mistaken," added Barouillet. "All this is the fault of an individual who is now in trouble with the law. He claimed to know...he convinced us, so to speak...we believed, for what he said was so precise and so concordant with the fact that it was impossible not to accuse you..."

Procas still did not understand. He was close to believing that it was a trick, and gazed anxiously at the two men, one of whom was his mortal enemy, who had unleashed the wrath of the crowd upon him many a time.

"Explain yourselves," he said. "What facts are you talking about?"

"You know very well," replied Barouillet.

"All I know is that I'm an object of horror, and that instead of feeling sorry for me you have all persecuted me.

You've insulted me and attacked me. I only had one friend left in the world, a dog, a poor lame animal, and you killed him. Why? What have I done to you?"

"You've done all kinds of wrong to you. I recognize that. But your way of living, your mysterious nocturnal labors…all that seemed suspicious to us, and when little Maurice disappeared, we thought..."

"What did you think?"

"That you'd killed him."

"But that's horrible! So you were able to think me guilty of murder?"

Fat Nestor and Barouillet bowed their heads without replying. They were now conscious of the infamy of their conduct, and could not find anything more to say.

"Come on," said Procas, "talk. Why have you come today to offer your apologies to me, whom you perhaps still consider to be a murderer?"

"No," stammered Barouillet. "We know now that you're not guilty. The child has reappeared. He was abducted at the Fête du Lion de Belfort by gypsies, but he succeeded in getting away from them, and yesterday, the police brought him home. You can understand now why we're here. We're honest men and we recognize our mistakes. Someone put it into our heads, and then everyone accused you. Someone found traces of blood in your back yard. The child was playing outside your door shortly before he disappeared. Put yourself in our place—what would you have thought?"

Procas had sat down, his head in his hands; he was sobbing.

So they had thought he was a murderer, and he had had no suspicion of it. He had thought that it was his ugliness alone that had aroused the mob against him. If he had known! Why had no one said anything to him? Oh, he understood everything now: the visit of the Commissaire, the search, the howls of rage that went up at his approach, the fury of the people who believed him to be guilty.

"Monsieur," said fat Nestor, patting him gently on the shoulder, "don't torment yourself. It's all over now, we know that you're a worthy man. You no longer have any enemies, I assure you. Everyone in the neighborhood is informed now…and they feel sorry for you."

Procas dared not raise his head to look at the man who was speaking, the enemy who he was previously execrated, and who was now apologizing…who was finally pronouncing the words of pity for which he had waited in vain and which might have encouraged him to live.

At the moment that I no longer have any enemies, he thought, *when those who were persecuting me have come to offer me their hand, the poison is on the march, circulating in the supply-pipes, perhaps already claiming victims.*

He stood up abruptly, looked the two men in the face, and exclaimed, in a hoarse voice: "No! No…if you knew…I've suffered too much…I've suffered too much!"

And he fled, at a run.

"Poor fellow," murmured fat Nestor. "He's mad. Not astonishing, after such emotions. Oh, he's seen people harsh, and they nearly had his skin. It's stupid, all the same. And it's all the fault of that swine Bezombes. Why did we listen to him? Père Grinchu was right…he was the only one who saw clearly in all this."

Barouillet made no reply. He took the apprentice butcher by the arm and led him outside.

Newsvendors were running through the streets, stopping, distributing a few sheets that were still moist, and setting off again, howling: "Mysterious disease! Full details! The day's deaths!"

Vengeance sometimes wields a scythe that mows down innocents. This is what had happened…

Procas had wanted to avenge himself on those who had made him so unhappy, but the fatality that had always pursued him seemed to have attached itself to him. His bacillus was now claiming victims, the hospitals were filling up with the sick, but it was not in the Montrouge district that the terrible epidemic had burst forth.

Procas had assumed, like many Parisians, that the Montsouris reservoir distributed the water of the Vanne and the Loing to the inhabitants of the fourteenth arrondissement, and that they would be the center attained, but it was the first, the second, the third and the fourth that had received the poisoned water, and were already counting many cases of affliction.

On the terraces of cafes, in the restaurants and in the houses, men, women and children were falling down and writhing as if seized by vertigo. The urban ambulances were going back and forth before the terrified eyes of the population.

The disease commenced abruptly with violent shivering and vomiting. The temperature rose very rapidly and reached forty-one or even forty-two degrees within two or three hours. The pulse increased to a hundred and fifty beats per minute. Neural phenomena were also very marked; many victims were seized by convulsions; the skin was covered with a viscous sweat; blisters appeared on the face and the limbs, filed with turbulent liquid.

And the people who had escaped the scourge thus far awaited their turn, anguished and trembling. The inhabitants of ancient Pompeii, seeing the descending lava that was about to swallow them up, could not have been more terrified than the citizens of Paris during those tragic hours.

Procas was now wandering the streets, crazily. The visit of fat Nestor and Barouillet had devastated him. Remorse had broken his heart. Could he allow people to die who had ceased to be enemies, who had recognized the wrongs they had done to him, and were only asking to be forgiven? He would go to tell the whole story, reveal everything, to the Commissaire, to have the water in the supply-pipes stopped. Perhaps there was still time?

Yes, but once he had confessed his crime, it was necessary that he disappear. His resolution was quickly made. He would return home and take the little bottle of potassium cyanide, which he had often thought of raising to his lips, from the shelf....

He would confess his crime...and immediately put an end to his life...

The cries of the newsvendors suddenly attracted his attention. A tremor took hold of him. He bought a newspaper, read it by the light of a street-lamp, and felt his legs give way beneath him.

So this was how it had ended! Killing innocents! People he had never seen, who did not know him!

A long sob rose to his lips. He wanted to run all the way to his laboratory, but this time the shock had been too strong for a man whose life was now only hanging by a thread.

A choking crisis gripped him; his heart abruptly ceased beating, and he collapsed like a mass, thunderstruck.

Meanwhile, the physicians had finally recognized that it was the water that was carrying death through Paris, and he epidemic had been halted. No one knew, as yet, that a man, in order to avenge himself, had poisoned the Montsouris reservoir, and there were long discussions regarding the causes of the contagion.

Procas, picked up on the roadside, was transported to the Passage Tenaille, and the following day, all of Montrouge followed the meager coffin that took him to his final dwelling.

The murderer had become a victim, and the crowd, *which did not know*, threw flowers into his grave.

Pity had finally awakened—too late.

Note

The story you have just read is a retrospective one. It is now utterly impossible to poison a reservoir, the water of which is analyzed every day with the greatest care by the city's chemists. May the citizens of Paris be reassured!

A.G.

Gaston de Pawlowski: *The Bankruptcy of Science*
(1909)

In those days, the Americans found themselves forced to push back the bounds of glory all the way to remote extremities of Alaska in order to permit Edison to collect the testimonies of the admiration of the entire world on his head, without being inconvenienced by them.

The great man's genius had rendered him master of all the elements, and it seemed to the least clear-sighted minds that the limits of science had been attained.

To him reverted the merit of having replace typographers in the great newspapers of New York by admirably trained chickens, compositing by means of printing characters shaped in the form of seeds. Also owed to him was the marvelous liquid permitting American dentists with overly rough hands to sensitize them before their operations. Was it not him, finally, who, surpassing all those endeavors, by means of prodigious improvements made to preceding inventions, had succeeded after unprecedented efforts in making Parisian telephones work.

But all that was not sufficient for his dreams. Carried away by the folly of grandeur, Edison wanted to push science beyond its natural limits.

The rumor spread one day in New York, with the rapidity of the engineer Jupiter's thunderbolts, that Edison had just invented a mechanical translator.

The apparatus resembled a phonograph, but prodigiously improved. One spoke English, for instance, into the funnel of the translator, and it promptly reproduced the sentence in French, German, Russian or any other language, at the whim of the operator.

The apparatus was disconcertingly simple. It was set according to the language to be translated, and then one inserted the scroll of the other language, composed of a certain number of membranes vibrating sympathetically with certain assonances and then converting the impressions received into a new language by a means so simple that describing it would be an insult to our readers.

The day of the official inauguration arrived; the room was full and the anxious audience was silent, expecting great things.

Edison, always smiling, was to operate the apparatus personally.

All the same, it was not without a slight emotion that he pronounced these words into the funnel of the translator:

"Hurrah for the glorious Edison translator, whisky, gin and soda, and the Lorisson girls."

That sentence was to be translated into French.

Calmly, the great scientist pressed the switch. There was a long pause. Finally, the mechanisms slowly began to speak, translating the sentence: *"Bravo pour le glorieux tran..."*

Then, abruptly, it stopped, and clearly pronounced the following words:

"Then again, in the end, you're beginning to annoy me. I know that I'm only an instrument, but you'll end up turning me into a blockhead with your unnatural inventions."

E.M. Laumann: *The* Alcyon

(1923)

At exactly thirty-seven minutes and three and a third seconds past ten a.m. on 15 November last, the watchman called attention to floating wreckage ahead on the port side. I am able to be so precise because, at that very moment, I was checking my watch against the ship's chronometer.

The officers assembled on the deck to discuss the matter; the advertised object seemed unusual, although it was scarcely visible in the water.

"A floating mine," someone aid.

"Don't think so," replied the captain, as lacking in loquacity as usual. "Man the dinghy."

Our speed was reduced and the helmsman was ordered to maintain the boat apart from the course that the wreck appeared to be following.

The dinghy was lowered, two men taking their places there along with the ensign. The sea was calm and smooth, ideal weather for such a maneuver.

We were all impatient, such a lucky find, at sea, always involves a series of consequences. At any rate, it's an event, and there's nothing better to break the monotony of on-board life.

With four or five strokes of the oars, the dinghy approached the wreckage, and we saw the ensign examine it at a distance, with careful attention. Then, in response to his order, the dinghy drew closer and one of the men got hold of the thing. Five minutes later, the dinghy was back on its davits and the ensign deposited the object on the captain's table.

It was a bottle approximately five liters in volume, made of thick glass almost black in color. The receptacle, which must have contained eau-de-vie, was carefully surrounded by tarred rope, lumps of cork and wood—precautions taken to protect the glass and ensure its flotation. At first sight we judged that it must have been in the water for a long time, for it was covered in zoophytes, including the stopper, which was constituted, as we discovered thereafter, by a roundel of wood, padding-material and tar.

Where had it come from? What course had it followed? The colony of zoophytes that had attached itself to the object revealed, in spite of the improbability of the fact, that it must have spent quite a long time in the Southern seas, for zoophytes are not found in the glacial waters where we were. Were we, therefore, required to surmise that the wreckage had originated in the great ocean and had been caught by the Arctic current, arriving in the glacial ocean after God knows how many months? The hypothesis could be complicated, though; it could have been thrown off the shore of Spitzbergen, tracing a contrary route, eventually to return here. Whatever the truth, its sojourn in warm waters could not be doubted.

The stopper removed, the bottle was tipped up and shaken. A piece of cloth carefully wrapped around a little eight fell on to the table. The sheet was carefully unrolled, exposing the characters of a handwritten scrawl to everyone's eyes, probably made with a piece of wood, liquid tar and soot.

The captain leaned over the thing, smoothed out its creases with the palm of his hand and read the first line:

"Aboard the *Alcyon*, 13 February 1820."

He stopped, emitted an "Hmm!" and, nonplussed, leaned further over, staring more attentively. Then he continued, slowly, confirming his first reading: "Aboard the Alcyon, 13 February 1820." Then, as if seeking consent, he looked at us and said: "The bottle's been in the water for ninety-eight years, then?"

There was silence.

"This is serious, Gentlemen," the captain added. "We'll draw up a formal statement of what's happening at this moment, and everyone will sign it. Lieutenant, fetch some headed paper. Take note, now, that this document has been written by different hands and by men of different education; the first lines are correct and in good handwriting, but the others—the later ones—are clumsy, indicative of hands not used to holding a pen. Let's press on quickly; I'm afraid that the air might cause these characters, so long held in the obscurity of that bottle, to fade and disappear."

Then the captain began to read slowly, his voice accompanied solely by the dull noise of the engines.

I don't know how to explain the general sentiment that weighed upon us, but I can't define it any better than by saying that the ship's cabin was like a mortuary chamber, and that invisible death was afloat in the room.

This, word for word, is what he read:

"We the undersigned, sole survivors, left Novaya Zemlya with a cargo of seal-oil on the 13 September 1819, setting course for Christiana as a first port of call, in moderate weather and a north-easterly wind blowing at six meters a minute.

"The *Alcyon* is a three-masted brig of 160 tons—solid and well-constructed it must be said!—holding steady in bad weather and headwinds. The crew was composed, on departure, of 25 men, whose roll-call was complete, including officers.

"Now, you who are reading these lines, listen and hear the plea that is addressed to you: twelve men are on their knees, their hands joined in ardent prayer, offering up their souls full of fear to Heaven, before throwing this bottle into the water, for it contains their last hope."

The captain raised his head again and fixed his gaze on us. His face, already severe in itself, had become even more serious than usual. Then he resumed reading, slowly: "You, whoever you may be, tell yourselves that twelve men, your peers, are in the process of dying in a funereal silence in the midst of strange and terrible things. Come to their aid, for the sake of our salvation, for the sake of those who are waiting for us!

"We raised anchor three days ago and were navigating with all sails lowered when suddenly, almost taking us unawares, the barometer fell rapidly and a great wind sprang up. At that moment we were at 48° 52' 40" north latitude and 0° 2' 45" west longitude. That is the last measurement we were able to make.[46]

"The wind was blowing from the east and drove us due north; we had the time to furl the sails and the sounding-line revealed depths that were entirely safe. The sea suddenly took on a strange milky color and he waves that the wind raised from the liquid mass became so high that they reached all the way up to the great yard-arm, like great white phantoms, and fell back very noisily on to the quivering deck.

"The deeps must have been tumultuous themselves, for long waves from the sea-bed sometimes brought strange creatures up to the surface: unknown, monstrous fish whose swim-bladders burst asunder in atmospheric pressure. The sea seemed to be steaming, solely by virtue of the water pulverized by the wind, perpetually renewed and in suspense.

"In spite of the precautions we had taken, the main-mast was plucked away like a wisp of straw and the top two-thirds of the mizzen-mast broken off. We struggled for hours, in spite of almost insurmountable difficulties, to free our unfortunate vessel of its ruins and establish two jibs with the aid of which we could maintain our heading. In the course of this work a man was washed overboard: Jean-François Crevat, from Binic.

---

[46] These figures place the ship just west of Paris, assuming that the captain is using the Paris meridian as zero longitude. If the apparent error results from a misprint, it is not obvious which figure has been misrendered, but given that the ship was headed from Novaya Zemlya toward "Christiana" (i.e. Oslo) the most likely hypothesis is that the first figure ought to be 78 rather than 48. If so, the fact that the ship is then driven due northwards suggests that its eventual resting place must be somewhere near the North Pole.

"Night fell, the tempest redoubled its fury; suddenly, without our being able to discover the cause, we were borne away with a prodigious rapidity, not by the force of the wind but at an angle to it; in that fashion, we lost what remaining sail we had. An irresistible current drew us on; the maddened compass no longer gave any indication on which we could rely.

"Soon, alas—forever accursed be that hour!—we heard the loud noise of surf, distant at first, but which increased in a frightful manner and came closer. We were in a watery tempest so violent that staying on deck, even if we lashed ourselves in position, was impossible. We were heading for the breakers; it was only a matter of minutes when, all of a sudden, it seemed to us that the ship was lifted entirely clear of the water and hurled forwards. We had the impression that it was riding on the crest of a wave. There was a dull impact, a prodigious splash, and then the external noises faded away. We sensed that we had quit the tumultuous atmosphere and were rotating gently on our axis. The darkness was too profound for us to be able to see anything, but we were safe and sound—for the moment, at least.

"Anxiously, we waited for daybreak. A particularly strange thing, explained to us by what followed, was that, although we could hear the frightful noise that the sea and the gusts of wind were making, we could not feel their effects.

"That disconcerting calm, after so much violence, filled us with an inexpressible dread; the crewmen told us, afterwards, that they believed they had died in the course of descending into the depths of the sea, and that they had quit life without perceiving it.

"Finally, the day broke—a cold, grey, dull and funereal day—and we understood everything, at a stroke. We were overwhelmed by fright.

"We were in the middle of a basin, and high walls of lugubrious black granite loomed up abruptly all around us. We could not see any beach, only a few ledges on which one might perhaps set foot, and a few holes in the frigid thickness of the granite filled with darkness, ominous and treacherous. The circle might have been a hundred or a hundred and fifty meters in diameter, and our poor vessel occupied its center.

"We remained immobile, unable to comprehend the event and the circumstances that had transported us there—but from that moment on the majority of us understood that we were lost, and that we could no longer dream of anything but eternal rest.

"The captain must have divined the mental anxiety behind our pale faces; he immediately set out to combat it by multiplying his orders and supporting them with the most terrible threats.

"A sounding-line that was thrown overboard when we emerged from our stupor yielded no definite result; the depth must have been enormous, our cable too short. Ultimately, we concluded on the basis of our investigation that we were in the middle of a chimney whose base was deep in the ocean.

"The men were put to work, with a view to events that we could not foresee, in making the *Alycon* as ready as possible to undertake, with the best possible chance of success, the adventures that we could not foresee. We had two anchors, and took the chain off one to add to the other; that gave us thirty-three meters of chain, which we let down without reaching the bottom—but it permitted us to hold the ship in place and to take account of things unhurriedly."

"I, the captain of the *Alcyon*, who is writing this, then let the crew have a necessary meal. The first mate and I went out in a dinghy to look for the fissure by means of which we had got in. Our short voyage could not have easier, as we were traveling over dormant water, but the conviction that we brought back was maddening. *There was no fissure!* The granite wall extended everywhere, high, solid and, at first sight, inaccessible, without any breach in its continuity. We decided to say nothing and our first concern, on coming aboard, was to take stock of our provisions. If no one died imminently, we had enough for 45 days.

"The following day, impelled by my conscience, I assembled the men and, after exhorting them to have courage, I shared the frightful truth with them. I encouraged them to search for a way out and all the boats were manned to that end. Their searches, like ours, were futile. An able seaman volunteered to scale the wall, planting iron spikes at intervals for use as footholds, proposing that, once the last spike was planted, a man should take up a pulley-block and secure it at the top, with the aid of which we could set up a rope-ladder. Then, piece by piece, we could lift up all the materials necessary for the construction of a raft, or even a boat. Hope blossomed in all hearts, and the work was begun. The chains were used to improvise the spikes, the ladder was rapidly fabricated, and we were already counting on success when it all came undone: the man at the pulley-block fell, carrying the ladder with him. We had nothing with which to make another.

"With the aid of the iron spikes, everyone went up to the summit of the gigantic wall. It fell steeply down to the sea on the far side too. Exhausted, overwhelmed again by despair, we came back down to the *Alcyon*, motionless in the calm water.

"The weary and discouraged men did not want to try anything else; they accepted the idea of their death with resignation. Only twenty days of supplies now remain to us...I assume, with horror, that things can only get worse!

"If our days are dismal and desperate, the nights are frightful, fertile in terror and nameless anguish. Enormous annelid creatures like viscous slugs emerge from the sea, emitting a milky light into the darkness. These slugs—for there is nothing else with which to compare them—are a foot long, as thick as a forearm; contact with them gives rise to pustules. The walls of our death-cell are full of them when night comes; they come there to suckle or graze on the sea-wrack with which its base is clad. They swarm over the deck of the brig, and then they cease to be luminous; it is as if they know that the light they emit reveals their presence. Two of our men, who mere merely touched by them, have died of a gangrene that made them into ambulant cadavers. By virtue of that, we gained a day's rations.

"There are also white shapes that fly slowly around us in the dark; their wings are also fins, for we hear and see them plunging into the sea, then re-emerging ponderously to hover a foot or two above the water. Their bodies give off a noxious odor of mud and their soft touch is cold and damp, like the cephalopods called medusae.[47] They have phosphorescent eyes, which, in spite of the light they emit, have the appearance of human eyes, but bleak and prey to an unspeakable sadness.

"We caught sight of them during a moonlit night and were able to catch one. They are flat creatures, their mouths surrounded by tentacles with suckers; they have two lateral fins and a tail terminating in a third. The whole thing quite palpably has the volume of a powerful devil-fish. Such is this vile beast, which is certainly unknown to science."

"Here there's a gap," said the captain. "I can read 'madness', then 'despair'. The text continues:

"It's terrible. A man went up to the deck in the night and didn't come back. In the morning, we found his corpse completely drained of blood, with a row of little round wounds on his throat, still exuding a little clotted blood. The creatures that fly and swim are vampires. The sea contains all horrors!

"Their flock surrounds the ship by night. No one dares go out. We no longer have any light or food-supplies. We can't catch any fish...

"A man, the strongest of those who are left, will climb up the spikes to the top of the wall. From there, he will throw the

---

[47] The term "medusae" would normally apply to jellyfish, but the reference to quasi-human eyes suggest that this imaginary creature is, indeed, a cephalopod than a coelenterate, the comparison subsequently made to a *poisson diable* [devil-fish] reinforces that suggestion, that being one of many familiar names attributed to the octopus.

bottle into the sea. We are waiting, without hope...but if God wishes..."

The ship's chaplain, who was present, began to recite the prayer for the dead in a low voice, and we remained silent until the final Latin words had emerged from his lips.

The captain raised his head again. He was very pale; he remained silent for a moment, then said: "There's nothing more but signatures and crosses, then a few incoherent words. Death was prowling around them. Let's bare our heads, gentlemen."

And we all took off our hats, before that piece of cloth unrolled on the table.

www.ingramcontent.com/pod-product-compliance
Lightning Source LLC
Chambersburg PA
CBHW060413030726
47495CB00003B/565